us and
usband
lo.com,

ist

n

'One of the few authors that can actually make me laugh out loud. I could sit here and fill a review with some of the lines that she comes out with. Nothing ... A brilliant book' *****
n.co.uk **@bookaddictshaun**

aracters – had me in stitches.
witty read' *****
pot.co.uk **@bookreviewbyrea**

doesn't disappoint ...
/10' **Press Association**

-turner' **Woman**

Also by Jane Costello

Jane Costello
Summer Nights
at the
Moonlight Hotel

SIMON &
SCHUSTER

London · New York · Sydney · Toronto · New Delhi

A CBS COMPANY

First published in Great Britain by Simon & Schuster UK Ltd, 2016
A CBS COMPANY

1 3 5 7 9 10 8 6 4 2

Simon & Schuster UK Ltd
1st Floor
222 Gray's Inn Road
London WC1X 8HB

www.simonandschuster.co.uk

Simon & Schuster Australia, Sydney
Simon & Schuster India, New Delhi

A CIP catalogue record for this book
is available from the British Library

PB ISBN: 978-1-47114-911-5
eBook ISBN: 978-1-47114-913-9
TPB ISBN: 978-1-47114-912-2

Typeset by M Rules
Printed and bound by CPI Group (UK) Ltd, Croydon, CR0 4YY

Simon & Schuster UK Ltd are committed to sourcing paper
that is made from wood grown in sustainable forests and supports the Forest
Stewardship Council, the leading international forest certification organisation.
Our books displaying the FSC logo are printed on FSC certified paper.

For Joy Wolstenholme

Chapter 1

Some things just don't work together. Chocolate and teapots. Straw and houses. Lead and balloons. Now I've discovered another combination to add to the list: high heels and the Lake District.

If we were tourists, we'd be forgiven for dressing like this to negotiate a landscape that's timeless, rugged and catastrophically ill-suited to four-inch strappy numbers. But my friends and I are not tourists: Cate and I have lived here for ever and Emily long enough to know better.

I should stress that we wouldn't ordinarily come out like this. Normally, you couldn't pick us out from lots of other women in their early thirties around here, the ones in slouchy tops, boho prints, combats, cut-offs and, an occasional necessity, given our changeable weather, waterproof jackets.

But Cate was convinced a different approach was required where we're heading tonight on a warm spring evening. And for a reason I can't quite remember, Emily and I listened to her. So, blossom-cheeked and perspiring, we teeter up one of Bowness's steepest hills, the vast blue-grey ribbon of Windermere behind us.

'Just so you know, Cate, even if I end up enjoying this, I'm not wearing these shoes again,' I tell her.

'They're dancing shoes. What were you expecting to wear – trail boots?' she grins.

'Converse would've done,' I protest.

'Oh, Lauren – not for *salsa night.*' The last two words are delivered in an unconvincing Latin American twang and accompanied by a J-Lo-style bum wiggle. I struggle not to snigger.

The reason we're en route to the class, on this evening in spring, is because a regular customer at Cate's florist's shop in Ambleside asked her to put a card in her window this week. It read: 'LEARN TO SALSA DANCE. *Experience the red-hot vibes of Latin America right here in Lakeland. Beginners and singles welcome.*'

Thanks to recent events, all three of us fall into both categories.

Which is why, despite the fact that I'm absolutely *not* on my way to meet the man of my dreams – I've already met him, even if I'm nothing more than a friend in his eyes – Cate has dragged me along tonight, when I'm not even remotely in the mood to mambo.

2

'I have to admit, Lauren,' says Emily, 'the shoes suit you. They're gorgeous.'

'What did I say? They're fantastic,' Cate adds, satisfied. She said the same about the false eyelashes she persuaded me to try out tonight, for the first time in my life. It feels as though my eyelids have been smothered in Pritt Stick and adorned with a catatonic tarantula.

'Fantastic or not, the chances of me being able to dance in them are slim, given that I can barely walk in them,' I say.

Emily, I hasten to add, didn't need the false eyelashes. The eyelashes nature has bestowed on her – just like *every* feature nature has bestowed on her, from her luminous blue eyes to her translucent skin – are already beautiful.

Nobody could begrudge her though, since Em is one of those rare creatures who are unequivocally lovely inside and out – something that was immediately apparent when I first met her four years ago, after she moved in next door to Cate's old place in Windermere. It's not only that she's easy to get along with, she's just incredibly *nice*: the kind of friend who sends cupcakes for your birthday, texts after a night out to check you're home safely, and doesn't even flinch when a check-out girl presses *yes* to the question *Is the customer obviously over 25?* If that isn't evidence of a soul entirely devoid of ego then I don't know what is.

'What time does this go on until?' she asks now. 'Only I've

got to be up at six tomorrow morning to take a group of Americans up Helvellyn and Striding Edge.'

Emily is originally from Derbyshire, but for the last four years has worked as a mountain leader for Windermere Adventures, taking hikers up some of England's most challenging fells. She's passionate about her job and entirely at home on the most treacherous crags, even those with names like 'Bad Step' and 'Sharp Edge', which as far as I'm concerned might as well be called 'Best Stay at Home With a Nice Cup of Tea'. She can turn her hand to everything from gorge scrambling to wild camping, for which there is an unfeasibly large demand. She's basically Bear Grylls, but with nicer hair.

'Are they aware of the torrential rain that's forecast?' I ask.

'No idea. Nobody ever enjoys it less when it rains anyway though.' She's apparently being serious.

'If you say so, Em.'

'I'll prove it to you – if I ever manage to get you up a mountain with me one day, Lauren.' She's aware the likelihood is minimal. I've lived here all my life and, although I'd only ever whisper this, have never wavered from the view that the mountains are best appreciated from a distance.

'To answer your question, the class itself lasts for an hour,' Cate says. 'But then there's a "social" afterwards, when we get to dance with all the gorgeous, single blokes who will *definitely* be there.'

Em and I flash each other a look.

Em's been single for a couple of months, having finally split up with a guy called Beck who was working in a hiking shop in Grasmere; she'd been seeing him on and off since last New Year. She'd made the schoolgirl error of assuming that being surrounded by crampons and camping stoves automatically made him the action-man type she always goes for, until she worked out that she never actually saw him *outside*. Not ever. The most dynamic thing he ever did was getting up to go to the bar in the Golden Rule, where he'd apparently set up long-term residency.

In Cate's head, the fact that Emily has been single for a couple of months, that she herself has been single for around the same time and that I've been single for so long there is virtually rust in my knickers ... means that we MUST ACT.

At times like these, it's just easier to humour her, not least because I can't claim I'd usually be doing anything more exciting on a Tuesday evening – unless you count marking Key Stage 2 literacy tests for the primary school where I teach.

'Why didn't we just drive here?' I ask, as we leave the outskirts of the town behind us and cross the road towards the Moonlight Hotel.

'Because it's launch night and there are free margaritas.'

'How many people are going to be there?' asks Emily. 'I just want to know if I'll be able to slip easily into the background.'

'Marion, the salsa teacher, is expecting forty or fifty. But for the record, you won't need to slip anywhere,' Cate insists, pushing her short blonde bob behind the four piercings in her ear. I used to have a couple myself in my late teens but Cate's never fully grown out of her alternative phase and never really wants to. 'Nobody's expecting you to be any good on the first lesson – none of us will be.'

As we crunch up the driveway, the pale stone towers of the hotel rise up above a watery sunset.

When I was growing up, I had a vague awareness of four types of holiday establishments here in the Lakes: campsites for the walkers; pubs for the walkers soft enough to want a hot shower; chintzy guest-houses overflowing with paper doilies; and grand, old-fashioned establishments like the Moonlight Hotel, with heart-stopping views, abundant history and gingerbread high teas served in bone china cups.

In recent years, much of the National Park's accommodation has been renovated for a younger, trendier, distinctly fussier market. But some of those older places have been frozen in time, refusing to relinquish their floral curtains and drag themselves into the twenty-first century. The Moonlight Hotel is one of them. And I'm glad.

It's nothing to do with the aforementioned floral curtains, but because this is not just any old hotel to me. It's part of my childhood, the backdrop to my most precious memories – of long summer holidays making dens in its gardens and mischief in the kitchens on the pretence of helping to wash up.

So despite the fact that I'm not here often these days – I've popped in with Mum for a tea a handful of times in the last five years – when I push through the door into reception, a rush of familiarity engulfs me.

Everything, from the austere oak walls and imposing reception desk, is exactly the same as it always was, only a bit quieter. Any evidence of throngs of people arriving for a riotous night of Latin-style hip-swivelling is thin on the ground.

Cate pulls out a business card from her purse. 'It definitely says the Moonlight Hotel, every Tuesday. Let's see if one of the staff can shed any light.' She pings an aluminium bell, or at least tries to. It sticks a couple of times, before responding with an unexpectedly loud *ting!*

A middle-aged woman with thick glasses and slightly greasy hair appears looking so stressed out you'd think she was on the trading floor of Wall Street. She isn't someone I recognise, although most of the staff who were around when I was a child have long gone. It's clear she has no time for pleasantries, so we're simply directed to the Lake Room at the back of the hotel. Not that I needed directing.

The door is firmly shut and it's deadly quiet when we reach it. Then suddenly, the throb of music bursts out from behind the door.

'There you go,' Cate declares. 'The red-hot vibes of Latin America – as promised.'

She turns the knob and flings open the door, and we stand mutely, surveying the room while our eyes begin to water with the volume. It's fair to say this was not what we were expecting. Apart from one couple and the teacher, we're literally the only ones here.

Chapter 2

'You came – excellent!' cries the woman I can only assume is Marion as she battles with the remote control from a music system, flings it down, then hurtles across the empty room. 'Come on in. Don't be shy!'

When I was a little girl, this grand room reminded me of the one in *The Sound of Music*, but it was only much later that I found out the house was built in 1895 as the private residence for an Austrian baroness – although what she was doing in the north of England I couldn't tell you. To my young and untrained eye, this was the kind of room where balls should be held, where elegant ladies should swish across the floor in silk gowns and white gloves.

This evening, soft light floods through the windows overlooking the lake and Langdale Pikes; the stucco ceiling and intricately patterned wallpaper are still just about intact. I don't know why they got rid of the old tables and chairs. Disappointingly, they've been replaced by the cheap, plastic kind you'd find in a British Legion club. Despite this, and the threadbare carpet and slightly crumbling walls, it's every bit the room I once knew and loved.

My dad worked at the Moonlight Hotel for more than two decades, having started here in his early twenties, shortly after he'd emigrated to the UK from Australia. For the last twelve of those years he was General Manager – and although he'd never class himself as a workaholic, you're not in a job for that long without passion and pride infusing everything you do.

'Hi, Marion,' replies Cate, with some trepidation. 'When are the others getting here?'

The woman responds with a protracted wince, as if someone's trodden on her bunions. 'It's not quite the turn-out I was expecting. But it's early yet,' she says, looking at her watch. I can't knock her optimism. Cate flashes a glance at Emily and me, which prompts a flicker of panic in Marion. 'You won't leave, will you?'

Cate claps her hands together. 'Course not. Right, where do I learn to have hips like Shakira?'

I realise I must have been holding some obscure preconception about what a salsa teacher might look like. I can't define this, except to say that it's in every way the opposite of Marion, who is the least Latin-looking woman on the planet, with her unruly blonde ringlets and short legs whose chubby, baby-faced knees peek out of a long jersey skirt, slit to mid-thigh. She offers us one of the dozens of complimentary margaritas lined up on a table. I take one – and come to the unavoidable conclusion that it's actually Robinson's Barley Squash.

'*Please* tell me you're beginners too ...' The woman addressing us is about three inches shorter than me, with scarlet lips, perfect flicky eyeliner and the sort of hour-glass figure that in the 1950s would have attracted wolf-whistles. 'Our only experience of salsa dancing is watching *Strictly*.'

'And that was painful enough,' adds her boyfriend. He looks six or seven years older and wears a sheepish smile to accompany the small spare tyre protruding over his cleanly pressed jeans. After a few introductions, we learn that the couple – Stella and Mike – are getting married in July. Preparations were going brilliantly until he dropped into conversation that, in the light of his two left feet, he *didn't think a first dance was necessary*.

'I had two words to say to that,' Stella tells us. '"AS IF". So here we are.'

'I've got four months in which to become a Latin lothario,' Mike grins.

Stella looks sceptical. 'Love, if we just get your legs moving without you doing yourself an injury, I'll be happy with that.'

'All right, ladies – gent,' Marion nods. 'How about we start with some basic moves? Let's get you all paired up.'

She turns on the music again and lowers the volume to a

level at which the windows are no longer vibrating. We stand in allotted pairs: Stella and Mike. Marion and Emily. Cate and me.

'No offence, Lauren,' she mutters, as she grabs my hand. 'But when I said I wanted to dance with someone dark-eyed and gorgeous, you weren't what I had in mind.'

'It could be worse – you could be in poor Emily's position,' I point out as our friend is forced to stand at the front of the 'class' and take part in Marion's demonstration. For Cate's sake I pretend to be disappointed that the room isn't a sweaty, bustling hotbed of male lust. But in truth I couldn't be more relieved, even if Marion isn't very satisfied with the situation.

'It's extremely difficult with only one man here,' she laments. 'In salsa it's the man's job to lead so I'm teaching you this the wrong way round. Which one of you wants to be the man?'

'It's been that long since I waxed my legs, I'd better volunteer,' Cate replies.

What becomes most apparent in the first half-hour of the lesson is just how difficult it is to master steps which are technically meant to be easy. They even *look* easy. But easy is the last thing they are, at least to me.

Even when we're trying to get to grips with the basics and follow Marion's instructions – to loosen the knees, move from the hips, keep the body central – Cate and I are a clash of ankles and giggling hysteria. This situation worsens significantly when Marion foolishly decides we're ready to move on to a turn.

We are instructed to ensure we're putting pressure on our feet each time we make a step, the idea being to get us wiggling the bottom half of our torsos and looking almost like dancers. I suspect we all look more like a pair of demented geriatrics on a waiting list for hip replacements.

Once we start taking this seriously, however, things start slotting into place. Although Marion seems to be under the impression she's tutoring *The Kids From Fame*, and doesn't find our haplessness at all amusing, she does get Cate and me moving in a vaguely salsa-ish way. Or maybe it's just that we don't look bad compared with poor Mike, who is not over-burdened with natural co-ordination.

As Marion turns her attention to showing him – again – how to master the basic mambo, Cate grabs me by the hand. 'What did Marion say this step was called? A kerfufla?'

'Enchufla,' I correct her.

'Bless you,' she replies. 'Whatever it is, I'm determined to crack it.'

Cate is nothing if not enthusiastic. She's always been like this. I've known her since we were little girls – we went to primary school together – and she was always the first to stick her hand up in the air and volunteer for just about everything. That was the case whether we were being asked to give out library books or, on one notable occasion, audition for a part in a TV advert for a breakfast cereal (she didn't get it; the producers said she had 'slightly too much personality'). Tonight, what we jointly lack in technical ability, my friend seems determined to make up with speed, joie de vivre and – it turns out – her innate ability to draw unwanted attention to us. To be absolutely fair, it's not Cate who manages to get one of the threads from the ailing carpet wrapped around her high heel – it's me.

'Cate!' I shriek, but she takes this as encouragement, grabs me by the waist and carries on dancing while the thread pulls against my ankle. Cate only becomes aware of my predicament when, in desperation, I reach out to try and stop myself from falling, a move that has the converse effect of making me lose my balance and stumble to my knees, taking my friend with me.

I attempt to scramble to my feet, aware that Cate is speechless with laughter and Marion has her arms crossed in disapproval. 'Sorry,' I mutter, pulling down my skirt as I sit up and start picking at the threads around my ankle in an attempt to release them.

'Oh, don't worry – at least no one's here to see us,' she sighs, as I glance up at two of the best-looking men I've seen in my life standing at the door.

In the excruciating moments that follow, I take in and process a succession of facts. The guys in front of us have that athletic, healthy look about them – tanned, muscular and with the air of being as at home in the great outdoors I would be in front of an episode of *EastEnders*. They are both wearing hiking boots, and one of them has on the instantly-recognisable bright red jacket of a Mountain Rescue volunteer.

I've noticed a certain trait in this kind of bloke over the years: they insist on *helping* people. It's not even a result of all the first aid courses they have to do. This is something in their genes that means they're physically unable to restrain themselves when there's anyone in need of assistance, whether it's a lone hiker cragfast on Skiddaw, a group of walkers attempting to decode their Ordnance Survey maps, or two women in strappy heels scrambling around to untangle themselves from a fraying carpet.

I respond to their attempts to help us up with the level of mortification the situation deserves – red faced, mumbling that none of this is necessary – while Cate holds out her hand as if she's Deborah Kerr in the *King and I* and rises elegantly on to her toes, with a demure smile.

As I brush myself down, I try not to look at the guy in front of me, although I've already caught a glimpse of clean-shaved skin, unusually symmetrical features and dark, brooding eyes that somehow look older than his face.

'You've got something on your cheek,' he says. I lower my eyes and follow the trail of a disconnected eyelash, before peeling it off and shoving it in my pocket.

Jane Costello

'Gents! Come in and join us! Are you beginners too?' Marion asks, seizing the opportunity.

The guy with the brooding eyes backs away. 'Actually, we're here for a business meeting. I have a feeling we have the wrong place though.' At that, his phone pings and he opens a text, before turning to his friend in the red jacket, who is almost as tall as him, with blond hair and a smattering of freckles across his nose. 'At least, we *did* have a meeting.'

'They've cancelled on you again?' asks the blond guy.

'Apparently so.'

Marion zones in on her chance like a heat-seeking missile. 'Don't suppose either of you fancy a go at salsa, do you?'

'Er, no, I don't think so,' the guy with dark hair says instantly.

But his friend is smiling: a broad, unashamed, distinctly flirty smile – aimed directly at Cate. 'Oh, come on,' he says. 'We're not doing anything else now, are we?'

To be fair to the two newcomers, they throw themselves into the situation. And the result, against all the odds, is quite an enjoyable evening.

I am more than happy to step aside and let Cate dance with the blond one, who's called Will, and Emily dance with the dark one, who's called Joe, while I stick with Marion. Meanwhile, Stella tries her very best to encourage Mike, despite the fact that every time I look over, his feet appear to be defying the laws of nature and going in opposite directions.

The lesson itself is over before we know it, at which point it's time for the 'social'.

Which isn't admittedly as 'social' as it could be given that there are still less than ten of us in the room. But after sticking to a fairly regimental set of steps under Marion's guidance, it's an opportunity to let our hair down and do a little more actual *dancing*, at least as I know it.

The kind where you get to loosen up, move with the music, enjoy yourself – although technically speaking, our salsa steps would never win Len Goodman's approval. Once the music is cranked up, it's easy to get into the swing of things, even if I am stuck with Marion while Cate and Will spin around the room laughing, and Joe gazes into Emily's eyes as he takes her hand and leads her, like we were shown earlier.

As the sky gets blacker and the moon shimmers outside, Marion looks at her watch and begins her appeal to drum up support for next week. 'I realise it wasn't as packed as we'd anticipated,' she says. 'But it's early days, isn't it?'

Cate places a reassuring hand on Marion's arm. 'It's been a great night. And once word gets round, you'll be packed out.' She turns to Will. 'But do us a favour boys: next week, can you bring a few friends?'

Chapter 3

I feel mildly groggy when I wake the following morning, which I could put down to antioxidant deficiency due to the absence of kale in my diet (which I read about online yesterday) but probably has more to do with drinking three margaritas on a Tuesday night, even if they didn't taste overly alcoholic.

Still, it is Wednesday. It is not raining. And I have a staff meeting this afternoon at which Edwin Blaire will be present. So life is good, in a bittersweet kind of way.

Which is how it has been in the two years since I've known Edwin, two tortured but sublime years in which he entered my life like a luminous blaze of fireworks . . . which I am soon to extinguish with a big bucket of water. Australian water, to be precise.

I am saving up to join my cousin Steph, who is currently on the Gold Coast doing little but sleeping with handsome but dubious men and topping up her tan, for a gap year.

I know I'm technically far too old for a gap year. But I've always wanted to travel Down Under. It's in my blood. Dad was born and raised just outside Melbourne, and when I was a teenager I was obsessed with the idea of living there one day.

As a result, my laptop is clogged up with bookmarks of travel articles for parts of the country I'm determined to see, including the town where my dad lived until he was twenty, when he and two friends came to the UK on a work visa and never looked back. Although he loved the UK, especially the Lake District, where he ended up after a short stint living in Shepherd's Bush, my dad remained unmistakably Aussie. Funny, outdoorsy and with a quiet strength of character that feels like a rarity these days.

Anyway, I've spent half my life in one long day dream about what it would be like to live, at least for a while, somewhere you could wake up knowing the sun would be shining, even though Dad said Melbourne's weather wasn't always that predictable.

So, disappearing to the other side of the world makes sense, even without my need to escape from my deep, all-consuming love for a man by travelling 10,000 miles away from him and never seeing him again. This, I'm afraid, is the only way of liberating myself from the shackles of an overwhelming passion that is – and this is the miserable nub of the matter – completely unrequited.

Edwin belongs to someone else. Fiona. Otherwise known as The Bitch.

It's an ironic soubriquet, in case you're wondering, because Fiona couldn't be nicer, sweeter, more fun and generally perfect if she'd been made in a cupcake factory and had a halo.

They are a gorgeous couple and they are never, ever going to split up.

I came to this realisation at our Christmas party before last, when Edwin confided in me that he was planning to propose in Paris on New Year's Eve, with an antique diamond ring that once belonged to his great-grandmother (spoiler alert: he went ahead with it – and she said yes).

There and then, after controlling the urge to cry for the rest of the evening, I decided I would follow in Steph's libidinous footsteps for an Edwin-free year of sun, freedom and possibly sex, although I have forgotten how to do that, or at least I would have without my *Game of Thrones* box set.

I have saved up £4,764.37, and estimate I have only another few months before I'm ready to depart. Which means torturing myself with Edwin's heavenly face for all that time, but at least there is light at the end of the tunnel. And I might as well enjoy the view in the meantime.

I clamber out of bed and pad across my tiny, creaky bedroom to look out of the window across the misty landscape and towards the whitewashed walls and seventeenth-century timbers of the Mortal Man pub. I can't deny I'll miss a view like this, whatever the Gold Coast has going for it. I open the window and breathe in the air, brushing away crystal droplets of overnight rain that have gathered on the windowsill.

Kissing Gate Cottage, which I've rented for the last five years, has two bedrooms, a tiny, old-fashioned kitchen, a bathroom and a living room. It's small but I love every nook and cranny of it, its slate walls and ancient beams and the fact that it always smells of the seasons: new grass and sunshine in spring, burning wood and spice in winter, admittedly with a little help from Ambi Pur.

It sits in a row of identical slate cottages in Troutbeck, which is quiet and scenic but close to the bustle of Bowness and Ambleside, both of which are short on the bright lights and action of a metropolis but have everything you could ever really need. There are pubs of every description, from the posh kind that serve thrice-cooked chips to the rugged kind full of muddy boots and wet dogs. There are boutiques that sell more than the obligatory hiking gear, old-fashioned cinemas – the kind where they have an interval and ice-cream sellers – and an exceptionally good chocolate shop in Ambleside, which probably just gives the place the edge for me.

Once I'm dressed and ready, I pick up my phone and spot a text from Emily that says, Did you enjoy last night? I loved it … though not sure if that's down to the dancing or gorgeous Joe! x I wish I could muster the same enthusiasm.

I hop into my aging Mini to make the twelve-minute drive to work, St Luke's and St Patrick's C of E primary school. Three other vehicles are in the staff car park when I pull in. One of them belongs to Edwin, who always makes it in at least fifteen minutes before me and will be in the staff room reading the paper already. I examine my appearance in the mirror, which is more unforgiving than in my dimly-lit bedroom, to see if it's suitable for his eyes this morning. The answer, immediately, is no.

The zit on my chin is not the most offensive I've ever had. That honour was saved for the one that graced my face when I graduated from university in Lancaster, which was like a second nose – and was captured for all eternity in the picture still on my mother's mantelpiece. But it's offensive enough. I noticed some kind of protrusion when I was putting on my foundation this morning, but in the thirty-five minutes since that moment it seems to have swelled up as if it's been sitting under the heat lamps in an industrial-scale cannabis farm.

I pull out a tissue and do the only thing open to me: give it a little squeeze. Then another one. Then, just when I'm getting really into it …

Knock, knock!

I leap up and bang my head on the ceiling of the car.

Edwin Blaire's beautiful face is staring at me. And at my zit. I open the door and smile awkwardly. 'Edwin! Good morning,' I say, swinging my legs over and shuffling out of the driver's seat.

'Gorgeous, isn't it. How are you today, Lauren?'

'I'm really good, thanks,' I tell him, surreptitiously holding my hand up to my face. When I remove it I notice a dab of blood on my finger. Perfect.

Edwin, physically speaking, is like nobody I have ever fancied before. When I was a teenager I went for obvious types – Ryan Gosling in *The Notebook*, or Keanu in *The Matrix*. The fact that Edwin is not some overblown dreamboat is part of his appeal. That's not to say he isn't gorgeous, because he is, but his frame is tall and slim, where I once sought out boy-band muscles. His eyes shine with kindness the more you get to know him, and the angular jawline and wide mouth grow more sensual with each snatched gaze.

His hair is glossy, his skin luminous and he always manages to dress in a way that's as original as it is impeccable. I remember thinking when he first started here, about a year after me, that the children might find the fact that he always wears a tie a little intimidating, but I couldn't have been more wrong. He is universally adored by the children – and the other staff, for that matter. Honestly, the rest of us don't stand a chance; Edwin is without question the most popular teacher in school. He is a complete natural: strict enough to command their respect, but so much fun that you know every one of them wishes he was their uncle.

'Your salsa class turned into a good night then?' he asks.

'Do I look that rough?'

He laughs his lovely laugh, the one that makes birds and butterflies and little pink hearts fly up around my head. 'You never look rough,' he reassures me and continues to make eye contact just long enough for my stomach to swoop a little. 'How did it go?'

'Oh ... it was fun. Though I was mainly paired off with Cate, which wasn't quite what I had in mind.'

'I'll have to come along one week and rescue you,' he says, as my cruciate ligaments threaten to give way.

'I wish you would,' I blurt out, then feel my neck redden. Fortunately, he changes the subject.

'Am I right in saying we've got a staff meeting later on? I had something in my diary but have managed to leave it at home.'

One of Edwin's gorgeous quirks is that, despite being only thirty-four and basically a genius – he has a degree from the London School of Economics – he manages to resist the frantic, twenty-first century scramble of technology that dictates all our lives these days. He's got a mobile, obviously, but prefers to organise himself with nothing more than a Mont Blanc fountain pen, Moleskine notebook and old-fashioned leather diary. He's not even on Facebook, which is quite inconvenient given how much I'd enjoy secretly poring over his pictures.

'We have, Edwin, yes. Three o'clock. Straight after the school bell.'

'Good job I've got you around,' he smiles, as I am hit by a ten-ton truck of longing, which has the strange effect of making me feel the need to move the conversation on. 'How's Fiona?' I ask as we stroll through the car park toward the main entrance.

Our school was established in 1861 and parts of the old building still exist, although they have been renovated internally – in about as sympathetic a fashion as was possible in the 1980s. Edwin is about to push open the door, but stops.

'Oh, Fiona's ... fine. At least ... I think so,' he says, as I register a meaningful look in his eyes.

'You *think so?*'

'Hmm.' He looks down, mildly embarrassed. 'I haven't seen her since the weekend.'

He pushes open the door and invites me to enter first as my heart starts thudding faster. 'Has she been away?'

'Er, no,' he replies dully.

'Oh,' I say, suppressing an urge to shout: '*Speak, man, speak!*'

He stops and turns to me, looking down again at his feet. 'The truth is ... I've moved out,' he confesses. 'And I can't deny it, I feel terrible about it.'

I realise my jaw is somewhere near my knees. 'You dumped her?'

He nods silently.

'Why? What happened?' I ask.

He glances around to check no-one's listening. 'When I proposed, I meant it. At that point, I didn't have a shadow of a doubt that I wanted to marry her. We would have done it last year, had Fiona not had so much on with work – it was her idea to leave it a couple of years. Anyway, in recent months, she started making wedding preparations and we went to see this venue in Ullswater.' I look up and realise he's started sweating. 'It was all moving along so fast and . . . suddenly . . .' he stops to draw breath before saying, 'I knew I was making a mistake. I had to put a stop to it. I had absolutely no choice.'

I don't know how to process this information. 'You're not getting married any more?' I croak.

He shakes his head. 'We'd been growing apart for a long time.' He looks at me, clearly worried I'll despise him, in some twisted act of sisterhood. 'Not that it had been *awful*. It hadn't. Fiona's a lovely person. A perfect girlfriend.'

I nod, feeling very hot. 'She is,' I agree, unable to deny it. 'She is unquestionably a lovely person. I can't speak for the girlfriend bit, obviously.'

'Well, she was wonderful,' he shrugs. 'Which is why I think I convinced myself I was in love with her . . . when I wasn't.'

'Weren't you?'

'No.' He looks into my eyes and my heart skips a beat.

'And you can't be with someone for the rest of your life when you're not in love. Can you?'

He's clearly looking for reassurance. You'd think I'd be bursting to give it to him. But I'm so shocked, I'm finding it difficult to say a single thing.

'Only *you* know if you've done the right thing, Edwin. But, you *should* be certain before you actually get married to someone,' I murmur, unable to meet his eyes. Then, before I can think about it, I place my hand on his arm as a gesture of solidarity. He looks momentarily surprised, then after a heartbeat, places his hand on mine.

I suddenly feel as if I'm dancing on poor Fiona's grave – and I'm not the only one. We both snatch our hands away. 'So you haven't heard from her? You don't know how she is?'

He deflates. 'OK, I confess: I was fibbing when I said that. She's devastated. She keeps sending me texts saying she's going to euthanise the goldfish in revenge.'

'That seems very out of character.'

'I think I've driven her over the edge,' he says.

'Poor Fiona,' I offer.

'Poor Fiona,' he agrees.

Then we stand, silently, wondering what to say next. 'Um ... I'd better get into class,' I splutter, and he nods as we scurry to the front door, a blaze of nervous energy firing up between us.

27

Chapter 4

The faintest hint of sunshine pushes through the clouds that weekend, apparently representing enough of a heatwave to convince Cate and Emily that the prime location at the Mortal Man on Saturday afternoon is outside.

I find Emily at a table in the beer garden, her teeth chattering and nose a peculiar tinge of blue. 'Isn't it lovely to see some sunshine? I feel like summer's only around the corner,' she says, huddling into her jacket.

'Yes, if this keeps up we might be able to remove our long johns in a few weeks,' I reply, taking a seat as Cate walks towards us with a tray, carrying three glasses, a bottle of white and a couple of bags of nuts.

To give my friends' sanity due credit, while the Mortal Man is a lovely cask-ale and high-beam type of pub, the greatest of all its virtues is the view: in summer, this little spot is a sun trap, surrounded by the craggy landscape of Troutbeck. It's the closest you'll get to heaven on earth without Tom Hardy and a tub of Häagen-Dazs.

Cate pours the glasses and raises hers.

'What are we toasting?' I ask.

She shrugs. 'Three soon-to-be-brilliant salsa dancers?'

We chink glasses as she hands over a bag of nuts.

'Not for me,' I reply. 'I'm on a diet. I've even started using MyFitnessPal.'

Emily frowns. 'I've never known you to diet. You don't *need* to diet.'

'You've never known me to diet *successfully*,' I correct her. 'I assure you I've got plenty of wobbly bits I need to get rid of.'

A look of glorious insight suddenly appears on Cate's face. 'Aha! This is because Edwin's single now, isn't it?'

I wonder about denying it, but that would prevent me from discussing the whole thing for the next hour, which I'm not prepared to relinquish. 'I still can't get over it,' I say. 'Fiona was perfect. I never thought *anyone* would split up with her.'

'Well the love of your life has,' Cate points out.

I suddenly feel slightly woozy, and Emily throws me a look. 'Deep breaths, Lauren.'

'Logically this might not mean much,' I tell them. 'Logically, if he'd been interested in me two years ago when we met, then he'd have dumped The . . . Fiona then.' I am appalled with myself for almost letting the word 'Bitch' slip out in the light of recent events, ironically or not. 'I've been tossing and turning for three nights wondering if . . . if . . . oh, it's ridiculous.'

'No, it's not,' Emily says. 'You and Edwin have been friends for two whole years. You've got loads in common. You spark off each other when you're together. I could totally see you as a couple. The fact that he hasn't thought about you in those terms until now just shows that he's a decent, honourable, one-woman type of guy. Now that Fiona is out of the way, it's time to step up your game.'

'You think I should ask him out?'

Cate considers this for a second. 'Under normal circumstances I'd say definitely. But Edwin's old-fashioned – in a good way, obviously,' she adds hastily, seeing my expression. 'I think it'd be better if *he* asked *you* out. You just need to plant the seed of the idea in his head.'

'How am I going to do that?'

'You'll think of something,' she winks. 'And if not, *I'll* think of something. Ooh, I've got a really good feeling about this. I bet all three of us will be hooked up by the end of the summer.'

'Still dreaming about Will then?' I ask.

'He is so unbelievably HOT,' she sighs, which I take as a yes. 'I've never been out with anyone from Mountain Rescue before. I wonder if he'd take me up in his chopper?'

I roll my eyes. 'Emily will have the same problem if she ends up with . . .'

'Joe,' Emily reminds me. 'But he's not Mountain Rescue. He's an *entrepreneur*.'

'Oh right,' I reply. 'The Alan Sugar kind or the drug-dealing kind?'

'I didn't ask,' she smirks. Then a thought occurs to her. 'Do you think he's out of my league?'

Cate tuts. 'Don't be ridiculous, Emily. Anyway, have you been practising your dance moves, Lauren?'

'Oh – do I really have to go to salsa again?' I ask, having conveniently forgotten about the whole thing.

The others look at me as if I've grown that extra nose again. 'Didn't you enjoy it?' Emily says, looking genuinely shocked.

'It was *all right*, but my shins are black and blue after five minutes with Mike, and now that you two are paired off . . .'

'I'd say that was a little premature, Lauren,' Emily chides me. 'We both fancy a couple of blokes, but that doesn't mean we're *paired off*. Besides, we're not there for the men. We're there for the fun. Aren't we, Cate?' She nudges our friend.

'What – eh? Yes, sorry,' she says. 'I was distracted.'

'By what?' Emily asks.

Cate narrows her eyes towards the car park. 'I could've sworn I saw . . .'

We spin round and follow her gaze when Robby, Cate's ex-boyfriend, appears and starts sauntering towards the pub door. 'Oh God, it *is* him,' she says, ducking her head down, as if this will save her from anything.

Emily chews her lip. 'Maybe he won't spot us.' At which point he starts waving.

Cate looks up, starts twiddling with the piercings at the top of her right ear and musters up a 'what a lovely coincidence' smile that is so unconvincing you'd think she'd just found fossilised squirrel faeces in the bottom of her glass. 'Shit. What do I do?' she hisses through clenched teeth.

'You just have a polite conversation and hold your breath until he's gone,' I tell her.

Robby is suddenly hovering above us. It's hard not to feel sorry for Cate's ex-boyfriend, and not just because she left him heartbroken when she dumped him. He's always had that feel-sorry-for-me way about him, which I think was part of the reason she eventually came to find him so strangely unattractive.

And it is strange, because Robby is unfeasibly good-looking, with the lithe, hard body of an underwear model, and a high blond Tin Tin quiff that is so daft it can only be cool.

Half-Parisian, Robby moved to London when he was eight, and then relocated up here to the Lakes last year for work. He's a bar-tender at the Damson Garden, an insanely luxurious boutique hotel where he's served cocktails to A-list film stars, Olympic sportsmen and the odd a chart-topping musician.

At twenty-seven, he's five years younger than Cate, and although he has everything going for him, he retains a strangely melancholic disposition, as if he's permanently mourning something that hasn't yet happened. Only, in this case, it has happened. Cate dumped him. And apparently ruined his life.

'How are things, ladies?' he asks, with a face that says, *I'm trying my best to keep a stiff upper lip*, DESPITE WHAT THIS FUCKING COW DID TO ME.

'Good, thanks,' Emily and I reply. Then there's a split-second silence in which everyone is thinking about asking him the same question, yet you can practically hear the cogs in our brains trying to stop us from doing so.

'And how are *you*, Robby?' Cate asks, clearly not able to stop herself.

He glares at her. 'I'll have to be honest, things are not so goo—'

'Would you like a nut?' I ask, thrusting the glazed almonds under his nose. He looks perplexed by this question. 'They're delicious,' I continue, before he can say anything. 'Lots of calories, mind you. Not that I'm suggesting you'd need to watch your weight. So have you served anyone famous recently? Tom Cruise been in? Or Katie Holmes? Oh, no – that could be awkward . . . '

A wrinkle appears above Robby's nose. 'Not really. I've had things on my mind other than work though. Personal things.'

He flashes another look at Cate, who is pretending to admire the view. He sits down next to her. When she turns round, she nearly leaps out of her chair. 'Things aren't going my way at the moment. I had my phone stolen yesterday.'

'Oh, I'm sorry, Robby,' Cate says, and he seems to leap on her sympathy and grasp it with both hands.

'I miss you,' he whispers.

Emily looks at her watch. 'Ooohh ... is it really nearly three o'clock?'

Cate throws us a glance that screams, *Do not go or I will never speak to you again.* Emily and I sit tight.

'Cate,' he repeats. 'I'd just like to talk about a few things. That's all. I – I know I'm not everything you want ...'

'It's not that,' she squirms. 'You're lovely, Robby.'

'Then why aren't we together?' he fires back. 'Because I think *you're* lovely too. I've said it enough, haven't I?'

Cate's face grows red. 'There's no point in going through it all again,' she says weakly. 'I think you're a wonderful man. But you and I ... I'm sorry, we're just not meant to be.'

His handsome jaw tenses. 'Okay,' he says flatly. 'I'm sorry I bothered you. See you around, ladies. Or ... not.'

And at that he gets up and walks away.

Cate draws a long breath. 'God, I feel awful. I'm not sure what's wrong with me. Most women would kill to have a man like that chasing after them.'

Emily shrugs. 'If you don't fancy him, you don't fancy him.'

Cate's eyes widen. 'You've seen him – he's gorgeous – but sometimes way too intense. You know how it is when you fall for someone: you either feel it or you don't. Think about how you feel about Edwin, Lauren. There's absolutely no shadow of a doubt in your mind about how madly in love you are with him. It's indefinable – the chemistry, the alchemy. And what you feel for Edwin, I certainly don't for Robby. Do you know what I mean?'

I take a sip of my drink. Because I know exactly what she means. My feelings for Edwin are rock solid. If only the same could be said of his for me.

Chapter 5

Our second salsa night is a revelation. It isn't just the sheer liberation of moving without the hateful shoes, which I abandoned in favour of my Converse, after Marion agreed they were acceptable.

It's that a decent number of participants turn up. We're still some way from forty or fifty but, following a piece in the local paper last week and Will and Joe asking a couple of friends, we're now up to sixteen.

This rush sends Marion into a quivering panic, which is abated slightly when the cavalry arrives in the form of her friend, who introduces herself rather formally as Lulu Mitford. Lulu is younger than Marion; she's in her late thirties, with a slim, fine-boned face and long eyelashes. Although she works for English Heritage, she's been dancing ballroom and Latin since she was a teenager, hence the fact that Marion has roped her along so she can split us into two groups: absolute beginners and those able to undertake more than the basic steps without risking a trip to A&E.

'How did you persuade your friends to come?' I ask Joe, as he takes my hand. His face breaks into a warm, easy smile and his eyes no longer seem as brooding tonight. Although perhaps all the hype from Emily about how lovely he was with her last week has simply made him seem a bit more approachable.

'They're mainly Will's mates from Mountain Rescue,' he explains. 'He says nobody was keen at first, then he told them the place was full of single women. After that, it was surprisingly simple.'

Lulu starts the music and asks us to begin with the same basic steps we learned last week. Joe, I'm relieved to see, is at about the same ability level as me: passable. Our footwork is a long way from fancy, particularly when Lulu introduces a new move – a turn outwards one way, then the other. There's the usual clashing of knees, for which we're both responsible.

'I might be wrong, but you don't sound as if you were born and bred in Cumbria,' I tell him.

'I'm a Londoner originally. I spent my childhood in Hampstead, but have lived all over the place since.' I mentally pocket this nugget of biography to fill in Emily later. 'I always knew I'd end up in the Lakes though, at least for a time. My dad fancied himself as a bit of an adventurer and so we'd come at least twice a year, to scramble up Scafell Pike or Great Gable. So when an opportunity arose a few months ago, I did that unforgivable thing the locals must hate tourists doing: I moved here.'

I raise my eyebrows. 'Well, I am a true, bona-fide local and I can say for the record that I'm totally at ease with the idea of welcoming people who've fallen in love with the place.'

'Really?' he asks dubiously.

'Yep. Until they all turn up, that is.'

He laughs and takes my hand again, but Lulu steps in. 'Time for a switch around,' she tells us. 'Move along now.'

According to Lulu, it's not the done thing to dance with the same person all evening, so over the next forty-five minutes, we shuffle promiscuously from partner to partner. The idea is to experience dancing with a range of abilities, rather than this being an elaborate prelude to a swingers' party. Marion also insists that it's the best way for us all to get to know each other – and I can't deny that collective cringing proves to be a remarkably effective bonding tool.

The only one who isn't convinced by the new system is Stella. I end up next to her while Lulu demonstrates a turn with one of the newcomers – a toned, olive-skinned guy with an accent I can't place. They make the steps look very remedial. 'Don't get me wrong – I get why we're doing it this way,' says Stella, as Will steps up and takes her by the hands and I'm joined by a sprightly man who must be in his seventies but looks good on it. 'I'm just worried that Mike is going to dislocate someone's kneecaps.' We both look over and wince as he attempts to unravel himself from Cate's ankles.

My partner, it turns out, is a former theology lecturer called Frank. He is three inches shorter than me, with a sweet smile and haphazard beard that resembles the bristles in a stiff boot cleaner. As we follow Lulu's lead, stepping and turning to the music, it's obvious he's significantly better at this than me. I start moving my hips a little more, in a bid to make more of an effort.

'How long have you and Mike been together?' I ask Stella when the music stops.

'Three and a half years,' she replies.

'He seems lovely.'

'Oh, he's a gem,' she says, wrinkling her nose affectionately. 'And I get on like a house on fire with his family. Or at least I did until the Monday before last.'

'Oh?'

'I thought I'd give Mike a nice surprise and recreate that scene in *Pretty Woman*. You know, where she sits on the table, naked except for his tie.'

'Ah,' I reply, unsure how else to respond.

'So I'm there: table set, candles on the sideboard, seabass in the oven. Only, after I heard a key in the door and whipped off my dressing gown, I discovered that it was actually his mum letting herself in to feed the cat. She'd thought we were still away for the weekend.'

'Oh good God . . .'

'I know. There I was with his M&S tie dangling between my knockers and in walks his mother with a bowl of Sheba. It was terrible.'

Tonight's newcomers make for an interesting mix. As well as the Mountain Rescue volunteers, there's Frank, the ex-theology lecturer, Esteban – who, it turns out, is twenty-five, a restaurant manager and from Peru – as well as a couple of nurses and a gorgeous blonde Ambleside College student called Jilly: Esteban can't take his eyes off her. There's also one couple from the Midlands who are staying at the hotel for a week's holiday and are salsa fanatics.

But our small band of new dancers are mainly locals, covering a vast age range that starts somewhere in the early twenties and ends with Frank.

All of which makes the whole thing so much more of an *event* than last week, that for a slim moment, I start to wonder if I might be enjoying myself. Although not as much as Cate.

She spent the first five minutes chatting with a couple of the waitresses – there is literally no one on earth she couldn't engage in small talk – before making a beeline for Will and being virtually inseparable since. Despite Marion and Lulu's efforts to get us all to swap partners, they've mysteriously ended up together at least five times.

'Before we begin, I need to say something to you.' Mike is

standing in front of me, offering me his hands before the dance begins.

'What is it?' I ask, taking hold of them.

He mumbles sheepishly. 'Sorry.'

'For what?'

The music starts and he steps forward . . . right onto my toe. 'Oh I see,' I gasp, hopping about, convinced that he's managed to chip my nail polish through a rubber toe-cap and pair of cotton socks. As Mike starts apologising again, Lulu appears.

Last week, Marion wasn't overly forgiving of Mike's ineptitude, addressing him like a disobedient child, as opposed to a moderately successful thirty-five-year-old IT manager. But Lulu appears to have taken a shine to him.

'You mustn't worry about it,' she says patiently. 'For some, this comes easily, for others it takes a bit of practice, but I've got no doubt you'll get there in the end.'

'I'm glad you're convinced,' Mike smiles at her.

'You just need to relax a bit,' she replies, moving his arms into the correct position as he reddens slightly. 'Though not too much – your arms need to be nice and tight. Remember, the man leads – *you're* the one in charge.'

'I suppose it had to happen one day,' he shrugs. 'Right, fancy trying one of these turns?' he asks me.

'Go for your life,' I say uncertainly.

Mike lifts up his arm, which is the cue for me to perform

the full 360-degree turn we learned earlier, in three quick, sharp steps. This is far harder than it sounds, although that might partly be because Mike loses his step and stumbles in my direction, leaving us a clash of arms and legs and red faces. The poor guy looks distraught.

'Don't worry, honestly. Bit of practice, like Lulu said,' I tell him, lying through my gritted teeth.

After the formal class, the half-hour 'social' kicks off, allowing everyone to do the one thing that is a priority in salsa: enjoying yourself. I step back and leave the eligible men to those who really want them – and so Cate ends up with Will again, while Emily is soon in Joe's arms.

I, on the other hand, dance with Frank again, who has increased in confidence so dramatically that he grabs me by the hand and yanks it back and forth as if he's trying to win three cherries on a fruit machine. As the steps become more familiar, I relax into the music and indulge in a blurred fantasy of what it'd be like to dance with Edwin. The thought sends a shot of heat through my body as I twirl round and stumble to a halt.

'Not bad,' declares Frank, grinning at me from behind his wire spectacles. My fantasy disintegrates.

When the class is over, we spill out into the floodlit driveway and head towards Cate's van, emblazoned with the logo of her shop, *Daffodils & Stars*.

The first part of the name is a reference to the William

Wordsworth poem, which he wrote in Ullswater; the latter a reflection of the fact that Cate will always be a bit of a hippy at heart, no matter how successful her business becomes.

'Did you pick up on some of the gossip among the staff tonight?' she asks me.

'No, what sort of gossip?'

She clicks the lock. 'The hotel is being sold,' she says tentatively, gauging my reaction. 'Apparently, it's been up for sale for nearly a year, on the QT. It's only now they've found a company willing to take it on.'

I feel a prickle of anxiety. 'So, who's the new owner?'

'They don't know who it is yet, but the rumour mill has gone into overdrive,' Cate replies. 'The staff seem to think it's going to be a disaster.'

'Why?' Emily asks.

'Word is, the new buyer is going for the jugular on the hotel. Plans to overhaul everything. The woman I got talking to seemed to think they were all going to be sacked and the place turned into Disneyland.'

I'd heard a rumour about it being up for sale, but that was months ago. Besides that, it's been on and off the market for years without anyone showing any interest, which is how I'd hoped it would stay.

Because, while I can't claim the place is thriving, the current owners at least understand the importance of keeping the fabric of the place intact, of retaining its history and

43

charm. The idea that someone's going to come in and tear it all apart sucks the breath out of me. Cate obviously notices.

'Sorry, that was really insensitive of me,' she says, putting her hand on my arm. 'They're probably exaggerating. I'm sure it can't be that bad.'

I glance back at the hotel. 'What if they're not?'

'Lauren, don't even think about it until we know more,' Emily says wisely.

And she's right. Of course she's right. When people's jobs are at stake, rumours like this have a tendency to spread like wildfire despite being dangerously inaccurate.

'Good night, ladies,' Will shouts, as he opens the door of a slightly dilapidated SUV.

Cate perks up. 'Night! See you next week?'

'Wouldn't miss it for the world,' he grins.

Joe lifts up his hand and opens the passenger door. 'Bye,' he says simply, as I realise Emily is mesmerised by him.

'Bye,' she replies, with a shy smile.

She's still unable to tear her eyes away as their tail-lights disappear down the drive. 'Is love in the air, Em?' I nudge her.

She glances up, shocked. 'Oh! No idea really . . .'

'Come off it. Things were looking seriously hot in there if you ask me,' Cate smirks as she starts up the van and we head out of the driveway.

'Do you really think he might like me?' Emily asks.

'I'd bet my Cuban heels on it if I had a pair,' Cate replies.

'Oh, while I remember, did you pick up one of the flyers Marion was handing round tonight? She's organising a two-night salsa holiday in Spain.'

'That's a bit optimistic, isn't it? She's only been running the class for two weeks,' I pipe up.

'I know but it's dirt cheap. I'm seriously tempted.'

'It's only your second class!'

'I haven't been abroad for three years and honestly, you couldn't get a week in Butlins for the price she's offering. If I'd known that learning to salsa would mean access to cut price holidays, I'd have signed up ages ago.'

'How does she manage to do it so cheaply?'

'Marion had been running a class in Manchester that'd been going for ages, and she's done the Spain thing for the last four years so has some sort of deal with the hotel. She swears it's a riot.'

'Cate – you hardly know these people. You might hate everyone there by the time the Spain trip happens.'

She takes on a dreamy expression. 'I doubt it somehow.'

'Well, don't look at me,' I tell her, glancing into the mirror of the van. 'Saving for Australia has put paid to any ideas of a holiday for me since I started.'

Emily spins round from the passenger seat and looks at me. 'I'm glad you're still saving,' she says. 'I was worried Edwin's newly-single status might have put you off the idea of leaving and following your dream.'

My heart misses a beat. 'Oh God, no. I mean, even if Edwin and I got together ... Oh God, what am I saying! Edwin and I are never going to get together. I wouldn't dream of planning my life around a schoolgirl crush that shows no signs of coming to fruition,' I say, wondering whether I'm lying or not.

'You never know, Lauren,' Emily shrugs. 'He definitely likes you. Now that Fiona is out of the way, who knows?'

I bite my lip, failing to suppress a surge of ill-founded hope. But Emily is right: it would be pathetic if I called a halt to all my Australia planning just because Edwin's love life has been thrown into disarray.

'Whatever happens, the trip to Spain sounds like a bargain, and I'm not prepared to let it pass me by, whether I've only just started this class or not,' Cate says firmly. 'What about you, Em? I can't think of anything better to do at the back end of Easter, can you?'

Chapter 6

Like my mum, I'm not one for diets. On the very rare occasions when I've dabbled, it's quickly become apparent that I have all the willpower of a starving elephant in a branch of Thorntons. I joined Weight Watchers – and left – in a record fifteen hours once, after one of the children brought in a humungous Minion-themed birthday cake with homemade buttercream that nobody but *a machine* could have resisted.

But things have got to change. Edwin Blaire is single for the first time in two years and this, finally, is my chance. I'm not going to let my wobbly inner thighs blow it.

I should say for the record that Edwin is not the kind of man who is shallow enough to worry about a few extra pounds on a woman. He is too emotionally intelligent for that. I'm almost certain of it. Just not certain enough to risk it.

Hence the fact that this morning's breakfast consists of plain porridge made with water, not milk – a dish not just entirely devoid of flavour and appeal, but so small it'd test Gwyneth Paltrow's resolve. I finish the bowl feeling like Oliver Twist, except it's so foul that even he would not have asked for more.

The drive to work is beautiful this morning. The sky is crisp and blue, sunshine shearing through the top of the Kentmere Horseshoe. It's the kind of day for picnicking and romance, a thought that trails into a day dream about Edwin and me sitting on the bank of Loughrigg Tarn, sipping something cold and sparkly and eating strawberries (hardly any calories!) between luxuriant kisses.

I flick in and out of a gentle reverie all the way to school, until I'm at the door of my classroom, ushering the children inside to join me and our new teaching assistant, Angela.

'Good morning, miss. Did you have a nice weekend?'

Tom Goodwin is at my side as he pushes his spectacles up his nose, soft tufts of pale brown hair at every conceivable angle. I know you're not meant to have favourites, but Tom is quite possibly the cutest, funniest child I've ever taught, an absolute sweetheart.

'I did, thank you, Tom. What did you do?'

'I went to my cousin's house for a sleepover,' he begins, removing his school bag from his shoulder.

'That sounds exciting.'

'Some bits were good. We watched *Ice Age* and ate loads of sweets. But then he called me *a brat*,' he tells me, blinking earnestly.

'Oh dear. What had you done?'

'Nothing! He thought I didn't know what a brat was.' He glances around, before leaning in and whispering, '*But I do.*'

'Do you?' I whisper back.

He straightens up, as though I've put him on the spot. 'Well . . . I know it's something with a tail,' he says.

I always wanted to be a primary school teacher. I had my first taste of how rewarding young children can be when I was basically still a kid myself, aged fourteen, and I volunteered to help out at a Sunday School at the church Dad intermittently attended.

It's been a while since I set foot in there these days – *sorry, God* – though I still believe and try to be kind, which is what Dad used to say was at the heart of it all, at least on the Sundays when he didn't make it there.

Anyway, it was only for a couple of years, for two hours a week – and I loved it. In fact now, even when I've been teaching long enough for the gloss to have worn off, I still can't imagine doing anything else. I only wish Dad could have seen me in this job, and come to the summer fairs and Christingle concerts as the family members of other staff do. He always knew teaching was where my ambitions lay, but by the time I got my first job, in a school in Kirkby Lonsdale, he was no longer with us.

Today, our first lesson is about the months of the year. We're attempting to order them correctly and discuss what happens during each one. Only, as ever, it's remarkably easy to stray off-topic.

'August is when my aunty gets married,' says Scarlet Cranston, who turned five last week.

'Oh, how lovely!' I reply. 'You'll have to bring something in for Show and Tell afterwards.'

'I will,' she grins.

'Now, onto September . . .'

'She's a lesbian,' Scarlet continues, turning to Tom next to her. '*That* means her husband is a woman.' He pushes his glasses up his nose as he considers this.

'You can't have a husband who's a woman,' Bethany Jones interjects.

'Yes, you can!' Scarlet argues. 'You can get married if you're a lesbian and you want a husband but that husband is also a woman. Can't you, Miss Scott?'

Trying to unravel this statement sufficiently to come up with an answer that is both accurate and politically correct makes my temples throb. So I make a series of ambiguous noises, before moving on to the time of the year when the leaves turn brown.

'Can anybody tell me the name of any more of the autumn months?' I ask.

'She's been married before,' Scarlet continues, apparently reluctant to drop a subject I can't deny is significantly more interesting than deciduous trees. 'That time it was to a man. He wasn't very nice though. He had a hairy back.'

'Thank you, Scarlet, let somebody else have a turn now.' I glance across the room to James Wesley, whose hand is thrust so high in the air he looks like he might give himself a hernia.

'Go on, James,' I encourage him.

He puts his hand down and thinks. 'I've forgotten the question.'

'Can you name one of the autumn months? What comes after September?'

'March,' he replies.

'No, not March, no. Anyone else?'

'January,' James shouts out again.

'Not January,' I reply, scanning the room.

'December? February? May?' James splutters.

'No, James, and you mustn't shout out,' I tell him, but it's too late, he looks ready to burst.

'WHAT ABOUT JUNE?'

The poor child appears distraught as I throw open the question to the class again and the first person to answer – Laura Cole – gets it right.

Little James looks so desolate after this turn of events, that I make sure when we move on to the subject of Halloween that he has the first chance to give it a go. Unfortunately, he doesn't want to answer my question, but ask one.

'Are *you* a lesbian, Miss Scott?' he pipes up, as I look at my watch to check how long there is to go until break.

*

Later, in the staff room, I recount this episode to Edwin who is looking unbelievably, earth-shatteringly attractive today. He's wearing brogues, with preppy chinos – a slightly more casual style for him than usual. It strikes me that Edwin could be a hipster in a certain light, although I should stress that there isn't a hint of pretension about him. It's just, he can carry off a waistcoat beautifully and he likes swing music and green tea, I mean *genuinely* – he doesn't just pretend to, like everyone else.

He's the only male in the room; indeed, he's the only male who works for the school. He and I are the youngest in here, although Maeve Barter, a Year Two teacher, sometimes acts as though she's sixty-three rather than thirty-three. As well as her, there's Gill Sumner, who's in her late thirties and is normally good fun but is in the process of a bitter divorce at the moment; this means she bites your head off at even the offer of a cup of tea. Then there's Joyce Bevan, who's looking forward to retirement next year and spends all her time between lessons reading books on her Kindle with names like *The Sheik's Tenacious Lover* and *Her Insatiable Italian Boss*.

'You're not, are you?' Edwin asks, glancing at me.

I frown. 'Not what?'

'A lesbian.'

I nearly spill my PG Tips as my head swims with the implications of this question. How, after knowing me for two years, could Edwin think that was a possibility? I know I haven't been out with anyone ... I know that I've had the love-life of a celibate mollusc ... but still. 'No,' I gulp.

'It'd be fine if you were, obviously,' he says.

'Of course,' I mutter, feeling my stomach sink further.

The fact that it'd be *fine* with Edwin if I was a lesbian, and therefore not even in the market for getting it on with him, does not sit well with me. Then I wonder, with a brief stab of hope, whether this simply adds an air of mystique and mystery to me, and means that I've hidden my feelings well. I decide to stick with that on the basis that the only alternative course of action is slitting my wrists.

'Of course it'd be fine. But I'm not. Just to be clear.' I smile and make a concerted effort to hold his gaze. To *flirt* with him. In an unequivocal, definitely-not-a-lesbian kind of way. It takes a second, but he does a double take and holds my gaze too. His back straightens in realisation. He doesn't move.

And for a quiet moment I am convinced that this unspoken sexual tension between us is finally being unleashed. I want him to know how I feel, or at least wonder about it, without saying a single thing. The moment is actually kind of perfect. Until my empty stomach decides to step in.

'*Ggggrrr,*' it gurgles.

It sounds as if someone is starting a rusty Harley Davidson from within the confines of my large intestine.

I gasp and put my hand over my stomach. '*Bllughhehae!*' it adds for good measure as I blush to my roots. 'Sorry about that,' I mutter. 'On a diet. Bit hungry. Better run.' I go to stand up.

'Don't run on my account, Lauren,' he says. I turn round again. 'Why don't you stay and share some cake? Not that I want to ruin your diet or anything.'

He holds out a Tupperware box and I realise I *cannot* pass up a moment like this: when the love of your life suggests you share his cake, calories don't come into it. You just get stuck in, for the sake of a higher cause. 'Are you sure you wouldn't mind?' I ask.

'Of course not, take some. My mum made it,' he adds, offering out the plastic box and handing me a wine-coloured napkin.

I don't know what type of cake it is beyond the fact that it's pale brown, cut into squares and covered in thick white icing. Even accounting for the fact that I am so ravenous I could eat a scabby horse with a pair of chopsticks, one thing becomes painfully apparent with my first bite: Edwin's mum is no Mary Berry.

'It's delicious, Edwin, thank you,' I say, trying not to gag as a chunk of raw, unmixed flour gets lodged in my windpipe. 'Is she . . . a keen cook?'

'She *was*. I'm not sure she's quite as good as she used to be.'

I muster a smile, swallow laboriously and pray that the flour

54

was the worst of it. 'So ... how are you, Edwin? You know, after the break-up?'

He sighs. 'Oh, I'm OK mostly. I've done the right thing, but I can't deny I feel a bit lonely lately. Fiona might not be the woman I want to spend the rest of my life with, but that doesn't mean I don't miss her. Does that make sense?'

'Of course it does. Sometimes, we all just need human contact, don't we?'

He looks at me and my cheeks heat up but mercifully he changes the subject. 'Maybe I just need a good distraction. Perhaps it's time for me to take up your offer to borrow that *Breaking Bad* box set ... as long as you wouldn't mind?'

'Of course not!' I've been extolling the virtues of Walter White and co since the day I met Edwin.

'Fiona never fancied it, but you convinced me.'

'I'll bring it in tomorrow,' I say. Then a tickle in my throat that makes me cough. And cough. So badly that at one point it sounds as though someone's polishing my tonsils with a feather duster.

Edwin stares at me with increasing alarm as, red-faced and eyes watering, my reflexes start to do everything they possibly can to eject his mum's cake in the most violent manner possible. 'Lauren, are you OK?' he asks in alarm.

When I fail to answer, he gives me several sharp thumps between my shoulder-blades. I wave my hands about, unable to speak, which finally persuades him to stop and start rubbing my back gently. I am slightly dazed from the experience, and the sensual feel of his hand against my spine does nothing to bring back my power of speech.

'Is that better?' he asks gently as I nod through bloodshot eyes, hook a finger into my throat and catch something on the end of it. Then I pull. And pull, gazing wonkily at my hand as I unravel a long, grey hair, which finally emerges from my mouth and dangles between my fingertips. He leans in to examine it.

'Oh God,' he winces, clearly mortified. 'That's one of Mum's. I'm so sorry,' he says, removing it from my hand and placing it in a napkin.

'Don't worry,' I mumble, composing myself. Then I realise he's looking at me peculiarly.

'Well, that was embarrassing,' he says. 'Mum'd be distraught.'

'Please don't worry, Edwin – honestly.'

He nods, clearly wanting to change the subject. 'So. Are these salsa classes you're doing fun?'

'Um . . . yes, actually.'

'I've always fancied it, you know. I love a dance. Not that I'm any good.' Unlike the first time he hinted at this, he looks like he could actually be serious.

'None of us are any good. You should come along,' I urge him, rather more desperately than I'd intended. 'You'd love it.'

He stands up, picks up his Tupperware box and turns to flash me a smile. 'I just might do that one day, Lauren.'

'I hope so, Edwin.'

And Mrs Blaire's hairball aside, I'm starting to think that today couldn't get any better.

Chapter 7

When we arrive at salsa night a few minutes early this week, Marion is pacing up and down with her arms crossed and a face like she's chewing a pickled wasp.

'Just when we get the class up and running – and a decent number of people turn up – I get told we've got to go,' she huffs, flipping back a wisp of blonde fringe.

'Go where?' asks Cate.

'Precisely! The new owner is going to rip this place apart. And for that, the hotel needs to close, probably for months, which means we've got nowhere to hold the class. It's all here,' she says, waving a piece of paper about. 'In a letter left for me at reception tonight from Gianni Battaglia . . . whoever he is.'

Cate looks over her shoulder. 'Project Manager of Wilborne Associates,' she reads.

'I've been talking to Janice the housekeeper,' Marion continues. 'The staff were called into a meeting last night by the current owners. The sale is due to be completed tomorrow. This place has been losing money for years and it's now reached a critical point. They didn't *want* to sell, but they had no choice. And the only buyers are these Wilborne people, who seem intent on destroying it.'

'Why would they want to destroy it?' Emily asks.

'They spin it as "bringing it into the twenty-first century". Which we can only assume means no more of these lovely ceilings and walls – and no more hotel for the next few months at least. It must be drastic if they need that amount of time.' She leans in. 'Wilborne Associates run other hotels, by the way – a budget chain called Travel Havens.'

My mouth gapes open as a wave of defiance sweeps over me. I feel like the miners marching in protest against pit closures in the 1980s. Like Emmeline Pankhurst at the gates of Parliament. I am burning with a righteous sense of indignation.

'Hang on, this is a listed building,' Emily leaps in. 'There are restrictions on what they can do. They won't be allowed to tear it apart.'

'They can't alter the basic structure but that won't stop them ripping out everything inside and putting in IKEA wallpaper,' Marion contends.

'Someone's got to do something,' I splutter. 'They can't allow this – the Moonlight Hotel is a piece of Cumbrian history.'

Cate frowns. 'So when is this all happening?'

'The new boss is going to be here tomorrow speaking to all the staff about their future,' Marion says ominously. 'What about the future of the bloody salsa class?'

In all honesty, the fact that Marion hasn't got a venue for her class is the last thing on my mind. I'm not even thinking primarily about the fate of the staff, although that'll be bad enough if people are out of their jobs. It's what's going to happen to the hotel. The thought makes my stomach swirl.

'I'll ask around Ambleside to see if I can find somewhere else, if you like,' Cate suggests. 'Shouldn't be too hard.'

'Maybe this isn't such a terrible thing,' Emily ventures. I glare at her. 'Obviously it's a nightmare for you having to find another venue, Marion, but this place is obviously in need of renovation.'

'Some TLC, Emily, that's all,' I correct her. 'Not for the entire character of the place to be bulldozed and all the staff to be sacked.'

The door opens and Esteban enters, wearing combat shorts and a luminous yellow muscle top that looks as if it belongs in one of Jane Fonda's 1980s fitness videos. 'Evening, ladies, how are things?'

Marion launches into a repeat of her tale of woe, virtually beating Esteban into submission until he agrees wholeheartedly how horrific the entire thing is. The others start to arrive shortly afterwards. The nurses aren't here tonight, but there's one new couple – a geologist called Andi and her husband, who I recognise from the local press as an environmental campaigner.

Then Lulu puts on some music – a salsa version of a Maroon 5 track – and Marion is forced to turn her attention to something other than winding everyone up. We start with the same basic moves on the spot that we've learned so far, and then move on to rotating back steps with a 'crossover'.

Lulu gives us a slow-motion demonstration with Esteban, before we all get to have a go ourselves. It feels good to be actually moving, covering some ground instead of being rooted to the spot.

'Couldn't Mike make it tonight?' I ask Stella, as Lulu thrusts Will in front of her.

'He's given up,' she says, making it clear that this isn't a decision of which she approves. 'He insists he's a hopeless case. Nothing will persuade him to come. Which means either I've got to do my first dance alone, or we don't *do* a first dance – *or* I find someone else to do it with.' She looks up. 'Do you fancy the job, Will?'

'Not sure what Mikey would make of that,' he grins, glancing down the row of dancers to Cate. She waves. His smile widens. And Stella begins dancing in the certain knowledge that her partner would rather be elsewhere.

*

As with last week, Lulu insists on us swapping partners and I find myself dancing with one of Will's Mountain Rescue friends, Luke, a divorced dad of three who's significantly better than me with the footwork.

During a short break, I go on chatting to Stella.

'How are your wedding preparations going?' I ask, keen to discuss something other than the future of the hotel. 'Apart from the first dance, obviously.'

'I hate to tempt fate, but pretty good really,' she replies. 'It's a big wedding but we're trying to keep things relaxed – you know, with a hog roast, instead of a formal, sit-down meal. Oh, and I went to see Cate this weekend to book her to do our flowers.'

'You won't regret it. She's awesome.'

'I know, I've seen her portfolio. Hey, are those two an item?' she whispers as Cate starts laughing at something Will has said, his playful eyes drinking her in.

'I think it's only a matter of time,' I reply as Lulu calls us to attention to watch a new turn and the men shift places until Joe is in front of me.

'I think a few of you ladies and gents are going to be ready to move into the improvers' class soon,' she announces.

My eyes widen. Then I become aware that my new partner is looking at me, with an undisguised smirk.

'What's so funny?' I ask, disconcerted.

'You,' Joe replies. Heat blossoms on my neck. 'You'd think

Lulu was trying to sign you up to the Olympic bobsleigh team, rather than move you up a class.'

'There's no way I'm up to it,' I protest.

'Ah, you'll be fine. Just wing it,' he says casually, taking my hands.

'Do you take that approach to all aspects of your life?' I ask.

He does the smirk again. It's got an *aren't-I-sexy* quality that is only not unbearable because he *is*. Sexy, that is. And nice. Not quite as nice and sexy as Emily, but the two of them are undoubtedly in the same arena.

'It's got me by OK so far.'

Lulu instructs us to repeat the turn as I wonder for a moment how I can twist the conversation to the subject of my friend. 'So are you single?' I blurt out.

He looks mildly surprised.

'I'm not asking for *me*, by the way,' I add hastily, as if I'm alluding to a fate worse than a slow death at the hands of a psychopath with a crochet hook. He frowns.

'I'm not saying you're hideous or anything,' I clarify. 'It's just that I have someone in my life already.' I realise this mysterious statement paints a significantly rosier picture than the reality. 'Kind of, anyway. The point is, *I* don't fancy you.'

He raises his eyebrows. 'Wow. That's a relief. But someone else does?'

'I couldn't possibly say,' I say coyly. Then it strikes me that subtlety is of limited use if I want to get things moving between him and Emily. 'At least, I'm not saying she *fancies* you – I wouldn't go that far, but if you were interested, then maybe she might be too.'

'Spit it out. Who?'

I glance over at Em, who smiles at me hopefully, then looks away. I instinctively know I need to be bold here. 'Emily.'

He doesn't reply at first, so I peer into his face as he contemplates the information, refusing to give anything away.

'So do you like her?' I ask, nudging the conversation along.

'She's lovely.'

'Why don't you ask her out? She might even say yes,' I grin.

'All right, Cupid. Maybe,' he replies, as I attempt a twirl but land on his toe again, mumbling apologies.

At that moment, I glance over Joe's shoulder and spot two of the waitresses huddled in the corner, talking with their arms crossed and brows furrowed. It doesn't take a genius to work out that they're gossiping about the future of the hotel and their jobs. Yet as we begin another turn, I realise that they're glaring in *my* direction. For a second I wonder if I've imagined it, but the longer it continues the more disconcerted I become.

'Is everything all right?' Joe asks.

'For some reason I'm being stared at. I'd assumed those two waitresses were talking about all the stuff that's going on with the hotel, but they keep looking over. I don't know what I've done.'

He glances at the waitresses, then takes my hand again. 'I wouldn't worry about it. It's not you they're looking at. It's me.'

'What?'

'They've worked something out, that's all,' he says, under his breath.

I step back and gaze at him in bewilderment. 'Worked *what* out?'

He lifts my arm up and I twirl around, landing haphazardly in front of him as he whispers to me: 'That I'm the new owner of this place.'

Chapter 8

I'm woken up at 5.45 a.m. the next morning by the deafening sound of my neighbour Agnes's hedge-trimmer. I tread to the window to see her in her dressing gown toting the power tool, attacking her rhododendrons as if she's the Terminator.

I shut the window – it's threatening to rain anyway – and flop back into bed, blearily picking up my phone, where I discover with a fluttering heart that Edwin texted me late last night. I excitedly open it up, only to find the following:-

> Don't suppose you could remember to bring that box set to school tomorrow? E xxx

I can at least take solace in the three kisses, which are the sole nugget of hope and affection in an otherwise devastatingly banal request, albeit a reasonable one given that I have entirely forgotten to bring it in since I promised to do so last week.

I log on to Facebook in time to see the latest Australia update from my cousin Steph. Steph is from my mum's side of the family, the youngest daughter of my Uncle Harry, who grew up in Birmingham. We were close when we were little, gravitating to each other during family get-togethers, at which we'd choreograph dance routines to Take That songs and make homemade rose perfume out of battered flowers and tapwater. I hadn't seen as much of her as an adult, but a few years ago, at a Boxing Day party, we discovered a mutual desire to travel Down Under and agreed that it'd be great to do so with a friendly face. She got there sooner than me, but is as keen as ever that I go out and join her as soon as I can.

This is going to get MESSY! she says, underneath a pic in which things are already looking messier than a rave at Mr Messy's house. She is surrounded by a host of tanned, ripped men, has a dodgy-looking cigarette drooping from her lip and is topless, except for two beer cans she is holding over each nipple. It's too early to scrape an appropriate comment out of the depths of my brain so I just hit Like.

A moment later, another comment appears, tagging my name. When are you getting over here, Lauren Scott? I've just shown several of my new hotties, sorry friends (!!!), your pic and they are all v. keen to show you a good time! Hurry up, girl!

It feels too early for that many exclamation marks some-how. Won't be long hopefully, Steph. Looks like you're having enough fun for both of us in the meantime. x ☺

I press Enter and hope that placates her, at least for as long as she remains conscious.

I try to roll over to get another forty minutes' sleep, but as soon as my mind starts working over last night's bomb-shell about Joe owning the Moonlight Hotel, drifting off again becomes an impossibility. I haul myself out of bed and try to put a positive spin on being up at this ungodly hour by pulling on my running shoes. A bit of exercise is exactly what I need after falling off the MyFitnessPal wagon yesterday.

To be fair, it is very difficult to adopt a kale-smoothie-based diet when you can't get your hands on any kale, so you have to make do with broccoli instead, an overdose of which can make you feel as if there's a helium balloon in your lower intestine.

Under normal circumstances, when I decide to go for a run, I open my front door, turn right and venture a mile in a straight line before turning round and walking back. But today I'm feeling ambitious, so decide to drive up to the Struggle next to the Kirkstone Pass Inn, where the views make up for the fact that its name is entirely appropriate.

I park and remove my car key from its ring, then step out, lock my gear inside and tie the key to the string at the top of my running pants. I set off underneath a pale grey sky, a wild mist twisting around the mountains, the air crisp as it hits the back of my throat.

I stick to the road, like I always do. A fine rain skims my face as I pound the rising gradient of the road and replay my reaction to Joe's announcement last night. Which wasn't nearly as hard-hitting as it ought to have been. I just kind of stood there, carp-mouthed and muttering, 'You? *You're* the new owner?' as I tried to think of a way to explain why I'd have greeted the news that he was the son of the Anti-Christ more warmly.

Of course I was polite. Or perhaps a wimp. Either way, I hid the contempt sizzling through my veins as, when quizzed gently by Emily, he said simply that he'd be going into further detail with the staff in due course, thereby doing nothing to abate anyone's fears about the fate of the Moonlight Hotel – otherwise known as Lakeland's newest Travel Haven. I shudder.

It goes without saying that this puts a wildly different per-spective on my views about him and Emily.

There is no way I'd have considered him as a potential love-match for my gorgeous friend if I'd known what he was up to. And despite the handsome smile and sexy swagger, one thing was absolutely clear last night: he can't be trusted.

Worryingly though, this is obvious to everyone except Emily, who refuses to be put off, despite my clearly-expressed rant on the way home.

I run for twenty minutes until the rain gets heavier, and by the time I've completed my circuit, there is steam coming off the skin on my arms. The second I reach the car and stop to catch my breath, cold encroaches on my skin, rain slicing into my cheeks.

I grab my car key and dig my fingers into the knot on my leggings to release it. Only, it doesn't budge. My nails are too soft from rain to be effective against the string, no matter how determined my attempts and colourful my profanities.

A gust of bitter wind nearly sweeps me off my feet and, with rain lashing against my face, the more I fiddle with the knot, the more it refuses to budge. I'm swearing hypermanically, sweating despair as the red raw skin of my fingers burns – until I am hit by a bolt of genius. I leave the key where it is – stuck to my midriff – and simply click open the lock. Then I slide into the seat, soaking, freezing, but with a temporary respite from the elements.

I briefly consider an escape attempt that involves twisting into a position that would allow me to put the key in the ignition while it is still attached to my belt. Then it strikes me that, in the absence of a lifetime's experience in circus contortion, it's out of the question.

In the end, there is no option but to whip off my leggings, drape them on the dashboard and start the ignition, thrusting the heating on high enough to recreate the climate inside a tumble dryer.

If you'd told me this morning that I'd have been relieved at the prospect of sitting in my car in nothing but a sweaty

Nike thong, attempting to bring my bum cheeks back to normal body temperature, I wouldn't have believed you.

But I tootle back home, reminding myself that it's a single-track road most of the way and, even if someone overtakes me, I'd only be visible from mid-shoulders upwards.

All goes well, until I pull up to a junction adjacent to a white hotel service van. I glance up anxiously – at the exact moment when the passenger, a bearded, heavily-tattooed bloke of indeterminate age, glances down.

His response when he sees that I'm near-naked from the waist down is not a subtle one. His eyes catapult out of his head. His jaw bungees to the floor. He even nudges his friend to have a look, to which I can only respond with the expression of an outraged *Carry On* matron before the lights change and I slam my foot on the accelerator.

The rest of the journey is incident-free. All I want to do when I pull up in front of the cottage is scuttle into the house, run to the shower and get ready to work.

Fortunately, Agnes seems to have abandoned the butchering of her shrubs and the coast is clear. So I creep out of the car, shut the door and prepare to make a dash for it. However, I haven't taken a single step when my elderly neighbour appears out of nowhere, brandishing her power tool.

'Your bush is terribly untidy, Lauren,' she declares.

I instinctively glance down, then realise she's referring to the greenery between our two front gardens. 'Oh, sorry,' I reply, cowering behind the car. 'I haven't had a chance to do much lately. I'll get on it at the weekend.'

She gives the hedge-trimmer a rev. 'Sure you don't want me to have a go? It's trickier when it's wet, but this bugger will cut through anything.'

'Honestly, Agnes, don't worry,' I reply, but she's already distracted.

'Oh, damn it, my wire's stuck,' she grumbles, pulling at the cable. I'd like to help, but my state of semi-nudity prevents me from leaping to her immediate aid. 'Well, come on, give me a hand!'

I glance around, then dive forward and hastily release the cable. I almost get away with it until she does a double-take and pulls a face as if she's swallowed a lit firework. '*Where's your skirt!?*'

'Long story, Agnes,' I wince. 'But I'd appreciate it if you could keep this between you and me.'

'And him,' she nods, as I whip around to see Edwin, standing in mute horror at the end of my path.

'Um … hello, Lauren. I only stopped by on the way to school to remind you about *Breaking Bad*. Is this not a good time?'

Edwin and I are both on playground duty at lunchtime. It is usual procedure to have a good old moan about this, at least when it's as chilly as it is today.

But when Edwin heads across the tarmac to come and talk to me, moaning is the last thing on my mind, unless you count the low noises that occasionally escape from my mouth with every painful flashback of this morning's mortification.

'Sorry to have just turned up at your house,' he says. 'I didn't mean to take you by surprise.' I fall in love with Edwin all over again for apologising for what was very clearly my own blunder. Today, perhaps because he's standing so close to me, he seems taller than usual. And he smells positively edible, a fact that can't solely be attributed to the Ferrero Rochers doing the rounds in the staff room earlier.

'Oh, don't worry. I don't normally spend my mornings like that in the garden,' I laugh, as lightly as possible, because the truth is I'd rather not have to go through the entire convoluted explanation again about why I was outside and trouserless at 8 a.m. 'I went to salsa again last night,' I throw in, hoping to change the subject.

'Ah ... quite the dancer these days aren't we?' he grins. I laugh again, probably a bit too heartily this time, as it seems to alarm him somewhat. 'Could you write the details down for me for the class?'

'You'd really like to come then?' I ask.

'Of course.'

I pat down my pockets.

'Here.' He removes his leather pad and fountain pen from his inside pocket and hands them to me. Our hands brush.

73

Pleasure flips in my belly and I find it inordinately difficult to hold the pen steady.

I finish the note and hand it to him, suppressing the wild hope soaring inside me that the next time I'm there, he might be too.

'It was at the Moonlight Hotel but it's moving to Casa Lagos in Bowness temporarily.' I catch his eye. 'I hope you come, Edwin. It'd be really good fun with you there.'

'Wouldn't it?' he agrees. A gust of wind picks up and I get a waft of him again. My reaction to this gorgeous smell is so primeval that it's all I can do to restrain myself from howling.

'That's a lovely aftershave you're wearing,' I mumble instead, which I hope is sufficiently understated.

A smile twitches on his lips. 'Thanks, Lauren. It was a Christmas present.'

'From someone with very good taste,' I say.

'Er, yes.' He clears his throat. 'Fiona.'

'Oh.' Discovering that the source of this heavenly, full-sensory-overload was his ex-girlfriend is comparable with complimenting a chef on his casserole, only to learn that you've actually just devoured a bowl of Pedigree Chum.

Fortunately, with excellent timing Tom Goodwin appears at my side. 'Miss!'

'What is it, Tom?' I ask.

'Is "twit" a swear word?' Ben Havistock and Jacob Preston come trundling up behind him. Edwin and I share a smile as I steel myself to deal with this with smooth authority.

'Hmm ... well, it's not a nice thing to call somebody, but it probably isn't an actual swear word,' I decree.

'What about "wally"?' Jacob asks.

'Well, again, not a swear word exactly but—'

'Nitwit? Numbskull? Plonk—'

'Yes – we've all got the idea,' I tell him. 'Your best bet is to not call anyone those names. Far better to be nice, don't you think?'

'Well, my mum says I need to think of something to call my brother other than "bellend",' Ben explains. 'So all those things should be brilliant, shouldn't they?'

'That is *definitely* a swear word, Ben – and you mustn't use it.'

'Brilliant?' Jacob asks.

'No! Look, why don't you all run along. Your playtime will be finished soon.'

When I turn back, Edwin is striding across the playground to check on a suspiciously quiet group of Year One children building a den. I watch as they all stop what they're doing to have a conversation with him – enraptured as ever by his words – before he heads back.

'Is everything all right?' I ask, realising he looks upset about something.

He stiffens his lip and nods. 'I'm just going to miss them.'

My brain struggles to process the words. 'What do you mean?'

He flashes me a look. 'You can keep a secret, can't you, Lauren?'

One of my defining qualities, I like to think, is my utter refusal to break a confidence. I honestly never have. The only downside is that lots of people feel the need to burden me with absolutely bloody every secret they've got. Including, it now seems, Edwin. And I'm getting a sudden horrible feeling that I might not want to know this one.

'Of course,' I hear myself say.

'Well, don't tell anyone at school yet … it's not official. But I'm leaving.'

My mouth suddenly feels too dry to speak, swallow, breathe or do any of the things it was designed for.

'Don't look so shocked Lauren. It's not for ages.'

I attempt to compose myself. 'Sorry,' I manage, trying to think of which of my 200 questions I should plump for first. 'When are you going?'

'The end of term,' he says.

Horror rises in my throat. 'But that's only four months away.'

'Exactly – ages.'

The playground starts spinning and my limbs feel as though they're made of marshmallow.

'Which school are you moving to?' I whisper, remembering that I'd heard that a primary in Hawkshead was looking for a deputy head. 'Are you staying in the Lakes?'

'Not exactly.'

I am engulfed in a sensation that my worst fears are being realised . . .

He's moving to Manchester!

'I'm moving to Singapore!' he announces. For a second I convince myself I can't possibly have heard him right.

'Miss! My nose is bleeding!' interrupts Jordan Carter. 'They're not allowed to play tennis with a football, are they?'

But I can barely answer. 'I . . . I . . .'

I don't get to finish my sentence anyway. Instead, I look up to see the offending football hurtling directly at my head. The thump – square between my eyes – is surprisingly, shockingly painful. But even accounting for that, the yelp I let out is less like a Jane Austen character swooning gracefully, and more like the noise a rubber duck would make if you stood on it in the bath.

And although I can hear a whistle and see thick drops of blood seeping into my favourite Oasis blouse, all I can do is pray that I'm so concussed that I imagined the entire conversation which preceded this event.

Edwin steps forward and takes me by the arm, leading me to the sick bay, before darting back to the playground. There I sit, sharing the edge of the bed with Shafilia Masood, who is awaiting the arrival of her mum after she vomited up the Spotted Dick on today's menu.

'Looks like both of us are in the wars, doesn't it, Shafilia?' She nods mournfully, her poor bewildered eyes overcome with shock and confusion. I know exactly how she feels.

Chapter 9

Almost a week later, Cate arrives to pick me up for salsa twenty-five minutes before she's due – which is a record as she's never early for anything.

Under normal circumstances it wouldn't be a problem, but I'm midway through applying some fake tan when the bell rings. I poke my head out of the window and see her at the door.

'How come you're so early?' I shout down.

'I'll explain when you let me in,' she replies. 'Come on, Lauren, it's raining!'

I throw on a dressing gown and race down the stairs to open the door. 'I needed to tell you what's just happened,' she blusters, heading into the living room and perching on the edge of the sofa. 'Robby turned up at the shop.' It's clear from the way she says it that her ex-boyfriend wasn't just popping in to buy a bunch of freesias. 'He wants to get back with me.'

I crumple my nose. 'That's hardly news.'

'I know, but he was different this time. He's ... *pissed off* with me.'

'You can't be pissed off with someone for failing to be madly in love with you.'

'Well, he is, believe me.'

I frown. 'What did he say? He hasn't threatened you or anything?'

'Oh, nothing like that. He just kept huffing and puffing, as if I was not grasping the logic of the situation. He always was possessive. Oh, I don't know ... I don't know why this bothered me so much, but it did. I wish he'd get out of my life, instead of having to see him all the time.'

'This is the one downside to not living in a big city: you never entirely shake off your ex-boyfriends.'

'Every time I see him, I get that same feeling you get when you wake up to a cold, leftover takeaway,' she muses. 'You know you must've thought it was tasty at some point, but it's impossible to work out why you fancied it now. Anyway, how are you feeling about Edwin's news?'

In the days since Edwin dropped his bombshell I have sunk deeper into a hole of depression. 'I know I was already planning to go to Australia. And I know I'd always said I needed to get away from him. But ... I thought I had forever to wean myself off him. Then, when he dumped Fiona I suppose a part of me hoped something might happen between the two of us.'

She puts her arm around me. 'This could be for the best. If Edwin is mad enough not to have snapped you up the second Fiona was out of the picture, frankly, you don't *want* him hanging around. As long as he's here, you'd never have the headspace to start thinking in romantic terms about anyone else.'

She is talking sense, but sometimes sense is the last thing you want.

'He might be coming along tonight,' I say, offering a nugget of hope.

She perks up. 'Ooh, really? Better get your lippy on then.'

I throw on my clothes and Cate and I jump into her van, before tootling along the road towards Windermere until we reach Emily's little slate-walled house, in a side road tucked away from the shops and cafés of the village. She waves at us from the window and skips out of the door in a tulip dress that sits slightly above the knee, ballet flats and a clutch of silver bangles that tinkle against her slim wrists.

'Have you caught a bit of sun, Lauren?' she asks.

'No, I just applied a bit of fake . . . Oh God!'

'What is it?' Cate asks.

'I forgot to finish applying my St Tropez. I only did my face, chest and one arm.'

'Just remember to do it when you get in tonight,' Emily sniggers. 'Your arms will match by the morning.'

The road to Bowness takes us past the driveway to the

Moonlight Hotel, which is now blocked by a No Entry sign. The hotel closed this weekend, sooner than anyone could ever have imagined, to begin a massive refurbishment programme that will leave it, if Cate's top source (aka Sally, one of the waitresses) is correct, 'unrecognisable'.

Sally was in Cate's shop at the weekend, and revealed everything the staff were told in their big meeting: The hotel is going to be turned upside down and will remain closed until the start of the summer season in July. And their jobs are far from safe. Although nobody's been handed their P45 yet, all are now answerable to the management team, headed by Joe and his right-hand man Gianni, under whom they're expected to take part in a massive re-training exercise, as well as get the new hotel up and running. And after all that, only a few will be guaranteed future employment. All of which serves to underline my instinctive belief that Joe Wilborne – Mr Travel Havens – is a Grade A arsehole.

'I wonder if your man is going to show his face around here after last week?' I ask Emily. She prickles at the comment, which I hadn't intended.

'I'm sure Marion will get over not being able to use the Moonlight Hotel for a few months. She's found somewhere else now,' she replies.

'It's not just Marion who's got the hump,' Cate replies. 'The staff are up in arms.' It's hardly necessary to add that I'm with them 100 per cent.

'They're keeping their jobs,' Emily says defensively. 'Nobody's being laid off for the foreseeable.'

'That's hardly much security, is it?' I argue. 'Especially not if they've got families to support. Plus, the fact that the hotel is closing for weeks on end means there'll be no tips.'

'I can't imagine they had too many tips anyway,' Emily replies. 'You need customers for tips – and there have been few enough of those recently.'

'I'm surprised he didn't wait until the winter season to close,' Cate remarks. 'It seems odd, doesn't it?'

'He clearly hasn't got the first clue about what he's doing – not with a hotel like this, anyway,' I grumble.

When we arrive in Bowness, Cate parks next to the Angel Inn and we make our way down the hill towards Casa Lagos, the little Spanish restaurant that will provide a temporary home for our Tuesday-night salsa. I am reluctantly forced to admit that it's an acceptable alternative, with more atmosphere than that massive high-ceilinged room at the Moonlight Hotel. The rustic, saffron-coloured walls, terracotta tiles and soft table-lights make the room feel intimate, the kind of room where this sort of dancing seems at home.

Presumably the owners are quite happy about the prospect of a room full of people buying drinks on a Tuesday night, which is comparatively dead. Not that I'm going to admit any of this out loud. Besides, I have other things on my mind now. Namely, Edwin.

I'm on edge as soon as I walk in, wondering if he'll be here. I reminded him of the change of venue at lunch and he responded with enthusiasm, saying he really hoped he could make it. And I can't help secretly pleading with God, Cupid, or whatever higher power has the capacity to get him here to do just that.

There are a few new faces tonight in Lulu's group, as well as the usual crowd. Which includes, to my astonishment, Joe. I deliberately shuffle to the opposite side of the room during the warm-up, but when the main lesson starts and Lulu sets us up with our first partners, by some hideous twist of fate, he ends up right in front of me.

'Hello,' I say stiffly.

'Hi,' he replies, his face breaking into that smile, the one I thought was sexy and self-deprecating when I first met him, but now just looks arrogant and smug.

'You're brave,' I mutter. 'After Marion's reaction to your bombshell last week, you're lucky she didn't chuck you out of the club.'

'On what grounds would she chuck me out?' No matter how coolly he responds, he's clearly mildly rattled.

I shrug. 'On the grounds that she wanted to pickle your spleen in aspic this time last week. And I believe she wasn't the only one.'

He lets go of my hands and looks at me. It makes me uncomfortable. 'I'm quite the villain, aren't I?'

'People are just worried about what you're doing to that

hotel – you know, that beautiful, historic building which has been part of the very fabric of Lakeland for centuries upon centuries.'

'Since 1895 actually.'

'And their jobs – the hundreds of people this is affecting.'

'Twenty-three members of staff. None of whom have lost their jobs.'

'*For now,*' I add pointedly.

His jaw twitches, before he is forced to concede: 'For now.' Then he draws a long breath. 'Well, I can live with being the bad guy. They get all the best lines anyway.'

I am about to respond with a stinging, quick-fire riposte, but Marion starts clapping and I'm just left to slink back, sizzling with dislike for him.

'I think it's definitely time we moved a few of you beginners up to the improvers' class,' she announces. 'Joe and Lauren – I'm fairly sure you two are ready for some of the more advanced turns. Can you come and help us do a little demo of some back steps and crossover?'

We exchange the kind of look you see before pistols are drawn. Then he reaches for my hand, as my heart flutters resentfully.

I tell myself to just blur my eyes, pretend I don't want to run a million miles away, and concentrate on what my feet are doing while Lulu counts our steps. 'One two three, tap, five six seven, back steps and open!' I'm making a half-decent job of it too, when the door flies open and I look up and catch the briefest glimpse of someone wearing a tailored jacket.

He disappears behind a pillar as I strain to get a look, my stomach lurching as I realise that I recognise the jacket. HE'S COME! Edwin's here and all is right with the world again!

The problem with happiness flooding your body is that it has a terrible effect on your co-ordination. My legs start to wobble, and I don't mean in a way that's good or sexy or cute. And instead of completing a fairly basic turn I absolutely know is within my capabilities, this time it's as if someone's trying to practise tying a slip knot in my ankles. Despite my best efforts to steady myself, I end up with my face momentarily stuck to Joe's T-shirt, quietly dying at the thought that Edwin might have witnessed this. Joe pushes me away, his lips twisted in amusement, as Marion thrusts her hands on her hips.

'I'm sure that's not *really* the best you can do, Lauren,' she says.

'Just … lost my concentration,' I mumble, wondering when and how I signed up to being critiqued, particularly when Edwin is here to witness it.

I look up again, my cheeks sizzling – and realise with a crunch of disappointment that it's actually Frank, the ex-theology lecturer, mid-way through battling with his combover, which couldn't be more of a contrast with Edwin's gorgeous hair.

'OK.' Marion purses her lips. 'We'll move you up to improvers' anyway, I think.'

Having been initially concerned that I wasn't ready to move up, this vote of confidence lifts my mood. 'You really think I'm improving?'

Marion looks at me doubtfully. 'No, love. We've just run out of space in the beginners' group.'

It becomes evident that the leap from the beginners' to the improvers' group couldn't be bigger if I dislocated both inner thighs making it. Which is an apt analogy, in fact, because I almost do. Particularly compared with some of those in the class who are endowed with more natural ability than me. Two of the nurses especially are fantastic, as are Andi and Joshua.

Part of the problem is that I can't stop looking at the door, willing Edwin to walk through it. And partly praying that he *doesn't*, given that being promoted to Marion's group primarily involves being contorted into a variety of positions that make us look like a tea party of pissed chimpanzees attempting to play Twister.

'You still can't persuade Mike to come back to salsa?' I ask Stella, my arm over my head as Esteban holds my hand, midway through a twirl.

'Sadly, no,' she says breathlessly. 'It's so annoying, particularly as he's throwing himself into everything else about the wedding.'

'Oh, how lovely. He's helping you choose the colours and things then?'

'I wouldn't go that far. But he has been on a healthy eating and exercise plan – lost ten pounds in two weeks. Wouldn't you just kill for that?'

'At the moment, yes,' I say, contemplating the abject flop that was my *Win Edwin Diet*.

I glance over and see that Emily is now partnered with Joe. There's so much sexual tension between the two of them you can virtually hear it.

By the time we leave the restaurant an hour later, Emily can talk of little else. 'I know you're worried about what's happening at the Moonlight Hotel, Lauren, but honestly – Joe's such a nice guy. And so funny and interesting. I found out tonight that he was in the army before he did this.'

'Unusual career path – from that to running budget hotels.'

'He's well-travelled and sweet and—'

'I believe you, Emily,' I interrupt, then regret it.

There's no point discussing Joe with Emily when she's so obviously smitten with him. It's my job as her friend to be happy for her, whether it sticks in the throat or not.

'Shall we go for a drink before we head for home?' she suggests as we pause in front of Cate's van.

'I'm up for it if the driver is,' I say, glancing back down the hill and seeing straight away that *the driver* is otherwise engaged.

I nudge Emily and she follows my gaze, letting out a spontaneous, 'Awww . . .'

Because Cate and Will are in each other's arms, kissing under a streetlight as if they never want to let each other go.

Chapter 10

There is little dignity in trying to woo the man of your dreams when he has already decided to bugger off halfway around the world and is apparently not even interested in a sneaky, no-strings snog in the meantime.

There is even less dignity in doing so with a fake tan application so mental that, naked and in a certain light, you're doing a very good impression of a Friesian cow. I completely forgot to even out my St Tropez last night. I was so distracted, too wound up, that it just disappeared from my head.

Worse, despite the fact that it has pissed down relentlessly for months, the lady on BBC Breakfast News gleefully announced this morning that today would be the hottest day of the year so far, a veritable spring heatwave, the likes of which hasn't been seen '*since records began*'.

This meteorological scenario is so unusual it even prompted said weather lady to opt for a distinctly daring – nay, plunging – dress, one that exposed her shoulders and will no doubt make the *Points of View* complaints email account melt. I, by contrast, have had to turn up to work on the hottest April day since records began . . . in a polo-neck.

Admittedly it's a lightweight affair – if I'd attempted a woolly one I'd be on a drip being treated for heat exhaustion by now. However, it's bad enough. I pull my Mini into the school car park, just as Edwin is about to head to the door. He too is not dressed for a heatwave: I've learned over the years that it would take some kind of nuclear apocalypse for him to let standards slip.

He turns and looks at me, his face breaking into this incandescent smile that's enough to make me catch my breath. If I didn't know any better, there are times when I think Edwin likes me.

Then the facts of the situation hit me: I've known the man for two years and he's not once made a sniff of an advance.

'Morning, Lauren,' he says, and a pang hits my throat at the thought that, come the end of term, I'll never get to see that lovely face on a Wednesday morning ever again.

'Hi, Edwin,' I smile, stepping out of the car.

'You're looking . . . *smart* today.'

This is a beautiful euphemism. Because I am not looking smart. If smart equals *an insane volume of clothing*, then I would concede the point. But it doesn't. 'My aunt used to wear a pair of gloves like that to church,' he adds, which was obviously *just* the look I was going for when I threw on the lace fingerless affairs I wore as a bridesmaid ten years ago.

'The eighties are very in at the moment,' I say, hiding them behind my back. 'This is what Madonna wore in that film . . . what was it?'

'*Saving Private Susan?*' he muses.

'*Desperately Seeking Susan*, I think,' I correct him.

'Oh God,' he laughs at himself. 'Movie trivia was never my strong point as you might be able to tell.'

I click the lock on the door.

'So, are you doing anything over the break?' I ask, deliberately avoiding any mention of him failing to turn up to salsa. 'It's a long one, Easter, isn't it?' The thought of an enforced separation from him for two and a half whole weeks doesn't bear thinking about.

'Lots to do to prepare for Singapore,' he replies. 'It'll be non-stop.'

'Oh yes. Not long now, is there?'

'About twelve weeks.'

'Twelve weeks and four days,' I blurt out.

He smiles and to his credit doesn't look at me as if I'm a bunny-boiler. 'It's getting exciting now, I must admit. You'll feel like this when you go on your big Australia trip too. I know you've got some way to go for that, but it'll come round sooner than you think.'

We reach the school door and he opens it for me, inviting me to walk in first. 'It's a shame you're so set on Australia really,' Edwin continues.

'Australia has been my dream since I was a little girl,' I reply.

'I've been to Sydney twice and it's amazing – wonderful place. But with somewhere like Singapore, you could just go tomorrow.'

I realise we've both stopped walking; he's facing me, looking directly into my eyes. 'What … what do you mean, Edwin?'

'They're crying out for English teachers in Singapore. The pay is great.' He looks at me with a quiet intensity that burns through me, and whispers: 'Why don't you consider it, Lauren?'

I try to swallow but my tongue suddenly feels too big for my mouth. 'Singapore? I … I don't know.' But the fact is, I *do* know. I want to leap into his arms, spin around three times and say, 'Singapore?! You're inviting me to Singapore? *WITH YOU, EDWIN?*'

Fortunately, I manage to restrain myself and pretend I'm still pondering the question for an acceptable period of time.

'Seriously,' he continues. 'If I'd thought for a moment you'd be into the idea, I'd have suggested it ages ago.' Then he touches my arm – or at least, my jumper. It sounds like a small gesture but the intimacy of this movement makes my heart leap into my throat.

'It does sound quite appealing, I must admit,' I croak.

'Do you know much about the country?'

'Oh, a little bit.' In fact, I've spent so much time Googling the place since Edwin mentioned it, I could probably get a job as the Singaporean Ambassador in any country in the world.

Then, the most amazing thing happens. He puts his hand on my chin and lifts it up gently, like Mills & Boon heroes do before they 'plant their lips' on the heroine. OK, he doesn't go so far as to kiss me, but the teasing glint in his eye as he says the next sentence is almost as good.

'If I didn't know any better, I'd say you were considering it, Lauren Scott.' I can feel his breath on my face.

'You can't be serious, Edwin?' I whisper, and obviously I know what I want the answer to be.

'Of course I'm serious,' he says, removing his hand from my chin. 'Come to Singapore, Lauren! There. I've spelled it out,' he grins, his arms open wide.

'Well,' I cough, trying to pull myself together. 'I'd have to give it some thought. It's a very big step. And as you know, my plans had always firmly centred on Australia.'

'Oh, I know. But you'd love it there, Lauren. I've even got a place to stay! You'd be welcome to bunk on the sofa until you found somewhere. Travelling is always better with a friend, and you and I get on so well together. We're totally compatible in every way – we love each other's company. At least, I do yours . . .'

He stops talking and there's an awkward silence between the two of us.

He grins. 'Just imagine – you, me, an exciting new country. I can't think of anything better.'

'OK. Don't get your hopes up too much, Edwin, but I'll definitely consider it,' I reply coolly, as I push open the swing door to the school and decide to finish this conversation on a magnificent, flirtatious high. 'I promise you that,' I add huskily, as the swing door flips back and hits me in the face.

On any other day, I would be quite bothered about the fact that I am dressed like a lunatic and have been smacked on the nose yet again. But this is no ordinary day. This is the day when I heard it with my own ears: Edwin Blaire invited me to move to Singapore with him.

No matter how much I try, I cannot bring myself to play down its significance. I mean, he hasn't invited any other members of staff to move to Singapore with him, has he? I don't see him asking Joyce to put down her copy of *The Well-Endowed Billionaire Prince* to jet off with him.

And OK, in the normal development of any relationship you might expect him to ask me out for a date at the Wild

Boar before inviting me to fly 6,500 miles to South-East Asia with him – but beggars can't be choosers.

I cannot deny that Singapore had never appeared on my radar before Edwin mentioned it on that fateful day. I know also that Australia is where my heart has lain throughout my entire life. The feminist in me would be slapping me round both cheeks right now. But *come on!* I have the means, I have the invitation, and judging by what Edwin says, I shouldn't have too much difficulty finding a job. It has to be worth looking into.

By the time I get to the staff room for break, I am literally itching to log on to my tablet and start Googling Singaporean schools. I'm partly glad that Edwin has a meeting with the Head because it means I can tuck into my Ryvitas (which I'm happy to eat now because *if* – yes, that's IF – I move to Singapore, I would have to be thin), and have a good look, in peace, at my options. It proves to be a positively dreamy break. I sit, pretending that I'm on the *Times Educational Supplement* website as I flick through a list of teaching agencies that advertise openings at Singaporean schools. They all sound wonderful. Then a pop-up advert appears for *Singapore's most exclusive wedding venue.* Honestly, I've never been one of these women obsessed with the idea of marriage. Finding life-long love, yes, but I'm no future bridezilla, I swear.

But it wouldn't do any harm to look at the ad, would it?

I click on the link and my stomach swirls as I take it in: it looks nothing less than magical. A bride's wispy silk veil floats upwards against the backdrop of a blissful sunset, her handsome groom leaning in to kiss her. I close my eyes and lose myself momentarily, when I am jolted out by a sound I can only compare to that of a cackling banshee on the set of *Loose Women*.

'You're a dark horse, Lauren! When are you getting married?' shrieks Joyce. 'Budge up and let's have a look. Is this the venue? Singapore. Oooh, Lauren's getting married in Singapore, everyone!'

'No, I'm not. I'm just . . . it's for a friend, honestly,' I cough.

'That's what they all say. Did you have any idea that LAUREN'S GETTING MARRIED IN SINGAPORE, EDWIN?' she adds, as the love of my life walks through the door. And I wonder if I am forever destined for a life of glorious humiliation.

Chapter 11

Over the next week, I bury my head inside my laptop researching jobs in Singapore and try to close my eyes and ears every time I pass the Moonlight Hotel or hear another rumour about what's going on there. And there is a *lot* going on. I'm not just talking about the vans that are perpetually coming and going, but also the adverts that have been doing the rounds for a new Head Chef – and the rumours about just how hard this Gianni bloke is making life for the current staff.

Cate and Will, meanwhile, are inseparable. When they're not working, they're going for picnics by the tumbling water of Aira Force or failing to emerge from one or the other's flat for days on end. When he's not around, she can talk of nothing but him. When he is around, they're perpetually locked together, hands clasped, foreheads touching as they whisper and smile – as if they know a secret the rest of the world couldn't begin to understand.

The only time they emerge from each other's embrace is for work, salsa night and a hiking trip organised by Emily up Coniston Old Man, for which Joe joins them. I declined. For obvious reasons – I don't do hiking and I despise Joe – and less obvious ones: they're all busy making plans for the Spain trip that's coming up at the end of the Easter break and to which I, alas, am not going. But I don't mind too much. I have other things on which to focus.

'Are you seriously thinking of going to Singapore?' Cate asks, as she adds a lush, heavy tulip to a bouquet.

'Do you think it's mad? The more I look into it, the more tempting it seems, I can't deny it. When I was planning for Australia, I'd aimed to save enough to allow me to travel round the country, without getting a job. If I moved to Singapore, I'd get a job and just soak up the local culture without moving.'

'Soak up Edwin, you mean.' I don't even attempt to argue. 'Don't get me wrong,' she adds. 'I understand your reasons. But you've been harping on about going to Australia for as long as I've known you. You were obsessed.'

'I know. But Singapore has got one trump card.'

'And he's called Edwin.' She stands back to examine the bouquet.

'I was actually referring to the fact that the pay out there is so good. Those flowers are absolutely beautiful,' I tell her.

'Thanks,' she grins, pushing back her armful of colourful

woven bracelets as she picks up a pen to write the card. 'Whoever Doris is, she's going to have an awesome seventieth birthday.'

She's done a tremendous job with Daffodils & Stars since she inherited the place from her Grandma Isobel three years ago. The fact that the old lady approved so wholeheartedly of the bohemian edge to Cate's refurbishment was the source of huge pride – even if Isobel didn't know it was all funded by every loan Cate could get her hands on – and one or two credit cards to boot.

She was always close to her grandma, who was a sweetheart – funny and kind, just like Cate herself. In fact, Cate had far more in common with her than she does with her own mum, so it was little wonder that she was devastated when Isobel died last year. But her legacy lives on in every bloom Cate ties, in every colourful corner of the shop – and in the huge black and white photograph that dominates the far wall, of her beloved Isobel arranging lilies of the valley.

Daffodils & Stars is one of those shops it's impossible to pass without stopping to look inside. Its high wood-framed shopfront is stained with a pale, moss-coloured paint, above which its name pops out in an elegant, yellow scrawl, a clutch of tiny stars bursting out from one side like popped champagne. The window is a riot of colour and scent, with flowers spilling on to the pavement whatever time of year: hydrangeas and roses in summer, berries and ivy in winter.

Cate's speciality is weddings and she's listed as a preferred supplier for some of the swankiest hotels in the Lakes. She tackles everything from large, formal arrangements in elaborate candelabras, to soft, floating trails of orchids that look perfectly understated on a summer's day – and she does it all with passion and skill.

The door pushes open and two elderly women walk in to have a browse. 'Good morning, ladies,' Cate smiles.

'Morning,' says one of them. 'Ooh, what a lovely shop! Look at these, Diana.'

Over the next twenty minutes, the two ladies proceed to coo over and sniff every other flower in the place while we carry on chatting. 'Can you still not be persuaded to come to Spain?' Cate asks me. 'It's been ages since we had a holiday all together.'

'There was our weekend in Dublin.'

'That was three years ago,' she argues. 'I think I'm owed one with you before you bugger off to Australia, or Singapore or wherever you decide to go.'

'Oh, come off it – you'll spend the entire time with Will. You won't want me there to interfere.'

'You're my best friend – your job is to interfere, so of course I do. And besides, I need a partner in crime to finally get Joe and Emily together.'

I look at her doubtfully. 'I don't think you need to worry there, Cate. I'm sure it's only a matter of time.'

At that, the ladies announce, reluctantly, that they're leaving – this has clearly been a sightseeing tour only. 'Nothing take your fancy?' Cate smiles gently.

'I think they're all a bit out of our price range,' one of them says. 'Beautiful though – worth every penny I'm sure. What a lovely place you've got.'

'Thank you. I think so too,' says Cate, glowing with pride as she pulls out a few stems from a vase and starts to wrap them up for them. I knew she would somehow. But I'm still not prepared for the subsequent meltdown the ladies have before scurrying out of the shop.

'You'll never become a millionaire businesswoman if you go giving away your stock for free,' I warn her.

'Yeah, I know,' she shrugs. 'But if you can't put a smile on an old lady's face once in a while, what can you do?'

On Easter Sunday, I head to Mum's for lunch. She lives an hour and twenty minutes away in Wasdale with her boyfriend, Barry – though 'boyfriend' feels an odd word, given that they're in their mid-fifties and not prone to scratching each other's names in their pencil cases, at least as far as I know.

If you thought where I lived was remote, it's like Times Square compared with this place. Personally, this would drive me insane, even if I can see its appeal: a view that gives you goose pimples, across the black abyss of Wastwater, England's deepest lake, up towards the mountainous stretch of Great Gable and Scafell Pike. Even I recognise why people come to be outdoors here, to spread their wings, fill their lungs, reflect and breathe.

I arrive at Fell Foot Cottage, where they've lived for the last five years, at 5 p.m., and step out of the car to see Mum emerging from the pub next door. She's dressed in her ubiquitous wellies and jeans, gilet over a long-sleeved black top, and is swinging something in one hand that's difficult to make out.

'What on earth is that?' I ask, although I am now close enough to have identified the offending item as a large, dead bird. Obviously. She comes to a halt and looks behind her, as if I've just alerted her to the fact that a herd of wildebeest is rampaging down the mountain towards us.

'No, *that*,' I gesture. 'In your hand.'

She lifts up her arm. 'Oh, it's a pheasant. I won it in a game of cards. Good, isn't it?'

'Never buy a lottery ticket, Mum,' I sigh. 'If you ever won a tenner it might blow your mind.'

My mum is fifty-six and looks kind of good on it in an earthy, athletic way – with slim, strong legs and the shoulders of someone who regularly does physical stuff. The tiny thread veins blooming on her cheeks are the result of working outdoors on farms all her life, although latterly she's been Head of Maintenance for a holiday park.

Whatever the opposite is of pretentious, she is it: a no-nonsense, no-bull individual whose friends admire her dependability, loyalty and the fact that she can hold her booze like a sailor. She's the most practical person I know. It'd never cross her mind to squeal if she saw a mouse, for instance – she'd just pick it up and chuck it out of the door in the way other people might deal with a leaf that had blown in.

'So how's Jeremy getting on?' I ask, as we head inside the limewashed walls of the building. 'Don't you miss having the house to yourself?'

'Oh, Barry and I don't mind,' she says. 'Although between you and me, I think he might be feeling a bit homesick.'

When Mum told me she was having her second cousin Helen's twenty-year-old son Jeremy to stay over for the summer, so he could work as a farmhand to save money for his next year at Bristol University, I did wonder how that might pan out. Particularly since, from what I hear, the closest the guy's been to the countryside before now was a trip to Center Parcs.

I enter the kitchen as the smell of freshly roasted chicken fills the room, and Barry is standing at the Aga, stirring something with a look of intense concentration on his face. He wipes his hands on an apron, takes a sip of cloudy ale and spots me.

'Lauren!' he beams, pushing his wire-rimmed spectacles up his nose as he dabs foam from his beard and comes over to kiss me on the cheek. 'Enjoying the Easter holidays?'

The real answer is: *No, because it's keeping me from Edwin*, but I decide not to even go down this route. 'It's been great, thanks, Barry. Ooh, something smells nice.'

'Roast chicken. Good for the soul apparently,' he winks.

'Well, I'd never say no to a bit of that.'

Fell Foot Cottage could be gorgeous if it were given the *Ideal Home* treatment, but my mum's never been much of a fashion victim of any kind. Its charm is innate though, soaked into the old beams, the thick slate floor-tiles, the big old stove. It's also helped along by Barry's love of pseudo-intellectual knick-knacks, the framed *Private Eye* covers, old Ramones posters and ethnic rugs. Mum's contribution to the house is more straightforward: wellies, paperback novels (thrillers mainly), and photos of Dad.

There aren't hundreds of them, just a few on the wall next to the stairs, nestled between other family photos – and the one on the mantelpiece in the living room that was taken in his early twenties. When I was little I never really thought of my father as cool – who does? But he unquestionably was, as the picture demonstrates; he's leaning on the motorbike he had for a couple of years, fringe flicked upwards as a cigarette droops from the side of his mouth.

Mum had been trying to get him to give up from the day

they met, and although he loved the bones of her she never quite got her way on that one. He was too headstrong, too focused on the present to worry about what turned out to be a fragile future.

Barry and I chat for a while as I help set the table; like me, he works with children – but as an ADHD specialist, helping kids and their families across Cumbria. Then we get on to the subject of his baking. Barry made his first batch of drop scones after episode one of *The Great British Bake Off* and has never looked back. Unlike other super-fans of the show I know (Edwin being one), Barry is no armchair cook, and from those humble beginnings, his ambition has known no bounds.

'I've got a beauty today, haven't I, Caroline?' he asks my mum. Then he disappears into the utility room and emerges a few seconds later with his latest construct. 'Ta-da! Can you tell what it is?'

It is, very clearly, his attempt at a magnificent recreation of an instantly-recognisable landmark.

Unfortunately, I haven't a clue what it is.

'It's a cake?' Mum offers.

Barry rolls his eyes. 'It's the Taj Mahal!'

She blinks at him. 'But it's brown.'

'That's because it's made of gingerbread,' he says. '*You* could tell what it was, couldn't you, Lauren?'

'Of course, it's obvious,' I reassure him, at which point the door opens and their house-guest walks in.

I've only met my mum's second cousin's son once, at the same wedding where I wore those bridesmaids' gloves, when he was about four years old. He was sweet and shy, as I recall, with ears like two shiitake mushrooms and a long fringe that kept troubling his eyes.

He's scrubbed up well, particularly considering he's spent the day dodging manure and herding livestock, and these days is unfeasibly tall and skinny, with a round face that's kind of handsome, if slightly foppish.

'Hello Jeremy,' I say, walking over as he reaches out to shake my hand. 'It's been such a long time. I'd love to say you haven't changed a bit, but I'm not sure how convincing that would be.'

Jeremy has the sort of handshake world leaders exchange at global summits: a single, elbow-dislocating chug, accompanied by eye contact that could singe retinas. 'Lauren. Hi. Good to see you again. You're a teacher these days, I believe?'

'That's right, I work in—'

'Hope you're better than some of the losers we had working in our place,' he declares, striding to the table. 'I hated them all.'

'Oh? What was wrong with them?' I ask, carrying on laying the table. Mum starts flicking through the *Westmorland Gazette*.

'I was predicted to get five A stars in my A levels, but as it is I ... performed below my clear personal potential, which

107

means I wasn't able to get into Oxford. I was *totally* let down by them. Who knows where I might've been if it wasn't for their fecklessness?'

Mum glances up briefly. 'But you might have missed out on shovelling shit all summer and staying in our box room.' Jeremy doesn't answer. She goes on: 'Before I forget, Lauren – your birthday.'

'What about it?'

'I need to give you my present.'

'But my birthday's in August. That's four months away.'

'I know, but Cate gave me a ring and made a suggestion, so I thought we might as well go with it. Save me having to bother in August,' she adds.

'What a lovely sentiment,' I mutter, as she heads upstairs, from where her printer, which I suspect may be gas-powered, springs into life and creates a similar sort of racket to one of Caractacus Potts' egg-boiling machines.

During this time, Barry and I have a discussion about football transfers before the conversation meanders on to the issue of whether Jeremy could have been a Parisian pastry chef were it not for an incompetent Home Economics teacher who forgot to remove his macaroni cheese from the oven.

Eventually Mum emerges with a print-out that looks as if it's been chewed by an Alsatian. 'Sorry – paper jam. This was the best I can do.'

I peer at the crumpled A4 sheet, trying to make it out.

'It's a flight to Spain for this salsa holiday your friends are going on,' she says, putting me out of my misery. 'It was a real bargain. You'd better go home and start packing.'

Chapter 12

The injection of a surprise trip into the school break lifts my spirits immeasurably, even if I feel slightly wary about how much I might need to spend while I'm out there. Despite Cate repeating constantly what good value it all was, I know there'll be a certain amount of alcoholic lubrication, which wasn't part of the plan, given that I am still saving. And I *am* still saving. Because, depending on what mood you catch me in, I am either chomping at the bit to fly off to Singapore with Edwin at the start of term, or spilling over with worry that I'm setting myself up for more heartache.

I also keep experiencing intense jolts of disappointment when I consider the prospect of not going to Australia. Which is nothing compared with the prospect of not going anywhere with Edwin, but I can't deny the empty crunch in my stomach at the thought of relinquishing the waterfalls and surf breaks of Great Ocean Drive, the lush vineyards of the Barossa Valley.

I suppose I just never imagined this scenario, even in my

wildest dreams. Six months ago I imagined nothing but Edwin and Fiona snuggling up into cosy matrimony. So despite the fact that the salsa trip smashes my budget into tiny pieces, I actually can't wait to get there and give my inner turmoil a holiday. Like Cate said, this is the first trip we've all been on for ages, and it feels like a fitting thing to do before I fly off to ... *wherever*.

We arrive at Liverpool Airport at an ungodly hour in the morning on Friday – hence the cheapo flight – as the sun is starting to rise in a beautiful clear sky. This is obviously not ideal because it is an unwritten law that any good holiday should begin by leaving behind the shittiest weather possible.

'How's the school break been for you, Emily?' I ask, as we find a parking space.

She throws me a look. 'Chaos, but fantastic. I took five eight-year-olds ghyll scrambling yesterday. Brilliant fun, although I was very glad to deliver them back to their parents afterwards ...'

Em's always been as certain that she never wants to be a mum as Cate and I are that we do, which sometimes seems a bit strange given how great she is with kids.

'Right, Em,' Cate declares after we've pulled up in the car park and she's dragged out her luggage. 'Lauren and I have had a long discussion and we are going to do everything in our power to get you and Joe together on this holiday. It's our duty. Our mission. And we have chosen to accept it.'

'He hasn't really made a move,' Emily replies dismissively. 'Maybe he isn't interested.'

'Of course he's interested,' Cate replies, then she leans in and scrutinises Em's face so closely you'd think she was searching for blackheads. 'You haven't met someone else, have you?'

'How on earth did you leap to that conclusion?' Emily asks, looking alarmed, but Cate is now too busy waving to the group outside the terminal building to respond. There's only a few of us who took up the offer of the salsa holiday; all of us, probably crucially, are single and without families. But we're joining several other groups over in Spain so hopefully it'll all be good fun.

As we head towards them, it strikes me how very British our tiny gang looks. This is despite Marion's attempts to salsa-fy matters by making us all wear bright red T-shirts that say *Caution: Hot Surface! Lakeland Salsa Club (tel 015395 6393 for details)*. We are, collectively, the direct opposite of what salsa dancers should probably be. There are no fireballs of burning, Latin energy. With the exception of Esteban, Will and Joe, who've all got passable tans, most of us are on the pasty side. Marion's perm is wilting after the strain of lifting her bag on to the trolley. Frank is eating a tuna sandwich produced from his rucksack, and even gorgeous Jilly is looking a bit flustered.

'I've obviously only come for the T-shirt,' Joe says, appearing next to me.

'Flattering, aren't they?' I reply, forgetting to hate him for a second.

He laughs. I decide to shuffle away before he gets the impression I'm prepared to tolerate him. The holiday starts in the terminal, before we get on the plane. I go to the bar and return to find that Marion has decided to launch into an impromptu group dance outside Boots.

It's excruciatingly embarrassing, until a security guard comes and asks us all to desist. 'These terrorism laws have gone mad!' Marion protests, until he explains that he just wanted to stop the children in Starbucks from crying.

Once we're on the plane, Joe and Emily sit together, and Cate and Will in front of them. Despite the fact that this is a budget airline – and the best they can do is a flaccid cheese sandwich and warm white wine – Cate and Will look so euphoric to be in each other's presence they could be in First Class on a British Airways flight.

Esteban, having been separated from Jilly during the rush for the gate, ends up sitting next to me. I'm not at all unhappy with this development – he's good fun, a nice bloke and it's fascinating hearing about his life back in Lima.

But two problems become apparent the second we take our seats.

Firstly, his biceps – which are so big that by rights they should each have had their own allocated seat – leave me with as much personal space as a family of hippos playing Sardines.

Worse, despite Esteban being seventeen stone and built like a brick privy, it emerges that he is terrified of flying – to the point of hysteria.

'I thought I was over this,' he whimpers, as sweat bubbles on his brow. The engine hasn't even started yet. 'But this ... this is terrible ... horrendous ... INSANE.' At that he begins hyperventilating.

'Esteban, don't worry. Take deep breaths,' I reassure him, as he grabs my hand and nearly breaks three fingers.

When the plane's wheels lift off the ground, the noise he lets out of his mouth is not even human; it's like the sound those creatures in *Avatar* make when they've been harpooned. And nothing I can say or do seems to help.

'Hold me, Lauren!' he implores, as Joe and Emily spin round to see what's going on. I smile unconvincingly as Esteban throws his massive arms around my neck and trembles with terror.

'Um ... how did you get to the UK? You must have flown here?' I mumble, my cheek squashed into his armpit, his hairs tickling my nose.

'Sleeping tablets.'

'Didn't you bring some this time?'

His eyes ping open. 'Good idea,' he breathes, rifling round in his bum bag, before producing a tablet the size of a nuclear warhead and washing it down with a bottle of sparkling spring water.

It doesn't just make him sleep. It sends him catatonic.

He slumps into his seat, and half of mine, with a lobotomised look in his eyes as I try and interest him in reading the in-flight magazine, just to check he hasn't slipped into an actual coma.

Still, he settles eventually – at which point I close my own eyes, put on my headphones and flick through the music, until 'You Send Me' by Sam Cooke comes on. I then allow myself to drift into the most blissful dream, in which Edwin and I are sitting in the sunshine on the terrace of the Raffles Hotel, sipping Singapore Slings with a cool breeze in my hair.

Edwin reaches over and touches my chin and is about to kiss me. His lips sink into mine as I experience a rush of warmth through my body – followed by a rush of cold *on* my body. My eyelids fly open as Esteban flails about, his sparkling water all over me, as it becomes apparent that he has realised we are about to land . . . and is no longer catatonic.

More's the pity.

Chapter 13

Despite the overblown title, the Grande Princess Royale Mar resort is a clean but uninspiring two and a half star hotel on the outskirts of Torremolinos. On the plus side, it overlooks the Bajondillo beach, with a sweeping view of the mountains and sea. It's early afternoon before we check in to the 'family suite' Emily, Cate and I are sharing. This arrangement was organised by Marion, who was either oblivious to the fact that Cate and Will are an item, or wanted to make sure that the only exercise in which they indulged was dancing.

The room consists of one queen-sized bed and a bunk apparently pilfered from the set of *Orange Is the New Black*. We toss a coin and I end up on the top. A brief try-out reveals a noisy squeak that gives the impression it's been left in the rain for sixteen years.

The rest of the afternoon is left free for the three of us to soak up some rays by the pool. In the evening, we head downstairs on to the terrace as a disco is in full throttle, belting out a medley of ear-splitting Europop songs as two dozen over-tired children and their beleaguered parents hop about waving their arms.

'Not much salsa dancing going on, Marion,' Will says mischievously. 'Unless we're meant to do it to "Gangnam Style"?'

'The dancing programme starts tomorrow, when there'll be a full day of it, so don't worry,' she replies.

Will flashes Cate a glance and, unable to stop himself, leaps up, grabs Marion by the hand and challenges her to a Gangnam-style salsa. To be absolutely fair to Marion, while the resulting dance isn't her best performance, it's as impressive as could be expected when surrounded by a dozen four year olds squealing 'EHHH . . . Sexeh laydeh!'

'Your new man is a nutcase,' I tell Cate.

'I know,' she laughs. 'A breath of fresh air from Robby.'

'Poor Robby,' I snort.

'There's no *poor Robby* about it,' Cate huffs.

'Oh I didn't mean—'

'No, I know you didn't. But let me show you why I no longer feel sorry for him.' She takes out her phone, clicks on to her messages and starts scrolling down. 'Look what he sent me about twenty minutes ago.'

I take a sip of sangria and peek at the phone, expecting either some schmaltzy message proclaiming undying love, or a text alerting her to the fact that he left socks at her flat last time he was there.

But there are no socks on this picture message.

In fact, there are no items of clothing whatsoever. There is just Robby, reclining on a sofa, one arm behind his back – and *completely* naked.

I realise I'm supposed to respond, but a piece of fruit from my sangria is wedged in the back of my throat and prevents me from doing anything other than spluttering several expletives.

'Shhh!' she says, glancing round. I look at the phone again. Then look away. Then look again. Then, convinced that my eyes are about to start bleeding, Cate says, 'Oh come on, it's not that incredible – at least his bits are covered.' This is technically true, although by 'covered' she is referring simply to the strategically-placed bottle of bleach on the table in the foreground.

'What's with the Domestos?' I whisper.

She shrugs. 'He was obsessed with cleaning so that was probably just the first thing we had to hand. And it was about the right size to cover him up.'

I park the issue of the unlikely proportions of the contents of Robby's trousers and ask a more pressing question: 'Did you take this picture?'

'Yeah, but ages ago. Sexting was Robby's favourite hobby,' she says, then catches my eye. 'Don't look at me like that. It's not *that* unusual these days.'

'I wouldn't know. The last time I had sex was before Alexander Graham Bell invented the telephone.'

'Well, this is what dating is like these days, believe me,' she tells me, pursing her lips. 'Loads of men go for it. Not that I've had loads of men, I hasten to add.'

I shake my head while contemplating this issue, which I'd never given a second thought to until now. 'Wow. "Shall I compare thee to a summer's day ... and get a shot of your boobs for posterity?" It hasn't quite got the same ring to it. Why is he sending it to you now?' I ask.

'Exactly!' she replies.

'Have you asked him?'

'I texted him right back. He *claims* he pressed the button by mistake,' she says dubiously. 'Which is bollocks – and does nothing to change my view of him as a Class A creep.'

Then, as the track changes to 'Oops Upside Your Head', she says, 'Come on, let's go and dance,' grabbing me by the hand before I get the chance to query whether her enthusiasm for this music is the result of a sharp blow to the temple.

Sometimes though, with a playlist as gloriously naff as this, all you can do is roll with it. So we do roll with it, all the way to Crapsville, taking a detour via 'The Birdie song', the 'Macarena' and a whole host of other audible delights with names such as 'Cim bombom!' and 'Chichi Wah!' By the time we get on to 'Barbie Girl' and Will dances up to Cate, I decide to head back to my sangria.

I put the straw to my lips, take a small sip and relax into the chair.

'"Barbie Girl" not your thing then?' I look up to find Joe sinking into the seat next to me.

I sit up uncomfortably straight and mumble, 'I've done the "Macarena" twice. I consider my work here to be done.'

'Me too. Besides, I can't shimmy as well as Will can.'

I don't know what his aftershave is, but the smell of him agitates me beyond words.

'So how's your room?' he asks, clearly not noticing that I can do without the small talk.

'Not quite up to the glorious standards of the heyday of the Moonlight Hotel,' I say pointedly.

He doesn't answer for a moment. Then: 'The Moonlight Hotel isn't up to the glorious standards of its heyday either, I suspect – and hasn't been in a long time. The place I bought is no reflection of what it was like years ago. Which is why it needs a bit of . . . vision.'

'So that's what you're calling it.' I slosh the straw in my drink up and down.

'It is. At least, I hope so.'

I remove the straw and take a large mouthful of the drink before looking away frostily.

'Will mentioned you have a family connection to the hotel,' he continues.

'Yes. My dad was GM for twelve years. So the Moonlight Hotel means a lot to me. And I don't like the idea of it being changed beyond recognition, I can't deny it.'

He singularly fails to leap in and reassure me.

Defiance starts to build in my chest and I feel the need to say more, to explain why what he's doing is so wrong. 'Look at this,' I continue, reaching into my purse and removing the photo I carry around of me and my dad.

I don't know why this one is so precious to me, why I keep it on me all the time; there are hundreds of other photos of us and this one's actually slightly blurry. But we're sitting in the place I loved more than anywhere: the gazebo at the bottom of the gardens of the Moonlight Hotel, right on the banks of Windermere.

I'm throwing one of my regular tea parties, with Dad as the only guest, forced to endure endless cups of non-existent beverages and to say 'Mmm . . .' while pretending to bite into cakes made of polyurethane.

I hand it over to Joe. 'I was five or six in that picture. Do you recognise where it is?'

He scrutinises it. 'I can't say I do.'

I have to stop myself from rolling my eyes. 'It's in the gardens of the Moonlight Hotel. Look – don't you recognise the tree?'

'Possibly,' he replies uncertainly. 'It was the gazebo that threw me. What happened to that?'

'No idea – I'd spend hours in it, though. I'd have lived in it if I could have.'

He smiles. 'I take it that's your dad?'

I nod but don't say anything.

'You look alike. You've got the same eyes. Although – clearly – he's a lot bigger than you.'

'He was a big guy, with a big personality. There was no one he couldn't make laugh.'

Joe looks hesitant, then asks: '*Was?*'

I decide it's time to put the picture away. 'He died when I was sixteen.'

'Oh. I'm sorry.'

'Anyway. I hope you can understand why I'm so worried about any plans to tear out all the character and original features and … well, just about everything that makes the Moonlight Hotel what it is. Does the world really need another Travel Haven?'

He looks taken aback. 'The Moonlight Hotel is *not* going to be part of the Travel Havens chain, Lauren.'

My back straightens. 'Isn't it?'

'No. We want to give it the kind of treatment we've done with a couple of the hotels we own in other parts of the world. They're a lot more upmarket.'

I wonder if he's showing off, but don't say so.

'Although, for the record, I'm very proud of the Travel Havens part of the business – it's what we're known for in the UK. But I can't deny I'd be disappointed if people thought the Moonlight Hotel belonged in the budget end of our company.'

'Well, you would say that, wouldn't you?'

One side of his mouth quirks up. 'I suppose I would. Look, Lauren, I'll be honest with you. I was in a difficult position when I first bought the place – on two fronts. The bank hadn't quite signed off the finance I needed to do what I wanted, so I've had to stay quiet about the plans. But, I'm presenting them next week to the staff and I'm confident that what we're doing will be far from average.' I can feel my jaw seize up. 'Having said that, I can't claim that we're leaving the place as it is. It's going to be *very* different. There's going to be a massive overhaul. It needs it.'

I bristle and take another large mouthful of my drink. 'Why don't you let me in on the secret, then? What *are* you doing with the place?'

He looks at me for a second, then takes out his phone, edging his chair closer to mine. I feel my heartbeat quicken and not in a good way.

The picture on the home screen shows him in climbing gear, his arm around a girl of about twelve or thirteen with orange hair, black nails and a T-shirt that reads *Yeah, I'm a weirdo*. They're both grinning from ear to ear. He sees me looking. 'That's my niece, Sophie. My sister's daughter. She's an angel. We had great fun that day. We'd been scrambling and … ' His voice trails off, clearly realising I'm not interested in anything other than the Moonlight Hotel. 'Sorry – the plans.'

He flicks on to his photos. 'I shouldn't be showing you on here. It does it no justice.' Yet he swipes his strong fingers over the screen before pausing – and then he offers me the phone.

The images are artists' impressions, which in my experience are never a wholly accurate representation. Even accounting for that, what I'm looking at prompts a clash of emotions in my head. It's still clearly the Moonlight Hotel, with its high ceilings and grand windows, but it's a weird and, what Joe obviously believes is wonderful, version of it: opulent and kind of funky too. There are huge chandeliers, antique books lining the walls, gold cornices above the windows – but they're juxtaposed against a glossy champagne bar, clever lighting and lush velvet furnishings. Joe, it's clear, wants to make a strong statement that this is no longer a fusty old hotel. This is a luxury hotel where newlyweds will while away their honeymoon and sophisticated travellers will feel right at home.

I sit silently, attempting to decode my emotions.

OK, I'm delighted – over the moon, in fact – that it's not going to be a Travel Haven. And I've no doubt that when the *Guardian* journalists traipse up from London to be plied with Veuve Clicquot and have their feet massaged with Jo Malone toiletries, before disappearing home again, they'll love what Joe Wilborne has done to it.

But *I*, Lauren Scott, will be unable to share their enthusiasm. I'll admit it: I loved that fusty hotel, just how it was.

True, the original features aren't quite being torn down like I thought they would be, but the whole thing is so vastly, catastrophically different from the place I grew up in, it brings tears to my eyes. The worst thing about this is it's going to be a success. That much is obvious. People will love it.

But I'm not people. And I won't love it. I loved it the way it was when I was six.

And as if to underline all this, I flick on to an image of what is no doubt to be a defining 'statement piece' of the hotel: hanging on the wall is a massive, spectacular – and very modern-looking painting . . . of a flying zebra. It's completely mad and I don't like it one bit.

'What do you think?' Joe asks quietly. And suddenly he looks so anxious about my answer, I can't bring myself to tell him I hate it. Because he clearly wants to make this place a success. He clearly is investing more than just money in it.

'It's certainly striking,' is all I can manage.

He presses his lips together as a second passes. 'Very diplomatic,' he nods, and I can tell he's got the message.

'You'll bring the guests in, Joe,' I concede. 'People will like it. Although, for the record, it is lunacy to even think about putting a flying zebra in the hall.'

He smiles. 'You think it's a bit OTT?'

'If you're prepared for people to think you're clinically insane, then I reckon it's fine.'

'Maybe when people see it for themselves, they'll be won

over.' His eyes search my face. 'I shouldn't really have shown you the plans – it's hard to see the place in its full glory on a bit of paper. It'll be different once it's completed.'

Which brings me to a question that's been nagging at me since I first found out about this.

'Why now, Joe? I mean, why are you closing the hotel as we're heading into the busiest season? It doesn't make any sense.'

'I didn't see any point in hanging around,' he says, and I can't shake the feeling that he's not telling the truth.

'How did you get into all this anyway? Emily tells me you were once in the Army.'

'Yes, it's been a circuitous route here,' he replies, clearly glad to be on an easier subject.

'I never had you down as the military kind,' I say.

'Why not?' he asks, and for a moment I can't work out why. Physically, Joe can obviously handle himself; he's big, muscular . . . all the attributes a soldier would require. But, rightly or wrongly, I'd always imagined guys in the Army to be excessively macho. And I can't quite square that with a man who's as concerned as he is with champagne-coloured upholstery. 'I just didn't have you down as the type,' I confess rather lamely.

He laughs. 'I hadn't thought you were the kind of girl who harboured stereotypes.'

'Neither had I. Sorry – go on.'

'Well, my dad was in this business, and when an

opportunity came up to develop a hotel in Chester, he wanted to put me in charge of it, to teach me the ropes. If I'm honest, my mum hated me being in the military. She lived in perpetual fear that I was going to come back in a coffin.'

'So you did it for them?'

'No, nothing like that,' he says immediately, then stops to think about whether his response is entirely accurate. 'It was the right thing to do,' he concludes. 'Though not a decision you take lightly. I'm glad I experienced life in the Army – I saw some incredible places and met some incredible people. But I'm equally glad to be out of it.'

I glance up to see Emily at the edge of the dance floor; she's looking in our direction. 'Emily's over there with nobody to dance with,' I tell Joe.

He looks up at her then back at me. 'Well, we can't have that, can we?' he says softly. Then he tucks his phone into his back pocket, drains his drink and stands up. 'See you later, Lauren. And don't say a word to anyone about those plans, will you?'

I force a smile and put my finger to my lips. 'Your zebra's safe with me.'

Chapter 14

I don't sleep well that night because even the slightest wriggle prompts a cacophony of violent squeaks which threaten to wake the entire room. As the sun finally shears through the edge of the curtains, my eyes flicker blearily open and I lean down to see if Emily's awake.

'Morning, Lauren,' she grins, looking inordinately happy.

'Emily, I am so sorry. You'd have got more sleep in an orchestra pit.'

'Oh, it's not your fault,' she says, with a long, languorous stretch. She rubs her eyes and, even with a glob of mascara underneath them, her hair mussed up on top, she still manages to look gorgeous.

'So, Em ... were you late back last night?' I ask, which is a subtle way of asking whether she and Joe ended up finally getting together. Cate is awake and has sat up to hear Emily's reply.

'Yeah, come on – spill the beans,' she grins, subtlety not being her speciality. 'Did you snog Joe?'

Emily responds with a giggle, before rolling over and snuggling down into her sheet. 'That'd be telling.'

'I knew it!' Cate shrieks, clapping her hands together.

'Yes, okay, Poirot,' Emily grins. 'You love all the juicy detail, don't you?'

'Right, all we need to do now is hook our Lauren up with someone and *all* our love lives are sorted. Easy. How about Esteban?' Cate continues.

I roll my eyes. 'I don't think so.'

'Why not? I don't think Jilly's interested – and besides, he seemed to be getting very cosy on the flight.'

'He had me in a headlock, Cate,' I tell her. 'There is a difference.'

The hotel might not look overly fancy, but breakfast is magnificent – and it therefore goes up in my estimation by about 1000 per cent. We feast on scrambled eggs and toast with a selection of pastries, washed down with hot, treacly coffee.

Will and Joe are already in the breakfast room when we arrive, so Cate, Emily and I end up on a table with three people from Marion's old Manchester salsa class. They've been on several of her trips abroad and their advice can be summed up by a girl called Keeley with cropped dark hair and a nose ring almost identical to Cate's. 'They're fab, as long as you don't let her bully you,' she grins, at the exact moment that Marion appears brandishing a class timetable.

It is clear that our esteemed teacher is taking this trip very seriously: there is not a scheduled moment of respite from the dancing, apart from an hour for lunch. 'When do we get to sunbathe, Marion?' Cate asks.

Marion looks as though she pities her. 'You can sunbathe *anywhere*. Why on earth would you want to do that, when you can dance?'

'I can't sunbathe *anywhere*, Marion,' Cate replies. 'I live in the Lake District, which isn't exactly known for its sub-tropical climate.'

In the event, the morning class is fantastic. It's also hilarious. I do realise that hilarity isn't supposed to be its key attribute, but it works for most of us. We start off by attempting some fairly advanced moves, including a loop-over lock with a barrel turn – which, yes, is as hard as it sounds and way beyond my ability. But, once we're over the fact that our collective failure to master this series of moves constitutes 'entertainment' for the Dutch and German clientele relaxing by the pool, there's no going back. Particularly when said clientele leap up and Marion nearly has a nervous breakdown while several men attempt to join in.

My mind drifts predictably to Edwin all morning. I

can't help thinking he'd love this. I've never been anywhere dancing with him, but you just instinctively know with some men that they'd be a natural, and he's one of them, at least I think so. Yes, I admit it's not immediately obvious, but Edwin's got so many hidden depths. I know – I categorically *know* – that, once he loosened his tie and grabbed me by the hand, he'd be unstoppable on a dance floor.

Lunch is big, long and mildly boozy, resulting in precisely zero takers for the afternoon class. All anybody wants to do is soak up some rays – apart from Cate that is, who wants to spend some 'quality time' with Will. Read into that euphemism whatever you like.

Emily and I grab a couple of loungers by the pool and lie back in the sun. Sleep-deprived as I am, I close my eyes and push my dilemma about Singapore from my head, and very soon, the red blur behind my eyelids disappears to nothing . . .

When I wake, God knows how much later, it is in the style of Basil Fawlty leaping out of bed, arms and legs akimbo, eyes wide, head spinning as I try to register my whereabouts. Emily smirks and puts her hand on my bare shoulder.

'How's it going, Lauren?'

'Eurgh, I feel a bit groggy. How long have I been asleep?'

'An hour, maybe an hour and a half,' she replies, as I register that she's fully dressed.

'Are you going somewhere?' I ask.

'I was going to suggest a walk along the prom if you fancy coming?'

I look down at myself and feel, frankly, wretched. 'I think I need a shower before tonight's activities to be honest, Em,' I reply.

She smiles. 'No problem. We've only got one key, though. Cate's got the other.'

'If you come up with me first and let me in, you can keep hold of the key. Then I'll just meet you here in an hour and a half or so. I presume Cate will have emerged from Will's love-nest by then.'

After a shower and rudimentary tart-up, I am feeling significantly more human so head back downstairs to wait for Emily and Cate over a coffee. I settle at a table by the pool and take out my notepad and pen, resolving to do my decision-making the *Cosmo* way: by making a list of pros and cons of going to Singapore. It ends up like this:

Pros

1. Guaranteed opportunity to spend immediate future with Edwin by:
   a. Holding a series of 'planning' sessions in romantic pubs.

b. Sitting next to him on a plane.

c. Once there, sharing accommodation, thus offering potential for Ross and Rachel-style romance in which two people *clearly* made for each other finally realise it. And, without getting too optimistic, potentially have *sex* of the non-self-administered kind.

2. Singapore looks lovely.

3. New life/adventure etc, with lots of brand new people – exciting!

4. Financially more viable than initial plan to bum round Oz.

5. Poss wedding at the Raffles Hotel? (Ultimately, *obvs*: but I'm all for deferred gratification.)

Cons

1. Real possibility of spending a week with Edwin before he finds new girlfriend, leaving me heartbroken and homeless.

2. I'd never even thought of Singapore until a month ago.

3. New life could = lonely, homesick existence with no cousin Steph for company, no friends and no enjoyment.

4. No Australia.

'Good day?' I look up and see Joe standing above me. I sit up in alarm and hastily stuff the note upside down under my saucer. 'Excellent day, thank you,' I reply.

I feel weird around Joe, I can't deny it. Now I know he's not turning the Moonlight Hotel into a Travel Haven I no longer hate his guts. And there have even been moments since he showed me those plans yesterday when I've thought that perhaps what he's doing to the hotel might not be such a bad thing. But they've been fleeting: I know in my gut that I'm not going to like it.

'What have you been up to?' I ask, as he doesn't seem inclined to walk away.

'I went for a run around the town. I'm not really the sun-bathing type, and I think a whole morning of Marion is enough for anyone,' he smiles. 'Plus, Will and I are sharing a room, so I thought I'd give him and Cate a bit of space. You know, just in case they weren't up there playing Scrabble. Would you like a drink?'

'I'm fine, thanks,' but as a waitress appears, he orders a Coke for himself and takes a seat.

'So,' he says firmly, as if he's about to broach an inordinately serious subject. 'Guy at two o'clock in the red shorts. What do you think he does for a living?'

I glance at Joe and wonder what the hell he's on about. 'I've got absolutely no idea – what *does* he do for a living?'

'Well, I've got no idea either. But I am fairly certain I can tell just by looking at him: he's a retired nuclear engineer.'

I raise an eyebrow. 'Really?'

'Only he gave it up to run a shop that specialises in cro-cheting jumpers made from the hair of people's pets. His name is Ludwig.'

I burst out laughing. 'OK. What about her ... lady in the blue swimsuit.' I nod over at a middle-aged lady with a jolly, jowly smile who is tanned to the colour of a conker.

'Dolphin-trainer,' he answers, without missing a beat. 'But she's recently moved on to squid. Wants to challenge herself.'

'Him,' I say, pointing to someone else.

'Trapeze artiste. Strong legs.'

'Her.'

'Goat-herder.'

'Couple by the tiki bar,' I challenge him.

'He's a golf-ball diver.'

'What's a golf-ball diver?'

'The guy who dives into the ponds on golf courses and retrieves all the golf balls. And she's ...' he frowns, pretend-ing to scrutinise her '... a sex-toy tester.'

I am actually laughing now, as I go to take a sip of my coffee. The cup is almost at my mouth, when a gust of wind whips past – and takes my pros and cons list with it.

Panic grips me as all I can think about is that reference to the fact that the only intimate encounter I've had in the last three years was battery-powered. Into the split second that follows, I cram a multitude of neurotic possibilities, which come down to my public exposure as a sad, sex-starved spinster who, twenty years after my first boxset, still wants to be Rachel from *Friends*.

I leap out of my seat and start frantically chasing the note across the terrace as Joe looks on, bewildered. As I repeatedly lunge for it – and fail to catch it – my inner hysteria intensifies, as Joe, clearly believing this to be of life-or-death importance, jumps up to try and help.

Just when I am almost weeping with desperation, the wind dies down and my note floats nonchalantly through the air towards the edge of the swimming pool. I hold my breath, praying that it stays still long enough for me to get it in my grasp. And it *almost* does.

The exact chain of events that follows is a frantic blur. All I know is that one minute, I've almost got the list in my hand … the next, it's rising into the air again and I'm stretching out to reach it.

But instead of clasping the note and tucking it firmly into a pocket, I feel the edge of it tickle my fingertips, and then my ankle twists and, as if I've been shot in the torso by a sniper, I find myself crashing side-on into the swimming pool.

The last time I ended up fully clothed in a stretch of chlorinated water was aged twelve on a junior lifeguard course.

And while the event gave me a basic grasp of life-saving, face-saving is another matter.

I splutter to the surface, my cheeks burning as I doggy-paddle to the edge and hoist myself up as Joe insists on reaching out for my hand and pulling me up with remarkably little effort.

'Are you all right?' he asks as the woman who makes a living as a sex-toy tester re-opens her copy of *Reader's Digest* and pretends not to have seen a thing.

Chapter 15

Cate and Will have finally emerged from the room he shares with Joe. Beyond that I have absolutely no idea where either of them is, because she's switched off her phone. Which means that, instead of going back to my room, drying off and curling up in my squeaky bunk to hide my mortification, I'm left with no alternative but to accept Joe's offer to do the drying-off bit in *his* room.

This is not a prospect with which I feel even a tiny bit comfortable, particularly given that the only dry clothes available are Joe's shorts and clean T-shirt, which hangs ludicrously off my shoulders. He smiles when I emerge from his en-suite.

'I'm glad I'm the source of such amusement,' I say.

'They kind of suit you actually,' he grins.

His room is slightly smaller than ours, but fancier, if you count the shower cap, actual bona fide vista (ours is a 'Garden View' which means it overlooks the car park) and remote control for the TV. He leans on the bureau and crosses his arms.

'So what was on the paper? All the passwords for MI6's security settings?'

'Far more important,' I tell him, sitting on the edge of the bed. 'Or more embarrassing.'

He laughs. 'I see.'

'Oh, not *that* embarrassing,' I insist hastily. 'I mean, it wasn't my list of top ten favourite Bros songs or anything, or membership of UKIP.'

'I should hope not.'

'It was ... well, it was just a list of pros and cons. About whether I should move to Singapore.'

'What's in Singapore?'

I sigh. 'Not what – w*ho*.'

'Go on.'

I squirm. 'It's just this guy at work, my friend. We're quite close, in some ways. I've had feelings for him for quite a while, only they haven't been reciprocated, because he had a girl-friend – until recently.'

'Now he's single?'

I nod. 'He dumped her and is moving to Singapore. Only, he's asked me to go with him.'

Joe raises his eyebrows. 'So you're an item?'

'Well, no. That's just it.'

He looks at me in a way that makes it impossible not to

continue. I sit on the edge of his bed and words tumble out of my mouth about my history with Edwin – my *feelings* for Edwin – in a way that's so cathartic I ought to be paying Joe by the hour.

When I stop talking, a rush of embarrassment fills my chest.

'Would you like some male insight into this situation?' he offers.

'Yes, please.'

'This guy *is* interested, all my instincts are telling me so,' he says. 'There's no way I'd invite a girl to fly all the way over to Singapore with me if I didn't think she was seriously special.'

'So why hasn't he done anything about it?'

'He's definitely not gay?' he says, and I realise he's being mischievous.

'He had a girlfriend for three years.'

'Could he be shy?' he ventures.

'That *could* be it. He's a little old-fashioned,' I agree. 'There's always the obvious though: he doesn't fancy me.'

'I don't think so,' he laughs. 'I'm going with your first guess. Which is fine – we all get shy sometimes. I used to be terrible when I was younger.' I find this difficult to believe somehow. 'But faint heart never won fair maiden, as the saying goes. He needs to man up.'

'He is *all man*,' I leap in defensively. 'Well, kind of.'

'Why don't you just ask him out?' he shrugs. I freeze in alarm and he looks surprised. 'Is that so controversial? I had you down as a feminist.'

'I am. But I've also read *The Rules*. I'm not going to fall into that trap.'

'Forget self-help books. I am a man – I know these things. Just ask him out, then you'll know categorically if he's interested. Mystery solved.'

Chapter 16

The salsa dancing comes into its own that night. Marion's lesson is fantastic. She shows us how to put together several of the basic steps we've learned in our Tuesday classes, and for the first time ever, the resulting dance looks vaguely as it should do. But it's the social when the whole thing really ramps up a gear: our small group joins the other salsa classes and everyone is up and dancing at one point – Frank and me, Jilly and Esteban, Will and Cate, Joe and Emily, along with throngs of other Brits from three other classes. As I take a seat, it's Joe and Emily I can't take my eyes off, the warmth of the day still hazy on my shoulders as she gazes into his eyes, clearly smitten.

He takes her hand and she makes several perfect turns; it's as if somebody from high above has come along and sprinkled fairy dust over the two of them. They're alive; they're electric. They really are made for each other.

'Why are you mooching over here by yourself?' Cate asks,

thrusting another drink into my hand as she sits down next to me.

'Just taking a breather,' I reply.

'You're here on a salsa holiday, you should be salsa-ing,' Will says, appearing from nowhere.

Then he grabs me by the hand. And before I know it, I'm on the dance floor, stepping, spinning, sashaying my hips, and feeling as if I almost know what I'm doing. I dance with Esteban. I dance with Will. And I dance with Joe.

'Right – loop-over locks with a turn. You ready?'

'I can't do that!' I protest.

'Neither can I, but I thought we could at least give it a go,' he says.

I step back. 'Go on then. You're the man. You lead.'

'Thanks a lot,' he laughs, before twirling me into a series of moves that we both agree afterwards looked about as slick as two knock-kneed goats.

'Think we might need a bit of practice first,' I gasp, as I get my breath back.

'And I think you might be right, but perseverance is the key.'

The rest of the evening is a blur. All I know is, we drink a lot, we dance a lot, we laugh a lot.

By the end of the night, Will makes a rash decision – and goes to reception to book a separate room for himself and Cate that evening. The two of them disappear off, giggling, leaving Joe and a very drunk Emily to stumble back to his room.

So I lie alone in the bedroom, while my two friends get laid elsewhere, feeling strangely horny, strangely unsettled but strangely happy. Because Joe's right. When I get home, I am going to make sure Edwin Blaire is under no illusions about what I feel for him.

I'm going to ask him out on a date.

Chapter 17

When I arrive at work for the first day of the new term, I feel mildly delirious. The cause of this could be anything, from lingering alcohol in my bloodstream to the far too late journey home (I didn't put my key in the lock until 11.45 p.m.). It could also be due to the fact that, despite my efforts to sit with anyone other than Esteban on the flight back, I ended up next to him again in yet another headlock, this time with him chanting a Mindfulness mantra down my ear canal as we took off.

Yet, when I woke this morning it was with a strong sense of destiny, and an even stronger sense of positivity. I have a task to do and I WILL do it. If Edwin says no to a date, I know exactly where I stand. If he says yes, then all is clear too – and amazing! Today, for better or worse, will give me clarity about whether the life I'm planning will be in Australia with Steph or Singapore with Edwin.

I park my car and gaze across the sunlight cast on the fells.

It's one of those days when heaven has taken up temporary home in Lakeland, when everything glitters, from the still water on the lakes to the dew on the grassy mountainsides.

'Miss Scott, I've got sausages for my packed lunch.' I spin round and see Tom Goodwin grinning at me through a gap-toothed smile.

'Ooh, lucky you,' I reply.

'It's not *just* sausages.' Tom's dad says, suppressing a smile. 'There are some healthy things in there too, I promise you.'

'Yes, there's a Fruit Shoot,' Tom tells me earnestly.

'I wasn't talking about the Fruit Shoot,' his dad laughs, ruffling his hair. 'There's an apple too.'

'I hate apples.'

'Oh good,' he sighs and I grin. I've never met Mr Goodwin before today – it's usually Tom's mum Jenny who does the school run. But I can completely see them together: they're both attractive in a bookish kind of way. He's big and muscular, with intelligent eyes and dark hair that shows the first signs of thinning.

'Daddy, this is my teacher, Miss Scott.'

Mr Goodwin looks taken aback by this, a reaction that's usually down to the kids having told their parents that I'm really, *really* old. 'Nice to meet you. I'm Nick Goodwin,' he says, reaching out his hand. 'I've heard an awful lot about you.'

'Really?' I'm pleased. 'Oh, well, that's nice to know.'

There's a moment's hesitation as I realise he's looking at me, as if he's trying to place me from somewhere.

'Can you point us in the direction of Breakfast Club, Miss Scott? It's normally Tom's mum who brings him in the morning. I'm a novice.'

As I show them in, I'm partly glad of the distraction, at least temporarily. Because by the time I reach the door of the staff room, my nerves begin to fail me. Excitement and dread are running in equal measures through my veins.

I'm holding my breath as I open the door ... only to find Joyce and Maeve alone and mid-conversation about *Hotter Than My Daughter*, which was on TV last night.

I flick on the kettle and wait for a break in conversation before saying casually, 'Edwin's not his usual early self today.'

'He's gone to the dentist,' Maeve tells me. 'Root-canal something or other.'

'Oh.' I feel myself deflate. 'Is he coming in later?'

'Think so.'

My buoyancy continues to unravel as the day unfolds and is replaced by something I can only describe as unease. It's lunch-break by the time Edwin appears, and across a crowded dining room. I am carrying a plate of chilli con carne large enough to feed several Mexican families, having been persuaded by Maureen the dinner lady to sample the one dish everyone else refused.

Edwin looks up and waves, beckoning me to the seat

opposite him. I glide over with trepidation rising in my throat. As I approach, the heat between us seems to radiate across the room and is only broken when I have to turn round and tell off a group of Year One pupils for playing football under the table with a strawberry jelly. I sit down, glance at Edwin's face and I realise his jaw is puffed up.

'I was leaped on by a gang of armed thugs outside and beaten to a pulp,' he says, trying to smile. I must look alarmed because he says: 'I'm kidding. My dentist decided to have a fight with one of my molars – and lost.'

'Ouch – that sounds painful. How do you feel?'

'Not too good,' he replies, pushing some mashed potato round his plate. 'Even with an enormous set of pliers, she hasn't managed to get the damn tooth out. I've got to go for an extraction operation before I leave for Singapore. In the meantime, I can't eat anything but this mush and am in a lot of pain. Plus, I look like hell.'

I meet his gaze over the mash potatoes. 'You don't look like hell, Edwin,' I whisper. 'Far from it.'

The hint of a smile appears from behind his swollen lips. The pupils closest to us are by now engrossed in a conversation about loom bands – and I realise it's now or never. I've got to ask him out. Unfortunately, I'm not quick enough.

'How's the chilli?' he asks, squeezing a small lump of mashed spud into his mouth.

I look down at my plate. So far, I haven't taken a single bite of my meal. So I lift a forkful of it to my mouth, instantly wondering where Maureen got the minced flip-flops from which to make it. The chewy sensation is followed rapidly by an astonishingly spicy kick, one that prompts me to start coughing.

I look up and see that Edwin is waiting for an answer. I can't let the kids hear me slag off the school dinners – I might as well invite the letters from the parents to come pouring in now – so I lean into him. 'It's not the greatest dish Maureen's ever—'

I'm halfway through my sentence, when Edwin is forced to duck out of the way of what are apparently overpowering spice fumes shooting from my mouth. I flush red.

'Sorry,' he coughs politely and holds a napkin up to his lips. 'You were saying?'

I hold my hand over my mouth. 'It's fine,' I mumble.

The rest of the meal is mildly excruciating and I don't get to ask my question, because that would involve getting closer and giving him the full force of my dragon breath again.

I'm also distracted by Ellie Sampson having what we euphemistically call a 'bathroom incident', Blossom Jones dropping her pasta salad on the floor, and being asked for input into a debate between two Year Two boys about whether it's possible that one of them *really* has a paper round, aged six, when he can't yet ride a bike without stabilisers.

I reach my classroom with an overwhelming sense of

disappointment in myself, something that must be written on my face, given that the first thing Angela, my teaching assistant, says to me is: 'Ooh, have you got a headache too?'

Still, I pull myself together and begin a lesson that involves painting a self-portrait on a paper plate; having tried this, I can tell you that it's significantly harder than it looks. I'm trying to persuade three of the girls to go easy on the sequins, when Tom Goodwin appears at my side.

'Miss Scott?'

'Yes, Tom?' I reply, slightly distracted by the sparkly embellishments.

'You're the best teacher in the world.' I stop what I'm doing and look at his sweet smile, my heart melting just a little.

'Oh, what prompted that, Tom?'

He shrugs shyly. 'I don't know.'

'Thank you, Tom,' I reply gently.

It's only a *little* confidence-boost, of course. But it's enough to make me straighten my back, fill my lungs and promise myself that I am *not* going to go home tonight without asking Edwin out. I couldn't live with myself.

So that afternoon, after I wave goodbye to the children and hand them back to their parents, I pop in my seventh Extra Strong Mint and stride purposefully to Edwin's classroom before he has a chance to leave.

'Edwin,' I say, knocking on his door. 'Have you got a moment?'

'Of course, come in.' I close the door behind me. 'Don't say it: I look like a gerbil,' he jokes.

'Of course you don't.'

'One of the pupils said I had cheeks like his pet. On the plus side, it's called Starlord, which I thought had a certain ring to it.'

'I hope you told him off for being cheeky,' I smirk.

He laughs. 'So what can I do for you, Lauren?'

My pulse thunders in my ears. Every instinct is telling me to come up with an excuse, turn and run. But I don't. I absolutely don't.

'I wondered if you'd like to go out with me one night?' Once the words are out, I'm so shocked that I've said them that all I can hear is my heartbeat filling every corner of the room.

I carry on speaking, just to shut it up. 'The thing is, I'm interested in Singapore and it'd be good to pick your brain about it,' I babble. 'There's so much for me to think about and . . . I thought it would be good to discuss the whole thing and—'

'Lauren,' he says, eyes glinting. 'Of *course* I'll go out with you. Singapore or no Singapore. I can think of nothing nicer.'

Then he smiles, one of his big, wide, *I-might-just-die-on-the-spot* smiles, which is all the dreamier given that he's having to manage it through a pair of distinctly pudgy lips.

It takes me a moment to respond. 'OK,' I reply coolly. 'In fact, *amazing*!' Which is not so cool.

151

'How about next week?' he suggests. 'Thursday would be good for me. We could go into Bowness, have a few drinks and take it from there.' He holds my gaze for a second or two.

'Sounds lovely. Right – well, we'll make the arrangements early next week then, shall we, but I'll keep Thursday free.'

He nods and I leave the room almost tripping over my own feet with happiness.

Chapter 18

I consider not bothering with salsa night on Tuesday now I have a date for which to prepare two days later (YES!!!), but Cate refuses to let me off the hook.

'They've got an offer on the tapas, Marion's going to introduce a proper routine tonight – and, more to the point, I need to hear all about how you ended up having a hot date lined up with Edwin this week.'

I give her and Emily a run-down on the way there that's briefer than I'd like, before we find a space to park and tramp down the hill to the restaurant.

'Will and I are going out on Thursday too,' Cate smiles, as we pass the candlelit glow from the window of Porto and continue along the limewashed row of shops.

'Anywhere nice?' Emily asks.

'Yes, actually,' she says, trying and failing to look cool. 'He's asked me to meet his parents.'

My eyes widen. 'Honestly? Oh, that's lovely, Cate! It was

obvious you were getting serious, but this is a big milestone.'

'Well, don't buy your hat yet, but I hope you're right. I can't wait. I'm nervous as hell too, obviously.'

'Will's lovely,' Emily tells Cate.

'He is,' she agrees. 'But so's Joe. And you've still got a spring in your step after your nights of passion in Spain.'

Emily blushes to her roots as we arrive at the restaurant and push open the door.

The class is smaller than usual, with only two of the nurses and none of the Mountain Rescue crew apart from Will. Even Frank's taken a breather which, unlikely as it sounds, I think qualifies us as the dedicated few.

'Hello, girls,' Stella says, lighting up when she sees us. 'How was the trip?'

'Good,' I tell her. 'It wasn't the most luxurious hotel in the world, but there was sunshine and salsa and quite a lot of booze so it definitely did the trick. Did you get a lot of wedding planning done?'

'Yes, but I wish I'd been with you. Instead, I was stuck at home saving up for the hog roast and making the silk bows on chair covers.'

'Do yourself a favour, love, and save the silk for your knickers,' Cate advises.

'If you'd once told me I'd be the sort of woman who gave a toss about what the chairs looked like, I wouldn't have believed you,' Stella replies. 'But I've been sucked into this weird world in which nothing but a pair of Jimmy Choos will do. This time last year, I was shopping at Primark.'

I look up in time to see Joe gazing lovingly at Emily next to me. He glances away, caught in the act.

'Shame you haven't persuaded Mike to come back to dancing again,' Emily says.

Stella shrugs. 'I'd have loved my big moment, but it's not going to happen. Anyway, he's too busy with other things these days – he's never out of the gym. Honestly, he's there all the time.'

'Wow. He must look amazing,' I say.

She scrunches up her nose. 'By rights he should have a six-pack like Wolverine. He's lost a bit of weight, but not that much.'

I laugh as Marion claps her hands. 'Good evening, dancers,' she says, as if addressing the cast of *Chicago*. 'Today we're going to have a go at putting together some of the steps we've learned so far, to create a routine. It'll be a doddle now you've put in all that practice on the salsa holiday! Right – I need a volunteer.'

She scans the room optimistically and is rewarded with complete silence.

'Thank you, Joe,' she says, grabbing him by the hand.

'Now. Let's start with a hammerlock, then break into a ladies' right turn. The lead and the follow end up back-to-back, from where you'll turn and go into a reverse salsa wrap. Got it?'

She lets go of Joe, who throws her a look as if to say, 'Is that meant to be a joke?'

Marion is right that the more you practise, the easier it becomes, but I can't ever envisage a day when we can put all that together smoothly – and, more importantly, remember it all.

Still, being coupled with Esteban gives me a bit of a head start. He's one of the few 'naturals', which makes it easier for me to be trailed around by him.

When we take a breather halfway through, Emily pops out to make a phone call as I go and buy us some drinks.

'So did you go ahead with it?'

I spin round with two glasses in my hand and see Joe looking at me.

'With what?'

'Edward. Whatsisface. Did you ask him out?'

'It's Ed-*win*. And yes, now you mention it.'

He waits for me to elaborate, which I must admit I'm dying to do. 'Come on, spit it out,' he grins, clearly fancying himself as some sort of relationship guru. 'What did he say?'

'We're going out on Thursday!' I blurt out, then it strikes me that if it wasn't for Joe, this joyous situation would never have even happened. 'I think I owe you one, Joe. I'd never have done it without your pep-talk.'

He looks strangely uncomfortable with this declaration, as if he's suspicious because I'm no longer being horrible to him about the Moonlight Hotel. 'Well ... good. Glad I could help.'

I nod, feeling slightly woozy every time I think about the date. 'I just hope it all goes OK. I'm a bit nervous.'

Then Emily appears at our side and he says, quite simply: 'I don't think you've got anything to be nervous about, Lauren. I'm sure you'll have a fantastic time.'

'Thanks,' I say happily. 'I think you might be right.'

Chapter 19

The preparations for my date with Edwin are so extensive you'd think I was getting ready for a wedding. As I heard Stella saying the other day, when she was debating the case for and against microdermabrasion, the aim is to be *the most gorgeous version of yourself*.

And OK, so I've put a few pounds on again lately after my Cadbury Marvellous Creations habit crept back in. But in other respects I am, if not exactly flawless, then as flawless as it's possible for someone as flawed as me to be.

I've waxed my legs. Tinted my eyebrows. Applied fake tan, this time with the precision of Michelangelo. And after racing home from work, I decided to go ahead and put my hair in heated rollers. I was torn about doing that, as it is obviously imperative that Edwin doesn't get the impression that I've done anything other than throw on the first thing that fell out of my wardrobe.

If he thinks I've made a big effort, that would leave me in

the heinous position of looking too keen, which is the last thing I want: I might as well change my Instagram username to Bunnyboiler87 and fall to my knees to ask him to have my babies.

We've arranged to meet at the Angel Inn, which is a landmark pub that sits right at the top of the hill, with panoramic views from its terraced gardens. I get a taxi into town and stop at the bottom of the hill to get some cash – not because I need some but because I'm somehow three minutes early and if I marched into the pub now it would make a mockery of my ice-cool façade.

The tumbling gardens at the front of the Angel Inn are largely empty this evening, aside from a few hardy souls wrapped in fleeces as they sip pints of bitter. We've arranged to meet in the front room of the pub which, like the rest of the place, is cosy but newly-renovated, with a roaring fire, polished wooden floors and a grand chandelier above.

He's there when I arrive, lounging on a sofa as he flicks through a copy of the *Westmorland Gazette*, a glass of red in front of him. In the small moment before he looks up, I allow myself to imagine what it'd be like to walk over, hold his face in my hands and gently press my lips against his.

'Lauren,' he grins, looking up.

'Hello, Edwin,' I reply, as he stands to greet me. He takes me by the hands and gives me the briefest of kisses on my cheek, before letting go and handing me the drinks list. My heart is in overdrive. I want his lips back on my cheek.

Instead, I manage to sit down in the seat next to him and focus on the list, scanning its contents.

'Did you get a taxi?' he asks.

I look up. 'I did.'

'Me too.' He flashes me a conspiratorial smile. 'What are you having?'

I look back at the list but I can't really focus on it. 'They've got quite a nice selection by the glass, haven't they?' I murmur.

'Yes, I thought so. Although,' I look up again, 'seeing as we both got a taxi, we might as well get a bottle, don't you think?'

'But it's a school night, Edwin.'

He leans in and whispers, 'I won't tell the Head if you don't.'

The evening progresses way too fast. We talk a lot about Singapore, which in my head is increasingly becoming my own personal Garden of Eden – though I try not to linger too long on thoughts of Edwin wearing a fig leaf as it just brings my neck out in blotches.

Edwin tells me that he's got a flat lined up, sharing with a girl who he went to university with, that he's run the idea past her of me bunking in and she was fine about it. 'You'd love Georgie,' he tells me.

'It wouldn't be awkward with the three of us? I wouldn't want to get in the way of anything.' I'd win no prizes for subtlety during these info-fishing sessions.

'It's a strictly platonic relationship,' he reassures me. 'She's a great girl, but not my type, romantically speaking.'

I take a large mouthful of wine and consider for a second if I've got the guts to say the sentence that's whizzing through my head. 'So, who *is* your type, romantically speaking?'

He looks at me with an expression I can only describe as intensely mischievous. 'Let me see. I like brunettes.'

I feel slightly hotter.

'Blue eyes,' he adds.

My hands start to sweat.

'Slim,' he says.

I breathe in, reminding myself to log on to MyFitnessPal again in the morning.

'And just ... I suppose someone with a personality I can really click with. You know, someone I can sit and talk to, while away the hours without ever feeling bored or uncomfortable.'

'It is nice when you meet someone like that, isn't it?' I agree. I realise he's looking at me. I also realise my eyelids have softened, my lips have parted slightly. Lust is rushing through my body as if it's been turned on like a tap.

'Are you all right? You look a bit faint.'

I sit up straight. 'I'm fine. Just a tad too much wine, I think.'

Actually, that's not far from the truth. The wine went ages ago and we then moved on to Old Fashioneds, at Edwin's suggestion.

'Hey, I've got an idea,' he continues.

'Oh?' I breathe, hoping it's that we stumble home to his place, rip off our clothes and make passionate love until the morning sun reminds us it's time to get up, go to work and take assembly.

'Why don't we head to the Royal Inn?'

I try to hide my disappointment. 'Great!'

'It's got a pool table.'

I lift up my eyebrows. 'Fab!'

'Are you any good at pool?' he grins.

'Well, it's been a very long time since I've played,' I prevaricate. It might be true that my last brush with a pool cue was in Butlins circa 2005, but I was absolutely brilliant at it. Not that I'm going to say that, just in case I've lost the knack.

'I might be slightly rusty,' I add, erring on the side of humility.

A smile appears at the side of his mouth. 'We'll soon polish you up, Lauren.'

The cold air that hits my cheeks as we push open the door to the Angel Inn has the dramatic effect of making me feel approximately ten times drunker.

It strikes me that, on paper, now might be a good time to call a halt to the evening because it's late and I'm smashed. *The Rules* would definitely advise it, and what's more, I have twenty-eight sets of parents coming in tomorrow to watch our assembly about 'Seasons' and I don't relish the prospect of doing so while still swaying from the previous night's intoxication.

But then Edwin reaches out and takes me by the hand, clasping his fingers around mine as I buzz from his touch. I drift along next to him in a state of bliss, feeling the warmth from his skin radiate through me.

As we arrive at the pub, he stops outside the door but doesn't push it open. 'Can I have my hand back, Lauren?' he says teasingly.

'Oh! Sorry,' I blurt out, releasing him from my grip.

I hang about behind him attempting to stand up straight while he orders two more double somethings and gets a token for the pool table in the back. The place is reasonably busy but we're in luck because the table has just been vacated.

I slip off my cardigan sexily, revealing my newly-tanned shoulders and newly trim-ish stomach. Then, with a seductive cowgirl-style sashay, I saunter over to the pool cues and grab one while he rolls up his sleeves. I watch, pouting, as he picks up the balls one by one, placing them in the triangle, before he stands back. 'Would you like to break?'

'Why not?' I murmur, gliding to the table and bending

over. I briefly consider feigning ignorance about the game and asking him to come and help with my positioning. Then I remember that I've already given him the impression that I'm a knockout – albeit a modest one.

Besides, Edwin is not the kind of guy to go for the bimbo act. I instinctively know he wants a smart, sexy cookie who is on his level intellectually *and* can whip his ass at pool. I close one eye to attempt to focus on the white, but it's surprisingly blurry as I take the shot. Yet, I feel sure as I go to tap the ball that something magnificent is going to happen.

The sensation quickly dissolves as my cue slips and the white trundles along as if it's run out of battery. When it finally touches the triangle of balls, it does not smash them across the table as I'd rather hoped, but simply jiggles one or two about a bit.

'Oh,' I say, genuinely bewildered as I go to examine the end of my pool cue to see if there are any obvious reasons for my faux pas, and end up with it momentarily up my nose. Fortunately, Edwin does not notice, for he's already in position, walloping the triangle so hard that he manages to pot two stripes.

'Well done,' I say, grabbing the chalk and putting plenty of it on the end, feeling sure that this must have been the issue.

'Oh – Lauren.'

'Yes?' I purr.

'Your nostril is blue.'

Once I've rushed to the ladies to excavate the chalk from my nose, the game resumes.

It turns out that Edwin is embarrassingly good at pool.

It turns out that I am just plain embarrassing.

OK, so I'm drunk. But that still does not account for the number of times I pot the white (four). Or the number of times I hit precisely nothing (seven). Or the number of times I casually pick up the chalk and start chalking up my cue, concentration deep in my eyes, before Edwin points out that I'm smothering blue stuff on the wrong end (one, which is quite enough).

I muster up my best *good loser* face, but frankly, I am struggling to deal with this. My performance is memorably humiliating; if Edwin isn't telling this story over dinner-party tables when he's in his fifties I'll be amazed.

The only thing that seems to help with combating my embarrassment is the vodka. And gin. And whatever else is in those drinks. The fact that it doesn't have a particularly positive effect on my performance is suddenly barely worth worrying about.

'I really enjoyed that, Lauren,' Edwin says, as he takes another perfect shot and trounces me for the third time. He puts down the cue.

'Sorry I wasn't much competishhion,' I reply.

The landlord appears in the doorway and politely reminds us it's time we were on our way, a point I concede when I look at my watch and realise that it appears to have developed six hands. We call a taxi and wait outside. 'Why don't we share?' Edwin suggests softly. 'We could go to your place first and drop you off. You're closest.'

The taxi pulls up, Edwin opens the door to let me in and, for some reason, I think it's a good idea to negotiate entry by going in head-first. It's only as I'm on my hands and knees on the back seat, tugging down my skirt so Edwin can't see up it, that it strikes me that this might not be the most ladylike approach; I've certainly never seen the Duchess of Cambridge attempt it.

As the journey home begins I open the car window slightly and let the breeze hit my face, while the orange glow of street-lamps whizz past and I desperately try to sober myself up enough to hold a conversation.

'Lauren.' He says my name in a slow, deep whisper that instinctively makes me realise he's about to say something serious. I sit up in my seat slightly.

'Yes?'

'I'd *really* love you to come to Singapore,' he tells me, with an intense, burning look. 'I just want you to know that.'

A wobbly smile trembles to my lips. 'Really?'

He nods and it strikes me that he's completely serious. 'And I also want you to know how much I've enjoyed tonight. So – thank you for asking me out. I appreciate it.'

'Oh, I'm glad you enjoyed it.'

'Well, I was thinking: *I'll* do the asking next time.'

My face breaks into an inane grin. 'I'd love that.'

'So watch this space,' he winks.

The car pulls up in front of my house. I tell myself there and then that if he kisses me – and I think he just might – then I'll invite him in for a coffee. By which I mean sex, and lots of it.

For a long, gloriously tense moment we sit in the half-light, our faces moving closer together. It's a moment so near to perfection I couldn't have dreamed it better.

Unfortunately, at the exact moment when I'm convinced the kiss is about to happen, Edwin kind of . . . twitches. Only slightly – so slight I'm not sure a split second later if I imagined it. But it's enough to ignite a moment of panic, when I convince myself that he wants nothing more than a kiss on the cheek. So I throw myself forward and do just that, crashing my face against his then darting away.

'Bye, Edwin.' I look up and register disappointment on his face.

It's so obvious and all-consuming that I decide there and then that the only possible action open to me is to lean in decisively and snog his face off. Unfortunately, by now he's got his wallet out.

'Don't suppose you've got two pound fifty? Sorry to ask – this is really embarrassing – but I didn't realise I hadn't got enough on me for the whole journey. I'll pay you back in the morning.'

'Of course!' I say, scrabbling about before producing a tenner and thrusting it in his hands.

And as I get out of the car and stand under the streetlight, I watch the taillights of Edwin's taxi wind up the road and over the hill. I touch my cheek where I collided with his and can feel it tingling, my body aching with happiness and frustration.

Chapter 20

I can genuinely say I have never had a hangover at work before. I've been a bit hazy on a couple of occasions, but nothing that matches this. I cannot tell you how hard it is to stand on stage, leading sixty-odd under-sevens in a chorus of 'All Things Bright and Beautiful', when all you want to do is run off and regurgitate your breakfast.

On the plus side, I catch Edwin's eye from across the other side of the school hall, just as he's leading out his class. He gives me a private, lingering smile, then mouths, 'You OK?' It makes my stomach flip, which isn't as lovely as it sounds given the waves of nausea rising up my throat as I nod and return to my attempt to get 1P back into something that resembles a straight line.

The following morning – Saturday – I wake up with a knot in my stomach, wondering when he's going to ask me out, like he said. We barely saw each other yesterday and logic tells me that no man, no matter how smitten, would follow up a first date by bursting through the staff-room door and taking me in his arms while Joyce chokes on her Swiss roll.

It's probably for the best that he didn't because, as I discovered throughout the course of the day, sudden movements had an alarming effect on my head.

Now though, it's all I can think about. Emily and I go shopping in Carlisle before she goes on a night out with the gang at Windermere Adventures. She advises me to put the whole thing out of my mind until Monday morning, when she's betting he'll ask. Which I know makes sense and is what I'd do if the shoe were on the other foot, at least I would if I could restrain myself sufficiently. Problem is, I know he has my mobile number and that fact alone means it's really quite hard not to wonder about whether he'll text.

Then I spot the most perfect art deco hip-flask in the window of an antique shop and I know – I just know – Edwin will love it so, feeling slightly guilty and a bit of a saddo, I go in and buy it for him, even though I'm not entirely sure there'll ever be an appropriate time to give it to him.

I'm busy over the weekend with various house-related chores, including pruning my bush to keep Agnes happy, but my mind constantly drifts to blissful, drunken flashbacks from Thursday. Then on Sunday night, I'm sitting in front of some gentle television, flicking through Facebook on my phone, when an instant message pops up from Steph.

I cannot wait til you get here, Loz! That's been her

nickname for me since we were little. I look at the clock and work out that it's 4 a.m. there.

Can't you sleep?

Shit! Only just realised the time – haven't been to bed yet. Got a flat full of people here.

You're still enjoying it there then? I ask, suspecting she's not yet ready to deal with the knowledge that I've spent the evening reading such articles as SINGAPORE'S BEST COCKTAIL BARS.

It's awesome. Wait till you see what I've got.

When Steph makes a statement like that it's usually impossible to predict what's going to come next. And my brain doesn't have the technicolour capacity for this one. Whaddaya think? An image pops up that I have to turn upside down several times in a bid to identify.

I eventually realise I am looking at a tattoo. I also recognise that the tattoo in question is some sort of representation of the Sydney Opera House. Only, it's slightly pink and looks more like a psychedelic sea creature that's just emerged from a bath full of Radox.

I am just pondering which part of her body this monstrosity appears on, when a second picture pops up, clearly designed to give me an alternative view, the way estate agents take pictures of a room from different angles. Only this particular alternative view is a massive photo of her bare bum.

I hesitate, at a loss as to how to reply, before eventually tapping out: Wow!

That's what the guy from the hospital said. Good, eh?'

What guy from the hospital?

The doctor.

Why have you been to see a doctor? A myriad of catastrophic health and safety breaches at the tattoo parlour burst into my head.

I fell over on the way out and scuffed my arm. Nothing serious.

I frown. So why were you showing him your bum, when you'd only broken your arm?

Duh! Shagged him afterwards.

That's the last message Steph sends, before disappearing,

presumably to either get rid of her house full of people or go to give her doctor a second viewing of her arse.

I hesitate, then flick on to the draft application form I filled in for the teaching agency in Singapore. I'd told myself that the second Edwin asked me out, I'd hit the Send button. But suddenly that seems slightly ridiculous.

Am I seriously making this monumental decision based solely on whether Edwin asks me for a *second date?*

I need to make this decision on my own. Romantic developments between Edwin and me should be entirely incidental. I open up the agency document and compose an email. Then I stare at it for ten minutes, reading it through for the umpteenth time.

I remind myself that applying doesn't commit me to anything. Nothing at all.

I glance at my phone for one last time, on the off-chance that Edwin has texted in the last thirty seconds to ask me out. But it remains blank.

So I attach my application, sign off the email and, before I can release my breath, press Send.

Chapter 21

An entire week and a half passes without Edwin showing the faintest sign of asking me out. My despondency must be apparent when Cate asks me – again – for an Edwin update in the ladies of Casa Lagos, five minutes before our salsa class starts.

'Do. Not. Panic.' She says this with the tone of a First World War reservist sent into the trenches after spending the first three years of service learning the art of embroidery.

'I'm not panicking *as such*,' I reply. 'I just am really disappointed.'

'It's weird, I can't deny it. But from what you've said, he spent the evening trying to persuade you to move to Singapore. *Plus* you almost kissed. Edwin is clearly just not very confident. I still think he'll get round to asking. I wish for your sake he'd get a move on, though.'

'Now I'm just panicking that I read things into the situation that weren't there.'

'I thought you weren't panicking?'

I sigh. 'I suppose that sending off an application to Singapore has focused my mind. Do you think I've done the right thing?'

She puts her arm round me and looks at me through the mirror. 'I *obviously* don't want you to go anywhere because I'll miss you like mad, but that's the case whether you bugger off to Singapore, Australia or Mars. You've got to have your big adventure at some point, Lauren. Wherever, and whenever it is.'

I decide to change the subject. 'So, tell me about Will's mum and dad.'

Cate and I have already exchanged innumerable texts on this subject after her first Sunday dinner with them, but she's clearly bursting to talk about it.

'Unbelievably nice people,' she smiles. 'Especially his older brother Peter, who's a detective inspector for Cumbria Police, and his fiancée Charlotte, who's pregnant. I swear you've never seen a guy as excited about becoming a dad. All he could talk about was things he'd seen in Mothercare. They live in Near Sawrey so we went to the Cuckoo Brow Inn first with their dog Wilbur, who is just the cutest ... and the house is really big and, you know, just nice. Homely. The kind of place where everything feels *right*.'

'And Sunday dinner was good?'

'It looked it, but I could barely eat anything. I hadn't realised how nervous I was. It honestly couldn't have gone better,

Lauren. I've even been invited to go to one of his cousin's christenings in a few weeks.'

'You're obviously part of the family already. When are you taking him to meet your parents?'

'It's going to have to be soon,' she grins. 'I know they'll love him.'

I actually think she's right, too – even if Cate's mum can be hard to please. I was always slightly scared of her when I went round for tea when we were younger. I don't think she ever told *me* off, but she was always terrifyingly strict with Cate and that was enough.

'Though there was something else,' she continues.

'What?'

Her face breaks into an enormous smile. 'He told me he loves me.'

'Are you kidding me?' I laugh.

She shakes her head. 'I'm not.'

'So what did you say to that?' I ask, though I don't really need to.

'I said I loved him too.' She looks at me. 'I really do, Lauren. He makes my heart feel like it's about to burst out of my chest every time I look at him.'

'Do you think he could be The One?'

'I just know I've never felt like this about anyone before. Ever.'

'Sounds like you've got your answer then.'

*

Salsa is brilliant tonight, exactly what I need to take my mind off Edwin. It's as if the evening has been sprinkled with an indefinable magic. Perhaps that's because even the most distracted of hearts couldn't fail to be lifted by Cate's mood. Perhaps it's the music, which thrums through my spine, making every bit of me tingle. Or perhaps it's simply because the group is so comfortable with each other now – we breeze through stumbles, trips and almighty fails on the dance floor without worrying. If I stop and think about the fact that everyone around me is falling in love – Cate and Will, Emily and Joe – it might depress me. So I don't. I just concentrate on my loops, locks, twists and turns – and *keep those knees loose*, as if Marion would ever let me forget.

'If you know anyone to drag along here on a Tuesday, please do,' says Lulu, during the break. 'We're out of beginners. All my new starters have done so well they've moved up to the improvers' class.'

I briefly wonder about asking Jeremy to come one day. It'd get him out of my mum's hair for one night a week, although I'm not overly keen on admitting he's a blood relative, however distant. It'd be a lot easier if Edwin would just walk through that door, swing me into a wraparound and dance the night away with me. Or even dance five minutes away – I'd take anything.

As the class resumes, Marion announces that we're going to 'nail' the steps she introduced last week, failing to notice that the introduction of this routine takes things more seriously than any of us ever imagined. Having already danced with Esteban, Luke and Frank, Joe appears in front of me. 'Can you remember how this starts?' he asks.

'Haven't the first clue,' I reply, peering at my own feet. 'I was counting on my partner.'

'Oh, I wouldn't do that,' he grins, as we turn towards Marion and attempt to copy what she's doing: a cuddle turn, then a ladies' right turn, then a few steps that bring us back-to-back, from where we step into a reverse salsa wrap. It seems so ludicrously fast, all we can do is stumble around as if attempting to break the world speed record in a game of Twister. I glance over at Will and Cate, who seem to be managing better than anyone else.

'Maybe it's easier if you're madly in love,' says Joe, who's clearly noticed too.

I suppress a smile. 'Will's *madly* in love then?'

'Oh, I would say so. A classic case. You know those trees planted in the shape of a heart just off the M6?'

'You mean Broken Gill Plantation,' I inform him. If you're driving past the landmark, it's unmissable – dozens of conifers planted on a hillside in a perfect heart-shaped formation, legend has it by a farmer devoted to his wife.

'I think Will's got it so bad he'll be doing the same soon,' he says. 'Although he doesn't own much land so she might have to put up with a few geraniums.'

I laugh. 'Personally, I'd be delighted with a few geraniums at the moment. Hell, dandelions would do.'

'Oh, *come on*. That's tragic.'

'It's true,' I shrug mournfully, only half-joking. 'I'd be happy with someone giving me their last Rolo. Or baking me a cake. Or knitting me a nice scarf.'

'Knitting,' he repeats. 'Ah, so this is where my romantic gestures have been going wrong all these years. I haven't *knitted* enough.'

'OK, maybe I'll take that one back. The point I'm making is, as long as they're from the right person . . .'

'Lauren and Joe! Don't you remember *anything* from last week?' Marion snaps.

Joe turns back to me. 'Every time I dance with you, I get in trouble.'

'Don't even *think* about blaming me. I'm brilliant when I dance with anyone else. It's only when you turn up that it all goes wrong.'

'Keep your core *strong*, Lauren,' Marion hollers.

Joe squeezes my hand, presumably as a demonstration of support as Marion instructs us to break while she huffily demonstrates the steps with Frank again.

I'm peering in, trying to get my head around how she slips seamlessly from a cuddle to a turn, when Joe whispers to me, 'So can I take it from your comment about the Rolo that your date with Whatsisname didn't go as hoped?'

The question instantly stops me from concentrating on Marion.

'*Edwin*,' I say. 'And no, actually, I was only joking about the Rolo. It was wonderful.' Clearly I'm not going to go into the fact that he's not followed it up by asking me out again.

'Glad to hear it,' Joe says, as the dancing resumes and he lifts his arm for me to spin under. 'You deserve to meet some-one nice.'

'You hardly know me. I might not deserve it at all.'

'You're still speaking to me after seeing my zebra. That's enough for me,' he replies, at which point I stand on his toes.

'It's not the zebra that bothers me most.'

He pauses before answering. 'Bothers you? Your reaction was underwhelming but I hadn't realised it actually *bothered* you.'

'It's hard to explain, Joe. There's no question that you've come up with a hotel that will get great reviews and people will enjoy staying there. I just prefer it the way it was. They're my childhood memories – and you're messing with them.'

His back straightens defensively. 'I'm determined that what we come up with will do you proud.'

I don't answer him because I know that's impossible and I also know that there's absolutely no point in saying it out loud. And OK, because I sound whingey. Which will achieve nothing, because if one thing's clear it's that I have very little choice about any of it.

'So are you going out again?' he asks.

I do a double-take. 'Going out?'

'You and Whatsisname.'

I suddenly wish that his attempts to make conversation would focus on something else.

'I'm not sure yet,' I mumble, as Marion claps and Joe, mercifully, moves on to his next partner, leaving me to dwell on that question yet again for the rest of the class.

Yet, after we've said our goodbyes and Emily, Cate and I are walking up the hill back to the van, something happens that makes all thoughts of Edwin pale into insignificance. Emily and I are comparing notes about our lack of ability to keep up with tonight's routine, when Cate takes out her phone and idly logs on. We're nearly at the van when the noise escapes her lips. It's almost like a gasp, but more guttural, more raw.

'What is it?' Emily asks, spinning round to see Cate's features, white under the moonlight, as she stands immobile, her hand on her mouth, whimpering 'Oh my God. Oh my God.'

'Cate, seriously – what's the matter?' I ask, walking towards her.

She doesn't hand over the phone, but she's powerless with shock to stop Emily from reaching out and gently prising it from her grasp. I suspect if Em'd known what was on it, she wouldn't have touched it.

The picture is on a website called meetmyexx.com. In it, Cate is gazing at the camera, her eyes heavy and flirtatious.

She is naked, next to a window I recognise as the one in her bedroom, her arms stretched up above her head, sunlight streaming on to her bare breasts.

In another context it would be a beautiful picture, arty and elegant, as opposed to cheap and porno. But I instantly know that whoever made it public didn't do so for artistic reasons. Instead, their motive was dark, twisted, more sinister. And presumably Cate realises the same as she stares at her phone, unable to speak.

Chapter 22

Cate's flat is directly above the florist's shop and reached via stairs running up the back wall. Its décor is as eclectic and lovely as the shop downstairs, a subtle clash of soft colours and fabrics. She pushes open the door and stumbles in, Em and I following, before I shut it behind me. Cate closes her eyes. But only for a moment.

'What the hell do I do?'

She marches to the living room, where her laptop sits on the coffee table, open but switched off. Emily and I follow her in as she thumps down on the sofa and presses its on switch with trembling fingers, waiting for it to load as she rocks backwards and forwards. Emily stands behind her and begins rubbing her shoulders supportively, but as she glances up, it's clear she's as helpless as I am.

'Let me get you a drink, Cate,' I say feebly.

In the kitchen, I fill the kettle, but immediately decide against it and open the fridge, where I find an unopened bottle of white wine. I grab three glasses, even though I've got no intention of drinking any myself, and return to find Cate desperately trying to change the default safe-settings on her broadband, which won't let her on to the website.

'What sort of bastard would you have to be to do this?' she yells, tears burning her eyes. 'I *dumped* Robby. That's all I did. I didn't strangle his cat or call his mother a whore or . . . anything. I *tried* to be nice. I tried to let him down gently. Did I really deserve this?'

'Of course you didn't,' Emily says, flashing me a panicky glance. 'It's . . . it's unspeakable.'

'How did you even know the picture was up there on the website?' I ask. 'Did Robby send the link to you?'

'No, I got an email from some vile creep saying . . . oh God, I can't even repeat what he was saying, except that he didn't want to get together for a jam-making session. And he *had my email address*. My own, personal email address.'

'How did he get that?' Emily asks, hastily pouring her some wine.

'God knows,' Cate mutters, before looking up at us, recognition blooming on her face. 'Robby must have put that on the website too. He's put my bloody contact details on.'

It takes ten minutes before she finally gets on the site as Emily and I watch in growing horror.

The image of Cate is about the tamest on there, but that's not what makes my stomach twist into knots. It's what these pictures represent that's so disturbing: the demented actions of hundreds of sad losers who can only vent their rage against women with this intimate revenge. It's clear as Cate becomes increasingly hysterical that someone needs to do something about this.

'Cate, listen to me,' I say, sitting next to her. 'The first thing you must do is contact the site and threaten them with legal action unless they take it down. Then we will take stock. Work out what to do next. And just remember that nobody you know is ever going to log on to a website like that.' I'm aware that this is a flimsy plan, but at the moment I just need to say something to try and get her to calm down.

It doesn't work. Because as we glance back at the screen and she hits the scroll button again, her own picture appears. Tears stream down her face and she thrusts her hands over the screen. 'Don't look!' she begs us. 'I'm so ashamed.'

'Oh, Cate,' Emily murmurs, as our friend slams shut the computer.

'We won't look,' I tell her. 'But you've got nothing to be ashamed of. You and Robby had sex. You are consenting adults. And he took a photo of you in the privacy of your bedroom. You did nothing wrong. And he is an utter shithead for doing this.'

'You said yourself people can't seem to just have sex these days. *You* said that, Lauren,' she sobs. 'And you were right. I can't believe I did it.'

Chapter 23

The following day at work is a blur of exhausted worry about Cate. It was stupidly late by the time I got home – the early hours of the morning – although at least I got some sleep, whereas I'm certain my best friend won't have had a wink. I've exchanged umpteen texts with her by afternoon break, and as I sit in the staff room staring at my phone, I'm running out of ways to reassure her that nobody will have seen the picture. That it's all going to be OK.

'Good afternoon, Lauren.'

I glance up to see Edwin sinking into the seat next to me, as I am reminded that it is thirteen days since our date. Thirteen whole days. Hell yes, I'm counting.

And despite the fact that we've seen each other innumerable times since, I still hold my breath in anticipation of what he might say, praying he utters the words I'm desperate to hear: *Come out with me, Lauren. Let's have another date. We can dance the night away and have the time of our lives and—*

'Would you like a coconut macaroon?'

I snap out of my daydream as Edwin holds out a Tupperware box lined with floral kitchen paper and filled with two neat rows of psychedelic pink cakes.

'Oh, um, I shouldn't. I had a big breakfast this morning. But thank you.'

'Actually, I don't blame you. I think anyone would have been put off after Mum's baking last time,' he says, suppressing a smile. 'For the record though, I would never have offered you one if I wasn't certain it was a one-off.'

'It's not that at all, Edwin, honestly.'

'I think you'd really hit it off with my mum, actually,' he goes on. 'She'd love you.'

I hesitate. 'Oh, you've twisted my arm, go on,' I say, diving into his Tupperware. 'They look irresistible.'

It's only as I have one cake in my hand and am about to take a bite that I spot the thick grey hair sprouting out of the top of it. I subtly lower it to my knee and attempt to maintain eye contact with Edwin while I try my best to surreptitiously pluck it out with my other hand.

'So . . .' he begins. 'I've been waiting for the right opportunity to tell you this – but I really enjoyed our night out together.'

'Oh, so did I,' I breathe, trying not to drop my eyes to the cake on my knee as I manage to grab the end of the hair and begin tugging gently.

'I was a bit … chemically challenged after all those Old Fashioneds, though.'

I laugh. 'Me too.' I realise with some alarm that the hair is not just long, like last time. This bugger is massive. And as I pull smoothly, it doesn't pop out as I was hoping, but keeps on coming, like a string of handkerchiefs emerging from a magician's sleeve.

'So,' he continues, as I give it a subtle yank. 'I've been thinking …'

I cannot tell you how tricky it is to focus half my attention on the hair and the other half on Edwin – or rather keeping Edwin on topic.

'What have you been thinking?' I say.

'Oh, just that it was fun,' he replies.

I decide to go for it. 'I agree, Edwin. And I think if we go out again, we should make it the weekend. Because I can't cope with a hangover like that again at work, that's for sure.'

He laughs and looks so deep into my eyes my pupils nearly start bouncing. 'Me neither.'

My throat grows hotter as I register that the hair is still not out of the cake, and it strikes me that if I don't get it out and at least put a morsel of the thing in my mouth soon then he'll start to wonder why.

'So I hope you don't mind me asking you this,' he goes on.

'Not at all, I'd be delighted. Name the day!' I blurt out.

He frowns. 'What?'

'What?' I repeat nervously.

It occurs to me that the only way to deflect attention from this potential faux pas is to tug out the hair once and for all and shove the cake in my gob.

So I do just that: tug. Sadly, this is not the deft movement for which I'd hoped and, instead of sliding out to make the cake edible enough to distract Edwin, the hair causes the cake to explode into two dozen pieces, spill all over my skirt and tumble across the staff-room floor.

'Oh no,' I mutter, as I jump down and begin scrambling round with a piece of kitchen paper, desperately trying to rescue Edwin's mother's culinary efforts.

'Lauren, seriously – don't worry,' he reassures me, as he leaps to help me gather it up. 'You should've just said if you weren't hungry.'

'No, I am! I wanted one, really. I'm desperate for one!' I reply, over-egging the pudding somewhat.

Only as I stand, watching Edwin on his hands and knees cleaning up my mess, the coconut cakes become a metaphor for my love for him. I get it into my head that if I really loved him I'd scoff the lot, even if there were more hairs in it than an Old English Sheepdog's sleeping basket. I discard the smashed-up cake in the bin as he holds out the Tupperware box again and I take one, refusing to look at it as I take a decisive bite.

'I was just going to ask,' he begins, 'if you'd applied to Singapore yet?'

I chew the cake slowly and nod, before swallowing. 'As a matter of fact, I have. I'm not certain that I'm going – not yet. But I thought applying wouldn't do any harm.'

Happiness sweeps across his face. Genuine, no-holds-barred happiness.

'Lauren, you're doing the right thing. I can't tell you how pleased I am. I can't deny I was feeling a bit intimidated by the idea of going by myself. Oh, I know there's Georgie, but she's just more of an acquaintance. To have a proper friend there – to have *you* there – well, it'll be amazing. Nothing less.'

My heart swells to twice its size. Why the hell am I worried about a second date when the guy wants to whisk me away to the other side of the world? This is ridiculous! My face breaks into a spontaneous smile.

He looks suddenly serious. 'Lauren,' he whispers, through a penetrative gaze.

'Yes?' I reply, sexual tension fizzing through me.

'I think you might have something stuck between your teeth.'

At which point I reach into my mouth and pluck out a small, grey hair. The whole thing really couldn't be more romantic.

All I want to do after the school bell rings is dart to Cate's place to see if she's OK, then go home, run a bath and let my thoughts about the imminent departure of Edwin – and possibly me – sink in. But I can't. Because it's parents' evening. The first parents to knock on the classroom door and squat down on to two foot-high chairs designed for five-year-olds are little Tom's.

As Jenny and Nick Goodwin flick through Tom's exercise books, I can't help noticing that she's more subdued than usual, barely responding when I explain what we've been doing this term and how Tom's done in various tests.

'He's a really lovely child, an absolute credit to you,' I say, trying to catch her eye. 'He's very polite and has lots of friends. A real joy to teach.'

She looks up briefly and allows herself the flicker of a smile that makes her pretty apple-shaped cheekbones appear. 'That's good to hear.'

Mr Goodwin glances at her briefly, then turns to me again: 'How's his spelling?'

'He's strong in all areas of literacy,' I tell him, producing his test results.

'He clearly gets that from his mum then.' Mr Goodwin glances at his wife again, but she looks away silently, lowers her eyes – and it's then that I realise, or at least suspect, that he's in the doghouse about something.

I feel the need to fill the silence. 'We're asked to suggest some areas where he could work on improving things, but in all honesty, he's a dream pupil. The only thing I could think of was that he could do with getting dressed a bit faster. He's always one of the slowest after PE. Not that that's saying a lot – it takes forever around here.'

The rest of the evening runs painfully slowly and culminates in the arrival of the final set of parents, Jacob Preston's mum and dad. Mr and Mrs Preston are the most physically mismatched couple you could ever meet. She is a female version of the Jolly Green Giant – unfeasibly tall, with the arms of a shotputter – while he is short, reedy, and looks as if a strong sneeze would make him fall over.

Not that I care what they look like – I only care that they're the last set of parents I have to deal with. So it's with a noticeable lift in my mood that I take out Jacob's file and prepare for our friendly chat. Only it's clear that Mr and Mrs Preston are feeling less than friendly.

'I wonder if you could explain something,' Mrs Preston barks at me. 'Why did my five-year-old son come home yesterday evening and call me a *tw* . . . a word that frankly I can't repeat. He tells me *you* said it was OK.'

My mouth drops as I recall the incident in the playground when the children thought they'd run an array of insults past me – including the word 'twit'.

'Well, no . . . that's not quite right. I said that he shouldn't call anyone names. It was just a group of children asking whether certain words were naughty or not. One of them was that.'

'I can't believe you think it's no big deal. You teachers with your liberal, airy-fairy views.'

I sit back, slightly in shock. 'I'm terribly sorry. I just thought—'

'You just thought it was acceptable for a five-year-old boy to call his mum *a twat*? What are you teaching him next? That it's okay to call his granddad motherfucker or his grandma a cun—'

'Mr Preston! I'm sorry, but there's been a terrible misunderstanding!' Only, by the look on both of their faces, they don't look much in the mood to listen to explanations.

Chapter 24

I phone Emily on my hands-free the second I get into the car as I'm on the way to Cate's. 'Have you managed to speak to her?'

'Only once,' she replies. 'I've been up on Striding Edge today, so had to wait until we got down the mountain.'

'How is she?' I already know the answer from the tone of her texts.

'Awful. That website has ignored the email we sent last night so the picture's still up there. And it turns out that as well as posting her email address on the site, her Twitter name's also up there, which meant she woke this morning to find dozens of messages calling her a slut and a whore and other things I don't even want to repeat.'

'That's horrible.'

'She's closed her Twitter and Facebook accounts this morning. I hate to say this, Lauren, but I've got a feeling this could be just the start of it. There are dozens of these websites. That picture could be all over the internet by now.'

'Has she been in touch with Robby?'

'She got through to him this afternoon but he's denying everything. He says the pictures were taken off his phone when it was stolen.'

'Oh, come off it,' I reply. 'If it had been some random scumbag who didn't know who she was, they wouldn't have been able to tag her on Twitter.'

'All that contact information was on his phone,' Emily replies. 'And I don't suppose there's any proof to the contrary.'

My head is spinning. 'Whoever it is, they can't be allowed to get away with this.'

'No. But to be honest, I don't think she gives a toss about someone getting away with it – she just wants to get rid of the picture. Listen, are you going round there tonight? I really want to, but it's my Nana's birthday and I'm driving home to see her. I've got the day off tomorrow.'

'I'm on my way there now,' I reply. 'I'll text you when I leave to let you know how she is.'

I arrive at the shop and head up the stairs to ring the doorbell. Nobody answers. I ring again and wait a minute before taking out my phone to try calling, when I hear footsteps.

I never expected Cate to look her usual, gregarious self, but I wasn't prepared for how destroyed she looks. She's in her pyjamas, her eyes reddened. I stopped off and bought her some chocolates on the way here, but I now suspect she won't be able to stomach a thing.

'Come in,' she mumbles, showing me through to the living room, where she slumps on her sofa and drags her laptop in front of her. 'I've spent the entire day reading up on "revenge porn".'

'Didn't you open the shop?'

'No. I had bigger fish to fry,' she mumbles.

I've never known her to shut the shop like that before, but at least she might have learned something practical to get the picture off that website. 'And what have you found out?'

She looks up. 'That basically, I'm fucked.'

I frown. 'I'm sure that can't be the case. There are laws against this sort of thing.'

'Yes, Lauren,' she says numbly. 'But that would involve going to the police.'

'Well, you should go to the police.'

She shakes her head. 'I can't.'

'Why not?'

She turns to me with glazed eyes. 'Will's brother is a detective inspector. He'd find out. He'd *see* the picture.'

I open my mouth to argue but then close it again. Obviously she wouldn't be reporting it to him directly, but the likelihood that he wouldn't find out is very small.

My mind races as I scratch round for a solution. 'Maybe you should tell Will anyway?' I say. 'Isn't he going to wonder why you've suddenly disappeared off Facebook otherwise?'

'Yes,' she mutters, as if this has suddenly occurred to her. 'I'm going to have to come up with some excuse. Oh, God Almighty, how can I possibly tell him *this*, though? He won't want anything to do with me.'

'Remember what I said, Cate. You haven't done anything wrong.'

A heavy tear slides down her cheek. 'Lauren . . . the picture you saw wasn't the only one.'

I let this information filter in my brain. 'OK . . .'

'There were more,' she whispers. 'Quite a few more. The one you saw was comparatively . . . restrained.'

'There are *explicit* ones?'

She nods miserably. 'Oh God, I want to die.'

'Don't say that.' I put my arm around her. 'Cate. One way or another, we're going to sort this nightmare out.'

I almost sound convincing. But secretly, my suspicion is that once photos like that are out there, they're never going to go away. They're going to follow Cate around for ever.

Chapter 25

Cate spends the rest of the week, and all weekend, in hibernation: in the back of the shop, or upstairs in her flat, feigning a chest infection so she doesn't have to face Will. I go over on Saturday night to keep her company, reassuring Emily that we'll be fine without her and that she should go ahead with her date with Joe – yes, on a *Saturday night*. I try not to be too depressed that she's got a Saturday-night date after about five minutes of knowing him, whereas I've entirely failed to bag one from Edwin, whom I've known for ever.

We sit for hours in Cate's flat as she proceeds to get quietly hammered in front of *The Wedding Singer*, weeping every time Will sends her a text, at a ratio of about six to one of hers. She's worked herself into a complete state, unable to sleep or eat with worry that the other pictures are going to appear somewhere, sickened by the emails she continues to receive; because although she can leap off Facebook and Twitter, she can't just close down her email address in case anybody important tries to contact her. All she can do is block the creeps propositioning her, one by one.

The following day, I'm on my usual Sunday supermarket trip, when I reach out to a rather sparse vegetable tray and clash hands with someone who has designs on the same aubergine as me.

I insist she takes it. 'Honestly, I'll get my five a day elsewhere,' I say, realising as she laughs that I recognise her from somewhere. She's in her early twenties with dark hair and long, feminine eyelashes hidden behind boxy spectacles.

'You were at the salsa night at the Moonlight Hotel, weren't you?' she asks. It's only then that I place her.

'Oh! Yes, that's right – you work there.'

'Waitressing, but only part-time. I'm a student. I believe the salsa's at Casa Lagos now. I wonder if it'll move back once the hotel's finished?' she asks.

'Oh, I'm not sure. From what I hear, I don't think anything is going to be the same as it was there,' I say. She doesn't take the bait. 'So is everyone having a nightmare with the upheaval? The training and job cuts must really be taking their toll on the staff?'

She pushes her glasses up her freckled nose and looks surprised. 'No, not really. The only staff member who has left is head chef Nigel – and everyone was glad to see the back him. Complete wanker,' she whispers conspiratorially. 'The place is looking amazing. Or at least it will, once it's open. And although I'd never claim the bosses are soft, I think most people think they're a breath of fresh air.'

'But what about the stuff being done to the building? It doesn't sound too sympathetic to the history of it.'

She shrugs. 'Personally, I think it'll be nice working for somewhere trendy.'

I shudder – and suddenly wish I hadn't relinquished that aubergine.

By the time salsa night comes around again, Cate still doesn't want to go. She says she can't face it, and instead wants to stay at home to email some American woman she discovered on a forum for revenge porn victims. Will arrives at Casa Lagos with Joe about three minutes after Emily and me, and heads over the second he sees us.

'How is Cate, Lauren?' he asks, dispensing with pleasantries.

'Oh, she's fantastic,' I reply, with terrific gusto.

He looks perplexed. 'Apart from the chest infection?'

'Oh, yes, apart from that,' I reply, reddening. 'That's absolutely *terrible*. You should've heard her coughing last night.'

He frowns. 'So, you've been to see her?'

'Um ... yes.'

'Oh. She refused to let me go over,' he says, clearly a little hurt.

'She's just worried about you catching it from her,' I leap in. 'It's a very nasty virus. Hideous, in fact.'

'But she was happy to let you risk it?'

'I only stayed five minutes. Besides, I'm at a lower risk of catching it than you.'

'Why?'

'Well, unlike when you go over, Cate and I don't do much snogging . . .'

Someone laughs and I turn round to see Joe.

'I'm sure she'll be fine in the next day or two,' I go on. 'In the meantime, I think she just needs a bit of space.' I regret the last part of the sentence as soon as it's out. You don't say a person needs 'a bit of space' when they've got the lurgy – you say it when they want to dump someone.

Paranoia visibly grips Will. 'It is definitely just a chest infection?'

'Absolutely. Nothing to worry about at all.'

His jaw tenses. 'Well, I wasn't worried until . . .'

'Honestly, Will. It's just a throat infection, nothing more, nothing less.'

'Chest,' he corrects me.

'Yes,' I add, never having been so relieved to hear Marion's clapping.

The whole night feels like a strange one, uneasy somehow. It's not even just what's going on with Cate that makes me say that; I can't put my finger on why the usual carefree feeling as the class begins seems notably absent.

Even Lulu seems jumpy. There's one point when Stella asks

201

if we can just learn a few more steps, rather than persevere with this single, rigid routine they insist we all do – and you'd think she'd mortally offended both of them.

'Look, it's just really important that you learn *one* routine. That's all I ask,' Lulu says, mildly exasperated.

Stella looks sulky. 'It just seems a bit odd to do an entire routine and keep going over and over it when there are still other steps we could be learning too.'

'There's no point moving on yet,' Lulu says. 'And nobody else minds, do they?'

'I'm not saying I mind . . .' Stella begins.

'Good,' Lulu replies, firmly underlining the subject before she instructs us all to switch partners.

Joe appears in front of me and takes my hands in his. 'So what's really going on with Cate?' he asks.

'Don't you start too,' I groan. 'Absolutely nothing. Anyway, I hear you and Emily went to that new restaurant that's opened in Bowness on Saturday. Any good?' I am keen to change the subject. Fortunately, he acquiesces.

'It was great – food was excellent, service impeccable. It'll be no competition for the Moonlight Hotel once it's open, of course.' He's clearly trying to elicit a response from me.

'Assuming you don't make a complete mess of it,' I reply.

'Well, I'm trying my best, Lauren.'

I sniff. 'Anyway, Emily said you both had a whale of a time,' I continue, sticking to a subject I'm comfortable with.

'She's a great girl.' Then he smiles that easy smile and it's obvious to see why she's becoming increasingly loved-up.

He has this quiet sex appeal; he doesn't flaunt it, like some sort of movie star. It's there, filling you up every time his eyes smile. Personally, I'd hate the pressure of going out with someone like Joe, although in the gorgeousness stakes, Emily can more than hold her own.

The song finishes and Marion addresses the class: 'Seeing as Stella's so keen to learn some new steps, I thought we could finish by trying out one of my favourites. In fact, it's the hottest move in salsa as far as I'm concerned. And I need some volunteers. Come on, who's feeling hot?'

Frank's eyes widen. Andi looks away. And, judging by the way everyone else slinks back, the answer is: no one. As Marion narrows her eyes and focuses on poor Stella, my phone beeps; I've forgotten to put it on silent. Marion spins round and glares at me.

'Thank you, Lauren,' she says, grabbing me by the arm. 'Up you come – and Joe, you too.'

Joe, who is patently not intimidated by anyone or anything, steps to the front while I visibly squirm at the mere thought of performing 'salsa's hottest move' with my friend's boyfriend, right in front of her. Emily however, seems to think the whole thing hilarious.

Joe takes my hand and a shot of heat runs up my arm.

Marion starts the music – a salsa version of 'Fever'. It's way too sexy to be anything other than mortifying.

I glance down and focus on Joe's wrists, because then I don't have to look at his eyes. Even his hands are handsome, if that's possible. They're not without their scars and rough parts: they've done a day's work. But his big fingers are tanned, with short, shapely nails. He wraps them around mine and I suddenly wish I'd stayed with Cate tonight.

The steps Marion proceeds to show us are intimate, embarrassing and distinctly uncomfortable. I realise I'm making it sound as if she's getting us to recreate a scene from *Fifty Shades of Grey*, but quite honestly she might as well be. My neck grows warmer as we twirl slowly into a half-turn, his arm crossing my body. I can feel his heartbeat thudding against my back, his body close against mine. I realise I'm breathing faster and glance guiltily at Emily, but she's busy whispering something to Esteban, the pair of them laughing.

We twirl back and, with Marion wittering on about loose knees and hips and thrusting our hands into position, we glide together until our bodies are pressed against each other, and I can feel every curve of his chest, his groin, his thighs. For some reason I can do nothing to prevent myself from looking up at his face.

He's already looking at me.

I have to avert my eyes.

'And *that* is how to do the hottest move in salsa,' concludes

Marion, as Joe and I burst away from each other. 'Right – can I check you've all paid your subs this week? I've got a mortgage to pay, you know.'

For the rest of the night, even after the class has finished and I've dropped Emily off, I can't stop humming the song. The low, sexy notes fill my head with thoughts of swaying hips, strong arms, that masculine, clean smell that lingered in a cloud above us after Joe had released my hands.

It's still there as I climb into bed, checking my phone to see if Cate has responded to the text I sent her on the way home. And it's just as I flick idly on to my emails, registering that the song's starting to annoy me, that something makes the notes fade away once and for all.

It's an email from a school in Singapore. I've got an interview.

Chapter 26

The next day at work, a momentary Edwin-shaped madness overcomes me. I can't tell you the reason for this, except that I woke in the night in a sweat, my pulse thudding, as flashbacks of that dance last night kept forcing themselves into my head. I took a big mouthful of water and turned over, reminding myself that this does not make me some treacherous bitch, and that the interpretation behind the dream is that I simply want to find out more about Joe's intentions with the Moonlight Hotel.

I feel qualified to say this after a period in my early twenties in which I repeatedly had X-rated dreams about my university professor – a sweet, but categorically unattractive sixty-something Geordie nicknamed 'Baldrick' on account of both his dearth of hair and his habit of coming out with phrases that made Blackadder's sidekick sound like Stephen Hawking.

Anyway, back to the momentary madness. Perhaps because I'm a step closer to going to Singapore with him, trying to get to the bottom of Edwin's feelings for me is all I can think about. I am itching with it, tingling with it, as if someone's lit a spark and I absolutely have to do something about it from the moment I get to school. I am wearing my favourite skirt with a lovely chic blouse that make me feel a bit like Miss Moneypenny (but after she became sexy) and the nicest underwear I own, a lacy set that treads just the right line between girl next door and certified sex bomb.

I read in *Cosmo* recently that you should wear underwear that suits your mood – and this is exactly the kind of image I want to give off to Edwin. Not that I think there's a chance of him seeing these knickers, not today anyway. But *I* know they're there, and that's all that matters.

When I see Edwin at lunchtime, I head directly towards him, after reassuring Salma Mahmood that I am absolutely 100 per cent certain that the school-mashed potato, no matter how lumpy, is halal.

'Edwin,' I announce, parking myself next to him and drawing breath.

He glances up and smiles, examining my tray. 'Oh, you went for the goulash.'

I am disproportionately flustered by this statement. 'Yes. Well, I've never had it before and felt like it was about time. Maureen twisted my arm.'

'She might twist your stomach too,' he smirks.

I laugh. Then I stop. 'Edwin,' I repeat, lowering my voice

before delivering a question as fast as I possibly can. *'Would-you-like-to-go-out-with-me-again?'*

He stops chewing his beef and quickly looks from side to side, before leaning in and whispering decisively: 'Yes. Very much so.'

'Really?'

'Of course,' he replies, which rather prompts the question 'Then why the hell didn't *you* ask *me* like you said you would?' – but I decide not to go down this route.

'Um … great then!' I splutter.

He lowers his knife and fork. 'Sorry I didn't get round to asking you, Lauren.'

'Oh, it's OK,' I reply, attempting to give the impression that the thought literally hadn't crossed my mind.

'I've been *so* busy this week. I've had something on every evening. And I was kind of … working out the best way to broach the subject. I wasn't sure if you were keen.'

'Edwin,' I say, locking eyes with him. *'I'm keen.'*

We burst into a fit of giggles as Margaret, the Head Teacher, walks past with a plateful of cabbage. This is part of a diet she's embarked on recently in a bid to squeeze into a costume she's required to wear while playing Daisy in *The Great Gatsby* – her latest role in the local amateur dramatics group.

By the time we've composed ourselves, it's just left for Edwin to whisper, *'I'm* keen too.' Then he holds my gaze and my insides go squishy and I'm so distracted that as I attempt to take a mouthful of goulash, instead of making it between my lips, it slides off my spoon and on to the table, where I'm forced to chase it round the Formica surface with a napkin, attempting to scoop it up.

'When do you fancy going out this time?' I ask eventually.

'Well, Saturday night would be ideal . . .'

'I agree! And I'm free this weekend!' I leap in.

'. . . but unfortunately I've got a wedding to go to.'

'Oh,' I reply, deflated.

'It's Fiona's brother. He's getting married to his childhood sweetheart.'

My heart sinks. 'Fiona?'

He nods. 'I know we're no longer together, and it's all ridiculously awkward, but I'd feel awful backing out of the wedding after I'd already responded with a yes.'

'But isn't that going to be difficult?'

'I wish I could get out of it. But I feel like enough of an absolute arse, having split up with her, without throwing her brother's wedding invitation back in his face.'

'I see,' I mumble. 'Well, there's always Friday.'

'Hmm. No, I've got to travel to Hampshire straight after work – I'm staying there the whole weekend. Sorry, Lauren. Hey, I've got an idea. Why don't I go to that salsa class I've been promising to come to?'

I hesitate. It's not that I don't want Edwin to come to

209

salsa – I do. It's just that I hoped for something a little more momentous for our second date, and I at least wanted him all to myself for it. Let's face it, if Saturday is the Veuve Clicquot of date nights, Tuesday's a Lambrini. And, more to the point, it's nearly a week away!

As quickly as that thought sweeps through my head I dismiss it: if I hold on until next Friday or Saturday, that'll be a full ten, eleven days.

'That sounds great,' I reply, taking what I can.

'I know we said we wouldn't do it on a week night again, but we could always go for a sneaky drink or two afterwards, don't you think?' And then, out of nowhere, his hand brushes mine, making my insides melt a little.

I return to the classroom with a spring in my step and call the children to order to begin our lesson about adjectives. I begin by explaining that an adjective is a *describing word* – and ask the class if they can think of any examples.

'Stinky!' shouts out Ameira Syed, as the class explodes into laughter.

Suppressing a smile, I write it on the whiteboard. 'OK, I'll give you that one. Any others?'

'Pooey,' says Michael Martin, followed swiftly by 'Farty,' from Jasmine Urquhart. I become aware that we're now on a train, and if I don't halt it soon, it'll become impossible to control: once a group of five year olds start talking bodily fluids there's no stopping them.

'Well, none of those are proper words, so let's try and think of some nicer ones,' I say. 'Some describing words, please, children.'

We have – variously – 'big', 'small', 'massive', 'gigantic' and 'catastrophic'; the latter strikes me as incredibly impressive – until Amber Smith, who came up with it, almost convinces the entire class that it's a reference to her new kitten.

As we head out to break, I realise that Tom Goodwin has barely said a word throughout the lesson.

'Are you coming out to play, Tom?' I ask, as the class heads out to the playground.

He gives me a long look, then whispers, 'I don't want to.'

'Why not?' I'm surprised.

He shrugs. 'I don't know.'

I walk over and sit down on my haunches, my face at his level. 'Is everything all right, Tom?'

'I don't know,' he repeats.

'If you're at all worried about anything, you can come and tell me whenever you want. You know that, don't you?'

He nods and looks away. I resolve not to push the issue further and to ask whoever's on playground duty to keep an eye out for him.

'Why don't I take you downstairs?' I say, standing and offering him my hand.

He reluctantly reaches out for me and pulls himself up.

And we head down the stairs, his small, warm hand in mine, as I wonder why so many people seem to be having a hard time of it at the moment.

My interview with Felicia Heng, from St Anne's Primary School in Yishun, Singapore, takes place at 5.30 a.m. the following morning, via Skype. Having gone to bed early last night, predicting that I'd be groggy at this time in the morning, I actually woke up fully wired at 2 a.m. and couldn't go back to sleep. Recognising that by 5.30 a.m. I'd be not so much groggy as catatonic without a little extra help, I swilled back four coffees in quick succession and now feel as though I need a man with a fishing rod to come and hoist me down from the ceiling.

The Skype meeting is only twenty minutes long, during which my interviewer leans forward, her head looming large on the screen, with concentration etched on her otherwise smooth brow as if she's playing an intense game of Kerplunk.

There are points at which I feel it's going well – really well, actually – but then she reveals what the salary is and I nearly fall off my chair. It's more than twice what I'm earning now. Putting aside any of the more spurious reasons I've got for moving to Singapore, this represents the job opportunity of my life.

Finally, she sits back in her chair and smiles. 'I think you'd fit in very well here, Ms Scott. Can I send you a prospectus via email? I'd love you to get a better feel of what we're all about.'

'That would be wonderful,' I reply, with a swoop of excitement.

'Any questions?'

'Um . . . when are you hoping to make your decision about who's got the job?'

'We've shortlisted eleven candidates and they're all very strong. You're our first interview, so we've got a long way to go yet.'

I think a lot about the interview throughout the day, partly because I'm not allowed to forget about it – Edwin grills me every moment he sees me. My mum on the other hand is mildly bewildered by the whole thing when I tell her about the possibility of Singapore for the first time that night, when she pops in en route from a trip to source some fencing.

'You sound pretty sold on the idea,' she says, clearly perplexed.

'Do I?' I ask. 'I'm still in two minds, to be honest.'

'I thought you were *dying* to get to Australia,' she points out. 'What about all your Australia scrapbooks from when you were a little girl? All the places you planned to visit?'

'I'll still visit them one day,' I protest, because the thought of not doing so is frankly inconceivable. I decide to change the subject. 'So, how's Jeremy getting on working for Gill and Jimmy Gavin? Is he a model employee?'

She takes a sip of her tea. 'I wouldn't say Jeremy and farming were meant for each other, put it that way.'

I snigger. 'No, he didn't strike me as the kind who enjoyed getting those beautifully manicured hands dirty.'

'You can talk,' she says. 'You've lived here all your life and you still treat those fells as if they're ornaments.'

'Don't start going on about my sense of adventure again,' I reply. 'And as a matter of fact, I go running outside sometimes these days. In *all weathers*. So I'm not completely immune to the great outdoors. And I'm certainly nothing like Jeremy.'

'I must admit I don't think I've ever met anyone quite so fond of . . . well, *moaning*.'

'I take it we're talking about Jeremy, not me, now?'

'I'm sure he's a good kid really. Deep down,' she continues, draining her tea and standing up to give her cup a wash in the sink.

As she places it down on the draining board, a thought filters into my head. 'Mum, do you remember the gazebo at the Moonlight Hotel – the one I used to have tea parties in with Dad? What happened to it?'

She looks at me, mystified as to why anyone would care. 'No idea. It must have been taken down after he died, but I couldn't be certain. If it was in anything like the state the rest of the hotel was in, it will have been torn down before it fell down. Why do you ask?'

'I was just thinking about it the other week, that's all. I was looking at that old photo I keep in my purse – the one of Dad and me.'

'Speaking of the hotel, have you seen what they're doing to it? There was a big spread in the *Westmorland Gazette* last week. They're absolutely gutting the place.'

'I know. God help us,' I mutter.

My mum looks surprised. 'You're joking, aren't you?'

'It's going to be completely different from how it was,' I tell her.

'Lauren, it's been in a state for years. It's crying out for someone to do something about it. It's far too old-fashioned,' she replies.

'It's meant to be old-fashioned. Old things are.'

She raises an eyebrow. 'Speak for yourself.'

The problem with having a mother like mine – or probably just having a mother *per se* – is this: no matter how certain you are that they're wrong, their opinion still manages to burrow its way into your head like one of those South American worms that feed off the human brain.

Over the next twenty-four hours, the possibility that she might be right about the Moonlight Hotel is something I have to battle with repeatedly. Maybe I am so fixated with my memories of the place that I can't recognise the need to move on. But the crucial fact is this: those memories are all I've got. And without them, without the happy times to think about,

I'm forced to remember something that frankly I just can't stomach, not on a daily basis.

The horrendous and yet humdrum circumstances of my dad's death still smother me with a blanket of sadness sometimes, sixteen years after it happened. He's not the first person to die of cancer and he won't be the last. But that's an irrelevance when the disease rips one of the most important people out of your life, far too soon.

I was on the cusp of taking my GCSEs when my creeping awareness that he wasn't well came hurtling into vivid focus. The cough had been there for weeks before I really registered it, and only then because mum's nagging to go to the doctor became too insistent to ignore. In the end, despite his waning appetite and unprecedented tiredness, the thing that made him go to the GP was a pain in his hip. He'd assumed it was a hairline fracture, or an inflamed tendon from wear and tear: a solid, dependable, normal problem. Certainly not a *big* problem.

The doctor sent him for tests straight away.

But in the midst of them, before results were confirmed and scans were scrutinised, I remember us going to my cousin Karen's engagement party. It was in my Aunt Julie's house, with a gathering of relatives and friends I vaguely knew, when I looked at him. I mean, really looked at him.

Instead of being on his feet, organising a game of charades among the little ones, or making the grown-ups laugh with a joke that bordered on the outrageous, he sat in the corner, nursing a drink that he hadn't touched. It wasn't just that he was quiet and withdrawn. The thing I remember most is the colour of his skin, the grey tones under his cheekbones.

And, although we knew nothing at all then, not officially, I knew. I knew just by looking at him, that the life was being sucked out of him, and that realisation came crashing down so hard on my shoulders I had to leave the room so no one could see me crying.

The diagnosis came less than a week later, and with one sentence everything changed: *Stage 4 lung cancer*. It became a question of when, not if. It had spread like wildfire. His body, once so strong and big, was riddled with it; it had crawled into every corner of him.

I hadn't known anyone who'd died before. Unlike Emily, whose brother was killed in a car crash when he was a teenager, I'd gone through life blithely untouched by grief.

The whole thing unfolded so fast and hard it was like being repeatedly punched in the stomach. Within nine weeks my powerhouse of a dad was lying in a hospice, skeletal and occasionally delirious from the medication, or the cancer, or probably both. It had reached his brain, infecting his thoughts, his ability to speak. Sometimes he didn't even recognise me.

Nine weeks. That's all it took.

My exams came and went and I didn't turn up for half of

217

them. Though on his better days, he was cross with me about that, even right at the end. I liked it when he was: I liked him having a go at me for fucking up my English Lit exam because it was the first bit of fight I'd seen in ages and it gave me hope.

Hope that proved short-lived.

The day of that conversation, after he told me he loved me and made me swear I'd re-sit, his hand tightened briefly around mine and he whispered something to me that no daughter ever wants to hear their Dad admit.

'Lauren, I'm scared.'

He left us that night, in my mum's arms.

And I sat at the end of the bed and felt my world silently implode.

Chapter 27

Cate has seen Will twice since she first became aware that her photo was on that website. And for the few hours they spent together on Thursday night, she says she almost forgot about the picture.

Then yesterday morning, as she rolled over in bed and checked her emails, the first one that loaded at the top of her inbox was some woman – yes, another woman! – calling her a whore. Which just goes to show that female solidarity isn't exactly alive and well in all quarters.

Will, she's certain, knows something's wrong.

It wouldn't take a genius, given that until now they spent every waking moment together and now – on a Saturday night – she's at home with me, watching *When Harry Met Sally*. Which strikes me as the only way to deal with a crisis you're powerless to stop: with romantic comedy of the finest order. The problem is, Cate spends the whole film crying, and I don't just mean at the bits she's meant to.

'Do you want a chocolate?' I offer.

She shakes her head. 'I might have one later,' she says, although I doubt it: she must have lost a stone in the last week. 'It was lovely of you to bring them. Shall we go and get some wine?'

'Why not? We can have a walk to the seven eleven – it's a lovely evening,' I suggest, deciding that encouraging her slide into alcoholism is a better option than her hurtling towards agoraphobia.

We pull on our sweaters and head down the steps of her flat, out into the dying rays of evening sunshine. It's one of those perfect late-May evenings when Ambleside is bathed in a golden light and full of people returning from a day on the fells with tired legs and bright eyes.

'I wonder how Emily and Joe got on in Ullswater today? They were going up Gowbarrow,' Cate tells me.

'More fools them,' I mutter, as we start walking down the hill.

'So tell me: why on earth is Edwin going to a wedding with his ex-girlfriend?' she asks. 'That's weird.'

'He's just trying to be a nice guy,' I reply, wondering why I'm defending him when 'weird' was the first thing I thought of too. 'You know what it's like when you've been together with someone for a long time. It's not just them you split up from. It's their family and friends too. And sometimes they're nicer than the person themselves.'

'If you say so,' she sighs.

'Well, I must admit I was a bit shocked myself, but—'

Then I become aware that she's no longer next to me and look back to find her immobile. I follow her gaze and see who she's looking at: Robby.

Cate's ex-boyfriend walks towards us with the most stupid expression on his face: part-amusement, part-swagger. 'Well, look who it is.'

'What are you doing here?' Cate asks.

'I'm walking down the street,' he replies defiantly. 'I think I'm allowed to do that, don't you?'

The despair in Cate's eyes is pronounced as she begins talking. 'You do realise that what you did with that picture is illegal, don't you, Robby?'

He grins, which strikes me as the least appropriate response possible under the circumstances. 'I told you, Cate. I didn't put that picture anywhere. My phone was stolen.'

'You told me you'd deleted those photos,' Cate tells him.

'I did, but my iCloud backed them up. I didn't ask it to. The whole thing's a pain in the ass – it clogs up space on my computer.'

I wonder for a moment if I should say anything, but I have a feeling it'd just make matters worse. So I hang back while Cate steps forward. Her demeanour changes. 'Please, Robby,' she begs. 'Please take the photo down. I'm really sorry if I hurt you, but I know you're not this kind of person, not deep down. This is killing me. All I want is to be able to get on with my life.'

He looks entirely unmoved. 'I can understand that, Cate.'

'Robby, if this is my punishment, then believe me, it's worked. But enough's enough. Please accept I'm sorry. Please let's just be friends and stop all this. Come *on*.'

He holds her eye for a moment and it's impossible to work out what he's going to say. Then he reaches up and brushes her hair from her eyes, a gesture that's too intimate for comfort. She doesn't move, though I'm certain his touch will be making her sick. 'I wish I could help you, Cate. But I can't. I'm sorry.'

Then he leans in and delivers a slow kiss onto her forehead, before turning round with a wave and disappearing up the hill.

Chapter 28

Edwin arrives to pick me up at 7.44 p.m. on Tuesday night, thirty seconds before he said he would. He has literally never been late for anything in his life.

I'm consumed by nerves before he arrives and have spent the evening tidying not just my eyebrows, bikini line and general appearance, but also the house – just in case he's so impressed with one of my right turns that he wants to whisk me back here and ravish me until dawn. I'd hate that to happen if I hadn't fully Dettoxed all my surfaces and had my posh, saved-for-best Molton Brown soap dispenser in the bathroom loo (the one that's been wheeled out on every special occasion since Christmas 2008 and is still three-quarters full).

He arrives at the door with his Volkswagen Polo parked outside, and it's fair to say that I'm mildly surprised by his appearance when I open the door. If I was laying it on thick, I'd go so far as to say 'alarmed'. I know Edwin isn't exactly a dedicated follower of fashion, but I've always considered him to be above all that; to have his own style that transcends it all, like Madonna or Dr Who.

Only tonight, I realise what a fine line he treads between looking uniquely stylish and plain bonkers. A line he's precariously close to crossing tonight. It's difficult to know what to focus on first, the billowing white ruffles of his shirt, or the trousers, which are such a vivid red that if he had a matching top I'd be concerned about children lining up to sit on his knee and telling him what they'd like for Christmas.

'Gosh, Edwin, you've dressed up,' I say, as he opens the passenger door for me.

'This is my favourite going-out outfit. You're honoured,' he says, and as he flashes me a smile I remind myself he could be wearing a bin bag and a set of fairy lights for all I care. This is the man I love and I'm not shallow enough to let a pair of red trousers put me off.

'So how was the wedding? I haven't really had a chance to ask you about it yet,' I say.

'About as much fun as I was expecting,' he says. 'Who wants to have to hang around with an ex once you've split up? It's not something I'd like to repeat, put it that way. And Fiona's changed.'

'In what way?'

'This is going to sound horribly cruel and I don't mean it

to be ... but she was so clingy. She wouldn't leave me alone for a minute.'

'She's obviously still upset about the break-up,' I offer.

He nods solemnly.

As we drive into Bowness, I begin to get the feeling that Edwin is slightly nervous about salsa and I can't deny that I'm a little twitchy too. I just hope he enjoys it, or doesn't think it's stupid. And, more importantly, that I don't make a complete show of myself, which is never out of the question.

My plan is to try and partner up with the better dancers in the group, on the grounds that their natural ability will carry me along. That basically means Esteban and possibly Joe – although the second I think of him, the idea of dancing with him in front of Edwin becomes too uncomfortable to contemplate.

Em is the first person to rush in and greet us as we arrive at the restaurant.

'Edwin, you remember Emily ...' If she is in any way unsettled by the ruffles, she hides it well.

'How could I forget?' he replies, and they shake hands.

'It's been a while though, hasn't it, Edwin?' Emily smiles enthusiastically. 'I think the last time I saw you was at the school Christmas fair. Have you ever been to a salsa class before?'

Edwin raises his eyebrows. 'I haven't. And I must admit I'm

a little nervous. I warn you, Lauren,' he says, turning to me teasingly, 'I am no natural dancer. There's every chance I might show you up.'

'Oh, you might surprise yourself,' I reply.

Edwin leans in to Emily and says: 'I think that's what you call wishful thinking.' Emily laughs. 'No, put me on a cricket field and I'll bowl you over. A dance floor is a different matter. I'll only knock you over.'

Marion calls the class to attention, before asking if there are any newcomers, then beckoning Edwin over to let him know the drill.

'He is *so* lovely,' Emily says to me, under her breath. 'I'd forgotten how funny he is. He's such a sweetheart.' I swell with pride at this and the trousers suddenly seem like a trifling matter compared to Edwin's sparkling personality.

'So how was your day with Joe on Saturday?' I ask. 'You two never seem to be apart these days.'

She gets this slightly reluctant look, like she always does when I ask about her blossoming relationship. 'Great. He's lovely.'

'Are you two getting serious?'

She looks around and whispers, 'Could be. Right, let's get some drinks and go and initiate your lovely Edwin into this madness.'

Edwin is in Lulu's beginners' group and, as I've brought him here, I get special dispensation from Marion to join him initially.

There are just three beginners and we're confined to a corner of the restaurant, which is a little lacking in atmosphere but has the benefit of privacy – a bonus when you're starting out. It's obvious that Edwin is keen to do his best. I've always admired this quality in him; he could never be accused of failing to give something everything he's got.

So we begin with the basic steps, just like on the first day we arrived. Lulu talks us through it slowly, demonstrating where Edwin's feet need to be. And even though it's not really been that long since I started, it all feels very elementary. I have to remind myself that I found this far from simple on my first lesson.

'Why don't we use Lauren and Edwin as our guinea pigs?' Lulu suggests, leading Edwin by the hand and inviting me to stand opposite. I lift my head and catch his eye as our fingers touch. It's one of those moments I've dreamed of since I first started this class – one that, deep down, I never thought would happen. Yet, I feel surprisingly un-flustered.

Edwin has the hint of a smile on his lips as Lulu instructs him to step back with his right foot, putting the weight on to that side of his body. It's the simplest move there is; it barely even counts as a dance step – it's just a *step*.

Yet when she counts, 'two three four' and he's supposed to

put his right foot behind him, he unfortunately – somehow – uses his left instead and his knee jabs into mine.

We laugh awkwardly. 'Sorry, Lauren,' he says. 'I *did* warn you.'

So we repeat the exercise.

And the same thing happens.

Then we do it again – and something else, equally wrong, happens.

After the ninth or so time, it occurs to me that Edwin might be either stoned, or playing some elaborate joke on me. But he's not laughing. In fact, he couldn't look less amused about the whole thing if he tried. He glares at his feet as if they're two disobedient children who absolutely refuse to do as they're told.

'It's fine, honestly,' I say gently. 'You'll get it.'

Despite the less than promising start, I'm confident as I say these words. Because to *not* get it is unprecedented; even Mike managed this bit. Yet, as the evening progresses and Edwin goes through innumerable attempts – and still fails simply to move his right leg back by six inches when instructed – I do start to wonder.

It doesn't seem to matter if he's with me, or Lulu or another partner – he just *cannot* master it without falling to pieces. Throughout this entire uncomfortable episode, I keep telling myself: *Oh, but at least we can laugh!* Only it turns out we can't.

The good grace with which I'd always associated Edwin is

nowhere to be seen. He gets crosser and crosser – at this situation, at life in general and, as I discover when it's my turn to be his partner for the fourth time – at Lulu, who he has convinced himself is responsible for the entire fiasco.

'She's so bloody bossy,' he hisses into my ear, when she's helping one of the other students get into position.

I couldn't be more ready for the break.

While Edwin retreats to the gents, I grab a Diet Coke and stand to watch the improvers' class finishing their turns. The music softens and my eyes drift on to Joe, dancing with Marion.

It's impossible not to notice how handsome he looks tonight, in the simplest of long-sleeved T-shirts and jeans slung low on his muscular hips. He's got one of those faces that demand to be looked at: not simply attractive, but beautiful, with playful eyes and a Brando-esque definition to the jaw.

I've noticed all this before. But tonight it unleashes a throb of pleasure inside me. It's almost a relief when Edwin returns and I can focus on reassuring him that it probably *is* just the lighting in here that's putting him off.

When the lesson resumes, Lulu announces that we're going to try a basic right turn – to which Edwin responds by diving in front of me and gripping my hand. 'I don't like being anyone else's dance partner,' he grins. 'You're the only one who'll tolerate me.'

I laugh as he pulls back. But as the evening draws on and Edwin's assault on my toes continues, I become aware of my attention drifting. And the fact that I keep thinking about Joe on the other side of the room disturbs me more than I can tell you.

I take my last mouthful of margarita as Lulu draws a line under the beginners' class – and when I realise that Joe and Emily are by our side, I feel my neck grow hotter.

'Welcome to salsa, I'm Joe,' he says, extending a hand to Edwin. 'We didn't get introduced earlier.'

'Edwin.'

They shake hands, but Edwin is significantly less buoyant than he was before the class started.

'Did you enjoy your first lesson?' Emily asks brightly.

Edwin forces a smile. 'It's safe to say I won't be coming again.'

Logically I know that I can't be held responsible for Edwin having a shit time of it, but I still feel as though I am.

'I don't think Lauren would want me, for a start,' he adds.

'Oh, that's not true,' I leap in, wondering how or why this man, with whom I've been in love for two years, needs me to beg him to come to the next class.

'It does take a bit of practice,' Joe reassures him. 'We were all awful when we first got here. The first time I danced with Lauren, her shins were black and blue.'

'Yes, you *were* absolutely dreadful,' I reply, unable to resist the tease, even though the truth is we at least were able to move together, unlike whatever happened tonight with me and Edwin. Only, when he laughs and our eyes connect, I realise, in this sixth-of-a-second moment, that my stomach is twisting.

I stop laughing and look firmly at Em. 'Would you two like to join us for a drink?' The words spill out before I can stop them; I don't even *want* Joe and Emily to come with us. All I wanted at the start of the night was to end up in a cosy pub with Edwin whispering sweet nothings into my ear while I smudged my lipstick on his ruffled shirt.

'Sorry, I can't,' Emily replies quickly. 'I need an early night. Big day of bouldering tomorrow.'

'Ouch,' I say.

Everyone looks at Joe, apart from me. I look at the floor, my heart thudding wildly as he considers his options.

'I'll pass, I think. I'm going to be on site at the hotel early tomorrow too. But you two have a great evening.'

Chapter 29

After a quick drink in the Royal Oak, Edwin drives me home. And through a combination of incessant babbling and complimenting him repeatedly on his trousers, I somehow manage to cheer him up. As a result of which, the car is filled with unspoken promise – and a big question mark over what is going to happen when we reach my house.

'Would you mind if I stop off at the garage to fill up?' Edwin asks. 'I won't get home otherwise.'

'No problem,' I reply.

As he steps out into the floodlit forecourt I look at his face in the wing mirror while he removes the petrol cap and starts filling it up. It's a harsh light, but he's still handsome. I idly watch him replace the pump as a small tingle of possibility warms through me.

I lean back and consider whether I could seduce Edwin tonight. Whether I should throw caution to the wind, invite him in to sample my Molton Brown handwash and make myself irresistible to him. A knock on the window nearly makes me leap out of my seat.

'Fancy some crisps?' he shouts through the window. 'I'm getting some prawn cocktail ones for myself.'

I shake my head. 'I'll pass.'

He smiles and a swoop of affection dances through me, as a sentence bubbles at my lips.

I must not think about Joe. I must not think about Joe.

Then –

Why the hell am I even thinking about not thinking about Joe?

My eyelashes flutter open to see Edwin join the end of a queue inside the shop. Deciding to take the opportunity to top up my lipstick, I unstrap my seat belt and kneel up to lean into the back seat to retrieve my bag, where I threw it when we first got in.

I'm on my hands and knees, my bottom on display through the windscreen, when I hear the click of Edwin's central locking. This wouldn't be an issue if it didn't also occur to me that he's activated the alarm at the same time.

I don't even get a chance to work out why he's locked me in: my mind is too busy fretting about how I'm going to get myself from my hands and knees, doggy-style, without setting off the alarm. I glance out of the window to see a woman in her late thirties pausing to peer in at me. I smile. She looks away and dashes to her car, clearly bewildered as to why a grown woman is undertaking a pilates class while poised over the handbrake of a mid-range Polo.

I am about to start panicking when the lock clicks off. I scramble back in the direction of my seat and am a foot away and positioned like an Egyptian hieroglyphic, when the alarm clicks on again. I freeze.

I dart my eyes in the direction of the garage shop and spot Edwin, fiddling with his car key and entirely oblivious to the fact that he's pressing it on and off.

A click interrupts my thoughts. I scramble into the passenger seat. Only it happens so fast, the contents of my bag spill out into the footwell.

I decide to sit it out and remain completely immobile until he's back. Then I glance down and realise that, not only have all my credit cards, loyalty cards, tissues, lip balm and any other number of items hit the deck, but there is also, right on the top, a tube of athlete's foot cream.

Edwin and I might have grown close over the last two years, but when I am teetering on the possibility of a seduction, shoving my fungal infection cream in his face is a step too far. I move forward – an inch – before the locks click back. I freeze. They click again and I repeat the exercise. This time, I make it a foot – before the click happens again.

Over the next minute I find myself edging forward between clicks, like someone attempting 'The Robot' after just coming out of a twenty-year cryogenic freeze.

I am finally poised in the footwell, frantically gathering up my cards and podiatry essentials, when the car door opens and Edwin appears.

'I took the liberty,' he grins.

'Oh?' I say, realising as I sit up and attempt to look composed that I have beads of sweat gathered on my brow.

'Wotsits,' he replies, chucking a pack on my lap. 'I didn't think you'd be able to resist.'

In the event, I do resist. Largely because, having successfully negotiated this evening without revealing any unsavoury podiatry disorders to Edwin, one thing is uppermost on my mind. Namely, whether after a two-year absence from any conjugal action whatsoever, it might be about to happen: I might get jiggy with him. Hell, I *want* to. I'm certainly not going to let any odd, short-lived thoughts about Joe throw things off-course.

I am contemplating a subtle way of asking him in 'for a coffee' as he pulls up outside my house. The key with Edwin, I'm absolutely certain, is not being too obvious. And 'coffee' could not be more obvious if I was holding up a big neon sign saying, 'Any chance of some sex, please?'

'So,' he says, switching off the ignition, before turning to me with a bright, wide-eyed look. 'Shall I come in for a coffee?'

The question leaves me momentarily speechless. 'Of . . . of course.'

He looks alarmed. 'Sorry Lauren. That was so presumptuous of me.'

'No, Edwin – it wasn't,' I leap in. 'I just ... of course, come in!'

'You're probably right,' he decides, backing away. 'It's a bad idea. It's late and it is only Tuesday.'

I am suddenly so hungry for Edwin to come in that I nearly grab him by the collar and drag him there. But I resolve to stay cool. Cool-ish. 'Edwin. I'd *love* you to come in for a coffee.'

A smile appears on his lips. 'Would you?'

I nod repeatedly.

He turns back to the windscreen, full of quiet contemplation. 'You know what? I think we should maybe save that for our next date. Don't you? On a Saturday this time. Let's do it properly ... *all of it*. Assuming you'd still like to go out on a Saturday?'

I nod again. 'I would.'

And then it happens. The moment I've been waiting for. Edwin leans over and kisses me. It's slightly awkward at the beginning because my leg is pressed hard into the gear-stick and the handbrake prevents a full embrace. But as our lips touch, softly, my heart races in my ears and it is, unquestionably, a great kiss. A wonderful kiss. A kiss that unleashes two years of pent-up longing.

Which is probably why, when he pulls away and gazes into my eyes, it feels over far too quick.

'You're an excellent kisser, Lauren Scott,' he whispers. 'I knew you would be.'

'I knew it too, Edwin,' I murmur. Then it strikes me that this sentence makes no sense whatsoever. 'Not that *I* would be . . . I always knew that. I mean . . . no, I didn't mean that. I mean that I knew, or at least thought, you'd be good too. And you are.'

'Goodbye, Lauren,' he says.

'See you in school tomorrow,' I grin, holding his gaze for a moment, before sweeping out of the car and doing my best job at sauntering sexily up the garden path.

When I'm inside, I close the door behind me and lean against it as my head swirls with thoughts. Then I plod upstairs, trying to work out how I feel as I pack the Molton Brown handwash into the cupboard. Because, although I obviously wanted Edwin to come back here, I can at least console myself with the fact that I'm now certain that something's going to happen between us.

I do my ablutions and, still tingling from the feel of Edwin's lips, I pull on my pyjamas and lie staring at the ceiling as I let my mind drift, and drift . . . on to something else entirely.

Joe.

Oh, *why* am I thinking of bloody, bloody Joe?

I don't even want these thoughts – in fact, I actively want to be shot of them. I close my eyes, but his body, his eyes, the way he moves when he dances ... they all push themselves back into my head, causing such a commotion that I'm forced to think this whole thing through, to reconcile it all with myself.

It's perfectly possible, is it not, to have a mild crush on someone – in the same way that I used to fancy Duncan from Blue – without ever believing anything will come of it.

I feel a degree of adolescent-style attraction towards Joe, I can't deny it.

But these are not real feelings like the ones I have for Edwin. They're just an instinctive human reaction to a person who's undeniably handsome, but also, I remind myself, going out with one of my best friends.

I decide to check my phone before I try to get to sleep. I go to Facebook first, waste seven minutes of my life on cute baby videos and news articles about a threatened global Prosecco shortage, then go on to my emails, where there's a barrage of spam and just one of any interest – from the agency in Singapore.

I don't know what I'm expecting as I open it – some feedback from the interview perhaps or, at my most optimistic, a message to say I'm through to the next round.

In the event I have to read it several times before it sinks in.

I have to read the words that say how impressed Ms Heng was, how she particularly liked the imagination I'd put into my lesson plans and how she was certain I'd fit in there. I keep looking for the 'but', before I realise that there isn't one.

> We would therefore like to offer Ms Scott the position
> of Elementary Head of Year.

I put down my phone with a thumping heart. I've actually got the job. And the prospect of moving to Singapore has suddenly become very real.

Chapter 30

Cate looks distraught when I tell her about Singapore, the following day after work. Despite her protestations that I must go and have a brilliant time, the look in her eyes consumes me with guilt. In only a few weeks, I will be moving nearly 11,000 miles away. Assuming I take the job.

'Don't look so worried, I'll be fine,' she insists. But she looks far from fine. She has lost so much weight, and when I went past the florist's shop to get to her flat today, she'd shut it early again. 'Besides, worse things happen, don't they? I've watched *Philomena* twice this week just to remind myself of that when I'm busy deleting emails inviting me to wank off strange men.'

I take a seat on her sofa. 'This happened to a load of celebrities a few years ago, didn't it? I know it doesn't make it any easier but you're not alone.'

'Sadly, I don't have Jennifer Lawrence's legal team to come down on the website like a ton of bricks.' She logs on to her computer, then exclaims 'Oh my God!'

'What is it?' I ask tentatively.

'I'm not sure yet ... give me a minute.' She starts tapping on her keyboard, frantically scanning the screen. Then she sits back in her chair and declares triumphantly, 'She's done it. She's only gone and done it!'

'What? Who? Who's done what and where?'

She pauses and takes it all in, then begins to explain: 'A few weeks ago I found a forum started by women who'd had exactly this happen to them. I got talking to a woman in Arizona who'd appeared on the same site I did, and was trying to get it closed down. She had the police and lawyers involved and ... well, I didn't think anything of it because time went on and it just stayed live.'

'But now it's not?'

I look at the computer screen as she clicks on to the website. There's a message reading: *This page no longer exists.*

'Now it's not,' she repeats quietly, and for the first time in as long as I can remember, a wide smile lights up her face.

There is a silence between us as one issue simmers in the air. Cate says it first. 'Of course it could still come back. And there are other websites '

'But there's every chance it could be the end of the matter,' I finish.

Relief floods through her features. 'Oh God, I hope so.' Then she shouts into the air: *'Lisa Delaney from Flagstaff, Arizona, I owe you one, girl!'*

I throw my arms around her, feeling tension dissolve from her shoulders as she sniffs away tears.

Then I pull back and look at her. 'Right. Now that's sorted, how about you put the kettle on and we make arrangements to go back to salsa again this week?'

She laughs. 'Fine!' She leaps up to head to the kitchen but stops in the doorway. 'You know what, Lauren? I think you *should* go to Singapore. '

'Really?'

'I hadn't finished,' she clarifies. 'I think you should go – as long as it'd still be attractive even if Edwin wasn't there.'

'The salary is twice what I'm currently earning,' I tell her.

Her smile wavers. 'In that case, you've probably got nothing stopping you.'

I don't know why but I feel nervous about telling Edwin I've got the job. I'm worried that, having idly encouraged me to join in his jaunt, he might think differently now the prospect of me tagging along is a reality. Or at least could be.

Particularly since I'd now be going not in the capacity of a friend, like we were when he asked me, but as someone he's kissed, which by definition is a lot more complicated. At least, I hope it is. There were tongues. Friends can't possibly still be just friends when they've engaged in tongue action. I know that, Edwin knows that, *everyone* knows that. Only, by Friday morning, I am fairly certain I can put it off no longer. I need to tell him my news before we go into the weekend.

"Thank God it's Friday, eh, Lauren?' he grins, striding across the staff car park.

'Um ... yes. Looking forward to the weekend?'

'Very much so,' he says. 'Are you doing anything?'

My heart skips a beat as I wonder to what this could be the prelude. I know *The Rules* would tell me to say, 'Yes, actually I'm extremely busy,' given that there are now less than thirt-six hours until Saturday night – but for some reason I can't bring myself to do so.

'Nothing special. Just a spot of gardening. Nothing planned in the evening though'

There is a pregnant pause in the conversation as I refuse to ask him for a date. I simply refuse to. Not this time. Yet eventually the pregnant pause becomes so pregnant it's virtually ten centimetres dilated and screaming for gas and air.

'Are you all set for Singapore?' I ask finally.

'It's coming together,' he replies. 'Got my visa. Handed in my notice. Flights booked. I just need it to happen now. Have you had any news from the agency?' he asks casually, pushing open the door to the school.

'Um ... yes,' I mumble. 'I got the job.'

'Bloody hell!' he grins, grabbing both of my shoulders. I drink in his expression and realise, to my surprise and relief, how happy he looks at this.

'So you're pleased?' I giggle.

'Pleased? Lauren, I'm *totally* delighted!'

His enthusiasm is infectious. And for a moment I know that if I had any doubt whatsoever, then it's now banished. In the last seven days Edwin Blaire has: kissed me, judged me to be an excellent kisser, and actually sworn when I told him I was coming to Singapore with him.

OK, so he still hasn't asked me for a Saturday-night date, but you can't have everything.

'Let me give you Georgie's details. She's the girl I told you about, the one who sorted the flat out. I've mentioned you to her and she's totally up for you staying with us for a while. It'd help with the rent, to be honest. How about I drop her a line tonight and you could arrange to speak to her? You could get to know each other; she'll be able to answer any questions.'

'Sounds great.'

We walk down the corridor and reach Edwin's classroom. 'Well, this is me,' he says awkwardly.

'Yes.'

I know he's not going to kiss me again here, not least because it'd get both of us suspended. But – irrationally – I wish he would.

'See you at lunchtime,' he says, pushing open his door.

I nod and smile and hold his gaze for a moment, backing away. 'See you.'

Then I head down the corridor as he enters his room.

A moment later, I hear the door open again. 'Oh Lauren,' he calls after me.

I spin round to find him skipping towards me. 'Yes?'

'Would you like to come out with me a week on Saturday?'

'A week on . . . Saturday?' I stammer.

'Yes. I'm tied up tomorrow night – my cousin Alistair's staying for the weekend. But next Saturday would be great. If you're not busy, that is.'

'Not at all!' I beam. 'Well, I mean, obviously it being Saturday I've normally got something on. I lead a very busy and full life,' I add, for the avoidance of doubt. 'But I've had a cancellation.' I have no idea why I am saying this as if he's phoned me up to ask if I can fit him in to have his roots highlighted.

'Good,' he smiles. 'I'll text you and we'll make the arrangements. How does that sound?'

'Brilliant.'

I head back down the corridor to my classroom where I sit and wait for the children to arrive, gazing out of the window at a cloudless sky and thinking about Edwin's reaction. And it's there and then that I make my decision, once and for all.

I'm going to Singapore.

Chapter 31

It is a bittersweet weekend. Having assumed I'd be going round to Cate's to keep her company like the last two Saturday nights, she has instead accepted Will's invitation to go over for dinner. Which I'm very glad about, obviously, as it's the first indication that the pit of depression she sank into after that picture appeared isn't going to cock everything up between them. Emily is of course out with Joe, which just leaves me, Netflix and half a bottle of Sauv Blanc.

My clear weekend does however mean that on Sunday I can tackle all the admin required to make my move to Singapore possible. So I apply for a work permit, check the notice period on my cottage (a month – which means I'll have to tell the landlord the week after next) and book my flight.

There's a good price available via a comparison site, and it's only a few pounds more to make it flexible if I need to change my dates later on.

Then I compose my resignation letter to work, swallowing the lump in my throat, and hit the button on my printer. As I'm waiting for it to print out, I log on to Facebook and find a picture posted by Joe at the top of my news feed, tagging 'Lawrence Wilborne' – his dad – in front the Moonlight Hotel.

It reads: Spent the day tackling the Kentmere Horseshoe with the old man. Now he's come to cast a critical eye over what I've done with our latest acquisition. Anyone would think he didn't trust me ;-)

There follows a long jocular exchange with various Facebook friends, in which some jest about whether they'll serve complimentary Custard Creams like in the Travel Haven, while a handful of women offer simpering compliments about how they're certain it'll be *amazing*.

An instant message pops up from Steph.

Oi, Loz!

I realise that there's no escape: I'm going to have to face matters and tell her what's going on. Hi, Steph – what are you up to?

Arrived in Bondi a couple of days ago. Playing beach ball with my new pal. Wanna see him?

247

A picture pops up on my screen of a buff bloke with teak-coloured skin, shiny pectorals and a grin like a 500-watt strip light.

He seems very nice, I write, which I hope covers all bases. What's his name?

I'll have to check. There's a short pause. He says, 'Magic Mike'. I'm not sure I believe him though.

I squirm, considering for a second if I should break my news to her via an email – a more personal version of the one I've just done for the school. Then I realise this makes me a complete wimp. And she forces the issue anyway.

> So how's the saving? Any idea when you're going to make it over yet? I've seen an amazing block of flats by Bondi. The one I've got my eye on is above a tattoo parlour – perfect. Hey, we could get matching tattoos so we'd always remember being here together! You up for it?

My fingers seize up and I find myself unable to type. I eventually compose, then delete, a message four times before I finally hit Send on the last one.

> Steph – I need to mention something. There might be a change of plan.

There is a gap of a minute before she starts writing again. What do you mean, Loz?

There is no easy way of breaking this to her. The thing is, I've been given an opportunity to go to Singapore. It's a really good job and, while I'd never even thought about Singapore before, they've made me an offer I can't refuse.

The response is unequivocal. *WHAT?*

I start writing something again, but nothing feels quite right – and she follows it up anyway. Loz, you've been banging on about Australia since you were a little girl. We BOTH have. That was the plan! I'm here by myself. Waiting. For YOU.

I know. I'm so sorry, Steph. But this is such a great opportunity I can't bring myself to say no. I feel awful for letting you down, I truly do. Although I hope it's not too much of a blow as you seem to be so settled there already. You've got so many friends. Although I doubt Magic Mike is the kind with whom she could spend an evening discussing relationships and shoes.

She doesn't respond for two whole minutes. They are torture. Are you still there, Steph? I write eventually.

I gotta go, she replies curtly.

I'm really, really sorry, I type.

But as I look up, the message hovers on the screen. She'd logged off and disappeared before she could receive it.

Chapter 32

For Monday morning's assembly, I'd asked the children to write their own prayers to thank God for what's important to them and to stand up and read them out in front of the school. It starts off well, with Bethany Jones citing 'food to eat' and David Smith 'my family'.

It's only when James Wesley, a sweet, studious boy, stands up and clears his throat that things start to go awry.

'DEAR GOD,' he shouts. I've been stressing how important it is to speak loudly and clearly, but suspect the Archbishop of Canterbury himself must be able to hear this one. 'FANK YOU FOR THE SKY ... AND SUNSHINE ... AND RAIN.'

I nod and smile and in common with everyone else, expect him to sit down. But then he decides to embellish the one-line prayer he wrote last week.

'AND FANK YOU FOR BIRFDAY PRESENTS ... AND CHRISTMAS PRESENTS ... AND PRESENTS YOU GET

IF YOU'VE BEEN GOOD … and … ANY OTHER PRESENTS.'

'Thanks, James,' I say, gesturing for him to sit down. But he doesn't.

'FANK YOU FOR … GRAPES,' he says, and it's apparent that he's now on a roll.

The Head glances over and frowns as I shift in my seat.

'AND CHICKENS.'

'Um …'

'AND MUMS AND DADS AND BROTHERS AND SISTERS AND AUNTIES AND UNCLES AND GRANDMAS AND GRANDADS AND COUSINS.' At this point, he goes to sit down, but decides against it at the last second. 'AND GREAT-AUNTIES AND GREAT-UNCLES AND STEP-MUMS AND STEP-DADS AND GRANDMAS WHO AREN'T REALLY GRANDMAS BUT JUST THE LADY NEXT DOOR WHO WANTS TO BE A GRANDMA.'

'OK, James, thank you,' I smile, scuttling over to him in a half-stoop, in an attempt to gently ease him back to the seat.

'I haven't finished,' he protests.

I sigh. 'OK. Just one more,' I concede, trying to avoid a scene.

He turns back to the school, 90 percent of whom we've now completely lost – yawning, playing with their hair or, in the case of one Reception child, picking something dubious from the sole of his shoe before giving it a good sniff.

'FANK YOU FOR MAKING X-BOXES … AND HOUSES FOR US TO LIVE IN … AND BAFFS SO WE ARE CLEAN … AND APPLES SO WE CAN EAT … AND BEDS SO WE CAN GO TO SLEEP … AND CLOTHES SO WE DON'T HAVE TO GO ROUND WITH OUR BUMS OUT.'

At which point the entire school bursts into uncontrollable laughter and there is a near-riot while James Wesley, finally satisfied, goes to sit down. Edwin, mercifully, brings his usual calm authority to the whole situation by clapping loudly and getting all the children to quieten down.

'Thank you, James, that was a very big list,' Edwin says, as the Head rolls her eyes.

'Scarlet, would you like to continue?' I add. 'And perhaps we'll restrict our prayers to God to just one item each?'

Clearly put out at this, Scarlet scrutinises the prayer she's written and spends the next ten seconds in silence trying to work out which of her four things she should prioritise. Finally, she settles on, 'FLOWERS,' before we move on to Benito Harper – but not before Scarlet puts her hands up, distraught, and says, 'Sorry, can I change that? I meant sunshine. I want sunshine. *Please can I have sunshine?*'

'Sunshine, it is,' I reply. 'Benito, off you go.'

The only child who seems completely decisive about what he's thanking God for is Tom Goodwin, who stands up, says simply, 'Dear God, thank You for my mum and dad,' then sits down again.

But as a result of the near-chaos I appear to have caused,

assembly runs over significantly. While the children file back into the classroom, Tom lags behind.

'Come on, Tom,' I say gently, noting that the rims of his eyes are pink.

I ask Angela to accompany the rest of the class back to the room, so I can speak to him alone. We take a seat on a bench and wait until the room empties.

'Tom, is everything OK?' I ask softly.

He doesn't reply at first, but it's abundantly clear as a tear slips down his cheek that everything is far from OK.

'Why don't you let me know what's wrong?' I say. 'Perhaps I can help.'

His woeful little face breaks my heart as he begins speaking. 'My dad might not be able to live with us any more.'

'What makes you say that?' I ask.

'They were shouting last night and I heard Mum say that they might get a divorce. I know what that means. It means that I won't see my dad again.'

I swallow. 'Have your mum and dad spoken to you about it, Tom?'

He shakes his head. 'I just heard them. It was after they were shouting. Daddy did something bad and Mum shouted at him. She's never shouted before but I heard it.'

'I'm really sorry, Tom. But I think you should have a chat with your mum. Because whatever happens, I'm certain that they love you very much. Both of them. And that will never change.'

His sobs become harder now and, before I can move, he climbs into my arms and hugs me, squeezing his little body into me.

And I sit, helplessly, as the tears of a little boy drip on to my skirt and rain starts to pelt on to the window, snaking down the glass as if the world's about to come to an end.

At lunchtime, I bump into Edwin. 'So have you done it yet?' he asks.

'Hmm?'

'Handed in your notice?'

'I've written my letter. I'm planning to do it after school today. I think it'll make the Head's day after the performance my class put in at assembly.'

'Oh, absolute guff – they'll be devastated to lose you.' Then he nudges me with a smirk. 'But tough – because now *I've* got you.'

I hold on to those words as I knock on the Head's door after school.

'Come in, Lauren,' she mumbles through a full mouth as she hastily shoves something into her desk drawer. 'Sorry! Absolutely starving at the moment. Have you ever done the cabbage diet?'

'No. I did try a broccoli smoothie once.'

She pulls a face. 'Well honestly, I cannot take any more cabbage. The human digestive system is not designed for it. I honestly believe that.' Then she hesitates for a moment, her hand on her stomach, before suppressing a massive belch, then sighing in relief. 'Sorry – terrible wind too. Never do it, Lauren. I've fallen off the wagon now anyway,' she says, opening the drawer again and taking a massive bite of a Mars Bar, pulling a private, orgasmic expression, before thrusting it back in the drawer.

'So . . .' she says, finishing her mouthful. 'Funny you wanted to see me as I've been trying to grab a moment to pin you down ever since Edwin handed in his notice.'

'Really?'

'As you know, he's Head of Year. I'm aware it doesn't mean much when there's only two classes, but still it's good for your cv, and a little more money. Would you like the job?'

I sink back into my seat. It's not as if it's the career opportunity of the decade. A nice little bonus maybe, but that's it. So I wonder why I find it so hard to say the next words.

'That's very kind of you, Margaret,' I begin, 'but I'm afraid I'm here to hand in my notice.'

She lets out a weary sigh, clearly naffed off about the thought of having to conduct a dozen job interviews to replace both me and Edwin.

'Oh gosh . . . Australia. You're finally going. Well, I can't say you never warned us – you always said it was your childhood ambition. Congratulations, Lauren. You need to live a little. I'm jealous.'

I squirm. 'Actually, it's not Australia. It's Singapore.'

I let this information seep into her brain, and recognition, followed by surprise, appears. 'Edwin's going to Singapore,' she states.

'Yes. And I'm going with him.'

Her eyes grow slowly wider. 'You? With Edwin? Are you . . . an *item*, Lauren?'

My jaw clenches. 'Um . . . no.'

'Oh, thank God for that!' I wonder for a second if this would breach some sort of contractual obligation.

'No offence to Edwin, obviously – I adore him, we all do. But I can't see you two together,' she guffaws.

I straighten my back indignantly. 'Really?'

'Oh God no!' she hoots. 'I always saw you being whisked off by some strapping hunk, not our Edwin.'

'Well, that'd make me a bit shallow, wouldn't it? Besides, Edwin's good-looking,' I say defensively.

'He's got a face his mother must love,' she laughs, and this is suddenly a conversation I don't wish to continue.

Chapter 33

Marion has been banging on for the last few weeks about her annual 'special salsa' night. She used to hold these in Manchester Town Hall, a setting that glitzified her usual class, allowed people to let their hair down a little and, so the idea went, attracted newcomers. Tonight, she's hired a room in the Willowgarth Hotel for her band of merry salsa dancers, for one evening only. It would almost feel like a party. Except it's a Tuesday.

Still, you can't have everything and the hotel is nice: homely but elegant and set high above lush gardens that tumble down to the south shore of Windermere. It's reasonably busy tonight, as you'd expect as we creep towards peak season. We have a function room to ourselves that spills on to a terrace, where fairy-lights twinkle above us and an early-summer breeze rustles through the trees. It's the kind of gorgeous, glittering evening that I hope makes Cate thoroughly glad to be back.

'Hello, stranger!' Frank greets her, spotting Cate as she clutches Will's hand. 'Where on earth have you been?'

'Bad chest infection,' she smiles, thumping her sternum. 'I hope I'm not too rusty.'

'Marion will soon whip you into shape,' he beams.

'Oh, hi, Stella,' Cate adds, as Stella responds with a hesitant smile. 'We need to have our meeting this week about your flowers.'

Stella nods. 'Yes. I'd forgotten about that.'

'Hopefully we can pin down those initial designs you liked and decide on a firm number of centrepieces,' Cate adds. 'Exciting, isn't it?'

'Er, yeah,' replies Stella vaguely, as a burst of salsa music interrupts them and Marion starts firing out instructions.

'Everything OK?' I whisper to Stella as we shuffle into place.

As her lip starts wobbling, I ask her quietly if she needs to go to the ladies. She nods and shuffles off, beckoning me to follow her.

When I push open the door she leans over the sink and looks numbly in the mirror.

'What's up?' I ask.

Her jaw tenses. 'There are less than five weeks to go before the wedding. The cake's ordered. My dress is paid for. I've got a Pinterest board with 50-odd types of DIY chocolate favours, 150 guests who've all accepted their invitations and ...

and ...' She looks down at her bag and pulls out a tub of Vaseline, sliding it on her lips and considering her next words. 'And I'm absolutely convinced that the groom is seeing someone else.'

My mouth opens, but I'm too shocked to speak.

'I'm sorry to spill this on you, Lauren. We hardly know each other. Problem is, all Mike's friends are my friends and I've got nobody to talk to.'

'Are you sure?' I ask incredulously. 'I don't know Mike very well, but I honestly wouldn't have had him down as the type.'

She sniffs back emotion. 'Neither would I. I've never been the possessive kind. But Mike used to have a quiet pint with his friends from work probably once a week, tops. Not any more. I hardly see him, Lauren.' She picks up her bag and starts twiddling with the zip. 'I'd thought nothing of it – assumed he was just enjoying single life before he tied the knot. Then this week, I bumped into his friend Richard, and *his* wife Alana. I mentioned something about them having been out at the Dog and Duck the previous night. Alana looked totally bewildered and said, "You weren't at the Dog and Duck last night – you were watching *Bloodline* with me." Richard looked distraught. It was obvious he knew something.'

'It might not be what you think.'

'That's what I thought. Then I asked Mike about it and I

swear I've never seen anyone look so guilty. It was ridiculous. He started blustering that Richard must've got mixed up, but he was beyond ruffled.'

I bite my lip. It doesn't sound good.

'It was then that I realised something: every time a text arrives on his phone these days, he dives for it – as if he's hiding something. It's been like that for ages. I've got no proof about any of this, obviously. And I don't want any of it to be true. I want someone to tell me that I'm imagining it all – and for me to believe them. But as it is, there's just over a month before I get married and I cannot shake this feeling. In fact, I'm certain. Mike's got another woman.' I spend the next couple of minutes trying to comfort Stella, before becoming aware that people might be wondering where we are.

By the time we return to the class and slip into the back, Marion is announcing that we're to practise the one routine she's been talking about for ages.

'Everyone find a partner, please!' she says. I look up as Luke gestures to me from the other side of the room and starts making his way over. But Joe steps in first.

When he smiles, a tingle of warmth starts in my tummy and spreads through me, before I pull myself up with a sharp stab of panic. 'How's it going?' he asks.

'Fine, fine,' I reply, apparently convinced that if I say it twice I'll appear less flustered.

'Cate seems to have made a good recovery,' he says. Then

he picks up my hands and lifts them into position as I feel myself grow hotter.

'Well, yes. She's been taking a lot of vitamin C.' I look down and study my shoes, wishing I could have thought of a slightly less moronic statement.

'Vitamin C always does the trick with me too,' he replies.

My eyes flick up and the second they connect with his, I feel my heart quicken. I swallow it back to whisper: 'It's good, isn't it?'

Then he just smiles this heart-stopping smile, as if to say that he knows this is the world's most inane conversation, but he's still happy to be having it. For a lingering moment, I find myself physically unable to look away from him. I'm temporarily spellbound, lost in those eyes as they refuse to break my gaze. I realise that I don't know what is happening here … but I *do* know it shouldn't be.

'Where is Emily?' I ask, finally pulling away my hands. 'She didn't want a lift tonight because she was going to be late home from work, but I hadn't thought she was going to be *this* late. But, you know Emily – she works so hard. She's really passionate about her job. She's absolutely a lovely person. Such a good friend.'

He listens to this soliloquy, watching my mouth run away with itself. Then he says: 'Lauren, I—'

Just then, the door from the function room bursts open and Emily emerges on to the terrace.

'Sorry I'm late,' she says, flustered, and with strands of hair stuck to her forehead as she slips in behind us, sees Joe and me together, and grabs Esteban by the hand.

When the music begins, dancing with Joe is far more pleasurable than it should be – in the most uncomfortable way. All I can think about, as I pretend to be entirely unmoved by this experience, is the heat between our bodies as the music throbs through my chest. Fortunately, my dancing is nothing like as awkward as I'm feeling.

Joe has become such a strong, confident dancer that all I can do is submit to his lead, lose myself in the dance, let the rest of the world disappear.

As he leads me into a turn then pulls me into his hips, I am, quite suddenly, forced to confront something I've done my best *not* to confront since the moment I met Joe.

This is more than a crush. I've got real feelings for Joe that go beyond a passing admiration for his biceps and sparkly eyes. The music stops and I breathe in the glistening heat from his neck. Then I snap away from him.

'So what's the latest on the train-wreck you're making of my dad's hotel?' I blurt out. I don't know why I sound so aggressive. But I feel the need to underline to him, to everyone else – and most of all to myself – that this is not a man I'll get my head in a tangle over.

'Well, it's all on schedule,' he says, almost as taken aback as I am. 'We've completed most of the major renovation works – all the behind-the-scenes stuff, like plumbing and electrics. And now the fun stuff has started: the decor.'

'Hmm,' I snort. 'I dread to think.'

'You'll get to see it soon, so you won't have to just take my word for it and rely on the artists' impressions.'

'I don't think I will be seeing it,' I reply, focusing hard on Marion as she yaps on about the state of everyone's core. 'I think I'd be heartbroken.'

When I look up, a wrinkle has appeared above his nose. 'Really? You wouldn't want to come and see it?'

'I'd prefer to keep the memory of the Moonlight Hotel as it was, to be honest. I'm sure you understand.'

Then we switch partners and I realise as he takes Emily's hands that I've regained the ability to breathe.

After the session Cate, Emily and I walk through the wind-swept streets of Bowness, glancing into the warm glow of pubs, the restaurants full of people romancing over candle-light. They're not the only ones who are feeling loved-up.

'Have you seen that amazing new hotel in Ullswater?' Cate asks me, skipping up the hill. 'It's super posh, all four-poster beds and fluffy dressing gowns. Well, Will's booked us in for a night.'

'Oh, that place is *gorgeous*,' Emily sighs. 'I had to pick up a group of travel journalists from there a couple of weeks ago. It's really special.'

Cate stops in her tracks. 'Oh, Lauren – you don't mind, do you? Two weeks ago I was dominating your Saturday nights. I don't want you to think I'm dumping you because I've got a better offer.'

'Cate, I'm enough of a realist to know that a four-poster bed in a posh hotel in Ullswater represents a much "better offer". Please don't worry about me. Besides, I've got a date with Edwin on Saturday night.'

Now Emily stops dead. She and Cate look at each other, incredulous.

'You've got a date on a Saturday with Edwin?' Cate blusters. 'How could you have forgotten about that?'

I suddenly want to change the subject. 'I thought I'd mentioned it,' I shrug, and continue up the hill.

'You don't seem very excited,' Emily says, to my alarm.

'I'm ecstatic!' I reply, probably too forcefully. 'Ooh, honestly, I can't wait. Ooh, gorgeous Edwin … ah, it'll be amazing!' Emily is frowning. 'I'm very nervous, obviously. But I mean, wow! This is everything I've ever wanted.'

I am unlikely to be nominated for a Golden Globe, but at least it seems to placate my two friends for the time being.

'How are you doing your hair?' Cate asks.

I have put about as much thought into how I'm doing my hair as I have the Theory of Relativity. 'I'll watch some Youtube videos tonight. I'm thinking an up-do would be good. Or maybe down. A down-do.'

'And are you still on your diet?' Emily asks.

'I've eaten nothing but celery sticks and raw spinach,' I lie, shoving my hands in my pockets and fingering my Kit Kat wrapper from earlier.

'Well, it's clearly all happening between you two, isn't it,' Cate says.

And as we reach the top of the hill and turn to look at the lake shimmering in the moonlight, all I'm certain of is that *something* is happening. But I'm not sure how much it's got to do with Edwin.

Chapter 34

I wake up at 6.40 a.m. on Saturday morning desperate for the loo and, having stumbled to the bathroom and supposedly relieved myself, notice I'm not feeling as much relief as I ought to. The implications of this are immediately clear: I've suffered on and off for years with mild urinary tract infections and, with a Saturday-night date ahead, I'm just not prepared to risk this going any further.

So I get straight onto the GP out-of-hours service, who dutifully provide me with a course of antibiotics and instruct me not to drink anything other than cranberry juice and water.

I'm home for five minutes when I hear footsteps outside and look out of my bedroom window to see Mum striding up the path. She's almost at the door, when she yanks out a stray hawthorn branch with her bare hands, chucks it over the fence and wipes her palms on her trousers, before ringing the bell.

I make her a cup of tea – builder's strength – before she asks about my preparations for Singapore, apparently having accepted that the change of plan merely reflects one of the myriad oddities about my personality.

'Well, I hope you have a better time of it there than Steph,' she concludes.

'Steph? Why, what's up with her?' I ask.

'From what Harry says, she's as miserable as sin,' Mum replies. 'She's not enjoying a minute of Australia.'

'I'm sure there must be a minute or two she's enjoyed,' I say, thinking back to the six-pack on that junior doctor.

'I don't think she's made many friends.'

'Are you sure?' I resist the urge to point out that she seems overflowing with 'friends' every time I see her.

Mum gives me a hard look. 'Yes, I'm sure.'

'I'm surprised, that's all. When I see her on Facebook, she always seems so … busy.' This is the politest euphemism I can think of for the fact that she seems intent on shagging half of New South Wales.

'It's apparently an act,' Mum says. 'The pictures on Facebook are just people she drinks with. They're not real friends.'

I lower my cup and realise that this probably *is* true. At best they seem to be drinking buddies or fuck buddies or buddies of any description except real ones.

'She spent last night bawling her eyes out on the phone to

Harry,' Mum continues. 'She's thinking of coming home. It's a shame. She was always a nice girl, even if she got a bit lost in recent years.'

'Maybe something will come up and she'll change her mind about coming home.'

Mum doesn't look convinced. 'I don't think so. She's too lonely.'

Which does nothing to make me feel any less guilty about the whole thing.

I meet Emily for lunch in the Lake Road Kitchen in Ambleside, a trendy little bistro with stripped-back floors, an open kitchen and an adventurous menu. We eat good food, laugh a lot and basically put the world to rights. Most of the time being around Emily feels like it always has done. But not always; not when I hear her talking about Joe.

'I shouldn't have eaten all that – Joe's cooking dinner for me tonight,' Emily tells me, as a waiter brings a coffee for her and a cranberry juice for me.

'Oh, lucky you.'

'His house is absolutely gorgeous,' she continues, picking up her cup. 'It must be brilliant to have such a knack for making places look good – he's obviously a natural. I know you're worried about it, but the hotel is going to be beautiful when it's finished.'

'So, is it a big house?' I feel myself flush as I say it.

'Not at all. Don't ask me why, when his dad flew in by helicopter the other week. It's only a three-bedroom cottage, a bit bigger than yours. But he's got one of those range cookers and a free-standing kitchen – it looks rustic but modern if that makes sense. And there's a lovely view from the garden. He's got one of those stone benches. You could sit and watch the sunset for hours.'

I picture Joe and Emily curled up on the bench, warming each other under a stretching sky.

'You sound smitten,' I manage.

'Joe's lovely,' she confesses. 'But speaking of lovely guys, shouldn't you be at home by now shaving your legs and with your hair in rollers?'

'Why?'

'For your date with Edwin, of course!'

'Oh, I've got plenty of time,' I say listlessly. 'Besides, we're only staying in.'

'That's even better, isn't it? When a man cooks dinner for you, you're in business, Lauren. You must know that, surely?'

She gestures for the bill as I hear myself asking something quietly: 'Has Joe cooked dinner for you?'

'Yeah, a few times,' she grins and I take a sip of cranberry juice to hide my stricken expression.

Chapter 35

Edwin's flat is on the top floor of a terraced house in one of the narrow, winding back streets of Windermere, and it's fair to say it's not what I was expecting. Considering this is a heterosexual man prepared to wear ruffles on a Tuesday night, the place is surprisingly drab.

I don't want to overstate this, as it's not awful. But Edwin's fondness for iconic style – the one that's evident at least in his taste in stationery – hasn't quite translated into his home. If I was being unkind I'd say it was reminiscent of a two-star guest-house, with a dark blue carpet fraying at the edges, white Anaglypta wallpaper and an abundance of dusty cabinets.

He invites me to sit on his sofa, which could well be original art deco, but looks like it's been fished out of a skip, courtesy of scratches from a cat, dog or possibly twelve gerbils. I perch on the end while I wait for him to open up the bottle of wine I brought and hand me a glass.

'Lovely choice of wine, Lauren. Hmm...' he takes a mouthful. 'Those crisp, starchy overtones really hit the back of your throat – it's like *liquid potato*. Not that I've got anything against that,' he smiles, and I wonder as I force out a laugh why I'm not falling to pieces like I would have done once.

'Whatever you're making smells tremendous, Edwin.'

'Hope so,' he replies, throwing his tea towel over his shoulder. And for a second he looks as attractive as I always thought he did. Those dreamy eyes. The lovely lips. I *do* still fancy him as much as always, I tell myself, taking a big slug of wine.

I'm not technically meant to be drinking. But the antibiotics – and five gallons of cranberry juice – have kicked in remarkably quickly and by this afternoon, my UTI was definitely on its way out. I predict it will be completely annihilated by dawn.

Under normal circumstances I would have stuck rigidly to the medical advice not to drink alcohol – but, obviously, the doctor didn't know the important circumstances of this evening: that I am on a Saturday-night date with Edwin. And therefore, the only option was to pop one last antibiotic before I left the house, and take it easy on the booze. The alternative – not drinking at all – isn't an option because firstly, after the years I've known Edwin he'd be aware this was out of character, and secondly, now that tonight has actually arrived, I'm unexpectedly nervous.

He apologises for the fact that his music system is playing up and puts the TV on low in the background. It's the *Britain's Got Talent* final. I'm not a massive fan, but I recognise the contestant who appears on the screen as she hasn't been out of the papers. She's a big girl, defiantly refusing to starve herself and succumb to the pressure the world seems to exert on pop stars.

'Blimey,' scoffs Edwin. 'She's got what you might describe as an *excellent personality*.'

I bridle at this. 'I think she looks lovely. Besides, she's got a great voice and the audience love her, so that's all that matters, isn't it?'

'Gosh, you've drained that already,' he replies, topping up my glass.

'I'll never say no to liquid potato, Edwin,' I reply, and he laughs as the phone rings.

'Oh, that'll be Georgie, calling about Sing.' I never did get round to calling her myself.

'I thought they were seven hours ahead,' I point out.

'She's back in the UK for a week so I suggested she call tonight. She can't wait to speak to you. Honestly, we're all so excited now.'

He answers. 'Hi, Georgie. Yup, she's here. She's excited too. Yep, I know.' He grins at me. 'I know.' He nods. 'I know,' he adds, as I wonder what the hell it is he knows so well that it's worth saying three times. 'OK, I'll put her on.'

He hands over the phone, grinning as he mouths: 'You'll love her.'

I smile and take the handset from him. 'Hello? This is Lauren.'

'Lauren! Lovely to speak to you!' Georgie replies, and I can't deny she sounds really nice. For about six seconds. 'So listen, I'm very glad you're able to join Edwin and me in Singapore and I'm certain we'll all get on like a house on fire.'

'Oh me too,' I reply.

'But I know you'll understand if I don't leave this to chance. So I've got a few ground rules I'd like to make clear from the very beginning. Hope that's OK?'

'Of course.'

'Right. All shoes to be left in the vestibule at the front of the flat to ensure no dirt is brought inside. All suncream must be removed with an exfoliating brush before entering the swimming pool. No nuts – I have an allergy. No eggs – I have an intolerance. No spray deodorant, only roll-on. No house guests.'

'O-kay ...'

'I haven't finished yet. No meat, it's against my religion and there's a well-stocked vegetarian supermarket down the road. Please do not leave any lights on in the middle of the night. If you need to get up to go to the toilet, use the light on your phone.'

'OK.'

'No music.'

I frown. 'None?'

'Headphones are fine, naturally.'

'Er . . . thanks,' I reply, but apparently this sarcasm is lost on her.

'So do you enjoy it out there?' I ask, deciding to make conversation before she can hit me with another rule.

'Oh, it's faaabbbulous! Have a look at my Facebook page – I never let anyone on who I haven't met in real life but I'll make an exception. You'll never want to live in the UK again. Every Saturday we have a champagne breakfast brunch at one of the hotels – the Greenhouse at the Ritz-Carlton's my fave. Though the W's pretty good too and they have Veuve on tap. Have you got your padi?'

'My what?'

'Can you scuba dive? If not, you *must learn*. Everyone does.'

'It does sound wonderful,' I reply.

'And you're lucky. You've got a friend in tow so it doesn't feel quite so daunting, does it? Not that you'd find it hard to make friends here, even if Edwin decided to drop you on day one.'

I scrunch up my nose.

'Not that I think he would. He speaks quite highly of you,' she adds, as if I've asked him for a reference to go and work in a shoe shop.

'Does he?' I say. Then I can't resist asking the next question. 'What has he said about me?'

'Oh um … let me think. I know – he says you have an *excellent personality*.'

Chapter 36

The *excellent personality* comment resonates with me long after I've tried to play down its significance in my head.

I remind myself that it's not even technically offensive, if you take it out of the context of the *Britain's Got Talent* contestant. But the thought that Edwin might find me as unsexy as he apparently finds the girl belting out her own version of Cher's 'If I Could Turn Back Time' makes something rise up in me: determination. Determination that this man – the subject of my most vivid dreams for two years – will find me irresistible tonight if it's the last bloody thing I do.

I arrange myself on the sofa seductively as Edwin busies himself in the open-plan kitchen. It's only as my elbow slips off the arm that I realise I'm feeling tipsier than I'd expect after a glass and a half of wine. Normally it'd take at least half a bottle before I started misjudging the depth of soft furnishings.

As Edwin chats away about whether we should have a joint leaving do, I surreptitiously check the antibiotics in my bag to see if I'd get away with pre-loading another one, when several words leap out at me. DO NOT DRINK ALCOHOL WITH THIS MEDICINE.

I draw a sharp breath as I attempt to focus on the words. I'd known I was being slightly naughty in straying from the cranberry juice and water, but I hadn't for one second suspected that the wine could react with the bloody medicine. Then I glance over at Edwin and tell myself to *relax*: I've already had a glass and a half and I feel really good. A little drunker than usual, perhaps, but as long as I don't go overboard, this will all be fine.

As it happens, the whole thing becomes more and more *fine* the more wine I sip. That helps me stop thinking about how much I liked the sound of the champagne brunches and how little I liked the sound of Georgie herself. That helps me stop thinking about what a date at Joe's 'gorgeous house' would be like. That helps me stop thinking altogether.

I don't even care that when I open my bag I also realise I'd failed to dispose of the urine sample I took along to the walk-in centre this afternoon. I didn't have a spare receptacle so had to wash out a bottle of Pepsi Max and put it in there. They then refused to test it because of some sort of contamination issues – as if traces of a soft drink could somehow result in me being misdiagnosed with Ebola.

The point is, as the evening progresses, I start to feel really, really happy. Ecstatic, actually. Why wouldn't I? OK, Edwin has not galloped up on a white stallion, flung me on the back and hurtled off into the sunset, ruffles a-billowing.

But he's spent all afternoon lovingly creating this dinner for me – seafood lasagne, which is *amazing*, by the way. And I decide, suddenly, that I actually *like* the fact that things haven't been straightforward between the two of us. That chasing him has been part of the fun.

'You've played terribly hard to get, Edwin,' I murmur, through a flirty pout, as I put down my knife and fork. We are sitting at one of those little fold-up tables in his living room. A ventriloquist's doll is singing 'Uptown Girl' in the background.

He looks at me, apparently surprised by this comment. 'Hard to get?'

'Don't be coy, Edwin Blaire. You couldn't have played harder to get if you were the size of a one-pence piece and stuck down the back of a sofa.'

He smiles, clearly enjoying the moment as he stands up to clear the plates. 'Well, I haven't meant to be like that.'

I roll my eyes and smirk seductively. It makes me almost fall off my chair. 'Yes, I believe you. Millions wouldn't,' I add, sounding sultry.

'Are you all right, Lauren?'

'Yes – why?'

'You sound a little hoarse. Would you like a Strepsil?'

I burst out laughing. 'Oh, you're so funny, Edwin! Let me help with the washing up,' I volunteer, standing up.

'I wouldn't hear of it,' he says gallantly, but by now I'm already up and concentrating very hard on putting one foot in front of the other as I head for the kitchen, the walls swimming in and out. 'Honestly, Lauren, you really don't need to.'

I place down the plates next to the sink, then spin round, throwing him a sensual look.

'Oh, but I insist,' I pout, grabbing the Marigolds on the drainer and snapping one on. He leaps back slightly. The scamp.

I turn to the sink, allowing him to admire my bum as I fill the bowl up with Fairy Liquid, then am mildly disappointed to see Edwin wandering back into the living room to collect the HP sauce. I turn back and find myself mesmerised by the bubbles, squashing them together between my rubber gloves then watching in fascination as I swirl the dish-cloth around the plates. My hips sway as I glance at the TV to see a small dog wearing pixie boots cartwheeling across the stage.

'Are you quite sure you're feeling all right?' asks Edwin, as I put the last plate into the dish-rack. I'm vaguely aware of the concern on his face and feel the need to do something to encourage him to relax; I'll never seduce him while he's this tightly coiled. So I start swaying my hips, all lap-dancer loose as if my pelvis has a life of its own.

'Shall I take those rubber gloves off you?' Edwin offers, and I glance down, having entirely forgotten that I was wearing them.

I instantly recall that scene when Marilyn Monroe sang 'Diamonds Are A Girl's Best Friend' – the stunning, curve-hugging ballgown, the long, sexy satin gloves.

OK, I haven't got the ballgown, but I *have* got the gloves, or the nearest thing. I put one finger on Edwin's chest and look into his eyes like Tyra Banks looking down a camera, before teasingly pushing him across the length of the kitchen until he's pressed against the units.

Then, finger by finger, my eyes soft and sexy, I remove the first rubber glove, then the second, flinging both over my shoulder before I turn my back on Edwin and sway into the living room.

I am momentarily aware of a delay as he scrambles around the electric hob, trying to peel off the gloves which, it appears, have melted on to one of the rings. Once he's got them off and sprayed a little Febreze to disperse the stench of burning rubber, he emerges into the living room and looks at me anxiously.

I pat the chair next to me and murmur, 'Come 'ere, lover boy,' though I realise a second later that any *Dirty Dancing* references are entirely lost on Edwin.

'I think you need more wine,' I decide, grabbing the bottle and topping up his glass. Then I pick it up, put it in his hands and encourage him to sip. Which he does.

His eyes meet mine and our gaze holds for a moment. It suddenly feels like one of those staring contests we used to have when I was a little girl. He breaks the gaze first and, before I can stop myself, I pump my fist and blurt out: *'Yess!'*

'Lauren, I'm wondering if I should get you an orange juice?' Edwin asks. 'You're acting a little oddly.'

I edge closer to him and smile. 'But I'm *feeling* wonderful,' I murmur.

'Only ... you're quite tipsy considering you haven't had that much to drink.'

'I'm not tipsy, Edwin. Just ... in the mood.'

'In the mood?' he gulps.

'For lurrrve.'

He straightens his back. 'I see.'

'Do you, Edwin?' I whisper.

His jaw tenses and he puts down his wine glass. And then, quite unexpectedly and quite wonderfully, he slips his hand behind my neck and draws my face towards his and kisses me.

It's stronger, more passionate than the first time. At least, I'm aware that he's pressing his mouth harder and he's using proper, full-on tongue; other than that, I must admit, my mouth feels a bit weird, a bit tingly.

'Lauren, how would you feel if I did this?' he says, his eyes glinting as he pulls back and looks at me, between kisses.

'Did what?' I frown.

He gestures downwards and I realise he has his hand on my breast and is rubbing it around like Mr Miyagi in *The Karate Kid*, when he's teaching Daniel Son to wax on, wax off.

He stops anxiously. 'Is that nice?'

'It's absolutely *awesome*,' I murmur, and before I even know what I'm doing, I am peeling off my top.

I attempt to do this sexily but the material gets stuck on the edge of the clip in my hair and I end up tugging and tugging until I nearly remove my ear, and my hair on the right-hand side feels as if it's been backcombed by a hyena.

'How would you feel if I did this, Edwin?' I breathe, unclasping my bra and allowing it to slip to the floor.

I can honestly say I've never witnessed a reaction like Edwin's before in my life. His eyes grow to about six times their normal size.

I can't stop myself from giggling. I've done it. I've seduced him. *Job done!*

'I'd say that was fine too,' he manages.

I stand up and take him by the hand, enjoying the feeling of unique brazenness that comes from standing in a man's living room with your bare boobs on show. I pull him up out of the sofa.

'Where are we going?' he stammers.

'To bed. Where else?' I whisper, leading him across the living room. He pauses briefly to turn the television off, explaining that he hates wasting electricity. I grab him by the arm and pull him in my direction.

Then I spin round and maintain his gaze as I start to wander backwards, a move that would be the ultimate in sexiness had I managed to avoid the handbag I'd left on the living-room floor.

As it is, I trip over a strap and almost go flying across the room, something that prompts a plethora of swearing before I bend over to pick it up. Unfortunately, instead of sweeping it out of the way, my Pepsi Max bottle – the one full of urine – rolls out and goes trundling across the room. I watch in horror as it traverses the blue carpet, 200mls of this morning's wee sloshing about inside.

'Oh God!' I shriek, which also turns out to be a mistake.

Sensing my panic, Edwin leaps over and, under the misapprehension that he's helping, attempts to grab it at exactly the same moment that I do.

The resulting scramble can only be compared to a miniature rugby scrum, except that one of us is semi-naked and the 'ball' in question is a modest bottle containing human bodily fluids.

There is *no way* I can allow Edwin to get to it first. So, I elbow him in the guts and grab the bottle, clutching it breathlessly to my naked chest.

'Are you that thirsty, Lauren?' asks Edwin, alarm in his eyes.

I nod as the implications of this question hit me. 'Yes,' I say feverishly.

He sighs. 'Go on then,' he says, waiting for me to drink the contents of the bottle.

Now, I am feeling strange. I am feeling drunk. But I am absolutely not feeling either of the above in sufficient quantities to emulate fourteen days at sea with drinking my own urine as the only option open to me.

Unfortunately, I *am* feeling both of the above in sufficient quantities to fail to know what to do. So I just wing it. I glance at the open window and, as Edwin goes to turn off the living-room lamp, I fling the bottle out of it, wincing as a cry of *Ow!* reverberates from the street below.

I stand in Edwin's living room, naked and cold and uncomfortable, and not really knowing what to do. Then Edwin approaches and kisses me. And that, I'm afraid, is the last of the evening that I actually remember.

Chapter 37

I struggle to describe the feelings that swim through my mind as I wake up in Edwin's bed.

First is the split-second realisation that I've been snoring loudly, as I wake with a grunt, genuinely shocked that the person who made the noise was *me*.

Second is the extreme physical discomfort of being even more desperate for the loo than I was this time yesterday, clear evidence that my UTI has failed to shift, which is little wonder given how far I drifted from the advice to stick to non-aggravating liquids.

Third is that Edwin is propped up above me on one elbow, grinning.

'Morning, Sleepyhead,' he murmurs, leaning down to kiss me. I reward him by clamping shut my lips, saving him from a distinct lack of minty freshness. But Edwin doesn't care. He just snuggles into me, nibbling my neck, pressing his body against mine. He is entirely naked.

'I'm sorry, but I'm dying for the toilet,' I say apologetically.

'Oh, let me get you my dressing gown.'

He stands and places his pillow over his groin – and the very fact that I am in bed, naked WITH EDWIN nearly makes my head explode. I've dreamed about this for years and yet I'm suddenly speechless, motionless, thoughtless.

He passes me his dressing gown and I slip it on. It's maroon velvet, has 'Christmas gift' written all over it, and smells faintly of Marmite.

I head to the loo and relieve myself, moaning with queasy relief as my bladder empties, before I check my appearance, realise it's beyond hope, then pop an antibiotic and plod back into the kitchen for some water to wash it down with. I look predictably awful. I feel predictably awful. Yet it's more than just the fact that the tablets I took, when mixed with alcohol, have a similar effect on human functionality as Rohypnol.

I am disappointed that my *first time* with Edwin wasn't as memorable as it should have been, in that I can't actually remember it at all.

Sheepishly, I return to the bedroom and slip under the covers. I can't deny it feels nice when he squeezes himself into me, but it's more the fact that I'm grateful that my strip routine with the rubber gloves – which is one bit I do remember – didn't make him disown me for life.

That turns out to be the last thing he wants to do. Edwin

has never been as enthusiastic or attentive or generally keen as this morning. Whatever the hell it was I did with him last night, it ought to be bottled and sold as a Viagra substitute.

'You look beautiful,' he murmurs, as I allow myself to be kissed by him.

'I find that impossible to believe,' I croak.

'It's true. Quite honestly, last night … the things you did … it was so unexpected. I've seen you in a new light.'

I freeze. 'What things?' I ask, but he just laughs.

'I don't know why you look so worried, Lauren. It was incredible. I'm walking on air today.'

'Are you?'

He nods and kisses me on the forehead and I feel overcome with worry. 'Edwin. Things are … hazy this morning. Did we *do it?*'

'Very funny, Lauren,' he laughs, which I can only interpret as a *yes*.

'It's just, I'm on these tablets at the moment and I think they reacted with the wine. Some parts of the evening are a bit hazy.'

'Not for anything serious, I hope,' he asks, a wrinkle appearing in his brow.

'No, no. Just …' I wrack my brains to try and conjure up something – anything – that I could feasibly have that isn't infectious, or mildly embarrassing like a UTI. 'Gout.'

'You've got gout?'

'Just temporarily,' I splutter, desperate to change the subject. 'So, the sex . . .'

'The sex?'

'Between you and me. Was it . . .' I try and think of a subtle way of asking this.

'Good?'

'No, penetrative.'

'Well, no, but it was magnificent as far as I'm concerned.'

'Oh right. Glad to hear it,' I reply, giving him another kiss and wondering how long I need to stay here before I can make my excuses and leave.

Chapter 38

Sunday is spent in a complete stupor, between my bed and the loo. By Monday, despite having largely recovered, I feel mortified every time there's a possibility of going anywhere near Edwin. This is problematic, given that our two classes are merged for 'Spanish Day'. The latter involves Gillian Holt, from the junior school, giving a lengthy talk on Madrid traditions – something a two-week holiday in 2009 has apparently qualified her for.

I sit in the corner, listening intently as she attempts to deal with the aftermath of her statement that, 'Chefs say you can put almost anything in a paella.' This led to a dozen hands shooting up in the air, and the children testing out alternatives such as, 'what about ice cream?' or 'chocolate cake?' or, my particular favourite, 'a football?'.

While this chaos goes on about me, Edwin keeps trying to catch my eye. Sometimes the pressure becomes too much to bear and I'll briefly look up, for him to flash me a smile I can only describe as *saucy*.

'You must be an absolute demon in bed,' Cate sniggers, as I fill her in that night.

'Please don't even joke about it,' I say, sipping water. Which is all I am going to sip ever again, for the rest of my life. 'I have no idea what went on between those sheets. From the way he looked at me in the morning, you'd think it had involved a black negligée and nipple tassels. Which it didn't, to be clear.'

'You saving those for the second time?'

All I can do is wince.

Cate narrows her eyes. 'So, was it good? You must recall an overall impression. You've been dreaming about it for bloody years so by rights it should've been off the scale.'

'I honestly do not know,' I say, shaking my head. 'I can't remember.'

'Is that why your feelings for Edwin have changed?'

My head snaps up. 'What makes you think that?'

She shrugs. 'I was just getting that impression. Sorry – I'm obviously wrong.'

'The date would have been wonderful, had I been conscious. I realise this sort of conundrum is all alien to you, given how well things are going with Will. I've barely seen you in the last couple of weeks.'

'Sorry,' she says sheepishly.

'Don't be silly, I'm over the moon for you.'

'Thanks, Lauren,' she smiles. 'So how's your Singapore planning?'

'Fine. I handed my notice in on the cottage last week,' I tell her, though just saying it makes a bead of sweat appear on my brow. 'I feel awful about letting my cousin Steph down though. I haven't even heard from her since I told her I'm not going to Australia.'

'Hasn't she posted one of her infamous updates on Facebook lately?'

'I don't know, now you mention it,' I reply, taking out my phone and clicking on the app.

I can see nothing from Steph though – just the standard Facebook guff I find so enticing: birthday wishes, wedding photos, new babies, humblebrags and rants. Plus one from my mum, who seems to think that if she writes, Hi Dawn, did you get the washing machine fixed? on her own wall that Dawn, whoever she is, will mystically pick up the message by the sheer cosmic force of the internet.

'My mother should be kept away from technology,' I sigh, as Cate reaches to the windowsill to turn the radio on. The song playing is 'Sweet Disposition' by the Temper Trap and it has the instantaneous effect of making her tap her feet as she finishes the washing-up, sunlight sheering on to her face as she sings, lost in the words.

And it's then, when I glance back at my phone, that I'm confronted by the picture. Not *the* picture – another one.

'Lauren?' Cate asks, but it takes a moment for me to register her voice. 'I was just saying I saw Stella for her final meeting and . . . what's the matter?'

The words stick in my mouth. But as it turns out, she doesn't need me to spell them out. She knows even before she's looked. She races over and takes the phone to glare at the photo that's been posted direct on her Facebook page – bewilderingly, from her *own* account.

This time she's in a kitchen. She's facing the camera directly, the hint of a smile on her lips as she lifts up her top to provide the sort of eyeful usually reserved for page 3 of the *Daily Star*.

She doesn't even say anything when she sees it. She just takes a slug of breath, deletes it – then slumps on to a kitchen chair and starts crying. I sink into the seat next to her and slide my arm round her, as her shoulders begin to shudder.

'It hadn't been on there long so very few people will have seen it,' I offer, though not with much conviction given that she has over 300 Facebook friends and that it had been there for twenty minutes.

Nobody had commented on it, nobody had liked it, nobody had presumably done anything but stare in disbelief – and possibly report it, although enough time clearly hadn't elapsed before Facebook got on the case.

Cate's phone starts ringing on the table in front of us, and

Will's name flashes up on the screen. She grabs it and turns it off.

'How could it have been on *your* profile?' I ask.

'I don't know.' She looks at me, terror in her eyes, her face red and wet from crying. 'I'm on Facebook with all my friends and all my family, as well as half the town. And ... and Will.'

'He probably hasn't seen it,' I comfort her.

'I'm sure someone will fill him in,' she sobs.

'Cate, I think you need to go to the police about this,' I tell her firmly.

She looks up with frenzied eyes. 'But – but Will's brother – the humiliation ... I'd feel like such an idiot and a slag. And what if it went to court and all the *other* photos were used as evidence?' It's clear this suggestion has sent her into an unstoppable panic. 'What the hell am I going to do?'

'It's going to be all right,' I whisper.

But as I pull her into me, her body trembling in my arms, it's hard to understand how.

The next twenty-four hours are a slow kind of torture. I spend the day at work getting texts from Cate, who tells me that *everyone* knows. I have no idea whether she's exaggerating but I suspect so, as the number of people on Facebook who will have actually seen the picture is minimal and, while gossip of any kind tends to spread like wildfire around here, I can't – or perhaps don't want to – accept it's as bad as she says. But then, I'm not in her shoes. And I'm sure it feels bad. I'm sure it feels worse than I can possibly imagine.

When the school bell rings and the children are safely deposited back with their parents, I leap into my car and head straight over to Cate's place. Daffodils & Stars is shut and she answers the door of her flat looking like death warmed up.

'It's everywhere,' she hisses.

'I'm sure that's not the case,' I say lamely.

'I went outside to fix some of the displays and heard two customers sitting outside the coffee shop next door talking about it. I couldn't believe it – I didn't even know them! You know when you overhear part of a conversation and think it must be about someone else … only it's not. I worked out how Robby could have done this too.'

'Oh?'

'He knew my password. It was the same one as for my emails – and I gave that to him once to check something for me when my phone wasn't working.'

I sigh. 'Have you seen Will since it happened?'

Will, we discovered from one of his texts, saw the picture with his own eyes, about a minute before Cate deleted it. She had dozens of missed calls from him by the time I left yesterday, but in the end he clearly gave up.

'Have you returned any of his calls yet?'

She shakes her head. 'No. And he's stopped ringing anyway.'

'Cate, you should speak to him,' I tell her.

'What am I going to say? "Did you like my home-made porn collection? Because there are more where that came from!"'

I frown. 'You should at least text him back.'

'Oh, what's the point! He's not phoning any longer, Lauren. He doesn't want anything to do with me. Why would he?'

'Well, because it's not your fault!' I reply furiously. 'And because he loves you! And because if he's a man worth his salt, he won't care about your past and will understand that you're a victim here and—'

I'm interrupted from my rant by the ring of her doorbell. She looks up, her lip trembling.

'Do you want me to get it?'

She nods. 'Promise you'll just get rid of whoever it is though? If it's Will, I can't face him. Make my excuses will you?'

I head to the door and open it to find Cate's mum, Liz. I feel instantly relieved. Cate and her mum have never been especially close, but I know that if there's one thing that's going to get a girl through this, it's having her best friend and her mum by her side.

'I take it she's in?' asks Liz. She's dressed in a smart pair of trousers and a cashmere throw, her short blonde hair swept softly out of her blue eyes. She looks upset, which is understandable.

'In the living room, Liz,' I say, closing the door as she walks ahead of me. 'It's just horrendous what's happened, isn't it?'

Liz turns to me and replies starkly: 'Yes. It is.'

Cate is curled up on the sofa, her cheeks streaked with more tears. She sits up when her mother enters and for a moment neither of them say a thing.

'Mum . . . I'm so sorry,' Cate eventually whimpers.

It takes a second for me to realise that Liz's eyes are not filled with the sympathy and maternal love that I'd anticipated. Disgust is apparent in the tightening of her lips. When she speaks, it's quiet and low – the whisper of a woman who considers herself scorned.

'I did everything I could to bring you up right, Catherine. I gave you everything a parent could be expected to. And your father and I are rewarded with *this*.'

Cate's face crumples. 'This isn't about you, Mum.'

'Oh, isn't it?' Anger radiates from the woman in thick waves. 'You think that when I have to walk into work tomorrow and face my colleagues that this doesn't affect me? You don't think that the fact that my neighbour has seen my daughter's body, flaunted about like some prostitute . . . you don't think that affects me? You don't think it's about *me* when I'm the one who has to explain to your Great-Aunt

Edith why everyone's gossiping, or to little Ellen why Aunty Cate – whom she loved and looked up to – is all over the internet with her clothes off?'

'Mum, I just didn't think—'

'*That's* your problem, Catherine. You have a rush of blood to the head and you *don't think*.'

Cate seems to shrink into herself. 'You're right – you're totally right. I'm so sorry, Mum. I just don't know what to say.'

'Neither do I,' says Liz, clutching her bag to her chest. 'All I know is that I'm having to come to terms with something I never dreamed was the case.'

'Come to terms with what?'

She glares at Cate with hard eyes. 'The fact that my daughter is a dirty slut.'

Chapter 39

It is no surprise that Cate doesn't come to salsa, given that she currently refuses to eat, sleep or move from her flat. But she's not the only one avoiding the place. I get a text from Stella as I'm almost at the door of Casa Lagos. Not coming tonight. Trying to work a few things out. x

I stop walking and compose a reply. Hope everything's OK? x

The second I've pressed Send, my phone rings and Stella already seems to be talking, clearly desperate to get a few things off her chest.

'The answer to that question is *not exactly*,' she breathes. 'I found a text on Mike's phone yesterday. I know who he's been meeting.'

'Who?'

'*Lulu*. The text was as clear as day: Hi darlin! See you at 8pm tonight – usual place?. Then xxx. Three kisses. Not one but THREE.'

'Lulu?' I repeat, incredulously. 'Are you sure?'

'I'm certain – I confronted him about it and he came out with some crap about one of his colleagues wanting to start a dance class, and him meeting Lulu to put them in touch. It was absolute bollocks. I just don't believe him.'

It's been months since Mike came to the salsa class, but now I think about it I can't deny that Lulu did seem to be giving him special treatment; I said to Cate at the time that she'd taken a shine to him. I never thought for a moment that there could have been more to it than that – but I must admit I'm at a loss to explain the text.

'So . . . where does that leave you?' I ask.

'With the wedding, you mean? Good question. Am I really going to marry a big fat cheating liar?'

'Oh, Stella . . .'

'I don't know what to do, Lauren,' she goes on, the words catching at the back of her throat. 'All I know right now is that I can't be there tonight, otherwise I might walk over and punch Lulu bloody Mitford in her pretty little face.' I hear a door slam. 'I need to go. Can I phone you this week?'

'Of course. In fact, come over if you want someone to have a glass of wine with,' I reply, despite feeling less than qualified to be an agony aunt for Stella or anyone else.

'I might,' she says hastily. 'Thanks, Lauren.'

When the call ends, I push open the door of the restaurant

and see Will and Joe on the other side of the room, chatting to Andi and Luke. Will looks up, spots me and marches over, his face full of questions.

'Is Cate coming tonight?' he asks.

'No, I don't think so. She's having a bad time of it,' I reply. His jaw clenches. 'I believe you know about the picture.' It's not a question.

'I think everyone does, don't they?' he says stiffly.

'Will, it's awful. It was her ex-boyfriend Robby who posted the picture. He hacked into her Facebook account.' This is clearly news to Will. 'She's extremely upset and feels totally humiliated. I'm sure if you gave her a call and—'

'Lauren,' he interrupts. 'I've tried to phone her a dozen times and got no response. Nor from my texts either.'

I lower my eyes. 'Yes, I know. She's in a bad way and . . .' My sentence trails off as I look around and realise that we're receiving some attention. It's not obvious, just the odd low-ered voice, or shifty glance. People *are* talking about Cate. And, in the absence of Cate herself, the focus of that atten-tion is her best friend and her boyfriend.

'Marion's looking like she's going to put us through our paces tonight,' Joe says, appearing next to us, mercifully dif-fusing the tension. 'She's limbering up as if she's about to run a 1500-metre race.'

'It'll be because *Dirty Dancing* was on telly the other night,' I reply. 'It will have given her a surge of enthusiasm.'

Joe gives a quick sideways look at Will, but he's not listening and, instead of joining in the banter, he just slips away.

'How's Cate?' Joe asks, as soon as we're alone.

'She's in a terrible state. It was her ex-boyfriend who posted the picture and she's distraught. I've never seen her so low.'

'How awful for her.' He searches my face and seems to register how worried I look. 'Impossible as it probably feels to Cate now, this will blow over, Lauren. I know people gossip and – if you're in the position she's in – that's horrible. I can't imagine how horrible. But they'll find something else to move on to sooner than you think.'

'I'm not sure I share your optimism,' I reply. 'And I don't think Will is as understanding.'

Joe looks surprised by this statement. 'Will hasn't had the *chance* to be understanding. The first he knew of any of this was when he logged on to Facebook and saw the picture on Cate's timeline. Now she won't return his calls.'

'None of this is her fault. This is revenge porn.'

'Of course it's not her fault. This sort of thing is illegal and her ex-boyfriend shouldn't be allowed to get away with it.' I can't exactly tell Joe why Robby very probably will – because Cate's terrified that if she kicks up a fuss, the other pictures will come out too. 'How was your weekend apart from that?' Joe continues.

I search for something to say that doesn't involve the real headlines i.e. I battled with a urinary tract infection and had sex with Edwin.

'Uneventful.' And then I have to look away, for fear that if he gets to see my eyes for too long, all my thoughts will unravel in front of us.

How I wished it had been him kissing me on Saturday night. How I wished it had been his skin against mine, his bed I woke up in. I cannot fully express how hideous these thoughts make me feel, especially when Emily turns up, breathless and slightly late.

It strikes me as the class begins, and Emily dances by my side, that I'd always considered myself to be a good person. A good friend. But if I was either of those things, the thoughts that keep infiltrating my head wouldn't exist in even the most fleeting form.

Yet, despite my feelings, I'm still determined to be the person I *want* to be. So when Joe addresses me in conversation, even in the most innocuous manner, I answer him politely but move on and talk to someone else.

The only problem with this tactic, of course, is that my acting skills have never progressed from when I was four years old and starred as a sheep in the school nativity play. And I feel certain that Emily notices. She's in a very odd mood tonight. Part of me worries that that is because she's on to me. She's guessed that I'm falling for her boyfriend.

'All right?' I ask, when we line up. But if I'm seeking reassurance from Emily, I don't get it. 'You seem a little tense.'

'Well, I'm worried about Cate,' she says stiffly. 'Aren't you?'

'Of course,' I reply, surprised and slightly defensive as I was the one who raced round there tonight.

'Sorry,' she says. 'I didn't mean to imply … oh, I'm a bit wound up about what I've just heard Marion saying in the loos about Cate. I quote, "Anyone who's stupid enough to have a photo taken like that gets all they deserve" and "Never appear in any photograph you wouldn't be happy for your grandmother to see". Must be nice to be as pure as the driven snow, mustn't it?'

'What a cow.' I scrutinise her face. 'Is there anything else?'

'It's just been a tough day – and I'm not feeling great.'

'Really? What's up?' It strikes me that she is looking tired. Still her beautiful self – but her skin is a little sallow, and she's thinner than usual. Not that she had much weight to lose in the first place.

'I think I'm coming down with something. Apart from that, everything's fine. Thanks, Lauren. I'm just glad I've got Joe,' she says, holding my gaze for the last sentence.

Yet, even Joe isn't enough to persuade Emily to stay for longer than twenty minutes. By the break, the class has started to feel like the *Marie Celeste* – no Cate, no Stella, and now Emily's disappearing early too, telling me that she just wants to go home and have a bath. She nips over to kiss Joe on the cheek and then disappears out of the restaurant.

And so we're left to Marion's technical melt-down: every time she tries to put on some salsa classic tonight, her music system blurts out a rousing rendition of the Can-Can – and as much as I'm enjoying these classes generally these days, I draw the line at that.

I studiously try to avoid Joe. Being around him and falling to pieces somehow feels even more treacherous when Emily isn't here than when she is. So when Marion launches into a practice of a turn, I dive towards Frank and grab his hands. Then when she asks us for a volunteer for a new step, I scour the room and spot Esteban, who is looking distinctly miserable since Jilly stopped coming so she could attend a karate class instead. I reach for him with such certainty that I manage to get my bracelet, which is one of my favourites, tangled up in his arm hair, forcing the two of us to dance our way under a lamp to remove it without giving him a full wax job.

When the class is finished, I leave immediately, anxious to get to my car and go home. My Mini, however, has other ideas. I put the key in the ignition and am rewarded with a noise that sounds like a defective combine-harvester.

A bang on the passenger side of the car makes me start. I look up to see Lulu staring through it – then wind down the window to talk to her.

'That sounds bloody awful,' she points out, and I really can't argue with her. 'I wouldn't try to drive that, Lauren. Are you in the AA?'

My heart sinks. 'I cancelled it because I'm going to Singapore. Oh God, I'm going to have to get a taxi.'

'I'd give you a lift if I could, but I've walked here tonight.' She looks up in the direction of the restaurant. 'Someone else'll help, I'm sure. Let me go and ask who's going in your direction.'

'Lulu,' I blurt out, stopping her in her tracks. 'Can I ask you something? In confidence?'

She leans into the window of the car. 'Of course. What is it?'

I hesitate, wondering if there's an easy way of putting this. 'You know . . . Mike?'

Just the mention of his name makes her freeze. 'Yes?'

'Stella found a text from you on his phone. And she felt a little uncomfortable about it. So she apparently confronted Mike and—'

'Are you telling me Stella *knows*?' she asks, her eyes wide. 'About what Mike and I have been up to?'

I swallow. 'I'm sorry.'

'Shit,' she says, standing up and running her hand through her hair. 'Who else knows?'

'Just me. Sorry,' I repeat, wondering why *I'm* apologising.
'Has it been . . . going on a while? You and him, I mean?'

'He started the lessons about a week after he gave up here.'

'Lessons?' I venture.

She sighs. 'Do not tell a soul, Lauren, please. Least of all
Stella. It'd ruin everything.'

'Tell a soul *what?*'

She leans so far into the window that now I'm concerned
she's going to fall in. 'I'm giving Mike private dance lessons –
for his first dance at the wedding. He's learning exactly the
same routine you guys have been working on. But it *has* to be
a secret or it will ruin everything.'

'You're not having an affair with him then?'

She starts spluttering as if she's got something down her
throat and needs a sturdy Heimlich manoeuvre. 'Of course
not! Mike's not going to be having an affair when he's getting
married in a few weeks!'

'Unfortunately, that's what Stella suspects.'

'You've got to be kidding? Why would she still be marrying
him if she suspected that?'

'Because she hasn't got proof. And because she loves him.
And she's already paid for a four-tier fruit cake and a Jenny
Packham dress.'

Lulu looks horrified.

'I think she just hopes she's wrong,' I continue.

'She *is* wrong!'

'Well, she'll be very glad to hear it,' I conclude.

Lulu throws me a stern look. 'Lauren, you can't tell her. You absolutely cannot.'

'Someone's got to,' I argue.

She narrows her eyes on me. 'Swear to me.'

'But, Lulu, it has seriously occurred to Stella that her future husband is having an affair. Surely that's more important.'

'She can't really think that,' she says dismissively. 'Mike obviously doesn't think so and he's the one who's paid all this money and put every spare minute into rehearsing. DO NOT ruin this for him, Lauren. He'd be devastated.'

I look up and see Joe and Will walking down the hill towards us.

'Everything all right, ladies?' Joe asks.

I'm about to say that my car has broken down but stop myself from revealing this in case he offers me a lift. 'Fine!'

'Apart from your breakdown,' says Lulu.

'Oh, I'm sure it'll start in a minute.'

'Go on, give it a go while we're here. We can't just abandon you,' Joe says. I reluctantly sit back in the car, turning the key and praying that the engine starts. 'I'll get a taxi,' I mumble.

'No need. I'll give you a lift,' Joe says decisively.

'No! It's fine. I really don't mind.'

'Neither do I. Come on. I'm only parked over here.'

I rack my brains to think of an inoffensive way to break it to Joe that I want to be a million miles away from him, when he adds, 'I'm taking Will too.'

It occurs to me that if Will's there it'll all be OK. 'Well, all right then. Thanks,' I reply, stepping out of the car and wondering how much of this pressure I can take.

There is an elephant in this Range Rover and it's called Cate. Throughout the journey, I keep waiting for Will to mention her again, but he is resolutely silent on the issue. Which means I have to think of something else to talk about. Anything.

'Have you seen they're opening a new restaurant in Hawkshead? Apparently they've got some Michelin-starred chef up from London. Problem is, they seem to be two a penny around here these days. It wasn't like that when I was a little girl, I can tell you. The food was all right, but I don't remember ever going to a gastro-pub. My dad used to take us to a place in Grasmere, but it wasn't really the done thing in those days to take kids into a pub. I don't even think children's menus had been invented.'

'You must be *very* old, Lauren,' Joe quips.

'Thanks for that,' I reply.

'Well, there'll be a kids' menu at the Moonlight Hotel, I

assure you,' he says. 'It looks fantastic: homemade fish goujons, fruit kebabs and mocktails.'

'I thought you were going for somewhere really upmarket,' I reply.

'Even The Ritz has a children's menu,' he tells me, then hesitates. 'I think.'

'Do you actually know what you're doing with this hotel?' I can't resist asking.

'I've got a very good project manager. Gianni won't let me down. He's worked in all my dad's hotels over the years – he's fantastic.'

Will turns round and looks at me. 'You need to go and see the Moonlight Hotel, Lauren.'

'I don't think so,' I reply.

'Well, I think you should reconsider,' he says. 'I've seen it every step of the way, right from the first time we were due to have a meeting there and ended up at this salsa class.'

'Why were *you* at the meeting, Will?'

'I just wanted an outsider's view of the place,' Joe explains.

'You might be surprised if you go and see it,' Will adds.

'I don't *want* to see it,' I snap. 'And I'm very happy to remain *un*-surprised.'

The car slows and Will unplugs his seatbelt.

'Cheers, pal,' Joe says, slapping him on the shoulder. 'Have a good one.'

'You too, and thanks for the lift.' Then Will turns to me

and looks at me, and for a moment I wonder if he's going to ask me anything about Cate. 'Good night, Lauren. See you next week.'

And then I'm left in the car, alone with Joe, and wondering how I'm going to stop my heart from leaping right out of my chest.

Chapter 40

I absolutely refuse to turn and look at him. Even though I'm dying to. Even though my neck muscles are on springs, pulling me in his direction. Instead, I snatch glances at the way his big, tanned hands move against the gear-stick, the way his thighs press against the seat and his muscles flex when he changes gear.

The chat revolves firmly around tonight's dancing and, although the conversation isn't forced, the journey seems to take for ever. I realise that the only thing that will stop my head throbbing with unwanted thoughts is to be away from him, in the comfort of my own bed, trying my best to focus on Edwin – who is now mine for the taking, after I've apparently worked the sort of bedroom skills that should take six months' intensive training under Madame Sin.

The more I talk, the more I panic that Joe suspects my dark secret, that my toxic attraction to him is written all over my face. My only tactic is to try and deflect attention from it.

'You and Emily make a fantastic couple,' I declare, as if I'm Len Goodman assessing their Rumba. 'You're so good together. I'm thrilled she's found someone like you. You're *so* well-suited!' I glance up, as we turn up the hill and I see that he's taken a diversion.

'Joe, this is the wrong way.' He doesn't answer and my heart trebles in speed. 'You've taken the wrong road.'

'Have I?' He looks at me sideways and concedes a half-smile.

'This is starting to feel like a scene from a movie in which I end up chopped into little pieces, put in a bin bag and thrown into a lake.'

He looks again, unnerved by this statement. 'Sorry. But I absolutely promise I'm not going to murder you. Or chop you up into little pieces. You have my word.'

'Great. Because axe murderers are trustworthy like that. So where are we going?'

But I already know. And even if I didn't, the sign for the Moonlight Hotel looms up on the horizon.

'I see. Well,' I huff, folding my arms across my chest, 'I did say I didn't want to see it. I don't know what makes you think I'm not a woman of my word.'

But he carries on driving until we pull up into a floodlit car park, the familiar lines of the building that is inextricably linked to my past rising above us. He turns off the engine, pulls on the handbrake and looks at me, the soft natural floodlight from the moon casting shadows across his face.

'If you really can't be persuaded, I'll take you home,' he says quietly. 'Obviously, it's up to you. But I'd be lying if I didn't say . . .'

'Say what?'

His jaw clenches. 'That I'm fairly desperate for your approval here,' he confesses, through a laugh. The sentence makes my heart surge. And for a split second as his smile dissolves and he just looks at me, I am lost, utterly, in those eyes.

'Fine,' I snap. 'Let's go and see what a mess you've made of the place.'

Mist swirls around the building, like in a gothic storybook. Spiderwebs cling to the trees and dew sparkles on the ground. Joe unlocks the colossal double doors at the front of the hotel and, with my breath hovering in my throat, I drift towards him, as if in a dream sequence.

I glance over my shoulder at the gardens that lead down to the lake, lawns I'd cartwheel across as a little girl. This was my own private playground, where I was happiest and most secure. The lock clicks.

'Here goes,' Joe whispers, as he pushes open the doors.

As I set eyes on the new lobby of the Moonlight Hotel, I know that this is a moment I shall remember for ever.

Stepping inside, my senses are heightened, my power of speech removed.

The old tiled floor has been refurbished, polished to a sheen, and upon it sits the plushest of furniture, in soft greens and greys, against a single, striking stretch of geometric wallpaper. Above us, the missing pieces of the dusty chandelier have been restored; combined with the subtle uplighters along the wall, it casts a warm light over everything.

There are original features everywhere; the history of the building sings out. But they sit amongst a labyrinth of modern, stylish elements, a visual lullaby of silvers and greens. And in amongst this is the zebra picture. Which looks as mad and brilliant as Joe promised it would.

The whole thing is stunning. And after all my whinging, I want to tell him that, so urgently, I feel as if the words are going to burst out of my mouth.

'Joe, it's—'

'Don't say anything,' he interrupts, pressing a finger to his lips. 'Not yet.'

He reaches out and takes me by the hand, to lead me to the next room.

'This isn't finished yet,' he confides, and releases my hand to open the door and walk ahead. I wish I felt relieved, but I don't. I want his hand back in mine.

'This is going to be the dining room. It leads from the

kitchens over there and we've picked some beautiful furniture for it which is arriving next week.'

Although the room isn't finished, I can see enough to know that it will be incredible. There's a stretch of intricately-patterned paper on some walls, plain sultry colours on others. It's a heavenly pairing of traditional and modern design – and nothing jars. It works so beautifully, I hardly know where to start.

'Joe, it's gorgeous.'

He allows a flicker of pleasure to pass his lips. 'Wait until I've shown you it all before you give me your verdict.'

I pretend to zip up my mouth. 'OK.'

If I was dazzled by the lobby, that's nothing compared to the room I was dreading and desperate to see, in equal measure: the ballroom. It's not finished yet either, but it's close.

Joe has turned a decaying room full of tired furniture and fraying carpets into something magical. The stucco walls are being restored, the floor returned to its original glory. It's the most traditional of all the rooms but there are touches that make it very clear this is a Wilborne hotel.

I step across the oak floor and take it all in as my head fills with memories. 'I used to practise all my ballet routines here when I was a little girl,' I whisper.

'Well, it's a room made for dancing,' he replies. And for a moment I wonder if he's asking.

I continue towards the window to prevent him seeing me

blush. 'I love the fact that you've restored so much,' I say. 'It's completely different from how it was when I was little, but there are touches … they're wonderful. It's going to be incredible.'

He shrugs. 'I've always liked the idea of finding pockets of history and bringing them back to life, so that's what I've tried to do.'

'Is it only this room that needs to be completed?'

'No, some bedrooms have barely been touched yet. One's done though and most are nearly there. Come on, I'll show you.'

He invites me to head up the sweeping, curved staircase. And the biggest thing that strikes me, as Joe walks me through each of the rooms, is how unfeasibly modest he is. Most people would be shouting their achievements from the rooftops, but there's a complete lack of hyperbole.

We start with a couple of the bedrooms at the back of the hotel; one is nowhere near complete, but has a bathroom suite fitted and all the old carpets and fittings torn out.

'Can I see the one that's finished?'

His eyes flick to mine. 'The Honeymoon Suite.'

I blush deeper. 'You old romantic,' I say, forcing a joke.

'Actually, I needed to get one bedroom done quickly so we could put it on our website. I have to get some weddings booked to make back some of the insane amount I've spent on this place.'

'More than pocket-money then?'

'You could say that. Depressingly, a lot of what we've spent isn't even on the stuff you can see.'

'What do you mean?' I don't understand.

He hesitates. 'This information isn't for public consumption because it could result in some negative press, but the reason we had to leap into this refurbishment so quickly – and close the hotel down in the run-up to peak season – was because of a potentially nasty case of dry rot.'

My eyes widen. 'What?'

'No other buyer would touch the place after they'd had it surveyed. But once I'd seen the potential of the place, I wanted to make it work – if we could. So we got our specialists in and they gave us a quote …and once I'd recovered from the shock and persuaded my dad it'd all be worth it, we took the plunge.'

'What would have happened if the dry rot had been left?' I ask.

'Well, untreated, it would have been disastrous. Dry rot can make floors and ceilings collapse – it's a nightmare. But I'm confident we caught it in time, so don't worry, you're quite safe,' he grins.

'You saved the Moonlight Hotel,' I say numbly.

'Well, I hope it'll be worth it,' he replies, pushing open a door. 'Because I'm broke, for the moment at least. If this place doesn't take off, I'll be on the streets selling the *Big Issue* by the end of the year.'

'Somehow, I don't think that's going to happen,' I say, as we step inside.

The Honeymoon Suite is exquisite, there's no other way to describe it – with a vast four-poster bed, smooth, cool sheets, an elegant dressing table and a carpet so plush your feet sink into it.

'Ah, Lauren,' Joe says. 'I've just realised I didn't switch a couple of things off in the restaurant, and if I don't go now and do it, I'll forget.'

'Shall I come with you?'

'You wait here and give this place a thorough inspection. Do your worst. I'll await your verdict when I come back.' And then he smiles the kind of smile that I know will stay with me for days on end and backs out of the door.

I glide through the room, examining every element, afraid to touch anything but desperate to do so at the same time. For so long, I wanted to find fault in what Joe was doing with this place. But seeing first-hand the love and attention that's been lavished on it makes that the last thing I want now. It'd be impossible anyway.

Every piece of furniture is bathed in honeyed light and I slide off my shoes and climb on top of the bed, closing my eyes and letting the softness envelop me. Time seems to tiptoe away as I lie there, drifting in and out of happiness.

Then my eyes flicker open and I sit up and slip off the bed, padding to the doors that lead on to the balcony. I hadn't expected it to open – none of them ever used to – but it does. The floor is cold against the soles of my feet as I prop my elbows on the thick stone rail and gaze across the gardens, towards the shimmering water.

If I imagine hard enough, I can almost see us there – my dad and me, running across that lawn as he chases me then picks me up, flinging me over his shoulder while I laugh so hard I'm crying.

I'm crying.

I realise I'm crying.

'You found the balcony then.'

I spin round, shocked, and sniff back tears self-consciously. Joe frowns and walks towards me. 'What is it?'

And then he does something I really don't want him to do, or at least I know he shouldn't do. Only, as his arms close around me and he pulls me towards him, I know these things are only designed to comfort me. And the thing is, they do. They make my thoughts dissolve until all I can think about is the thudding of his heart against my ears.

He pulls back, but only slightly. Not enough. And he looks at me and whispers, 'Is everything all right?'

The truth is, everything isn't all right. I feel delirious and out of control and as if nothing and nobody can stop me from wanting him to stay just where he is. In the event, he doesn't move. He just looks at me and I look at him until the pleasure and pain of the gaze is unbearable.

As we embrace in the silence, I know exactly what I must do. I must leave.

But I don't.

After one frozen moment, I become aware that we're moving closer together. The expression in his eyes is heavy with desire. *I must leave*.

But I don't.

Not when his mouth is so close to mine that when I breathe in I can almost taste him, the mint he ate in the car and the scent on his throat.

Not when his lips touch mine, the lightest of touches, brushing so gently at first that I wonder if I might have imagined it.

I don't make a conscious decision to kiss him back; it's pure instinct drawing me into the heat of his mouth, desire pumping through me as my lips soften against his. I slide my hands up his neck and pull him closer, and he responds by wrapping his arms tightly around me.

It isn't just desire that I'm feeling. It's pure, white-hot exhilaration. The rights and wrongs of this don't even enter my head. There's no room for them. Not when instinct on every level is making me submit to this unprecedented kiss, a kiss that leads to both of us tumbling on to the bed.

We are soon devouring each other, my hands running

across his back, heat pulsating through me at the feel of him. I wonder how a touch that's so bad can feel so good.

And it's that thought which makes me falter, for the first time.

So bad.

So very bad.

I pull away and sit up, trying to catch my breath. 'I can't believe that just happened,' I gasp, the back of my hand against my mouth.

When he doesn't respond, I look round.

'Why?' he says defiantly.

I look at him, incredulous. 'Because of Emily! God Almighty . . . I've never done the dirty on anyone before. It's not the type of person I am. I just can't—'

'Lauren, stop,' he interrupts. 'My relationship with Emily is—'

'Emily is crazy about you.' He's about to object, but I'm too fast. 'You might not realise it, but it's true,' I say, scrambling for my shoes and thrusting them on my feet. 'I need to go,' I tell him urgently, as I stand and dart for the door.

'Lauren, please,' he calls out, but I don't stop. I hurtle down the stairs ten to the dozen, realising he's right behind me. When we reach the door I start fumbling with the lock.

'Here, you need a key,' he says, pulling a fob from his back pocket and starting to unlock it. I cannot be out of there quickly enough.

'You can't just go running into the night, Lauren,' he says, opening the door. 'At least let me give you a lift home.'

'I'm fine,' I say, because if I remain in front of him for a moment longer I'm just not sure I'll be able to bear it. 'I can walk.'

'It is *miles* to your house.'

At that, I am forced to admit that getting home from here on foot is a near-impossible task. So I have to endure waiting while Joe switches everything off, locks up and jumps into his Range Rover. As he drives me home, we sit in excruciating silence. There just isn't anything to say, and I'm too appalled with myself to bear to hear my own voice.

'Thanks for the lift,' I say when we finally reach my house. I go to open the door, but he grabs my hand.

'Lauren—'

'Save it, Joe. Please,' I reply, and walk up my path engulfed by a wave of guilt and shame. And the knowledge that, contrary to everything I've ever assumed, I am possibly the worst friend in the entire world.

Chapter 41

I text Joyce the next morning to ask for a lift into school, given that my car is out of action. She spends the entire journey discussing Zoella, with whom she has developed an obsession after her niece introduced her to the delights of YouTube. When I get to school, I phone Brian, a mechanic friend of my mum's who runs a garage in Windermere. He agrees to go and look at the car and ring as soon as he knows the (presumably expensive) score.

But it's at lunchtime when the thing for which I've been longing, for more than two years happens: Edwin asks me out. Although it would be more accurate to say he *begs* me. I can almost see him salivating as we stand next to each other in the lunch queue, waiting to be served.

It's stew and congealed rice pudding today, as if I hadn't lost my appetite enough already.

The problem, apart from the rice pudding, is that despite Edwin chomping so hard at the bit he's on the verge of dislodging a filling, I can't even focus on the fact that he actually wants me now.

All I can think about is Joe and last night. And what I've done to Emily. My loyal, lovely friend who has been with me and Cate through thick and thin. I've always felt that she knew what I'd been through when Dad died after her brother's death in a car crash. It was Emily and Cate who got me through The Edwin Years, as much of a damp squib as they turned out. And now, what kind of friend have I become that I'd allow her boyfriend, even for a second, to put his lips anywhere near mine?

What's worse than any of this is the fact that I wanted it, not just in the half a minute or so when it was happening. I wanted him to continue. *All night.*

I take a spoonful of rice pudding and wonder if what happened in the Honeymoon Suite of the Moonlight Hotel represented some bizarre displaced affection on my part because he's filled my dad's hotel full of nice cushion covers and kept the chandelier – and OK, saved the place from certain dereliction? Perhaps it was the hotel, the memories that I fell in love with, not Joe and—

God, what am I saying? *Love?* Seriously?

There's only one man I've ever used the L word about – ever – and he's sitting in front of me now, trying to persuade me to come over tonight to watch *The Great British Bake Off* with him.

'It's pastry night. Though I do realise it's sad that I know that,' he smiles.

'Not at all – I love the *Bake Off* too,' I reassure him.

'I wonder how long it'll take Paul to complain about some-one's soggy bottom? He hates them. Though don't we all,' he smirks.

I force a smile and he looks terribly disappointed with this reaction, as if it's worthy of a voluminous guffaw. Like he's used to.

'OK, Edwin,' I say decisively. 'I'll come and watch the *Bake Off* with you. It's a deal.'

He sits up a little straighter. 'Excellent. I might get some Prosecco in. Or I can cook for you again if you like? I honestly don't mind.'

'Oh, no – don't go to any trouble.' I squirm.

He sits and holds my gaze until it becomes a bit uncomfort-able. 'Nothing is too much trouble, Lauren,' he says in a low voice. Then, to my alarm, he reaches over to whisper in my ear. 'If I could kiss you right now, I would.'

I realise a group of Year Ones are looking at us.

'I need to fetch something from the staff room,' I announce, standing up and grabbing my tray. 'See you later, Edwin.'

'See you at 8 p.m., then,' he winks. 'And don't be late, or you'll miss the technical challenge. Though I could always set you a technical challenge all your own . . .'

I get back into the staff room and take a call from Brian,

who tells me that my car just had a flat battery and, as a favour to Mum, he agrees to tow it to school for me and get it going again. I'm ending the call, overflowing with profuse gratitude, when a text pings on to my phone. I somehow knew Joe would be in touch. But it doesn't stop my stomach from lurching when I open up his message.

> Sorry if it got a bit weird last night – because I don't want things to be weird between us. Can we have a chat? x

I compose a text back. Joe, I feel sick about what happened last night and the only way I can think of to deal with this is by staying as far from you as possible. I hope you can respect that.

As I press Send, I am reminded that I am going to Singapore in a matter of weeks. Which is good. Because that's when my world is going to get back on track. This is what's going to happen: I'll end up with Edwin. And Emily will stay with Joe.

I am suddenly gripped by a panicked thought: that he might tell her what I did. What *he* did. Then I tell myself not to be so stupid. He's hardly going to confess to her that *he's* been unfaithful, is he? He might be a cad – and me a disloyal bitch – but neither of us are complete idiots. And neither of us, I suspect, could bear the effect this revelation could have on Emily.

I sit on one of the soft-back chairs and close my eyes, desperate to try and think for the ten minutes left before my next lesson. But as the coffee machine drips, my head just seems to spin harder – until my thoughts are interrupted by the beep of my phone. This time it's from Emily.

Can you talk? I know you're at work, but this is urgent. Will you give me a ring? It seems uncharacteristically blunt and unfriendly.

I hastily gather my things and head outside into the car park, where I dial her number. She answers after one ring.

'I need to talk to you, Lauren,' she hisses, clearly trying to keep this conversation private from whomever she's with.

I swallow. 'What about?'

'It's not something I can discuss on the phone. Can you meet me?' Her voice is strangled.

'Sure, when?' I ask.

'Straight after work?'

'Of course, no problem at all. How about at the Wateredge Inn?'

'OK. Good,' she replies. 'I'll see you then, shall I?'

'Yep,' I say. 'And Emily – is everything all right?'

She pauses. 'No, Lauren. I can't honestly say it is.'

Chapter 42

The rest of the afternoon is torture. All I can think about is Emily and how the conversation might unfold when I meet her. I'm so fixated on the issue that, as I dart out of work as early as I can get away with and climb into my car, I almost don't hear my phone ring. As I register a muffled tone, I wrestle it out of my bag and see Mum's name on the screen. I press answer.

'I'm just phoning to see if Brian managed to fix your car?'

'He did,' I say, feeling too distracted to add anything further to this conversation.

'Did he charge you?'

'No, he didn't, unbelievably. Thanks for putting me in touch with him, Mum.'

'He's a good bloke.'

'I'll drop him an email to say thank you again,' I reply. 'Listen, Mum, I'm sorry to run but—'

'Before you go ... I found out about the gazebo you were asking about.'

I put the key in the ignition. 'Really?'

'I bumped into Brenda McCullum. Do you remember her?'

'I'm afraid I don't.'

'She was your dad's deputy for a while. She had a son with autism and they lived in Coniston, and—'

'So what did she say?'

'There was a fire, shortly before your dad became ill. It was only after she'd said it that I remembered. It wasn't a big one, no one was hurt. But part of the gazebo was damaged and had to be torn down. Your dad had been trying to persuade the owners of the Moonlight Hotel to let him order a replacement. Then he became ill and everything overtook it.'

'I don't remember any of this.'

'No,' she says softly. 'We had other things to worry about at the time, didn't we?'

I arrive at the Wateredge Inn, at the apex of Windermere and, seeing that Em isn't here, buy two glasses of wine to take outside to the beer garden. There's a table in front of the marina, where I set down the drinks and sit, unable to stop my fingers twitching against the wood legs as I wait. There are a handful of swing benches across from me, all occupied by couples gazing across the sunlit water and suppressing smiles at the two young boys playing hide and seek behind the bushes.

A shadow appears on the table and I look up to see Emily

standing above, her jaw clenched. She lowers herself on to the bench, refusing to look at me.

'I don't want that,' she says flatly, gesturing at the glass of wine.

And that's all it takes for me to be certain: she knows.

She knows what's happened between Joe and me and she hates me for it so much she can't even bear to share a drink with me.

I can hardly blame her.

I brace myself for the conversation we're about to have, the confrontation and the absolute knowledge that I will get down on my knees and beg for her forgiveness. But as she starts talking, the words that tumble from her mouth feel woolly and disjointed, and it's hard to process them.

'You know how sometimes, you're on your little path,' she begins, 'and things might not be perfect, but you're so happy and grateful to be with someone that the thought that something might happen to throw everything into disarray doesn't even cross your mind?'

I nod and feel tears gather in my eyes.

'That's how I've been feeling lately: head over heels in love. Knowing that this is the strongest and hardest and best I'll ever feel about another human being. And, not even looking to the future, because I was so incredibly exhilarated by the present.'

'Is that how you feel, Emily?' I manage.

She looks down at the ground. 'That's how I *felt*.'

'But something's changed?'

She nods. 'Everything's changed.'

My spine seems to chill.

'I've found out something and I honestly don't know how to handle it, Lauren.' She looks into my eyes.

'I understand.' I wait for her big eruption. For the drink thrown in my face. For the shouting, the screaming, the cries of what a bitch I am and how I've ruined her life, her relationship. All of which I'd deserve.

But when I lift up my chin, I see that she's not doing any of those things. And as a single, salty tear slips down her face, she looks up and says the words that change everything.

'I'm pregnant.'

I feel as though I've been winded. I can't talk, but neither can Emily. She just sits, sobbing quietly as I walk round the bench, sit down and embrace her, my mind twisting and turning.

'Does Joe know?'

She wipes away the tears. 'Lauren, I don't want Joe to know. Not yet. You mustn't say anything.'

I frown, taking this in. 'OK . . .'

'I don't want *anyone* to know. Not until I've decided what to do.'

It takes a second for the meaning behind her words to filter through. 'You're thinking of having an abortion?' As soon as I've said it I wonder why I'm surprised. Emily has never wanted kids and she doesn't have a desk job where she could put up her feet and look forward to maternity leave. She quite simply couldn't continue to climb up mountains while pregnant.

She starts sobbing again. 'I don't know what I'm going to do. This is such a mess.'

I clutch her hand. 'When did you find out?'

'Last night, after salsa,' she sniffs. 'I've been puking up my guts for the last week – I can't keep a damn thing down. Then I stopped off at Booths and bought a pregnancy test on the way home. I did it as soon as I got in the house.'

The irony hits me with a queasy punch that I could well have been kissing Joe – rolling around in the Honeymoon Suite with him, no less – while Emily was busy discovering that he had fathered her first child.

I feel sick with guilt. Sick with disgust. Sick with hatred – for Joe, but most of all for me. My treachery.

'What am I going to do, Lauren?'

'Surely ... Joe is the first person you need to discuss it with.'

'Lauren, *no*,' she says, glaring at me defiantly. '*Nobody* can know. Not Joe. Not Cate. Not my mum. Not anyone.'

'OK. I've got it.' I take another slug of wine. She reaches for hers, then hesitates, before pushing it away. Her mind is clearly not made up on the future of this baby.

'I want you to know this,' I tell her. 'Whatever you decide to do, Emily, I will be right behind you. I'll support you. If you decide to have the baby—'

'I can't contemplate anything that far ahead. I just need to *think*.' She reaches over and clutches my hand again. 'Thanks for being such a good listener, Lauren. I don't know what I'd do without you.'

'Don't say that.' This is the closest I've ever come to wanting to die on the spot.

'But it's true,' she insists.

I look out across the lake as the two little boys find a free swing bench and start pushing it far harder than it was designed for. And one thought engulfs me: how impossible it would be to stay here – with Emily, Joe and their baby – and for me ever to be able to live with myself.

Chapter 43

I arrive at Edwin's house forty minutes after we'd arranged and he answers the door in a state of breathless pandemonium. 'They're already on to the second challenge. The first was a Princesstårta.' He shuffles me through the door urgently. 'It's a tart made with custard, whipped cream, marzipan and a bright green covering. Quite the thing if you're at a Swedish dinner party. Quick – can't miss the next one.'

He darts into the living room and leaps over the back of the sofa, in time to catch Paul Hollywood confide that he 'prefers the big ones', something I can only assume refers to the batch of macaroons in front of him.

As I approach the sofa, the scene is similar to the kind you'd expect from a bloke during the FA Cup Final. Only Edwin's version is rather different. He is not surrounded by cans of Stella but there's an empty bottle of Prosecco lying at his feet, along with half a plate of *bruschette al pomodoro*, garnished with rocket. I can tell before I sit next to him that he's tipsy, and for a moment it feels nice to be the sober one after the fiasco last time I was in this flat.

'You look gorgeous,' he declares, taking a bite out of a bruschetta.

'Thanks, Edwin,' I reply awkwardly as he tears his eyes away back to the television. I have no wish to be here after what I've just learned from Emily, but I didn't want to let Edwin down. Also, I thought it might distract me from the urge to throw myself under a bus. 'Should I help myself to a drink?'

He is momentarily torn between good manners and Mary and Paul.

'Of course. What can I get you, hun?' he replies and, putting aside my abject shock at being called 'hun' by Edwin, I tell him I'll have a glass of water but insist on getting it myself.

When I return to the sofa for the rest of the *Bake Off*, it's fair to say that I'm fighting a losing battle for Edwin's attention against seven Austrian tortes and a batch of rosemary-infused drop scones. The thing is, I don't mind. I'm actually relieved that Edwin is so distracted, because it takes the pressure of his gaze away from me, at least until Mel and Sue say cheeri-bye and the closing credits roll.

'Brilliant television,' he concludes.

'It's a great show,' I nod, though all I've done is let my eyes roll in and out of focus as I battle with thoughts of Emily, Joe, the baby . . . and last night.

He peers at my glass. 'Oh, I forgot – I bought some fizz for us,' he says, picking up the bottle. Confusion simmers on his brow as he realises it's empty. 'I must've spilled some. Sorry, Lauren.'

'It's absolutely fine,' I reassure him.

He tuts. 'Well, I'm annoyed with myself. I'd wanted everything to be perfect. I thought we'd do the *Bake Off* then chat about Singapore and ... get to know each other even better.' He holds my gaze. '*Like the other night.*'

'Yes, about that ... ' But I can't bring myself to go any further, even though I'd love to know what actually happened.

He leans in, gazing into my eyes, his mouth dropping as if lust and gravity are directly related. 'Hmm.' He focuses on my lips until he's nearly cross-eyed.

'I've been thinking about what happened,' I cough. 'Or what *might've* happened.'

'I can show you if you like?' he offers.

I freeze, engulfed by the certainty that I *do not* want to rediscover first-hand what happened with Edwin the other night.

It's not even that my attraction to Edwin has diminished. It's more than that. I am actively *un-attracted* to him. He is suddenly about as gorgeous as a fungal toenail infection.

If you'd told me I'd ever feel like this six months ago, when my feelings for Edwin were passionate and overwhelming – I might have almost felt relieved at being unshackled from these emotions. But I don't. Instead, I feel terrible.

How can I *not* find Edwin attractive any more, just because I've slept with him, even if it was non-penetratively? What does this make me? A *toxic female* probably – because if some bloke had come along and done this to one of my friends, I'd unquestionably say that he was a commitment-phobe who loved the thrill of the chase. That he was a sad, pathetic cad who'd had his wicked way, then gone cold.

Well, here I am, doing exactly the same. And what's worse, I can't even remember the wicked way. All I know is that Edwin no longer sends me into fits of rapture when he looks into my eyes. He just alarms me. The manifest problems that this unravelling situation presents is enough to make my head ache. It's not just in his flat, here and now, with him going in for the kill. It's Singapore. It's everything. It's . . .

'It's all too much!' I say aloud and he looks up, shocked.

'What is?'

And although I can't untangle the most pressing issue in my life right now, I can at least attempt to put things straight with Edwin. 'Look, I've been attracted to you for quite a long time,' I confess.

He grins. 'I know.'

'And . . . well, I suppose deep down part of me thought something like this would never happen between us.'

'Well, I'm all yours.' At that he opens his arms wide and goes to lean back on the other end of the sofa, but instead falls directly off it – and plonks, bum first, on the floor.

'OHHH GODDD!' he shrieks.

I scramble down to his side. 'What's the matter?'

'It's my coccyx!' he exclaims, and it takes a moment before I realise he's not referring to the thing I apparently got to grips with last week. 'It's no end of trouble,' he continues, clutching his lower back as he winces in pain.

I try and help him up, feeling as if I'm in a nursing home and about to give him a bed-bath.

'I'm afraid this might put paid to anything too physical this evening. I'm so sorry.'

'What a shame,' I exclaim.

He does a double-take. 'Lauren, can I ask you something?'

I cough. 'Of course.'

'Have you gone off me?'

Oh my God. This is my get-out clause, but suddenly saying this directly to Edwin seems horribly harsh.

'I'm extremely fond of you, and er . . .'

'You've gone off me,' he concludes sulkily. You could never accuse Edwin of being stupid.

'Edwin, you'll always be my friend . . .'

'I don't want to be your *friend*, Lauren,' he hisses. 'I don't want pity. You've led me on for two years, you do realise?'

'I wasn't leading you on,' I argue.

'I dumped my girlfriend for you!

'I didn't have anything to do with that!'

'You had *everything* to do with that,' he fires back. 'I would never have looked at another woman had you not come along fluttering your eyelashes every morning and pretending you liked my mum's baking.'

'I wasn't trying to lead you on. My feelings for you were real. I felt very strongly for you.'

'*Felt?* Forgive me, Lauren, for noticing your use of the past participle. Come on, tell me: What have I done wrong?'

And as I sit, self-loathing once again sweeping over me, I'm not sure I can answer that question.

Chapter 44

I try to avoid Edwin the following day, although to be honest, he is the least of my worries. All I can think about is Emily, with whom I exchange several texts throughout the day – about how she's feeling even sicker, is in turmoil about what to do and how I *mustn't* tell anyone, words she can't seem to repeat enough.

By the time the bell goes and I drive over to Cate's, my head is pounding with it all.

I don't bother giving Cate an update about Edwin when she asks, I just mumble something about not feeling the same about him any more. In other circumstances, she'd have me pinned down on a chair, grilling me for information about this volte-face, but she has other things on her mind. Including wine.

I deliberately refused to bring something so she could self-medicate herself into a stupor, but now she wants a drink it doesn't feel like the right time to deny her. The pub is out of the question, so I suggest we go for a walk to the convenience shop. I suspect it's the first time she's been out – and not cowering in the back of the shop or her flat – since the picture reappeared on Facebook on Tuesday.

It's a sunny evening, but the air is heavy with moisture when we step out of her flat, and by the time we're at the bottom of her road, the light drizzle has become heavy enough for me to push up an umbrella. The glimmer of a rainbow appears on the horizon as we turn the corner. It hardly feels appropriate to our mood. We reach the shop and Cate slows outside the window as a woman serving at the till, who looks to be in her early sixties and has blonde, bobbed hair, looks up at us. Her expression changes when she recognises Cate.

'Here's the money,' Cate mutters, thrusting a ten-pound note in my hand. 'You get the wine and I'll wait outside?'

'But don't you want to get out of the rain?'

'I'm fine with the umbrella,' she insists. 'And I've got my hood.'

I find a bottle of white on offer and wait in a lengthy queue before I'm served, though not by the woman who recognised my apparently infamous friend. When I emerge, Cate is itching to return to the safety of her flat.

And as we walk through the streets, I realise why: people *are* looking at her. Not everyone, not even most people. But you can see the occasional sideways glances; the snatched looks. Cate's notoriety is no mere figment of her imagination.

'You shouldn't be intimidated about the idea of seeing people you know,' I hear myself saying as we tramp back up the hill.

She frowns at me, looking suddenly hurt, as if I don't understand.

'I completely get it, why you feel like you do,' I add hastily. 'I'm simply saying that you mustn't go into hiding. You haven't done anything wrong.'

'I've come out tonight, haven't I?'

'If you count the Spar as "out", I suppose so,' I say gently.

'And I saw Will this afternoon,' she adds.

I stop in my tracks, shocked that she's only just mentioning this. 'Good. Great, in fact. So . . . how is everything?'

'Fine,' she shrugs, taking her keys out of her pocket as we approach the flat. 'He came over. I made him a coffee. He went.'

'Is that all?' It strikes me that they had a significant amount of unaddressed business to catch up on, not just a coffee.

We plod up her stairs and she puts her key in the door, then her shoulders slump. 'No, that wasn't all,' she says. 'Come in.'

We get inside and the story tumbles out. Will came over and they talked about the pictures, despite how mortifying Cate found the entire conversation. He looked confused and pitying and angry and sad. But they ended up kissing and for one sweet, fleeting moment Cate convinced herself that it was all going to be OK.

'Then he went to the loo and a text arrived, from his mum.' She lowers her head. 'I didn't even mean to see it, but it beeped and I just rolled over and instinctively picked up the phone.'

'What did it say?'

'It said, I feel awful about upsetting you earlier, but I promise I'm only thinking of you. You need to stay away from girls like that, Will. The whole thing will come to no good. Give me a ring if you want a chat – love Mum xx.

'Oh God.'

'Exactly.'

'Well, Will's obviously heard what she thinks about you and decided he shouldn't stay away.'

She sniffs. 'He didn't know I'd seen the text, but when he picked up his phone and read it, everything changed. He left shortly afterwards. I don't blame him in the slightest.'

'What makes you say that everything changed? What did he say?'

'It was nothing he said. I can just tell, Lauren,' she says, dropping on to the sofa. 'He hasn't been in touch since then.'

'It *was* only yesterday.'

'I agree with his mum,' she says defiantly. 'He could have any girl he wants, not someone the whole of Twitter is calling a slut and who can't walk round her own town any more without knowing that every second person has seen that picture. His mum's totally right: it can come to no good.'

I'm about to protest, when the bell rings. 'Do you want me to get it?' I offer.

She thinks for a moment, anguish etched in her forehead. 'Don't worry.' She pushes herself up and heads into the hall. I can hear Will's voice, even though I'm in the next room and the door is shut. I turn on the TV to try and drown out their conversation and give them some privacy. But as the volume rises, it's impossible to avoid hearing the entire sorry saga unfold.

'Cate, why are you pushing me away? I've come to try to get through to you, to tell you that I love you. To *show* you that I love you. What more do you want me to do?'

'Not raising your voice at me would help for a start,' she fires back, apparently oblivious that she's significantly louder than him. 'I don't need you swanning in here, Will, having spent twenty-four hours clearly wondering what the right thing to do is. I can see this isn't easy for you. But let me reassure you, I'm fine by myself.'

'So I'm surplus to requirements now? There is absolutely nothing I can do – nothing at all – that is any use to you?'

'Just don't do *this*, Will . . .'

'Do *what*?'

'You know what. Make a big thing of this. Don't you think I've got enough going on in my life right now without you acting like this?'

'When did *I* become the bad guy, Cate?' He sounds incredulous. 'Aren't I the guy who's standing here, in front of you, despite everything? Aren't I the guy who doesn't give a fuck what photos there are of you out there? Aren't I the guy who's shown nothing but loyalty and determination to get through to you that I think you're the most amazing woman on earth? What more do you want from me?'

'For you not to be standing on my doorstep yelling at me, for a start!' she shrieks.

And, even before the next words are out of her mouth, I know what's happening. I can see it coming: she is about to screw this up with Will. Irreversibly.

'You seem to think you're some sort of fucking hero, Will. Well, congratulations! You're in the "great guy" club – you've got a girlfriend who's a slag and who everyone looks down on *but you don't mind!* You're not shallow enough to dump her . . . yet.'

His silence can only be explained by disbelief. And I'll admit I'm with him on that one.

'OK, I give up,' he says finally. 'You win, Cate. I'm out of your life.'

Chapter 45

That night I am forced to think hard about an unavoidable and increasingly pressing issue: Singapore. There's no escaping it. I might have handed in my notice at work, convinced everyone around me that it's where my destiny lies and even booked a bloody flight there. But one fact remains. It's the last place on earth I want to be.

Ironically, I wish this wasn't the case. The urge to get out of here – and away from Emily and Joe – is overwhelming. And that's still got to happen. But it won't be to Singapore, where there is nothing for me, except a psychotic flatmate whom I've no desire to meet and Edwin, who hates me.

I set my alarm for half an hour earlier than usual so I can phone Ms Heng to break it to her that I won't be coming to work at St Anne's Primary School in Yishun any time soon. It's fair to say she's not very pleased.

'A series of very, very unfortunate personal circumstances have emerged that means I'm tragically unable to take up the position,' I begin, hoping I sound suitably distressed enough for her to not pry any further. 'I'm terribly sorry to do this. But it's completely unavoidable.'

'Has somebody died?' she demands.

'No, not exactly – '

'Are they terminally ill?'

'No. They're really . . . family circumstances.'

'A divorce?'

'Well, no.'

'So *you're* ill?'

'It's not something I'd feel comfortable going into. I hope you understand,' I reply, aiming to give this the impression that she's hit the nail on the head but it's too sensitive for her to delve further.

'Well, you've let us down with weeks to go. So I hope *you* understand why it's fairly important I know what the issue is. So what is it?'

Wildly, I come up with: I have irritable bowel syndrome, which at least has the benefit of shutting her up.

I make it through the day without bumping into Edwin, and decide, on a whim, to go over to Mum's house after school. I arrive to find her on her hands and knees at the back of the house, attempting to unblock a drain. I won't go into the smell, beyond the fact that I'm convinced it singes my nasal hairs.

'Wouldn't you be better calling a plumber?' I ask. She looks at me as if this is as ludicrous a suggestion as hiring John Frieda himself to come round and personally apply her Head & Shoulders.

'Don't be daft,' she says, stuffing her rubber glove down further, before looking up at me expectantly, and asking meaningfully: 'Did you want to help?'

I look round, hoping she must be talking to someone else. 'I'm ready to give you all the moral support you need,' I say, and she grunts. 'How about I go and make some tea?'

I'm in the kitchen straining the tea bags when she walks in, streaks of mud on her cheeks as if she's about to go on a mission with Rambo. 'There,' I say, handing a mug to her.

'Cheers,' she replies, taking a slurp. 'To what do I owe the pleasure?'

'I just thought I'd stop by, that's all. And ... I thought I'd let you know that I'm no longer going to Singapore.'

I actually feel ridiculous saying it, a sensation her perplexed expression does nothing to abate.

'I thought you were excited about going to Singapore?' she says. 'What happened to it "definitely being the place for you"?'

'I made a mistake,' I mumble.

'Right,' she says, in this oddly flat tone that conveys the message 'nothing surprises me about you any more'. 'So does that mean you're staying here? Or that the saving for Australia's back on again?'

'Australia,' I mumble.

And although it's been on, then off again like a defective boiler, at the moment it's my only option. Because if Joe and Emily *do* become parents, I cannot be here to watch. I just can't.

'Well, I'm not sure I understand, but there's nothing new there,' Mum philosophises. 'One thing's for sure though: Steph'll be pleased.'

And so I stumble back into planning to save for Australia again. Although, obviously now that leaving ASAP is a priority, I also need to get a job out there, so have registered with a teaching agency and am keeping my fingers crossed that some interviews come up soon. I am consumed with worry about leaving Cate, but it's impossible for me to hang around here any longer.

Planning to go to Australia again feels like crawling back to an old boyfriend after you've betrayed him. But it's the best option I've got. And it at least gives me something to think about, something to plan for. Something to dwell on that isn't Emily and Joe's baby.

I've had a creeping certainty, ever since she told me, that Emily will decide to keep the baby. I know my friend. Emily might never have actively wanted kids, but she's always been the type who believes in fate, that things happen for a reason – something she actually said in one of her texts to me yesterday. I'm equally certain that, although Joe tried to convince me his feelings for her didn't amount to much, he'll try to make a go of things with her. As a family.

I find my mind drifting every so often to thoughts of what Joe would be like as a father.

If you'd asked me before our kiss in the Moonlight Hotel, I'd have imagined him to be made for it, one of those guys you can effortlessly picture kicking around a football with his young son, or hoisting his little girl on his shoulders on a sunny day. You only had to see how proud he looked when talking about his twelve-year-old niece. But that kiss made every perception about him unravel. He's not the fine, upstanding potential dad I believed him to be. Though, come to think of it, what do the events of the last few days make *me*?

'Miss Scott?' I snap out of my contemplation and find Tom Goodwin at my side, while the other children complete the self-portraits I'd tasked them with.

'What is it, Tom?'

'Miss, I've had an accident.'

I look down to see a dark patch on the front of his trousers, distress etched in his little face. 'Oh dear. Not to worry, Tom,' I say gently. 'Let's go and get you cleaned up.'

I leave Angela in charge of the class and take Tom down to the toilets, collecting his PE kit en route so he can change into a clean pair of jogging bottoms.

'Did you forget to go to the toilet at break, Tom?'

'I don't know,' he says, under his breath. 'It just happened.'

I've been teaching Tom since last September and, until two weeks ago, he'd never wet himself. Now it's happened three times. Sometimes, with children of this age, this just happens; there's no particular explanation for it beyond the fact that they're easily distracted. But I can't help wondering about Tom, how sad he's been lately – and what he tells me is going on at home.

'I want you to make sure that at the start of every break-time you go to the toilet,' I remind him. 'And when you think you've finished, you need to squeeze your tummy muscles to make sure there's absolutely none left. OK?'

He nods slowly, then his eyes flick up to mine. 'Miss?'

'Yes, Tom?'

'If my mum and dad get divorced, will I be the only one in our class whose dad doesn't live with them?'

I reach out briefly to pat his little shoulder. 'No, Tom, you wouldn't be. I grew up without my dad around too.'

He looks up, surprised, as if it had never occurred to him that I'd have parents too, that there was a time when I was a little girl. He doesn't answer, as I wrap up his wet trousers in a plastic carrier bag. Then we wash our hands, he picks up his PE bag and we head into the corridor together. 'Have you spoken to your mum like I suggested?' I ask. 'About what you heard her talking about with your dad?'

He looks down and shakes his head. And I realise I'm going to have to have one conversation that's just no longer avoidable.

Jenny Goodwin, Tom's mum, is chatting to another mum at home-time. She looks thinner than when I last saw her, her wisps of blonde hair brushed back from her pale, pretty face. I wave at her through the throng of parents and when she spots me she comes straight over.

'Hello, Miss Scott. Everything all right?' she asks.

'I wondered if I could have a quick chat before I send Tom out.' Her expression becomes anxious. 'Nothing to worry about.'

Mrs Goodwin and I find a quiet corner of the assembly hall while Tom plays in the after-school club room with the other children. 'What is it?' she asks immediately, clearly not buying my 'nothing to worry about' line.

'I wanted to let you know that Tom wet himself again today. And I thought I ought to tell you about a conversation I had with him.' It's impossible not to feel awkward. 'He was upset afterwards. He didn't really want to tell me why, but he referred to some ... changes that were happening at home.'

She bites her lip. 'What changes?'

It takes a moment to think of the right way to say this. 'He seems to think you and Mr Goodwin are getting divorced.'

Her breath is released in a long trail, her expression agonised.

'Oh God … he must've heard us arguing. Children pick up so much. You think you can protect them, but you can't.'

'I didn't know whether to say anything, Mrs Goodwin – it's really none of my business,' I find myself blabbering. 'And I should stress that there are other children whose parents have divorced in the school and they've taken the whole thing in their stride. So it doesn't *need* to be difficult for a child and, I mean, it's a fact of life these days. But I just thought I ought to mention that Tom's aware of it, because it's clearly on his mind.'

When she looks up at me there is a film of tears on her eyes. 'I'll talk to him,' she says, her breath catching in her throat. 'But, just so you know, we're *not* getting divorced.'

'Oh, right.' I feel temporarily relieved that Tom might have got the wrong end of the stick.

'I'm determined we're not,' she goes on. 'I'm going to do everything I can to keep this family together.'

I simply nod. I don't want to know the ins and outs of what's going on at home; I just want Jenny and Tom's dad Nick to try and do the best for their little boy.

'We've been going through a rough patch, that's all,' she tells me. 'But Tom's dad and I, we're still in love. We've made amends.'

'That's good to hear,' I conclude, but she wants to convince me.

'He gave me this at the weekend.' She holds out her hand and displays a diamond ring. I'm no expert, clearly, but it doesn't look cheap. 'You don't give that to someone if you think nothing of them, do you?'

'No, I don't think you do,' I reply.

She pushes her hand into her pocket. 'I know what you're probably thinking. This is just a thing. But it means more than that to me. And I think it does to him too. I love my husband and son more than anything else on earth. And I know Nick loves me too. It'll take more than a rough patch like this for him to break up our family.'

I nod. It's time to end this conversation.

'Well, like I say, I just thought you'd want to know about Tom. So maybe you could have a chat with him?'

'I will,' she says hastily, clutching her bag into her chest. 'And thank you.'

That night, Steph Skypes me. Which I'm glad about because I've been putting off sloping back to her with my tail between my legs to tell her my trip's back on. Contrary to Mum's prediction, she doesn't greet the news with unrestrained joy.

'I believe you've decided to come,' she says, with mealy-mouthed satisfaction. 'Well, the flat I'd earmarked in Bondi has gone. We might end up with somewhere away from the beach. Somewhere quiet, where hardly anything's going on. No all-night parties. No tattoo parlours. No *fun*.'

'I'm sure we can make our own fun. Or just walk to all those places, don't you think?'

Her expression softens. 'So . . . you're definitely coming?'

'Looks that way.' I smile tentatively.

She is briefly silent, before exploding into peals of laughter. 'Oh, Loz! OK, I'll admit it. It's been shit since you said you were backing out. I mean, I've met people here, but it's not the same as family. Or friends – real friends. You had me worried. I thought I was going to have to go to all these beach barbecues by myself. Or at least with Jimbo here,' she grins, hooking her arm round a thick, tanned neck and planting her lips on its owner's cheek.

The guy pulls back. 'It's Jason,' he corrects her.

'Whatevs,' she replies, jumping on him again and clicking shut her laptop.

Chapter 46

I don't go to salsa the following evening; nor does Cate, nor Emily, all of us absent for different but equally horrible circumstances.

The following day after work, I've pulled up in front of the house when the phone rings and I glance down to see Joe's number. My heart trebles in speed as I consider for a moment not answering it. But before I can think enough to stop myself, I pull on the handbrake and press the green button.

'Hello, Lauren,' he says, clearly surprised I picked up.

The roof of my mouth feels like a sandpit. 'Hi.'

'I know you said you didn't want to talk, but I need to explain a few things. How things have been with Emily, for example and . . . well—'

'I *know* how things have been with Emily,' I interrupt fiercely, not wanting to hear him try to justify his actions by explaining he's somehow gone off her. 'I don't need you to explain anything at all.'

He doesn't answer at first. Then, when he speaks, my chest contracts, as if my heart is physically breaking. 'What you don't know is what I feel for *you*, Lauren. You can't possibly know.'

Tears gather in the rims of my eyes as I answer with the weakest excuse in the world. 'I'm sorry, Joe, but I've got to go. I've got stuff to do.'

'Lauren, please,' he begins, but I put down the phone before I have to say another, strangled word.

It's the weekend before I get a chance to cancel my flight to Singapore. That makes it sound like a straightforward affair, though it's anything but. Although I'd gone for a 'flexible' fare, what they don't tell you is that the flexibility required seems to be from *you*: you've got to jump through more hoops than a performing seal to get your cash back.

Still, I feel a lot better once there's an email in my inbox confirming that the money has landed back in my account at teatime on Saturday, just before Cate and Emily come over. There isn't time to book my Australia journey until the morning, but I've found it and have it saved on my browser: an Emirates flight to Sydney, via Dubai, leaving at 7.45 p.m. on 20th July, four weeks from now.

It's evident as soon as Cate arrives that she's not on what you'd describe as peak form. Which is no surprise; she looks worse every time I see her. Emily, meanwhile, seems better.

Tired still, slightly lost, but at least her smile when I open the door is a genuine one – even if the thought of what's behind it makes sweat gather on the nape of my neck.

As the only person in whom she's confided about the pregnancy, I know she needs me right now, and that in itself makes my betrayal weigh heavier on me than I can possibly describe.

Nevertheless, after a few drinks and a good chat, there are moments when I could close my eyes, take a bite of a Dorito, and imagine things are exactly the same as they used to be, long before any of this stuff happened to us.

'I must admit, I'm as surprised as Edwin is that you've gone off him,' Emily says as she curls up her knees on the sofa, taking a sip of the elderflower water I've surreptitiously put in her glass each time she needed topping up. It seems to have done the trick because Cate hasn't commented on why Emily is the only one not drinking and has assumed it's the same cheeky Sauvignon that she's knocking back. 'Although how he thinks ranting at you about it is going to help is anyone's guess.'

'My feelings just . . . altered, that's all. I can't really explain it. He didn't do anything wrong.' I thrust another Dorito in my mouth and wish they'd change the subject.

'You've met someone else, haven't you?' Cate asks, and although I can tell she's half-teasing I can feel my face blench.

Emily notices. '*Have* you, Lauren?'

'Of course not. I think I'd have mentioned it before now, don't you?' I smile unsteadily, standing to go to the kitchen. Cate picks up the remote control and starts flicking through channels as I head out, but I become aware as I reach the sink that Emily has followed me. She pushes the door gently closed.

'How are you feeling?' I whisper.

She shrugs. 'Not too bad. Well, sick as anything. But OK. And I've made a decision about the baby.'

'Oh?'

'I'm going to keep it.' I realise I'm holding my breath. 'It took a couple of days to get used to the idea. But now ... I can't imagine anything else. I feel ready – to be a mother I mean. I really do.' She says the words as if she can barely believe them herself.

'That's wonderful. I bet Joe will be delighted,' I manage.

She looks down at her hands. 'Do you think I'm doing the right thing?'

The answer sticks in my throat. 'I think you're going to be a wonderful mum, Emily. I'm really happy for you. How've you coped with work?'

'I feigned a foot injury and asked to be put on duty in the climbing shop,' she says. 'I'm going to have to think of a better excuse soon though, because that one won't last long.'

'Oh, Lauren,' Cate shouts through, 'any more of that fizzy stuff I brought?'

Emily flashes me a glance. 'I'm determined to keep it under wraps for now, though – so please don't tell anyone. If I can get away with it, I want to wait until the twelve-week mark before I tell a soul. It's only about seven as far as I can work out.'

'Of course,' I promise as she heads back into the living room, while I remove the bottle of Prosecco from the fridge.

Then, as if I've been grabbed from behind, I'm engulfed by an electric flashback of Joe's lips on mine. Adrenalin races through me as I slam shut the fridge door and my doorbell rings.

I find Stella on my step. She's wearing a tea-length dress with white and bright pink spots. It strikes me as the kind of dress you'd put on to cheer yourself up, or perhaps I've just noticed how forced her smile is.

'Are you sure I'm not gate-crashing?'

'Don't be silly, you're more than welcome,' I tell her, showing her in.

'I just needed to get out of the house for a bit.'

As we head into the living room to join the others, Emily looks up. 'How are you, Stella?' she asks warmly.

Stella lowers herself tightly on to the sofa, placing the bottle of wine she's brought with her on the coffee table. 'Fine, thanks,' she replies miserably. Then she leans forward and puts her head in her hands.

'Stella, what is it?' Cate asks.

'I can't go on pretending things are fine between me and Mike,' she says, lifting up her face. 'It's not *natural*. He's been seeing another woman, for God's sake!'

'Who?' asks Cate.

'Lulu,' Stella says sombrely. 'Oh, he denies it – keeps reassuring me there's nothing in it, but I don't believe a word of it. I spent last night tossing and turning, asking myself if I could make this work. If I loved him so much, could I try and . . . I don't know, be a bit more *European* about the whole thing. A bit more modern. Turn a blind eye.'

Cate and Emily exchange glances.

'Then I realised what I was doing: trying to avoid cancelling the wedding.' She sighs, her face stilled in sadness. 'Yet, can I commit the rest of my life to a man just so I don't lose the money we've forked out on five bridesmaids' dresses and a hog roast? The answer is, I can't. I *can't* go ahead with it.'

I sit forward on the sofa and give her what Paddington Bear would call a hard stare. 'Stella. Do not cancel the wedding,' I say firmly.

She sinks back, resigned, and looks up at me with crimson-rimmed eyes. This is suddenly feeling horribly serious. 'But he's sleeping with someone else, Lauren. It's that simple. No matter how much I love him, I need to let him go.'

I dig my nails into my hands. 'Before you do that, Stella, I have to tell you something.'

All three of them glare at me. And it strikes me that not every secret is better left unbroken.

It's gone 11.30 before Cate and I pack Stella and Emily into a taxi and wave goodbye.

'Interesting night,' Cate says. 'Poor old Stella. Fancy thinking Lulu and Mike were having it away with one another. You did the right thing, by the way.'

'Yes, I think I probably did, didn't I?'

'Unquestionably. And, thanks for letting me stay tonight. It means a lot.'

'No problem at all. Nice to have a girls' night before . . .'

'Australia,' she finishes for me. 'Listen, I want you to know how glad I am that everything's worked out for you on that score. Australia is where you're meant to be. Besides, I want to visit you in Sydney far more than I ever fancied Singapore.'

'Are you going to be all right, Cate?'

Her jaw twitches and she looks away, hiding the emotion in her eyes. 'That's not your worry, Lauren. My problems are my problems – and Oz is your future.'

'You wouldn't think of joining me, would you?' I already know the answer without her saying it.

She shakes her head. 'And do what with Daffodils & Stars? I'm not saying I couldn't *ever* go anywhere because of it. And hell, yes, the other side of the world has never looked more attractive than it does right now. But I'd need more than three weeks to find someone I trusted enough to run this place for me, for Grandma Issy's sake as well as mine. And that's before we even get into the issue of a work permit.'

'Have you heard from your mum or dad lately?'

'Dad's been in touch and we had a chat on the phone. It was terrible, to be honest. He's not like Mum – he's not angry at me, just heartbroken. It's far worse.'

'Nothing from your mum then?'

'I tried to get in touch again today, but she says she doesn't want to speak to me at the moment. And I'll be honest – I'm not sure I can face her either.'

She then spots her phone on the coffee table, picks it up and scowls angrily at the screen.

'Robby's texted me.'

'At this time of night?'

'He sent it over an hour ago but I hadn't realised while the girls were here. He says he wants to talk.'

'I take it you're going to tell him to sling his hook?'

'I can't, Lauren. Whether I like it or not, he's not someone I can afford to ignore.' She takes a deep breath and, with trembling fingers, clicks on his number before walking through into the kitchen to make the call.

I switch on the TV and stare at a vacuous action film, trying to imagine what he's saying to her. Unlike her conversation with Will, there are no raised voices. It occurs to me that she wouldn't shout at Robby quite simply because she's terrified of him, or at least what he's capable of.

She's gone less than five minutes, and when she returns and sinks into the sofa, her cheeks are wet from tears.

'What is it?'

'He's got all the other photos,' she says, her voice thick and helpless, like a wounded animal. 'He's not even trying to hide the fact that it was him. He finally admitted it. I actually think he's proud of it.'

'So what did he say? And what did you say?'

She stares into space, mascara streaking down her cheeks. 'They're so much worse,' she says quietly, not even hearing me.

'What are?'

'The other photos,' she croaks. 'He's got them all.'

'What . . . what's in them?' I ask quietly.

She doesn't turn to look at me when she replies. 'I can't even bring myself to say it. I'm doing stuff in them, put it that way.'

'Legal stuff?' I ask tentatively.

Her head snaps round to me. 'Of course legal stuff! Just the last thing you'd want anyone to see. *Ever*. They were all his bloody idea.' She shudders. 'I feel like killing myself, Lauren. I just feel like ending it now.'

I leap over and throw my arms around her. 'Please don't say that. Please,' I whisper.

'This is never going to end, Lauren. I can't give him what he wants. I don't *have* it.'

I pull back slightly. 'What does he want?'

The words tremble out of her mouth. 'He says he's been offered a job in France but moving there is too expensive. But if I was prepared to help him out . . .'

'What does he want, Cate?' I repeat firmly.

'Five thousand pounds in cash,' she whispers. 'For every last photo to disappear, along with him.'

For a second, I'm speechless. Then: 'He's *blackmailing* you!'

'Give it whatever name you want, he's calling the shots.'

'Cate, I'm serious, this cannot go on. You need to go to the police. What he's doing is definitely criminal. He's got to be stopped.'

'How are they ever going to know about that phone call?' Powerlessness seems to anaesthetise her vocal cords. 'I didn't record it. He'd just deny all knowledge of it. Besides, how can I go to the police? Even without the issue of Will's brother, this is all shameful enough. I just need these photos to disappear. I need them to go. I need *him* to go.'

'So what are you going to do? You can't seriously be considering paying that money.'

She turns to me, looking deadly serious. 'If I had the means, of course I would. But I haven't anything like that amount of money and I have no access to it. I hit my credit limit long ago when I refurbished Daffodils & Stars. I tried to get a loan for a new van last year and there's no longer a bank in the world that will touch me. But the answer to your question is yes. Definitely. If I had that money and could make all of this go away, I would pay Robby off, this very minute.'

Chapter 47

The decision that I'm going to help Cate – I mean *really* help her – isn't one I make the second she leaves my cottage the following morning. But as I log on to my bank account, I realise that I'm the only person on earth with the power to make her problems disappear.

My train of thought might be madness.

But I've never felt a stronger need to prove to myself that I am a good person, a good friend – after all I've done to the contrary in the last couple of weeks.

So by Monday morning, I know exactly what I've got to do: give Cate my travelling money to get rid of those pictures, get rid of Robby and let her live her life. There's just no alternative.

The practical implications of this are impossible to compute: I'll be out of a job in a few days' time. Not only that – I'll be unable to escape.

I haven't heard from Joe since I put the phone down on

him last Tuesday. That was six days ago. But I've thought about nothing else since – nothing except him, Emily, their baby ... and the burning fragments of that night in the Honeymoon Suite of the Moonlight Hotel.

I am sitting in the staff room at lunchtime, staring into space as another one of my regular, vivid images flashes into my head – of my hand sliding up the back of Joe's shirt – when my phone beeps. I rip it out of my handbag and see that he's texted me. I open up the message with my heart thrashing against my chest like a caged bird.

> Sorry to have to text. But one of the staff found your bracelet on the stairs of the hotel. Can I drop it off at your house? I'm in Ullswater, but could come later after you've finished work?

I remember that the clasp on that bracelet was loose after I got tangled up with Esteban; I can't believe I dropped it there though. I chew the side of my mouth and start to compose a text, as the staff-room door opens and Edwin enters. The look he throws me is icier than a Mr Whippy van in January, before he backs out of the door again.

Joyce looks up from a book called *Her Libidinous Billionaire Cowboy*. 'What's up with Edwin? He's got a lip on him like my front step this morning.'

'Maybe he's just sad about leaving,' I say weakly.

'Well, I'm not surprised. I'm sure Singapore's got a lot going for it but when you live somewhere like this, sometimes you need reminding that the grass isn't greener. Not that I think you're doing the wrong thing, obviously.'

'Hmm,' I reply, having neither the energy nor inclination to explain that I'm not going anywhere fast except the Job Centre.

I click on Joe's message and press reply. Hi. I'll come and collect it from the hotel straight after work – no need for you to be there if you just want to give it to a staff member.

He responds less than a minute after I've pressed Send. OK. I'll give Gianni a ring and ask him to meet you at the gate. I'll forward his number if you could text him when you're on your way?

I try to think clearly over the muffled buzz in my ears. I tell myself that going back to the scene of my indiscretion is at least better than Joe turning up at the cottage tonight. Because I honestly don't think I can face him again. Ever. For a multitude of reasons, including the one I'm trying to stop bursting into my head: that I want him so badly my entire body aches with it.

The rest of the day at work ticks by torturously. And that evening, despite the fact that I know he won't be there, as my car crunches up the drive of the Moonlight Hotel, I can feel myself grow tense.

A high, midsummer sun casts a saffron light on to the pale

walls of the building. Like the last time I was here, I'm momentarily winded when I see it, memories unfolding in my head as I draw closer.

I step out of the car, as I realise that someone is approaching. When I'd heard Gianni's name mentioned previously, for some reason I expected a sharp-looking Italian guy in his mid-thirties. In fact, he looks to be almost sixty, but good on it, with intelligent eyes and a flat, toned torso. When he reaches me, I notice that his shirt smells freshly ironed.

'You must be Lauren,' he smiles, offering me his hand.

I shake it, feeling inexplicably embarrassed. 'Yes, that's me. I believe I left my bracelet here?'

'I believe you did. Why don't you come with me?'

I prickle at the suggestion, wondering why he couldn't have just brought the damn thing out to me, saving me the turmoil of being here longer than necessary.

'I understand your father was once the General Manager of this hotel?' he begins, as I follow him through into reception.

'Many years ago. It was completely different then.' My eyes skitter around the room as I realise the furniture is now *in situ*. Still covered in plastic, but all in place.

He stops and turns to me. 'Mr Wilborne is putting his heart and soul into this project,' he says quietly. 'I've worked with his family for twenty-three years and . . . I've never seen anybody so passionate about a place.'

I don't answer him. It's not a conversation I want to get sucked into. So I simply follow, thoughts whizzing through my mind so fast that at one point, I don't actually remember how I got to where I am: through the double doors at the back of the hotel, overlooking the gardens that stretch down to the lake.

I look at Gianni, waiting for an explanation as to why we've come outside again. 'Your bracelet is down there,' he says with a perplexing smile, before glancing at his phone. 'Sorry, I have a call to make. You'll find it just down there,' he repeats. 'In the gazebo.'

He walks away before I can answer, not that I'd know what to say anyway. I simply stand, feeling bewilderment crinkle on my face. And then I start walking across the lawn. My steps quicken before breaking into a gallop as I approach the trees at the shore, disbelief searing through me as I see it appear behind them.

My gazebo.

Or at least, a replica of it. I walk towards the structure in a trance, holding my breath. I place a foot on to the step and pull myself up into it, inhaling its new, woody smell as I run my fingers along the rail. Then I sit down on the beach, in the exact spot where my little pretend café was, and close my eyes.

My heartbeat slows and the birds quieten around me as I can almost feel my dad sitting beside me. Sipping a non-existent drink in my tea set and murmuring approval at my plastic cakes. Laughing as I played see-saw on his leg. Cuddling me into him as we fed the ducks.

When my eyelids flutter open, hot tears spill down my cheeks so fast I can feel a drip on my knee. Then I glance down and see the envelope my bracelet has been left in. I sniff back tears and pick it up. My bracelet is in there, along with a letter, handwritten in black ink on thick, white paper.

Lauren,

I've thought of little else but what happened between us last week – or rather what didn't happen. And why. In fact, I've thought about it so much and still failed to work it all out that the only thing left to do was stop thinking and start acting.

I know you're going to Singapore with Edwin and I want more than anything to just wish you a glorious, happy life together and really mean it.

But I'm seriously struggling, Lauren.

I'm struggling because I can't help how I feel about you – and wanting things to have been different.

But I won't dwell on it as I'd only embarrass myself and I've done enough of that. In fact, I might be about to do it again. I've never claimed to be brilliant with words, but I did something that expresses how I feel about you in the only way I know how – and I couldn't bring myself not to let you see it.

I started building your gazebo weeks ago, but finished it this weekend. I told myself that I was doing it because I'd simply wanted old elements of the hotel to be restored, to keep the history of the place alive.

But I was lying to myself. I was doing it because I wanted to give you something, to <u>make</u> you something, with my own hands – to <u>show</u> you how I felt, when I couldn't say it.

None of this was selfless, by the way: it made me feel good. In fact, it still does, every time I set eyes on it. So, I hope you like your gazebo and get to enjoy at least a few moments in it before you fly away.

It'll be yours, for ever. And when you find yourself at home, visiting your mum or whatever, I want you to know that your seat here will always be reserved, just to come and think, or even throw a tea party, if it takes your fancy.

Joe x

I put down the envelope and stand up, focusing on the ripples of water lapping against the shore. I don't want to leave. I want to just stay here, and breathe the air in my happiest of places.

The thought makes me despair – of everything. And it's then that I turn around and spot the little plaque on the bench I'm sitting on.

It says, LAUREN'S PLACE.

As I try to make sense of it all, one thought keeps pushing its way in.

Joe. Why are you making it impossible for me not to fall in love with you?

Chapter 48

To say Cate is shocked when I tell her I have the solution to all her problems – in the shape of £5000 – barely covers it. She looks at me open-mouthed across the counter in Daffodils & Stars and a piece of gold ribbon drops from her fingers.

'*What* did you say?' she whispers.

'I still think you should go to the police about Robby. This doesn't change that.' I reach out and take her hand. It's trembling. 'But the money's yours. If this is the only way you feel able to get him out of your life, then I want you to have it.'

She shakes her head violently. 'No, Lauren. Don't be ridiculous. I absolutely couldn't. You've spent years saving this up. It'd mean you couldn't go. And you *have* to go – you're out of a job, aren't you?'

'There's always supply work,' I tell her, which is true, less than ideal as it is. 'I won't starve. Some things are more important.'

'No,' she says again, her eyes darting about as the implications of my offer sink in. 'I couldn't do it.' Her chest reddens as the next words catch in her throat. 'You're such an amazing friend to even offer . . . thank you so, so much. But it's not fair. This is my problem, not yours.'

'And you're my friend – the best friend I've ever had. Which is why I'm doing this for you. I've already transferred the money to your account,' I say.

The plump, salty tears that follow are the best kind of tears, ones made up of relief and happiness and the knowledge that you're loved and protected, no matter how shitty others can be towards you. I walk round the counter and pull her into a hug.

'I'll pay you back really quickly, I swear,' she says, sniffing. 'I'm going to get a bar job or something and, month by month, I'll put it back in your account. I absolutely promise you, Lauren.'

'Take all the time you need.'

As Cate's face continues to go through a whole range of emotions – disbelief, guilt, elation – something else is flickering behind her eyes the entire time: relief that her nightmare is going to end. What she doesn't know is that a nightmare of my own is just beginning.

But I still think I'm doing the right thing.

*

Cate phones me the following day to say she's arranged to make a cash withdrawal from the bank – having told them the money was to buy a car – and to meet Robby on Saturday to hand it over.

But none of that lessens the private hell I'm going through in having to stay here, with Joe's words throbbing in my head when, unbeknownst to him, he is about to become a father. And when the mother of his child is one of my best friends.

That night, I sit at my bedroom window, gazing past my curtains as mist swirls around the trees, and I try to work out a solution to this. One that makes Joe Wilborne completely unable to think of me as someone he even likes, let alone anything more.

I pick up my phone and scroll to his name in the contacts book. Then I dial it with a heart that thrashes harder and harder with every ring.

It goes to voicemail.

I sigh and click off, lying on the bed as my adrenalin subsides.

Then it rings. I scramble to a sitting position and glance at the phone. It's him.

With my breath hanging in my chest, I pick up.

'Hi, Lauren.'

He has the kind of voice that makes your skin tingle: masculine but warm, with rolling vowels and an accent that's only apparent with every other undulating lilt. I force myself to stop thinking like this. The only emotion that is ever going to be possible between the two of us from now on is dislike. No, that's not enough.

I need to make him hate me.

'Hello, Joe,' I reply coldly.

'I believe you got your bracelet.'

'I did,' I reply, summoning the strength to say the words I've planned to say. 'I saw your gazebo too.'

'Well, it's your gazebo really . . .'

'No, it's not. It's not my gazebo at all.'

He doesn't answer at first. Then he asks, not unreasonably, 'What do you mean?'

'*How insensitive can you get?*' I spit out the words as if I can't bear the taste of them in my mouth. 'Did you seriously think you could build some crappy replica of the place where I used to spend days with my dad? Was it some kind of cruel joke?'

'Of course not.' He tries to say this dispassionately, but the hurt in his voice almost – *almost* – makes me take it back. Then I think of his baby, of Emily's determination to make a go of it, and steel myself to deliver a further onslaught.

'I think you're *sick*, Joe,' I rant on. 'That's the only explanation for it. I don't know why anyone would do something like that.'

'I'm . . . I'm sorry,' he replies, with pain in his voice.

'I didn't mean to upset you,' he continues, 'and I apologise if I did. I thought it would be something you'd like. With hindsight, you're right. It was crass.'

My heart breaks a little more, as I say, 'Yes. It was upsetting and stupid, and well, like I said, Joe – I just don't want *any-thing* to do with you any longer.'

'Well, you're not going to, are you? Given that you're leaving the country soon.'

'As it happens, I'm not going just yet,' I mumble. 'There's been a setback so I'm stuck here. And that's precisely why I wanted to let you know – because of this – that it's just impossible for you and me to be friends.'

'OK, I've got the idea,' he says stonily.

'And in case you're wondering, I'm quitting salsa,' I go on.

'Yes, me too,' he replies.

That rattles me. 'Really?'

'There wasn't any point in going any longer.'

I let this sentence filter through me then brush aside my innate desire to decode it.

'So, it seems like we're probably not going to bump into each other anyway from now on,' I conclude. 'Which suits me fine. I'm certainly not going to be heading anywhere near the Moonlight Hotel after the stunt you've just pulled.'

'I'm sorry, Lauren,' only this time, he doesn't say it as if he is sorry. He says it as if he's pissed off in the extreme – and who could blame him. But I can't let him know that. 'Like I say, it was meant to be a nice gesture, it was meant to—'

'Yeah, well, it didn't work.'

'Yes, I've got it, Lauren,' he snaps. 'I've got it completely.'

Chapter 49

Steph has a friend – a real one, someone she spends time with and tags herself with on Facebook, at the beach, or having coffee.

She's called Rosa and is twenty-four, Italian and the daughter of a former priest. When I heard that last bit I couldn't help but wonder if the chap in question realises who his daughter is socialising with but, surprisingly, Steph seems to be changing her ways. Last week, she put something on Facebook about being on a detox. I dread to think what this could do to some of the bar takings around Bondi.

'Don't tell me, you're not coming,' she says when we Skype on Thursday night. She has a twist in her lips designed to underline that she thinks I'm dangerously eccentric. 'Seriously, Loz – you don't need to say a thing. It's written in your eyes.'

'The thing is, Steph, I really want to come to

Australia – and I will some day. Definitely. But at the moment, I've got a few things I want to sort out. A few … cash-flow issues.'

'Loz, it's fine. You don't need to worry. I know Mum had mentioned to your mum that I was having a hard time of it, but things are looking up. And I'm sure you're right … you'll get over here one day. Don't leave it too long though, eh? We want you young enough to still be in a bikini without scaring anyone off.'

The last day of term is a strange and sad one. Strange because, while the children are typically hysterical with excitement, for me the day has none of its usual uplifting effect.

Matters aren't helped by the fact that I am backed into a corner during a conversation with the Head – and find myself forced to confess the inglorious news that I'm no longer going to Australia, Singapore or indeed anywhere.

I can't tell her or anyone else the real reason, so just have to mumble something about 'domestic matters'. She responds by looking at me as if I am flakier than a Greggs cheese and onion pasty.

'I hope you don't expect to get your job back. We've already filled it,' she says curtly. I never expected anything else.

I always knew I'd be spending my summer job-hunting, in the hope that by September, when my pay runs out, I'll have somewhere to go. If not, it'll be supply work for me, which I don't mind at all, apart from the fact that it's intermittent, involves lots of travelling and will look like an odd move on my CV. Which I suppose is exactly what it is.

What I feel most sad about though is saying goodbye to the children. The end of a school year is always bittersweet; saying cheerio to a bunch of little people you've grown fond of, knowing that their funny little quirks will be absent from your life, at least for the near future.

Only this time, I'm not going to see them next term. I'm not going to watch them progressing and growing and turning into the person they're destined to be. This time, I'm probably never going to see them again full stop.

'What are you eating, Georgia?' I ask a little girl in her last day of Reception year.

She looks up at me with wide eyes. 'Some chewing gum.'

I reach into my pocket for a tissue and hold it out. 'Pop it in there, please. Chewing gum's not allowed, even on your last day.'

'I didn't know,' she says, looking slightly worried. 'I just found it stuck on my shoe.'

Scarlet Cranston tugs at my side. 'Miss, when are you going to open our presents?'

'Oh ... you want me to open them now, do you?'

'YES!' they all shriek.

I laugh. 'OK, right … well, look at all these lovely surprises!' I say, though in reality we are fairly light on the surprise front around here at the end of term.

Last year I ended up with four plants, seven Body Shop gift sets and fourteen boxes of chocolates, which were responsible for me putting on three quarters of a stone over the summer.

'Oh, how lovely! I never would've expected one of those!' I declare, unwrapping the first present to reveal a box of Roses.

'Do you like it? That was from me,' James Wesley tells me proudly.

'It's extremely kind of you, James – I love it. Please thank your mummy and daddy.'

'My dad got them from a man in the pub,' James tells me. 'They were really cheap because they're out of date.'

'Oh, right.'

'They're OK though,' he reassures me. 'Apart from the orange ones. The orange ones gave my Auntie Rachel the trots.'

'I'll remember that, thank you, James,' I say, moving on to the next box.

My stack of booty amounts to an unusually large number of plants this year (six), something I briefly wonder could be attributed to people noticing how dramatically my arse had ballooned by the time I returned to school last September.

And as the children file out to go to lunch, Tom Goodwin appears.

'My mum forgot to get you a present. She forgets a lot of things these days.'

'Tom, it's absolutely fine, please don't worry. It's been gift enough to me being able to teach you.'

He goes to shuffle out but pauses and turns back to me. 'I'm going to miss you,' he says.

I've replied in exactly the same way dozens of times today. Only this time, to my surprise, the words catch in the back of my mouth. 'I'm going to miss you too, Tom.'

On Saturday night I have never felt less sociable, and certainly in no mood for Mum and Barry's 'farewell dinner' to Jeremy. Having decided that the farm-handling job isn't for him, he's taken a job shovelling shit of a different variety, at an accountancy firm in London.

Helen, Jeremy's mum, told my mum that the pay is minimal, the prospects are abysmal and that he'll be lucky if they'll let him near the photocopier, but he's said yes because he gets to wear a suit and never has to see the business end of a sheep again. To listen to Jeremy, you'd think he was taking over from Richard Branson.

'I'm going to be in charge of a twenty-nine-million-pound portfolio,' he tells us with a self-congratulatory grin, as Barry walks to the kitchen table carrying his latest culinary masterpiece: a recreation of the Swedish Ice Hotel, fashioned primarily out of marshmallows and Fox's Glacier mints. 'I cannot tell you how glad I'm going to be, to be out of this place.'

'I'm sure Jim and Gill Gavin will miss you too,' Mum says. To the untrained ear, it's impossible to work out whether she's being sarcastic or not. I'm not sure that even I can tell.

'You must be so hacked off that your Australia trip's fallen through,' Jeremy continues – and I grit my teeth because I could do without discussing the subject again in front of Mum, who seems to think my 'change of heart' can only be explained by some sort of mental breakdown.

'I don't know how you've been able to stand living round here all your life, Lauren,' he goes on. 'I'm not saying it's without *any* appeal; it's pretty enough, if you go for that kind of thing. But after a while, all this fresh air is enough to make you sick. And the hills – Jesus! I cannot wait to walk somewhere without my calf muscles burning. Even the buildings . . .'

'What's wrong with the buildings?' asks Mum wearily, clearly used to this kind of rant.

'This is a lovely home, Caroline, but it's so . . . old,' he says, as if the word is interchangeable with the phrase, 'rife with infectious diseases'. 'If I have to duck to avoid another doorframe I think I might just *die*.'

Mum finishes off her dinner and resists the temptation to invite him through to the sitting room, which would involve passing through a doorframe several inches lower than his forehead.

'The big city is where it's all at and it is calling me. The cocktails. The parties. The glamour and energy, the sheer thrill of it all!'

'So did you manage to get that bedsit in Streatham you were after?' Barry asks.

'Um . . . yes.'

'The two ladies sound nice you're moving in with. How old are they again?' Mum asks.

'Early eighties,' he coughs. 'That's just a stop-gap though.'

'Of course,' Mum says.

'Well, we'll miss you, Jeremy,' Barry says heroically, as he dishes up the Ice Hotel cake. 'And you're always welcome back here, whenever you like.'

'I wouldn't hold your breath,' Jeremy mutters, before taking a bite of his cake as Barry awaits his verdict.

Instead of murmuring his approval – or more likely turning his nose up – my mum's second cousin's son instead launches into a cataclysmic coughing fit, turns the colour of a varicose vein, sprays marshmallow halfway across the kitchen and, most disconcertingly, seems unable to breathe.

We are collectively stunned into inaction, at least for a moment, until Mum leaps up.

Just as he looks as though his vital organs are about to burst out of his belly, she grabs him round the waist and gives him several sharp thumps, before a shard of glacier mint torpedoes out of Jeremy's mouth.

'Oh. My. GOD.' Jeremy's chest trampolines up and down, as he clutches the side of the chair. 'Your cake nearly killed me!' he shrieks at Barry.

Barry stands there, unable to speak. But I'm afraid I'm not. Something rises up in me as I fix my glare on him.

'Jeremy,' I say tightly. 'Barry and Mum have shown you nothing but kindness and hospitality – you'd do well to remember that. *You* might not have enjoyed your time here, but it's not their fault if you come out in a rash every time you approach so much as a tree.'

'Don't give me that, Lauren,' he splutters. 'You're as desperate to get out of this place as I am. It's written all over your face.'

'That's not true.' I stand there, mute for a moment, and wishing I could fire back the real explanation: that my desire to leave is far more complicated than he – or anyone else here – realises.

But of course I can't say that. So I am left to slink back into my chair and simply watch as Jeremy spins on his heels and attempts to flounce out of the room. It'd be a good flounce too – with big, theatrical strides – if he didn't come undone at the kitchen door. As his forehead smacks on the beam between the kitchen and the living room, it nearly shakes the foundations of the house.

Then he stumbles backwards and lands on the floor. He is out cold for a second or two, before his eyes flutter open. Mum turns to me and lets out the long sigh of a woman in whose vocabulary 'panic' does not exist. 'I think one of us had better drive him to hospital,' she says. Her eyes flick up at me. 'Assuming they'll have him.'

Chapter 50

The hospital is forty minutes' drive away and I'm sorry to say that I'm the one doing the driving. Mum and Barry had both had a couple of glasses of wine, but I'd abstained because I wasn't staying over.

Jeremy is appalled by the fact that we didn't call the air ambulance for a full-scale rescue involving ropes and stretchers and frantic shouting. Instead, he sits groaning like a burst radiator valve in the back of my car, a bag of frozen peas pressed against his temple.

'Because I've had a head injury, it's very likely that they'll consult with *you* to find out what's happened,' he tells me. 'In case I'm delirious or something. So, can I just say now that it's important we present a united front and *do not accept* anything less than an MRI scan.'

'Hadn't you better see what the doctors say first?' I suggest, glancing in the mirror.

'I don't like doctors,' he declares. I wonder if there's anyone

Jeremy does like. 'They'll fob you off with anything, particularly in some small cottage hospital like the ones around here.'

'The hospitals around here are fine,' I tell him. 'Once you get used to the rusty pliers or neat whiskey they use as anaesthetic.'

'I'm not the being-fobbed-off kind,' he continues, ignoring me. 'I've read about this sort of head injury. About people getting a bang to the head and on the surface feeling completely fine. But in reality internal bleeding is going on and hours – literally hours – later, they wake up DEAD.'

'I promise I won't let you wake up dead,' I tell him, as I turn on to the A road. 'Although don't be too disappointed if they send you away with two Paracetamol and tell you to go and get some rest, will you?'

'There is absolutely no way they're going to do that, Lauren. Absolutely no way. LOOK.'

He thrusts his head between the two seats like that alien that burst out of Sigourney Weaver's torso and points at a massive purple egg between his eyes, apparently unconcerned at nearly forcing me off the road.

We pull up in the hospital's car park and, as I rustle round for some change for the Pay and Display, Jeremy staggers to the front door of A&E, convinced there is no time to waste. I follow him in a minute later and find him at reception, where he is laying on his injuries thicker than Cara Delevingne's eyebrows.

'I do feel I'm facing a life-or-death situation here,' he tells a receptionist who, despite the pleasant expression, looks distinctly unmoved. 'I'd hate you to get in trouble or end up in some sort of terrible litigation situation. Seconds could count.'

'OK, lovely,' she replies, with a sunny smile. 'No probs at all. Take a seat and the triage nurse will be with you shortly.'

He fails to move. 'The fact that we've driven here ourselves might give the impression that I'm in a better physical state than the reality is,' he continues. 'I did explain to my hosts how dangerous head injuries can be. How they can go from seeming innocuous one minute to DEATH the next. But they're not trained medical professionals, so—'

'There's a drinks machine over to your right if you'd like to take a seat,' the lady adds.

'A drinks machine?'

'In case you fancied a brew while you're waiting.'

'I don't think you're quite grasping this . . .'

As Jeremy continues explaining to the receptionist how his situation is ten times more pressing than absolutely anyone else's here, I take a seat and settle down to what I suspect is a lengthy night. I've just taken my phone out of my bag to see if I can get enough of a reception to log on to Facebook, when a text arrives from Cate.

Cash handed over. All pics deleted from his files and the websites – he did it in front of me. He's going to be out of my life for ever, Lauren. Can't tell you how relieved I am – but more importantly, how grateful. I will pay *every penny* back to you, I swear. xxx

I text her back.

Glad it's sorted. Now put that arsehole out of your head immediately and go and see your gorgeous boyfriend x

She responds.

R really is an arsehole: The first thing he said was, 'this money means nothing, not compared with how much I want you'. He still took it though – bloody loser. Anyway, am so lucky to have a friend like you – don't know how to thank you, sweetheart. xxx

I close my eyes, feeling an uneasy sense of relief.

Belatedly, I realise that I'm not as convinced as she is that this will be the end of it. What happens when the money runs out and Robby decides he wants more? He could easily have backed up those photos somewhere else. And even if he has deleted them, the nature of this particular beast is that copies of it will still be out there, ready to emerge at some point on some dodgy website.

But, if it makes Cate feel well enough to start rebuilding her life, and it's enough to get Robby to move to France, then it'll have been worth it.

'This place is run by a bunch of yokels!' Jeremy says loudly, stomping over and plonking himself next to me. This has the unfortunate effect of making it impossible to pretend I'm not with him.

I spend the next hour and a half trying to get a signal so I can log on to Facebook and ignore Jeremy, which unfortunately – after the triage nurse has made some rudimentary tests – is exactly what the emergency team have to do after we're told they've admitted two climbers in a far more serious condition.

When Jeremy is finally called in, he musters up a brave face and tells me graciously that I can wait in reception.

So I wait . . . with nothing but my thoughts for company.

It is saying something, but after twenty minutes, even being with Jeremy is suddenly looking like an attractive alternative. I decide to head out into my car to find a magazine I think I might have left in the boot, when the double doors open and a figure shuffles in, huddled in a massive coat, head down. I barely give them a second glance; indeed, am about to stride out into the car park when I hear my name spoken in a low whisper.

'Lauren?'

When I look up, it takes a moment for me to realise who it is.

'*Emily?*' I reply. 'What are you doing here? Has something happened?'

The fear on Emily's face is stark as she nods her head. I put my arm around her shoulders and usher her in through the door, out of the cold.

'I've been bleeding,' she confides, her bottom lip trembling. 'I think it's the baby.'

She looks to be in shock. 'Come on, let's go and see the receptionist,' I say.

Emily gives her details before we take a seat. 'What happened?'

She swallows. 'I'd been feeling really ropey all day but put it down to nothing more than the pregnancy in general. So I thought I'd just, you know, go for a walk, take it easy. I didn't overdo anything, I swear.'

'Of course not,' I reassure her, clutching her hand.

'Then tonight . . . we'd had dinner and, obviously, I wasn't drinking and all we were doing was watching a film, but I got up to go to the loo, and that's when I felt it – this pain in my belly. It wasn't even that bad – just like period pains. I went to the bathroom and it was then that I realised I was bleeding. Not just a little bit, either.'

'Is it still happening now?' I ask quietly, glancing round, wishing the triage nurse would come.

'No. Maybe,' she says, shrugging. 'Not as much. The thing is, Lauren, I know I wasn't sure about the baby at first but that was because it was all so unexpected. I couldn't get my head around the whole thing. But now I have. Now I really want it. I hadn't realised how much.'

'I'm no expert but I'm sure I heard that this can happen in early pregnancy and it doesn't necessarily mean anything bad has happened,' I tell her. 'Don't leap to any conclusions.'

She nods. 'Part of me doesn't know why I'm here. They're not going to be able to do a foetal scan or anything tonight. I just . . . I was scared. I didn't know where else to go.'

'You've done the right thing.'

The triage door opens and a nurse comes out and calls Emily's name.

Em nods and stands up. 'I'm coming with you,' I tell her.

But she hesitates. 'What is it?' I ask.

'It's OK, Lauren, I don't need you to come with me. I'm not by myself. He's just parking the car.'

My stomach sinks as I realise Joe is about to follow her in.

'Then you're in good hands,' I say quietly. 'I know Joe will look after you.'

She doesn't move. She just looks me in the eyes and says a series of words that are laden with meaning – a meaning I don't grasp.

'My baby's father brought me, Lauren,' she says.

'That's what I said, Joe brought you.'

She looks at her hands and whispers her reply. 'Not Joe.'

The double doors slide open and we both look up.

And standing there, with panic in his eyes, is a man I recognise instantly but never in a million years expected to see in this scenario.

He walks over, barely registers my presence, before slipping his hand in Emily's and walking towards the door with her, as incredulity sweeps over me and I attempt to put together the pieces of the jigsaw in my head.

The man who Emily has just told me is the father of her baby is not Joe. It's Nick Goodwin. Little Tom's dad.

Chapter 51

Emily and Nick Goodwin are only in with the triage nurse for a matter of minutes. When the door re-opens, Emily shuffles over to me immediately. 'I've been sent straight in. I can't really explain.'

I nod, then my eyes flick up spontaneously to Nick. But he can't bring himself to look at me. 'I'm going to get your bag out of the car,' he says, and squeezes Emily on the arm. She nods and he heads outside.

When we're alone, Emily turns to me, a glaze on her eyes. 'Don't hate me, Lauren.'

'Of course not,' I say, though I can't deny I'm completely bewildered by all this; by when Nick came into this equation – and where Joe fits in. If he fits in anywhere . . .

She lowers herself on to the seat next to me. 'You and Cate assumed so much about Joe and me, but we were never serious,' she says, as if reading my thoughts. 'I liked him a lot – fancied him at the beginning . . . but we went on a few dates, went walking a lot and became friends. Friends who both enjoyed the mountains and each other's company, but nothing more than that.' She pauses to think.

'Then I met Nick – he's friends with one of the other guys at Windermere Adventures and came on a couple of nights out at the Golden Rule. We just kind of clicked and got to know each other and ...' She looks up at me, trying to read my face. 'It all happened so quickly. I fell completely in love with him.'

I am speechless, there's no other word for it.

'I let you believe there was more to Joe and me simply because I couldn't tell you about Nick. I felt ashamed,' she says, lowering her head miserably. 'I feel ashamed. Not just because of the affair, but because I know Tom is in your class. I know how fond you are of him – I remember you telling me that story about his cousin calling him a 'brat' and he thought it meant some little animal ...'

I didn't even remember telling Emily about that.

'It became *impossible* to tell you, Lauren,' she goes on. 'And I knew that if I'd told Cate she couldn't have kept it from you. She's never been any good at keeping secrets, not like you.'

'So you and Joe ...'

'There isn't a me and Joe. Like I say, we went out on dates at first, then became friends. We carried on with some climbing every so often, but it's nothing like the big romance I let you think it was. I didn't mean to lie to you. I just never corrected you because it became so much easier not to. I'm sorry.'

'I … God …' A dozen questions are bubbling up to my lips. 'But Jenny – Nick's wife … '

'Nick's leaving her,' she finishes.

'What? But he can't.'

Defiance shines in her eyes as she hisses, 'He's about to become a father with me, Lauren. And more to the point, he loves *me*.'

I can feel my jaw clench as I think about Tom's sad little face, how upset and quiet this gorgeous, bright little boy has been lately. If Emily had any idea what this would do to him …

'I know it won't be easy for Tom,' she adds. The words trip off her tongue so effortlessly I have a feeling that the truth is, she doesn't. 'Kids get over it though, don't they? People divorce all the time. And their marriage is over. It was over long before I came on the scene.'

It strikes me that now might not be the time to remind her that *they all say that*.

'Even before Nick found out about the baby, he knew that was what he had to do. The baby just makes everything clear. But even if …' she looks around, remembering where she is. 'Even if something awful happened, he's leaving her – to be with me.'

I am mute, unable to know what to do or say, entirely unable to share the triumph in her voice.

'Emily Costa?' The doctor pops her head round the door again.

'I need to go,' she says urgently. Nick appears, skulking at the door, glancing at me with shifty eyes, suddenly looking far less of the man he was.

I look back at her. 'I hope everything's all right,' I manage.

She nods, takes Nick by the hand, and they disappear into the emergency room.

Chapter 52

Jeremy is dispatched from the A&E clutching two Paracetamol and an ice pack. The only thing missing is a Mr Bump sticker and a lollipop. By the time I've driven to his temporary hovel i.e. Mum's house, then home, I'm too wired to sleep.

The events of the last twenty-four hours ricochet around my head, making me toss and turn, with I can do nothing except sit up and switch the light on. First there's Emily and the fact that she's been having an affair with Nick Goodwin. An actual affair, with lies and secrets and clandestine meetings ... all of which is about to add up to the destruction of Tom Goodwin's world.

I've never considered myself the judgemental type. And I'm trying not to judge Emily. But it bothers me how flippant she sounded about Nick and Jenny's marriage break-up and its effect on Tom. Perhaps it's because I'm Tom's teacher, but I can't feel anything other than distaste for what Emily and Nick are doing, no matter how in love they say they are.

Then there's Cate and the money she's given to Robby, something I feel more and more uneasy about. Even if he does disappear to France, and those pictures are never to be seen again, I can't shake a sense that the bad guy has won.

But more than any of those things, I cannot stop thinking about Joe.

Beautiful, kind, generous Joe who wasn't even remotely doing the dirty on Emily when he tried to kiss me. Gorgeous Joe, who built me a gazebo and made me fall in love with him . . . only for me to throw it away like a piece of dirt.

I have no idea how I can ever show my face in front of him again. I wanted him to hate me – and that's exactly what I made him do. I finally plunge into a dreamless sleep at around 4.30 a.m., but even then it's not for long. When my eyes flutter open, sunlight pushing its way through my window, the clock reads 8.14 a.m.

So, I flip off my sheets and push myself up, feeling a need to at least repair one of the relationships in my life right now. It might not be the most important one, but it's a start.

The woman who answers Edwin's door is tall and fine-boned with a silk scarf caressing her neck and a long suede coat in a violent shade of purple. I don't need her to introduce herself as Edwin's mum – they're so alike.

'Can I help?' she smiles, clearly wondering if I'm selling something.

'I'm a friend of Edwin's,' I announce. 'I've just come to say goodbye before he leaves.'

'Oh!' she exclaims. 'You must be Sarah.'

'Um . . . no, I'm—'

'Gillian!'

'Er, no.'

'Diane?' she tries.

'I'm Lauren.' Not even a flicker of recognition passes her face.

'Oh, Mum, there's a crockery set here.' Edwin arrives behind her and looks at me. 'Oh.'

'Hi,' I say, smiling uncomfortably.

'Come in, come in,' he says, beckoning me. 'Mother, this is Lauren.'

'I know, I can't keep up!' she hoots, as he reddens slightly around the ears. 'Darling, I'm going to leave you now – but you're coming over for breakfast before you go, aren't you?'

'I will, Mum,' he says, kissing her on the cheek.

'Nice to meet you, Mrs Blaire,' I smile.

'You too, Lisa,' she says, closing the door behind her.

Edwin looks at me. 'Just a little going-away gift,' I say, handing over my present: the art deco hip-flask I bought him months ago. 'You can open it now if you like.'

He doesn't exactly crack a smile, but beckons me over to the sofa, where he proceeds to unwrap the gift. I can tell he likes it, even before he says so.

'I'm sorry about the way things turned out,' I say.

'There's no need to be, Lauren. There really isn't. Things have worked out fine.'

'I know I've let you down over the flatmate thing – that I've left you in the lurch.'

'No, you haven't,' he tells me. 'I'm not going to Singapore either. Fiona and I are back together.'

I feel my eyes bulge. 'Really?'

'After everything that happened, it made me realise that excitement isn't all it's cracked up to be.' For a man whose idea of a wild night is getting drunk in front of *The Great British Bake Off*, this strikes me as quite a statement. 'Fiona isn't the most thrilling woman on earth, she'd be the first to admit that. But she and I ... I think fundamentally we're made for each other.'

'Wow.' It's all I can manage.

'So we're moving to Hampshire, to be closer to her family. I'm going to do some supply work and see how it goes. But I think I've really discovered what I want in life.'

Six months ago if he'd told me this, I'd have been devastated. Now, I'm so relieved I could weep. Edwin and Fiona are back together and it feels as though *some* equilibrium is restored in this world.

'You know what, Edwin, I hope you're really happy together. I genuinely mean that.'

He smiles. 'Thanks, Lauren. Or should I say . . . *Tiger*.'

I look at him blankly.

'That's what you asked me to call you that night. Tiger.'

'Oh! Oh, of course I did. Ha! Well, it was . . .an experience, wasn't it?'

'It certainly was.' He adjusts his trousers and sighs.

'Well, I'd better be going,' I say, standing up. 'You've still got a lot of packing to do, by the look of it.'

'I have,' he says, showing me to the door. We embrace in a suitably brief manner, before releasing each other. I turn to leave when it occurs to me to ask him something.

'Edwin, who are Sarah, Gillian and Diane?'

He shrugs. 'Oh, no one. Just . . . people on Tinder.'

I raise my eyebrows. 'Tinder?'

'Nothing ever came of any of them,' he reassures me. 'And I never *did* anything with them. Not like you and I did. But it was all very time-consuming at one point.'

I finally realise why getting a date with Edwin was harder than getting an audience with the Pope. He was a serial dater. 'Anyway, Lauren. I really appreciate you coming over here. And, for the record, that night we spent together . . . I honestly don't think I'll ever forget it.'

I haven't got the heart to tell him I don't think I'll ever remember it.

Chapter 53

Emily has lost the baby. It happened a few hours after her hospital visit, something confirmed by a scan this morning. She tells me in my living room, as she clutches a cup of untouched tea later in the afternoon.

I knew she was coming over because she texted en route to say Nick was dropping her off, but that still didn't prepare me for the broken figure on my doorstep, the one whose pale skin seems to cling to her cheekbones. As she'd rightly guessed, the A&E couldn't give her a definitive answer last night, so she had to wait to go to the maternity department this morning, where her darkest fears were confirmed.

'I'm so sorry,' I say helplessly. But the words don't seem big enough.

'I just feel … sick. I can't believe this has happened. This was a baby I never even knew I wanted.' The words scratch at the back of her throat. 'Now, I'd give anything – literally anything – for her to have lived.'

I lower my eyes. Emily had no way of knowing the sex of her baby, but she'd obviously convinced herself she was having a daughter.

'This doesn't change anything between Nick and me though,' she continues. 'He knows I need him more than ever.'

I pick up my tea, but can't bring myself to drink it. 'Nick's definitely leaving Jenny then?'

She stiffens at the use of his wife's name. Then she looks down. 'Tonight.'

I can't think of a thing to say that's appropriate.

'He loves me, Lauren. And I know there's a child involved, but from what Nick tells me, Tom is a sensible little boy. I'm certain this can all be done without disrupting anyone too much.'

She pulls her legs up tight on to the sofa, pressing them against her chest.

'How do you feel?' I ask, which is a silly question to ask someone after a miscarriage, but she misinterprets my motive anyway.

'A little nervous, I must admit. But I'll be glad when he's done it. This whole thing has been kept quiet for so long, I'll feel relieved when it's out in the open. When we can be a normal couple. Stella's said it's OK for me to bring someone to the wedding.'

My head jolts up in surprise.

'Why are you looking at me like that?' she frowns. 'There's

no sit-down meal or anything. It's a very relaxed affair, that's what she keeps telling us.'

'I know, sorry. I didn't mean to ...'

Her jaw tenses as she takes in my expression. 'You think this is wrong, don't you?'

'I'm worried about you,' I confess. 'About *this*. And, yes, I'll admit it – I can't stop thinking about poor Tom.'

She clearly doesn't appreciate the statement. 'Marriage breakdowns happen all the time, Lauren. It happens to loads of kids.'

'I know,' I say gently, conscious of what Emily's just been through. 'I'm just not convinced this won't have any effect on Tom. He knows something's been going on. He's told me.'

A pulse appears in her neck. 'What does he know?'

I don't tell Emily the whole story. The last thing I want is to upset her further today. But I tell her enough. Enough to make it clear that this is not the victimless situation she's convincing herself it is. That this is not something she can shrug her shoulders about and say, 'no harm done'.

'What's Tom like?' she asks eventually. I have no idea if the question has only just occurred to her, but I can only answer honestly.

'He's lovely. Funny, very sweet, full of personality. One of my favourites, actually.' I wonder if I've gone too far.

She sighs. 'You don't think Nick should leave, do you, Lauren? You don't approve of any of this. I knew you wouldn't.'

'It's not for me to approve or not approve. But I suppose I can't get out of my head that, when you've got a family and you've made a commitment to someone . . . well, I believe in the idea of sticking it out, of trying to make it work.'

'What if he has tried to make it work? Their marriage is dead.'

'If that's the case, then yes, you're right. If it's dead, there's nothing can be done.' I pause before speaking again. 'Although . . .'

'Although what?'

I have no idea if I'm right or not to say my next words: 'Jenny told me that, although they were having difficulties, they were making a go of it.'

'When did you speak to her?'

'Tom was wetting himself at school. He'd heard them discussing divorce.'

She swallows. 'That's surely all the more reason to end it. She must realise that Nick doesn't love her any more.'

I can feel the inside of my lip between my teeth. 'It's just that he'd bought her a diamond ring. She'd thought it was a way of proving he loved her.'

Part of me expects Emily to throw back another protestation, but she looks momentarily crushed.

I suddenly wish I'd kept my mouth shut. Yet, I feel the need to explain myself, digging myself into a deeper hole.

'I think the problem is that he's leaving them after meeting *you*,' I say. 'If Nick's marriage had broken down without someone else being around – without *you* being around – well, of course, these things happen sometimes. A ten-year marriage is never going to be as thrilling as a brand new romance – but that doesn't mean you just throw it away. Not when there's a child involved. Nick might ultimately decide that that's the only option open to him, but if so, he ought to come to that conclusion himself, without you being ready to leap in with both feet.'

Then she starts to weep. And I'm hit by an overwhelming wish that just sometimes I could keep my big mouth shut.

Chapter 54

In the following few days, I'm consumed by the question of what to do about Joe.

When I'm thinking straight, I'm certain I've been so spectacularly awful to him that there's no going back. And the idea of being brazen enough to attempt to approach him makes me cringe so much that I almost shrinkwrap myself onto the sofa.

Despite this, I clutch on to the pathetic hope that *something* I could say or do might make him forgive me, even if I can't imagine what it could be. The fact that he's a guest at Stella's wedding, this Saturday, leaves a rather odd set of possibilities open.

The first is to do nothing and say nothing. Ever. Just keep my head down, let him think I'm a nutcase and get on with his life. Which is the option I'd ordinarily be most comfortable with, on the grounds that I feel sick every time I think about what I said. And it would work if it wasn't for something else: I think I'm in love with him. I really think it's happened. I've totally fallen for a man who now despises me.

The second option is to wait until the wedding, hope he's drunk enough to engage in conversation, then fall to my knees and beg forgiveness, even if he might by rights ask why I'd waited until then.

Which brings me to the final possibility: to seek him out now and do everything within my power to tell him that I am, categorically, an arsehole – and that he is, categorically, the most incredible man on earth. Which doesn't make us a match made in heaven, I admit. But it's all I've got.

So, I spend the days before Stella's wedding trying to take the third option. *Trying* being the operative word.

I turn up at salsa night in the vague hope that he was bluffing about calling it quits. Only, he's not there. I end up attempting Marion's trickiest routine – the cuddle left turn, ladies' right turn, back-to-back and reverse wrap – with Frank. The results would be hilarious if I was even remotely in a laughing mood.

The next morning I decide to text him.

But deciding this and knowing the right thing to say are two different matters. I compose, then re-compose my message so often it's a wonder my fingertips aren't bleeding. My first text is so long my phone instructs me to turn it into an email. But an email feels like the wimp's option, so instead I determine to say something face to face.

I open a blank text again and write: I am so very sorry. And I'd like to explain why I reacted like I did, if you'd be willing to talk? x

Even that seems intensely crap, but I send it anyway and pray that he's willing to listen, despite owing me nothing.

I check my phone on average every three minutes.

But as three minutes become six minutes, then six minutes become nine minutes and, somehow, using this bizarre counting technique, I end up hitting the three *days* mark, I am forced to come to a devastating conclusion.

He is never going to text me back. He really does hate me.

By Friday, I am tearful and wracked with self-loathing and regret.

There's only one thing left. I have to try, one final time.

I drive to the Moonlight Hotel in a bid to seek him out.

As my car crunches up the drive, my heart is racing as if I've just sprinted. I park in the forecourt, and I head into reception as I realise that the hotel is finished – or as near as damn it.

'Oh hello, madam. We're not actually open until next week, I'm afraid. Can I help you at all?'

It's the same receptionist who greeted Cate, Emily and me when we first started at salsa all those months ago – but a significantly new and improved version. This time, she actually smiles.

I clear my throat. 'Um . . . I'm wondering if Joe Wilborne is available at all?'

'I can certainly find out for you. Who shall I say is looking for him?' she asks, before I give her my name and she radios through to another staff member.

Through a crackly blur, I hear someone offer to go and find him. And I wait, anxiety racing through my veins, before the radio springs back into life and I hear someone explain, with deliberate vagueness, that he's tied up and won't be able to come up to see me.

I don't leave a message. I can't think of anything else to say. So instead I am left to skulk out of the building, wishing I'd never come. I click open the door to my car and am about to step in when something stops me. Checking that nobody's looking, I tentatively walk round to the lake side of the hotel, to the window that overlooks the ballroom.

I press my hands against the glass and peer in, feeling my breath leave me as I take in the sight.

It's finished. And it's magnificent. Every corner of it glitters in the sunshine, the walls incandescent and glorious. It looks how it used to when the place was booming. When impossibly glamorous clientele – at least in my eyes – would spill onto the terrace and summer nights at the Moonlight Hotel were the stuff of legend. I could stay there all day and just look at it. But instead I tear away my eyes and head back to my car, knowing one thing for certain: my dad would have absolutely loved it.

*

As Cate gets ready for the wedding, I'm reminded of the person she used to be, when we'd dance round my bedroom during our teenage sleepovers. She even has the rollers in her hair, though this time she's actually got somewhere to go to when they're out, instead of just staying in my room, which was what we used to do, watching *Notting Hill* and trying not to crack our face packs from laughing.

This Cate has changed over the last few weeks, inevitably. But she's no longer consumed by panic, or by despair. She turns round at one point and flashes me a small smile of recognition, before turning up the volume on 'Groove Is in the Heart' by Deee-lite and starting to dance around the bedroom, luminous-eyed and energetic.

As the song comes to an end, she leans into the mirror and begins filling in her eyebrows with a pencil. 'With hindsight,' she muses, 'I could tell Joe only thought of Emily as a mate.'

I don't question why she never mentioned it until I filled her in earlier today, with Emily's permission.

'It's obvious he's got the hots for you, or at least it has been lately. Poor Edwin didn't get a look in.'

'*Poor Edwin* has been through half of Tinder, from what his mother said. But … really? Obvious?'

'There were a couple of nights at salsa when the two of you were virtually sizzling. And when I say "you", I mean both of you. I suspected weeks ago that if Joe had ever had feelings for Emily, they were yesterday's news.'

'Why didn't you say anything?' I ask.

'Same as you,' she shrugs. 'Because I thought he was going out with Emily. I wasn't going to encourage you. Besides, after a while I became too wrapped up in my own problems to even think about anything else. Sorry.'

'Have you seen Will yet?' I ask.

She sighs. 'No.'

'You know he's going to be at the wedding?' I ask.

'Yeah. Not sure how I'm ever going to face him though.'

I take a sip of tea and don't need to tell her I know exactly how she feels. I decide to change the subject. 'So how was Stella this morning? Nervous?'

Cate spent the morning delivering flowers to the venue – the gorgeous, rambling Swan Inn at Newby Bridge – and then to the bride and her bridesmaids at home.

'Very, but also ridiculously excited. *And* quite plastered,' Cate tells me. 'Her bridesmaids were already plying her with champagne and it was only 10 a.m. I'll be surprised if she doesn't stagger down that aisle.'

I glance at the clock. 'Hey, we'd better get going. We need to be at the hotel in less than an hour.'

'I'm ready!' Cate replies, as she throws on her heels. She looks beautiful today, with the tendrils of her hair curled, a gorgeous short silk dress, and slim, athletic legs. We grab our bags and stumble down the stairs in clatter of heels. I'm looking for my keys as Cate idly takes her phone out.

'I thought you'd given up on social media after the last few months,' I say.

'I had, but I missed all the funny cat videos,' she grins.

I laugh and finally find my keys, checking my hair in the mirror. But I don't feel excited, not even vaguely. I feel sick – literally sick – at the thought of what might be about to happen. I open the door, and wonder why Cate isn't behind me.

Then I spin round and see her slumped against the wall, staring incredulously at her phone. And then I know exactly what's happened. The picture is back.

All my instincts were right: Robby couldn't be trusted. All he really wanted was Cate, not the money, so when she continued to reject him, right until the end, it only made him angrier, more bitter than ever. And unwilling to relinquish the one, twisted bit of power over her he had left.

Chapter 55

Cate refuses to come to the wedding. The transformation in the space of minutes only serves to underline how fragile her recovery was. I spend the next ten minutes begging her to come, to no avail.

She insists it's because she needs to contact Facebook about the picture, but it's obvious as she crumples on the sofa that it's about more than that. Once again, her world has come crashing down on her. She knows that if she walks into that hotel today, half the guests could have been treated to yet another humiliating glimpse of her body. A picture that should have stayed private, a body that should have remained hers and hers alone. But, thanks to Robby, didn't.

With the clock ticking towards 2 p.m., and in the absence of any other ideas, I have no option but to leave her to drive home to her flat, hugging her silently before jumping in the car and driving like a maniac towards the hotel. I screech into the car park and stumble through two glass doors – just in time to see guests filing in from the bar to the ceremony room. I scan my surroundings to see if I can spot Emily, but someone taps me on the shoulder.

'Hey.' It's Will. He looks very alone without Cate by his side.

'Hey, how are you?' I say warily.

'Not bad. Are you by yourself?' he asks – and I can't tell by looking at him if he's seen the picture on Facebook or not.

I nod. 'Yes. Cate's had a bit of a . . . crisis.'

He looks perplexed. 'One of the pictures has reappeared on her Facebook feed.'

From the shock on his face he apparently didn't know. Beyond that, I can't work out what's going in his head. 'She didn't mean all that stuff she said the other night, you know,' I tell him.

'I know,' he says in a low voice.

A momentary silence descends on us. Then I ask: 'Are you here by yourself?' It couldn't be more obvious that this is code for: *Where is Joe?*

'Yes,' he replies. 'Joe's had to step into a babysitting crisis.'

I feel myself deflate. 'He's looking after a *baby?*'

'Well, Sophie's twelve. Joe's sister Mel is over for a few days with her, only some big work crisis erupted yesterday afternoon and she had to fly to Dublin until this afternoon. So Joe's had to back out of the wedding.'

'Oh. Oh, I see.'

'I think he's disappointed not to be here. He wanted to say goodbye to everyone properly before he leaves.'

The air seems to be vacuumed from the room. 'Where's he going?' I ask, as we approach a row of chairs at the back of the ceremony room.

'It's meant to be confidential,' Will says. 'But I can tell you, Lauren. Now that the Moonlight Hotel is in the shape it's in, he's got a buyer lined up. His plan is to sell, then go and manage another project.'

'Where's he going?' I repeat, more urgently this time.

But as the toastmaster appears and asks for hush before the ceremony, the room quietens.

'I've said too much already,' Will whispers.

I fix my eyes on the front of the room, feeling emotion rise up into my throat as I focus on the ushers. Mike is in his tails. Even from here I can see the sweat glistening on his brow, his feet shuffling from side to side as he tries to keep a lid on his nerves and fails entirely.

I glance at the door, awaiting the arrival of the bride, but Emily appears first. She slips into the back, looking mildly flustered as she takes the only seat left in the row behind us and clutches her little silver bag. She's alone as far as I can tell, though I check back a few more times afterwards to see if Nick turns up. But all that happens is she catches my eye and gives me a stiff smile.

Then the string quartet at the side of the room open with the Bridal March. The guests turn round and after a few beats, Stella appears with her dad, three bridesmaids and a flower girl with nail varnish so glittery it could be seen from Outer Space.

Stella's dress is gorgeous, a vintage ivory gown that's fitted at the waist, with delicate, chiffon sleeves. It's demure and angelic and a little bit sexy all at the same time. Her face lights up with excitement and nerves, before she starts walking up the aisle faster than she should, until her dad gently tugs her by the elbow. She giggles and slows down, clearly reminding herself that it isn't a race.

When she reaches her groom and turns to look at him, the light in their eyes makes the back of my neck tingle. Stella's younger brother James stands up to deliver a reading, telling the guests with a slight croak in his voice that it was written by Bob Marley. It begins: 'He's not perfect . . .' It's a lesson in the art of loving. It's simple and beautiful and perfect. And I can hardly bear to listen to it.

As the ceremony unfolds, I think about Joe's letter to me, the gazebo, the feelings he very clearly had for me. I didn't just let him slip through my fingers. I didn't even just push him away. I banged my fist on his chest like a spoiled child and hurt him in the worst way possible. And yes, I thought I was doing it for the right reasons, but the fact that it's too bloody late now is inescapable.

It's not just that Joe's not here that makes me want to cry. It's that, after what I've done, he's *never* going to be here. I've lost a part of my future. And in its place is a world without Joe, one devoid of colour and music and the way he made me feel every time I danced with him. As if every bit of me was smiling.

My throat feels thick with despair as Stella and Mike take a seat to sign the wedding register and a thought kicks inside my brain: *What an almighty fuck-up you've made, Lauren!*

I fix my gaze on a ribbon on the chair in front of me as the registrar starts speaking again. I don't even hear most of the words, until I'm jolted by one sentence.

'*This day will form a milestone in your lives. You will look back upon it with love and happiness, as the start of a new life together.*'

I make the decision as the sentence is still hot in the air, floating over our heads. Today I need to make my own milestone – one way or another.

But it's not until the register is signed, the happy couple are pronounced man and wife and they're skipping back down the aisle as Pachelbel's *Canon* rings out, that I lean into Will and say, 'I need to know where Joe is.'

'What?' He can barely hear me.

'Where's Joe? Is he at the hotel?'

'Why?' The closing music rings out triumphant, as a deafening applause launches through the room.

'Because I need to go and find him.'

He looks at me as if I'm completely insane. 'But you're at a wedding.'

'Yes, but this is important. Besides, everyone will just be milling round for a couple of hours now, while the photos are taken. Nobody will notice I'm gone. I can be there and back in two hours.'

'Not where Joe is,' he tells me. 'Not without seriously pushing it.'

Chapter 56

'Do you believe me yet?' asks Will. 'About this being a bad idea, I mean.'

We are standing underneath a 'tree trekking' course at one of the activity centres on the east shore of Windermere. I'm vaguely aware that it's been here for a few years, but it's not the kind of place I'd normally go anywhere near. The mere thought brings me out in a cold sweat.

The course is apparently designed to test balance and endurance. I've never felt the need to do either – why would you? It consists of rope ladders, trapezes, zip wires and about twenty-odd other challenges – all of which are suspended 25 feet in the air.

'We've got an hour and a half before the group photos are taken, according to the Best Man,' I tell Will. 'So as long as we're back before then, no one will ever know we're gone.'

'The guy in the office said Joe and Sophie are in the group that's just set off,' Will says, and I remind myself to thank him later for indulging me in what he clearly thinks is a ludicrous endeavour. 'The course meanders along here then heads down to the lake. So if we follow it from the ground and keep our eyes peeled we should, in theory, be able to find them.'

'Great. This way then,' I say authoritatively as I attempt to stride off, high heels a-clattering, past a family in head-to-toe North Face gear.

It's fair to say that Will and I don't blend in here, not today at least. The fact that we're the only people in sight who are *not* wearing climbing boots and waterproofs and harnesses is only the half of it; between the heels and floaty Karen Millen jumpsuit I couldn't look more out of place if I was wearing a bowl of tropical fruit on my head.

'They're there,' Will announces as my eyes dart up, momentarily blinded by a shard of sun before I see him, straddling the two steps on a bridge that looks straight out of an Indiana Jones movie.

'JOE!'

It's Will who shouts his name as both Joe and the girl in front of him – who I can only assume is Sophie – freeze. While Joe clings on and peers down, Sophie loses her step and falls briefly into her harness, scrambling back into position with the help of her uncle.

'What are you doing here?' he shouts down eventually.

I realise he's directing this at me, but find myself suddenly mute.

'Go on then,' Will urges me.

I clear my throat. 'Joe, I really need to talk to you,' I yell, as heat shoots to my face. 'There's so much I want to say—'

'Excuse me, love.' I spin round to see one of the staff marching towards me. 'You can't have a conversation from down here. It's not safe. When someone's on that course, they need to concentrate. You'll have to wait until they've finished.'

'How long will it take?' I ask desperately, looking at my watch.

He looks up. 'Hmm ... from where they are, I'd say forty-five minutes or so. If they're quick.'

'Oh, that's no good,' I tell him. 'I've got a wedding to go to.'

Judging by his expression, I can tell that he fails entirely to see the relevance of what I've got in my diary this weekend.

'She could always meet him at the bottom of the zip wire, couldn't she?' Will suggests. 'That's halfway round the course. Am I right in saying you can pay to only do that part of it?'

The guy shrugs. 'Yeah, she could do that. You'd be with them in about fifteen minutes then.'

'There you go,' Will concludes.

'Brilliant!' I agree, then: 'Sorry, but which zip wire are we talking about?'

At that moment, a hideous, ear-piercing roar echoes

through the air and I look up to see a grown man above me in a harness, travelling at the sort of speed Concorde used to reach.

'Surely to God you don't mean that one?' I say.

'No, not that,' Will laughs. 'I mean *this*.' He beckons me up a small pathway until we're standing at a higher point on the hill.

And it's there that I first set eyes on the precise zip wire he's talking about. Only to call it a 'zip wire' is misleading, at least in my head; for that implies something fun and whizzy and significantly smaller. *This* is beyond the realms of sanity. Something completely out of the question.

'It starts at the top of the four-storey tower and runs 250 metres down to the lake,' he tells me. Then he takes in my expression. 'It's fun. Whenever I've got friends with kids over I recommend this.'

'*Children* are allowed to do this?' I clarify, feeling mildly delirious.

'Of course. They have no fear at that age,' he adds casually.

'I can't possibly do that, Will,' I announce.

He shrugs. 'It's up to you. We can just go back to the wedding.'

I realise I'm chewing the side of my mouth so hard I can taste blood. I have never felt a greater urge to get something off my chest. To sort something out. The possibility of me *not* addressing this issue – right here, right now – is unthinkable.

'Isn't there some sort of age restriction, or height restriction, or something?' I enquire, as we start heading back to our original point.

'Are you over five?' the staff member asks.

'Yes,' I squeak.

'Then you're in.'

'Lauren!' I look up and see Joe. 'I've got to go.'

I watch as Joe disappears into the woodland above, following his niece, along with all hopes of me ever making it up to him before he disappears off somewhere. Then a sentence fires from my mouth before I realise I've even thought it. 'Right, I'm doing it. I'm definitely going to do this.'

'I take it you have some suitable footwear before I go and get you harnessed up?' The guy looks at my shoes. They were purchased in Kurt Geiger and have a four-inch heel and two straps similar in consistency to dental floss.

'I've got something in the boot that'll do,' Will offers.

We scarper back to the car and he hands me a pair of wellies, which would be an ideal choice of footwear, except for them being a size 11 and a half.

'Who do you think I am, Bilbo Baggins?' I ask.

'I've got socks too. They'll stay on with a bit of padding.' And so, I pull on a pair of thick socks, followed by my giant boots and try to convince myself I am channelling Kate Moss at Glasto, rather than a Hobbit with a limp. Then I trip over myself all the way to the office, pay £12 and, as confidently as possible through my warbling tonsils, ask to be harnessed up for the zip wire.

The staff are polite enough not to question why I look as though I've raided a dressing-up box, as I climb up the four-storey tower to reach the platform for my safety check.

Will is behind me, as he has been the entire time. In amongst the gazillion thoughts whizzing through my brain is a swell of affection for a man who would have been fantastic for Cate, had her circumstances been different. It proves to be a fleeting sensation after I turn and register that he's suppressing a smile. 'What's so funny?'

He straightens his face. 'You don't really want me to answer that question, do you?'

'Probably not.'

'Seriously though – good on you,' he adds.

'What do you mean?'

He looks awkward, as if he's struggling to say the right thing without offending me. 'I just mean … you screwed things up with Joe. Big time. Like, irreversibly. I don't actually think you've got a hope in hell of him telling you anything other than to sling your hook. Sorry.'

I listen to this with my eyes stretched, as I suddenly find myself at the front of the queue being strapped up on to the zip wire.

'Is this supposed to be a pep talk?' I grunt, as the instructor performs safety checks and my heart nearly flies out of my chest.

'The point I was about to make is this: you're still giving it a go.' Will grins. 'You're a true romantic, Lauren. Hat's off to you.'

I look into his eyes one last time and say: 'I'm not sure I'm a true romantic. I think I'm just like you. I know that some people are worth fighting for.'

He doesn't answer.

I spin around to find myself facing a wooden board that appears to be controlled by some sort of lever. I am in a harness, with so many clips and contraptions securing me to the line that I know – of course I know! – that I am safe. Statistically, the chances of me being the first person to die a hideous and gruesome death in this way are probably fairly slim.

But while the sensible part of my brain keeps repeating that, another instinctive part can only focus on the fact that I am miles from the ground. That if that rope broke, I'd be face first in a field of mud with my knees twisted at a right angle around my ears.

These are the cheery thoughts going through my mind as a team member gives out his instructions, his words threading through one ear and out the other, drowned out by the thudding of my heart, and Will's words swirling around my head.

Then the lever lowers. I look ahead. I cannot see Joe. I cannot see *anyone*. The end might be in sight but it's way too far away to make out more than a handful of dots – which I assume are people – in the distance. It's at that point I realise that the whole thing is so far beyond my capabilities that the only option is to ask to get off. Now.

'Can I go first?' I look to my right to see a girl of about eight, who's so ice cool I am virtually sizzling as I stand next to her. I close my eyes and tell myself that if I am ever to win back Joe, and prove to him how sorry I am, I need to focus on this. Focus hard.

'WHEEE-EEE-EEE-EEE!'

The little girl is off, hurtling in the direction of the lake, clearly having a whale of a time. I don't want to shout 'WHEEE-EEE-EEE-EEE!' I just want to *have* a wee; my control of all bodily functions has never felt flimsier.

'Ready when you are,' the instructor tells me jovially, obviously wondering why I'm still here. I hesitate. 'Any time you like.'

I close my eyes and inch forward. Then, before I black out in panic, I step off the ledge.

The experience of flying towards the lake at a similar velocity to the Millennium Falcon during a meteor shower takes seconds and feels like forever.

My heart is the size of a beach ball, thumping violently

inside my ribcage. Only that's nothing compared with that stupid bloody woman who is SHRIEKING at the top of her lungs and . . . oh, that woman turns out to be me.

My knuckles aren't so much white as on fire, as I clutch on for dear life, my legs knotted together as I perch on the harness in a constipated position, all the while hurtling towards the end, gaining in speed and wondering how THE HELL THIS IS EVER GOING TO STOP.

When I think the experience cannot possibly get any worse, I note to my horror that the harness I'm in is starting to turn – slowly, ever so slowly – in direct contrast with my approach to Windermere. Eventually I'm facing in entirely the wrong direction and heading, arse-first, to the landing pad.

I desperately try to start spinning myself back the right way, yanking my head in the right direction – just enough to spot a group of people, one of whom is Sophie, gathering at the spectator ledge in front of where I'm due to land.

I'm still some way from the landing pad, when I register that a malfunction is occurring.

My right welly is slipping off.

I lift my leg to the side and start jerking it in an upward motion, hoping this will do the trick. And this tactic might have worked if I was on the ground and hopping on one foot, but when you're flying through the air at this speed, it's another matter altogether.

After several sharp thrusts upwards, which results in me looking like a life-size, eccentrically-dressed marionette, the welly has edged itself back slightly on to my foot and I'm attempting to grip it in place with just my toes.

At this point I know that there is one option open to me: this is make or break time. So I close my eyes and give my leg a single, massive kick upwards, designed to return the welly firmly to its rightful position back on my foot.

The result is catastrophic.

The boot flies off my foot and soars across the field, at such a tremendous speed that at first glance it resembles a giant, rubber bird of prey. A group of Girl Guides run for cover.

I don't actually see the welly land, since by this stage the harness has spun me round again and I seem to be gaining in speed, if that's possible, as I reach the end. Screeching and breathless, I close my eyes and wait until the rope reaches the end of the line, which it does with a whiplash-inducing flop.

A staff member runs up and grabs me, pulling me to a spot where I can put my feet down. She's an earthy, sporty type who, it appears, has not run towards me to check if I'm still conscious and breathing.

'Enjoy that?' she grins, clearly not noticing that my face is the shade of an avocado bathroom suite.

'Wonderful,' I croak as I look up and see Joe. I disengage from the zip wire and hobble towards him as Sophie informs me helpfully, 'You lost your welly.'

'I know,' I reply apologetically. I can no longer feel my legs. Or face. In fact, I can barely speak. 'I need to go and get it.'

The three of us silently plod out of the way of the zip wire and I begin limping across the field, my foot squelching so I'm ankle-deep in mud every time I put it down. I had so much to say to Joe and now, suddenly, my head is empty.

Sophie races ahead. 'If I fetch the welly, can we go and get some ice creams, Uncle Joe?'

'I'll buy you a whole van,' I interject, as she laughs and runs away.

Joe and I continue walking behind her, as I try and find some words. 'Joe . . .'

We stop and he turns to look at me, briefly, but it's clear my performance has done little to impress him. He is reluctant to meet my eye, so I do the only thing I can do: keep talking. Words tumble from my mouth faster than I can really think about any of them. But the thing about them is this: I really mean every single one.

'Joe, I don't know where to begin, except to say that I am sorry. For everything I said. I must've come across as a selfish, unhinged idiot – although I promise you that I'm not one. Not in the slightest. It was totally out of character. The thing was, I was convinced you and Emily were an item. More than an item, actually. She was – well, I'm not meant to say anything, but I thought – wrongly – that you and she were . . . I thought she was pregnant. But she isn't. It turns out ... well, it doesn't matter why now, but that's what I thought.'

He looks stunned by this outburst.

'We never even slept together,' he tells me simply. 'We just went on a few dates, then became walking buddies when it became clear that we had both become distracted.' His eyes bore into me. 'And, yes, I'm talking about you, Lauren. I became distracted by *you*.'

Tears fill my eyes; I don't know what to say. 'Every time I think about that gazebo, it breaks my heart.' And it's true. 'I can't bear to remember the things I said to you about it. I'm so ashamed, Joe.'

'Well, you don't need to worry about the gazebo any longer.'

'You haven't taken it down?'

'It's happening this afternoon.' And then, because there doesn't seem to be anything else to say, he turns to walk away from me. The sight of him leaving makes my legs buckle.

'Joe, please!' I hobble after him, as one bare foot sinks further into the mud with every step. 'I cannot believe I would do this – say this – to a man I've ... *argh!*'

I am suddenly unable to take another step. And so I find myself sitting in the mud in my posh jumpsuit, wearing a lone welly, mascara smeared down my cheeks and an overwhelming sense of despair. Time seems to stand still as I gaze across the lake, helpless, cold and miserable to my very bones.

What the hell am I going to do now? About everything. Hot tears sting my cheeks as I sit, sobbing.

'Oh, for God's sake, you can't stay there.' I look up on hearing his voice. He's walking back to me and then tugging me to my feet. Then he's square in front of me.

I'd forgotten how big he was until now, something I'd noticed on the very first day we danced. The thought that he'll never take my hand again like that makes my chest contract.

'*To a man you've what?*' he whispers urgently.

'Eh? What?' I blub.

'To a man you've *what?* You were about to say something. I'm too intrigued – or maybe just weak-willed – to walk away and not find out what the rest of that sentence was.'

Through my tears, I see that his expression has softened and that very fact – the way he looks at me – makes me pull myself together. Sometimes, I decide, you've just got to spit it out. Throw caution to the wind and lay yourself completely bare.

'Joe, this is what it comes down to,' I say, taking a deep breath, before declaring loudly, 'I would knit you a scarf.'

We stand gazing at each other as the meaning of this sentence filters into his head, and his face is lit up by a wide, spontaneous smile. I take this as encouragement. 'And I'd plant you some trees,' I sniffle. 'And bake you a cake. I would even give you my last Rolo.'

He tries to maintain his cool but he's glowing – and his smile warms every bit of me up. 'Seriously? Even the Rolo?'

'Yeah,' I grin nonchalantly. 'Even the Rolo. Well, probably.'

He laughs now, a big wholesome laugh that gives me a sliver of hope – that there's a possibility that he'll forgive me. And then the most miraculous thing happens.

He slides a warm hand behind my neck and leans down to kiss me. Only this is not a kiss like the last one – not one we fall into then have to stumble out of. When his mouth touches mine, it's as if every nerve in my body has been diverted to my lips. His body feels hot and strong and his neck smells faintly of earth and salt and aftershave. And the whole experience, his mouth hard on mine, his big arms around my back ... it's so passionate and all-consuming and blow-your-socks off awesome, that it makes me feel weak at the knees for reasons that go beyond the fact that I am only wearing one welly.

I am lost in the moment, in this eternal place and time, with the sun high over the trees and fells, as the sky swells with light. Then he finally pulls back and brushes my hair away from my face with his fingertips before releasing me. I watch as he wrestles with his harness and finally manages to extricate his phone out of his jacket.

'What are you doing?' I ask.

He reaches down and takes me by the hand, and together

we start walking to the exit, as Sophie appears from behind a tree, clutching my welly.

'Putting a call into Gianni,' he replies, squeezing my hand. 'To see if I can rescue your gazebo.'

Chapter 57

Will and I get back to the wedding, after a quicker-than-ideal spruce-up, before Stella has even noticed our absence. She's too caught up in the whirlwind of the day. Joe arrives about half an hour later – after his sister has arrived to collect Sophie.

I'd tried phoning Cate while we were on our way back to the venue, but her phone went straight to voicemail. *I wondered how you are, sweetheart? I say. Please let me know you're OK. I'm worried about you.*

'Where's your Karen Millen jumpsuit?' asks Emily, in front of the mirror in the ladies.

'I thought I'd have a quick change. Just call me Lady Gaga.' She forces a smile.

'How are you, Emily?' I ask.

'Oh, look, I know I was barely even pregnant. And I know that lots of early pregnancies end in miscarriage,' she says. 'I just . . . I feel shit. Completely shit.'

I put my arm around her and hug her. 'What made you decide not to bring Nick along today?'

It takes her a moment to say, 'I've called it a day with Nick.'

'Seriously?' I didn't know what I was expecting her to say but it wasn't this.

'Do you know what it was, Lauren?' she asks tremulously. 'It was the ring you told me about. That sounds stupid, doesn't it, but afterwards I just kept thinking to myself, *this doesn't add up.* He'd told me his marriage was as good as over. I'd already had my suspicions that that wasn't the whole truth, and the ring just added to them. You don't buy a token of love for someone you feel *nothing* for, do you?'

'Maybe he was confused,' I offer, wondering why I'm trying to come up with an explanation for him.

'I've no doubt he was. It was clear when I discussed all this with him that he still had feelings for Jenny. He just couldn't deny it.' She glances down at her pale hands. 'If I'm honest, I wanted him to tell me you'd been mistaken about the ring and that the relationship was as he'd always told me: irretrievable.'

'He didn't?'

She shakes her head. 'He admitted that part of him still loved her.' Her voice chokes. 'But then he said that part of him loved me too and that he suddenly didn't know what to do.'

'Oh, Emily . . .' I clutch her cold, delicate hand.

She goes on, 'I don't know if it's possible to love two

people, but I do know one thing: *I* can't share someone's affections. And if there's a chance he can make it work with Jenny, then ... as much as it kills me to say it, he *should*. I grew up in a family with a mum and a dad and, although I've never sat and meditated over that, I know I was privileged to do so. If Nick ends up leaving Jenny, leaving Tom, then that has to be his decision. I don't want to be any part of it. And I certainly don't want to be the cause of it.'

'That's really brave of you, Emily.'

Her shoulders move involuntarily upwards. 'I can't switch off my feelings for him. But all I've done for the last twenty-four hours is think about this. I've told Nick he should try and be the best father he can. And that means staying put. Trying to work things out. And never seeing me again.'

'He'll come after you,' I tell her. I can see how much her face crumples with emotion, how hard this has been for her. She really does love him.

She sniffs away tears and tries to hide them as the door pushes open and Stella's mother walks in. 'We'll see,' she whispers.

Then we head outside, spilling into the hotel lobby, out of earshot of anyone else.

'You're going to find a man who's perfect for you,' I promise her. 'And he'll be all yours.'

She nods. 'Thanks, Lauren. Speaking of which, you and Joe ...'

I tense up. 'You know about me and Joe?'

'I saw him reach out to hold your hand when he came in just now,' she smiles. 'I'm really happy for you, Lauren. I knew he liked you.'

'Really?'

'Yes. I didn't know *you* liked him, of course – I thought you were still obsessed by Edwin and moving to Singapore. But Joe and I have done a lot of talking on our walks in the last few months, and you've been a topic of conversation that's barely left his lips. I want you to know that if I'd even remotely known that you were interested in him, then there's no way I'd have kept up the charade that we were together.'

'Well,' I shrug. 'Edwin and Singapore turned out to be my little charade too. Part of me hoped to convince myself I *was* still mad about Edwin – it would've been so much easier had I been.' My phone beeps. 'That could be Cate.' I take my mobile out of my bag and read her message.

> I'm fine, honestly. Just enjoy the wedding and please don't worry xxx

I sigh. Because, somehow, I don't believe a word of it.

The wedding is an absolute riot. Esteban seems intent on breaking a world record in chatting up bridesmaids, before lingering on Stella's older cousin Jasmine, who takes one look at his biceps and seems unable to lift her tongue off the floor.

He's not the only one who's attracted attention today. As Will joins me, Joe and Emily on the lush terrace that runs alongside the meandering River Leven, I take a sip of champagne and notice when most of the guests spill out of the double doors that he's winning admiring glances from every direction. I honestly don't think he's even noticed though.

'The weather's meant to be good next week, Will. Fancy tackling Great Gable?' Joe asks.

'Why not,' he answers.

'We might even persuade Action Girl to come with us,' Joe adds with a smirk. I realise he's referring to me.

'Very funny,' I reply, feeling my cheeks heat up.

'Hello, you lot!' Stella heads over, sloshing champagne about so haphazardly there's only about an inch left in her glass by the time she reaches us.

'Stella!' Joe says, standing up to kiss her on the cheek. 'Congratulations. You look beautiful.' The rest of us heartily endorse this statement, because it's completely true, despite the fact that her tiara won't stay on straight.

'Oh, I thank you, I thank you! So the burning question on my lips is this,' she says, turning very serious. 'What did you think of the organza chair tie-backs?'

The men look at each other blankly. 'I made them myself,'

she adds proudly, failing to cover the slight slur in her words. 'Seven bloody hours it took to get those bows straight.'

The hint of a smile appears on Will's lips. 'Well, I can say categorically that those bows were definitely straight. That's what I said to you, Joe, didn't I? "Look at the bows on these chairs. They're sooo ... *straight*."'

Stella purses her lips, suppressing a giggle. 'I hope you're not being sarcastic.'

He laughs. 'Congratulations, Stella. It's been a great day.' Then he glances self-consciously at the rest of the group and excuses himself to go to the gents.

A thought buries itself in Stella's brow and she turns to me with a frown. 'Where's Cate?'

I squirm. 'Oh, um, well ... '

'She's there,' Emily whispers.

We all look up. Conversations are being cut short, heads are turning, and a sizeable number of guests have their eyes on our friend.

As Cate scans the crowd, searching for us, I wave to her and go to leap up before she can change her mind and dart home again.

Only before I get there, something surprising happens. She straightens her back, draws a fortifying breath into her lungs and looks, for the flicker of a moment, every bit the confident woman she always was. Then she walks towards the guests, her head held high.

Instead of slinking away from people – people she knows could well have seen her picture – Cate does what she does best: she starts chatting. She's making small talk with Stella's mum when I reach them, discussing posies and button-holes and how she's not a fan of gypsophila as she thinks it looks dated. I join in briefly, nodding my approval about the choice of colours, when the mother of the bride is politely swept away to take part in another family photograph.

Cate forces her mouth into another stoic smile when she sees me, then she leans in to give me a hug. 'Hello, you.'

'You came.'

She responds with a tight nod. 'I did.' Then she braces herself to add: 'I have spent the afternoon with the police.'

'Oh my God – really?'

'I had to,' she concludes. 'You were right, Lauren. There was no other option left. I have to face the fact that everywhere I go, anywhere I go, people might have seen that picture. And that is horrendous. But there comes a point when you have to say to yourself: *I* didn't do anything wrong. Nothing at all. So I refuse to let my life be ruined by a vicious little prick like Robby.'

I squeeze her arm. 'That's the truth.'

'Well, I'm still dying inside just being here,' she confesses. 'But I won't be bullied. Not by him and not by anyone. So if anyone here has anything to say about the fact that they happened to see my boobs on Facebook this morning, bring it on.'

I'm about to respond when I become aware of someone tapping Cate on the shoulder. It takes me a second to place the woman, but when I do, recognition is instant: it's the shop assistant from the convenience store near Cate's flat – the one with the blonde bob who froze when we went to buy wine that time. Cate's jaw tenses.

'Might I just say something,' she says sternly.

'Please,' I leap in. 'If you're going to say anything detrimental about—'

'No,' she replies, horrified by the suggestion. 'On the contrary. I was just going to say . . . we all know what's happened. It must have been awful for you. But nobody who's worth knowing thinks any less of you.'

For a moment, Cate looks as if she might burst into tears of gratitude. Instead, she manages to mutter a thank you – or several – before the woman disappears to re-join her husband.

Cate lifts up her glass and clinks it against mine, her lip trembling slightly as she says, 'Amen to that.'

Then she looks up – and freezes. I follow her gaze until I see Will standing with the rest of the group again. He looks away and continues to make conversation with Joe.

'Any bright ideas about what I say to make this right?' Cate asks me.

For the sake of brevity, I don't fill her in on everything I've been through this afternoon. But I do say simply: 'I'd recommend starting with one word. *Sorry*'.

Stella and Mike's first dance is the most brilliant spectacle I think I've ever seen in my life. It's not just that Mike is putting on a miraculous attempt at dancing without risking the two of them ending up face first on the starlit dance floor. It's not just that they're spinning round, twirling and salsa-ing like the best of them.

It's the performance Stella puts on in order to convince Mike – and everyone else – that she had *absolutely no idea* that he'd learned to dance. She gasps, she coos, her eyes are wide in amazement – as Mike looks thoroughly delighted at the 'surprise' he's given his new wife.

I'll be honest and say I'm amazed people are taken in by Stella's acting job, which is hammier than a Peperami factory. But somehow they are. I can only put it down to the dim lighting and flowing booze.

'I think he's pulled this off, don't you?' Lulu asks from the edge of the dance floor as we watch. I glance over to see if she's being serious. She appears to be, deadly so. 'I'm so glad you decided not to tell Stella,' she goes on. 'It would've ruined the whole thing.'

I redden around the gills. 'All's well that ends well,' I grin nervously.

Then I glance over at the corner of the room and see Cate and Will standing opposite each other, talking.

I have no idea what they're saying. But the sparkle in Will's eyes makes me suspect that they might just be able to have their new start, after all. He takes my friend by the hand and leads her to the dance floor, and it's as if the two of them were never apart.

'Now that's nice to see.' I spin round and see Joe behind me. He reaches out for my hand, sending a shot of excitement through me.

'It is,' I agree and it strikes me that tonight, somehow, *everything* feels right. Except one thing.

As the song draws to a close, the beat of another song takes over. 'Shall we get some air?' I suggest.

Joe leads me outside, where we kiss under a black sky, alight with stars. And although I know it'll kill the mood, I need to raise something now – because if I don't, it'll just eat away at me. 'Will mentioned that you were planning to leave,' I say.

I feel him tense up. 'Oh … he told you.'

'He said you had your eye on a new venture.' He does not reply, just looks into my eyes as my lips tremble and the warm breeze ruffles my hair.

'At least I got a proper snog out of you, I suppose,' I say, forcing a laugh. 'Before you left.'

A million things are whizzing round my head, but the main one is this: I want him to say he's not going. That he's changed his mind. That he's going to stay and we can make a go of things and—

'It *is* time for me to leave, Lauren,' he says, as if reading my thoughts. 'I've never stayed anywhere as long as here. And much as I love it, from a business point of view, there's nothing else around for me at the moment. I've looked.'

I nod. 'I understand.'

'Everything I can do for the Moonlight Hotel is done. I don't *run* hotels – I set them up.'

'You don't have to explain,' I whisper.

He reaches out, clutches my hand. 'This is what I do, Lauren. But I promise you the Moonlight Hotel will be in good hands, if that's what you're worried about . . .'

I look at him, incredulous. 'I'm not worried about that at all. I had no doubt about it. I just . . .'

'What?' he asks.

I look into his eyes and feel compelled, by alcohol or adrenalin, to confess something. 'I'll miss you. And I'd have loved to . . . just *be* with you. And I suppose it's this simple: I don't want to lose a man I've kind of fallen for . . . ' I feel a swell of emotion as reality comes crashing down on me.

'You've kind of fallen for me?'

I redden and roll my eyes. 'Don't ask me to repeat that.'

His hand slips behind my waist and pulls me closer to him. 'It's OK, I won't. But for the record, I've kind of fallen for you too.'

'Have you?'

He nods. I just want – there and then – for him to kiss me and for it to never end. But he doesn't. Instead he says: 'Can I ask you something, Lauren?'

'Of course.'

'This is going to sound really sudden. Stupidly sudden. Except in my head it's not, because it's all I've thought about for the last few months – even if we only technically got together three hours ago. I wondered if you'd consider . . . well, would you consider coming with me?'

My heart nearly stops. 'Coming with you where?'

'Well, that's the thing. I haven't decided yet. And we don't need to go immediately, but I would like to start making plans, putting things into place.' My head starts spinning again. 'There's a place we're looking at in Pembrokeshire, and another in Cornwall. But there's also the possibility of somewhere further afield.'

My eyes flicker upwards. 'Australia?'

He lets the word filter into his brain and starts laughing. 'Well, I've got no experience out there, but we *have* got hotels in other countries . . . '

'Oh, don't worry, I never for a second thought—' I start to protest, feeling silly for even blurting it out.

'Don't apologise. It's not beyond the realms,' he says clearly surprising himself. 'I think, Lauren, that you may have just planted the seed of something. Something insane, I should add.'

Our faces are inches apart, and although there are other people milling out of the doors now, it's just impossible to hold back from kissing him. Fortunately, he seems happy to oblige, at least at first. Eventually, he whispers, 'OK, I'll do you a deal. I will give due consideration to this mad idea of yours if you do something for me.'

'What is it?'

'You and me. The Langdale Pikes. In two days' time.'

I burst out laughing. 'You want me to climb up a mountain with you?'

He nods, deadly serious. 'Yes, I do.'

I shake my head and cover my eyes before sighing, 'I suppose it had to happen at some point.'

Just then, the door to the balcony bursts open and Cate appears, beckoning us in. 'What are you two doing out here? Every one of us from the salsa class is up dancing. Except you!'

Joe squeezes my hand and says, 'I think we need to get in there pronto.'

I giggle. 'I think so too.'

We head through the doors and on to the dance floor, where the throb of music vibrates through my chest. Joe takes my hand and we start moving in time to the song.

'You know I can't do this bit where it gets to the reverse wrap,' I protest, following his steps into a basic turn.

'Yeah, I know,' he replies. 'But we've got to keep trying. You can't let these things defeat you.'

'Well, when you put it like that … I never have been the kind to accept defeat.'

He looks at me. 'I noticed.'

At that, he sweeps me into an embrace and twirls me round into a series of moves that normally leave me tripping over my own feet. I don't know why it is, but tonight, they almost work.

The song draws to a close and another higher tempo song takes over.

Yet Joe and I ignore it.

As music and laughter and dancing and celebration clash around us, I simply sway in his arms – where I've never felt happier to be.

Acknowledgments

Thank you to the brilliant team at Simon & Schuster who, ten years since I signed my first publishing deal, remain not just enthusiastic champions of my books, but a complete pleasure to work with too. Special mention must go to Clare Hey, Suzanne Baboneau, Sara-Jade Virtue, Ally Grant and Dawn Burnett – thanks so much.

Thanks also to Lulu Mitford, who made a donation to a charity that helps children with cancer in order to have her name mentioned in the book. Your generosity is hugely appreciated and I hope *my* Lulu did you proud.

Thanks, as ever, to my fabulous agent Darley Anderson, as well as Clare Wallace and Mary Darby. And to my parents Jean and Phil Wolstenholme, and my uncle Colin Wolstenholme for the number-crunching.

Finally, thank you to the people who make my world go around when I'm not writing: my husband Mark and my three brilliant boys, Otis, Lucas and Isaac. I love you all. x

Jane Costello

The Time of Our Lives

It was supposed to be the holiday of a lifetime …

Imogen and her friends Meredith and Nicola have had
their fill of budget holidays, cattle-class flights and 6 a.m.
offensives for a space by the pool.

So when Meredith wins a VIP holiday at Barcelona's hippest
new hotel, they plan to sip champagne with the jet set, party
with the glitterati and switch off in unapologetic luxury.

But between a robbery, a run-in with hotel security staff and
an encounter on a nudist beach that they'd all rather forget,
the friends stumble from one disaster to the next.

At least Imogen has a distraction in the form of the gorgeous
guy who's always in the right place at the very worst time.
Until, that is, his motives start to arouse a few suspicions …

Hilarious and heart-warming by turns, T*he Time of Our
Lives* is Jane Costello at her romantic best.

**'Funny, sexy and moving - a hilarious holiday romp
with a heart. I loved it' Sophie Kinsella**

**Paperback ISBN 978-1-47112-923-0
Ebook ISBN 978-1-47112-925-4**

Win a Suite Treat for two
at the Beech Hill Hotel & Spa

Beech Hill
HOTEL & SPA
on Windermere

One lucky reader could be in with a chance of winning a three-night stay for two people at the 4 star Beech Hill Hotel & Spa, overlooking Lake Windermere & £250 worth of spa treatments in the hotel's Lakeview Spa.

The winner will receive three nights in the luxurious Wordsworth Suite, including dinner and breakfast.

The impressive Wordsworth Suite marries extravagantly tasteful design with those essential modern touches. The room is adorned with antique furniture including a seven-foot, antique oak bed. To continue the opulent theme, there are two leather chairs facing the floor-to-ceiling panoramic windows. The luxury continues outside, where your private garden area offers superb views over the lake, an attractive seating area and a relaxing hot tub. You will be able to simply open the glass doors, breathe in the fresh Cumbrian air and enjoy the unrivalled views of Windermere.

To enter visit www.simonandschuster.co.uk/competitions

books*andthe*city
the home of female fiction

BOOKS | NEWS & EVENTS | FEATURES | AUTHOR PODCASTS | COMPETITIONS

Follow us online to be the first to hear from
your favourite authors

bc
booksandthecity.co.uk

books and the city

@TeamBATC

Join our mailing list
for the latest news, events and
exclusive competitions

Sign up at
booksandthecity.co.uk

Buy your next book
directly from

Sparkle Direct
to receive 25% off & free P+P!

Call **01326 569 444**
or visit **sparkledirect.com**